"*W*hat are you waiting for?" she whispered.

He leaned down to kiss her pouting mouth again. "Do you really want to give yourself to a man like me?" he asked softly.

"Only to a man like you," she said without hesitation.

He closed his eyes. "You honor me, Chloe."

"I don't want to honor you, you scoundrel. I want you to . . . to finish what you started. Dominic, for God's sake, have a little mercy. I have *never* felt like this before."

"My God, I hope not." The thought was intolerable to him. If he had met her before his life had fallen apart, he had no doubt he would be approaching her brothers for her hand. "Chloe," he said, the intensity of his expression easing, "you're the best thing that has ever happened to me. I'm afraid the same does not hold true in reverse."

"You're wrong," she whispered. "And you aren't going to change my mind."

"God help me," he said in a low voice, "I don't intend to."

The Love Affair of an English Lord

A Novel

Jillian Hunter

BALLANTINE BOOKS • NEW YORK

2010 Ballantine Books Mass Market Edition

Copyright © 2005 by Maria Hoag
Excerpt from *The Wedding Night of an English Rogue* by Jillian Hunter copyright © 2005 by Maria Hoag

Published in the United States by Ballantine Books, an imprint of The Random House Publishing Group, a division of Random House, Inc., New York.

BALLANTINE and colophon are trademarks of Random House, Inc.

Originally published in mass market in the United States by Ivy, an imprint of The Random House Publishing Group, a division of Random House, Inc., in 2005.

ISBN 978-0-345-52341-9

Cover illustration: Jon Paul

Printed in the United States of America

www.ballantinebooks.com

9 8 7 6 5 4 3 2 1

This book is dedicated to my mother-in-law,
Phyllis Cotton, with love and admiration.

Chapter 1

England
1814

The late Dominic Breckland, Viscount Stratfield, was returning to life in a sea of women's underwear. From ear to ankle he fought a sensual undertow of lacy shifts and white silk stockings, his muscular arms tangled in the ties and tapes of lavender-scented buckram stays, his heavy thighs wrapped in a pair of dainty French percale pantalettes. Like a wounded beast of the night, he had eluded capture and taken refuge in the last place his pursuer would think to look.

Summoning a primitive instinct for survival, he had climbed the sturdy oak tree outside the manor house and hauled his bruised and bleeding six-foot frame over the windowsill. Hopeful he had outwitted the man who chased him, he had then collapsed—into an open trunk stuffed with personal female attire and frivolous accessories.

He was not too exhausted to appreciate the irony of the situation.

For now at least he had managed to escape the man who was hunting for him. Yet moment by moment his life's blood was saturating an unknown woman's muslin petticoats and blush-pink stockings. Pain seared his upper body. Gritting his teeth, he unraveled from his elbow a flimsy lawn chemise embroidered with blue silk forget-me-nots. His gaze unfocused and brimming with deviltry, he examined it in the moonlight.

If he was going to die, for the second time in a month, he might as well go out on a rousing sexual fantasy. "Well," he murmured, "what sort of woman are you anyway? Fast or merely fashionable? Do I have a choice? Then give me fast."

Unfortunately the maidenly garment failed to inspire a potent sexual image in his mind. The owner did appear to possess a decent pair of breasts, although Dominic was admittedly not capable of objective appraisal in his current condition.

God help them both—the poor woman would suffer a heart seizure when she found his carcass buried in her drawers. It seemed to him that he had once owned this creaky old manor house, at some time in the murky past, and he tried to remember who had bought it from him. To his frustration his brain refused to focus, images flitting elusively behind his eyes like moths in the shadows.

A retired sea captain, wasn't it? Sir Hickory or Humpty Something, his wife and daughter. Their names escaped Dominic at the moment. Bleeding to death, he hoped he would be forgiven the lapse in manners.

"Humpty Dumpty had a great fall," he muttered. "But who the devil was his wife?" If he was wallowing in the women's underclothes, he ought at least to know her name.

Many would remark that Dominic being found dead

in a trunk of petticoats was not surprising for a former English scoundrel who had thumbed his nose at society. His closest friends might even have chosen to bury him in a shroud of female underclothing as a loving tribute to his past sins.

Except that Dominic had been officially "buried" a month ago, mourned by a few, cursed by many. Aside from the persistent rumors of his ghost popping up in the oddest places and doing the naughtiest things, no one really expected to see him again.

Not his servants or scattered acquaintances.

He trusted only one person. The man who had helped him arrange his own funeral.

The late-evening silence of the country estate was marred by thumping footsteps, a bucket being kicked over, and an irate male voice coming from the front of the house.

"Somebody open the bloody gate!" the gardener shouted from the driveway below. "The carriage is coming over the bridge!"

"The bloody gate has been open for an hour!" the groom shouted back.

"Company," Dominic said with a mordant sigh, tossing the embroidered chemise over his shoulder. "I suppose I ought to tidy myself up—if I'm expected to entertain."

He looked like a nightmare cast up from hell, and he knew it. His lanky frame had lost flesh. The hollows below his cheekbones gave his masculine face a dangerous gauntness. The lugubrious pattern of surgeon's stitches that crisscrossed his chest and left shoulder had been torn during his tree-climbing escapade. Taking a breath that burrowed into his lungs like talons, he felt with his uninjured arm for the windowsill and hoisted himself upright for a few moments of enlightening agony.

His gray eyes widened in approval as he took stock of his surroundings.

"Well, isn't this convenient?" he said, clenching his teeth against a wave of pain. "A room with a view."

His own estate lay across the swathe of moonlit road on a wooded rise. Warm beams of candlelight glowed from the bedroom window where he had been brutally stabbed "to death" three weeks ago. His uncle, Colonel Sir Edgar Williams, had already taken possession of the house, and if Dominic had access to a spyglass, he could have identified the shadowy figure standing behind the curtains.

The taunting silhouette belonged to a woman, he thought in cynical detachment. Of that he had no doubt. But whether she was the same lady who had shared his bed while he was callously being stabbed, he could not say. Nor did it matter now. That love affair belonged to a past life and had died along with his previous identity. His feelings for his former mistress were as dead as she believed him to be.

The *clip-clop* of approaching horses, the churning of carriage wheels on the road, interrupted his troubled reflections. Pray God whoever owned this trunk would not decide to explore her dressing closet tonight. For if he was any judge of women's underwear, and it so happened that he was, then the delicately proportioned owner of these garments would quite indelicately scream her head off when she discovered a ghost in her intimate garments.

*   *   *

From the stuffy depths of the lumbering carriage, Lady Chloe Boscastle could discern one of her undergarments dangling like a banner of indecency from her bedroom window. She leaned forward, her body frozen in disbelief, her face turning pale. The bulk of her personal belongings had arrived from London just that morning. She and the maid had barely started to unpack them, let alone put them on display from her window.

She attempted to close the carriage curtains in a casual manner, hoping the other passengers would not notice this disconcerting sight. Not that anyone would be surprised by such a faux pas from Chloe at this point. She had brought the inglorious label of troublemaker with her from London and was almost expected to continue her worrying ways. Far be it from her to disappoint her growing critics.

The errant undergarment—heavens above, it rather looked like her favorite chemise—could only mean that her scapegrace brother Devon had come and gone while she had been carted off to a country ball in a cavernous cobwebby hall.

And what had the rascal pilfered from her room this time? she wondered in alarm. He had already pawned off a good deal of her jewelry to pay off his debts. But surely he had not stooped to stealing her underthings. . . .

A more amusing thought jolted her upright. Could Devon be walking about the countryside disguised as a woman? Or had he found a female companion to give him shelter? He was supposed to be lying low with an elderly relative in the next village. Chloe realized her brother, a nobleman who had overnight become a sort of heroic outlaw due to a stupid prank, felt a little desperate. Being a Boscastle, she was a very liberal person herself, but even so, there were limits to decent behavior. Devon seemed to be dangerously testing those limits beyond what a wicked Boscastle would usually dare.

She turned away from the window as the ancient carriage labored between the rusty iron gates of the modest estate, making enough noise to raise the dead. A furtive glance at the endearingly blank faces of her aunt and uncle, also ancient in her eyes, reassured her they had not noticed the wayward article in the window of their wayward niece's bedroom.

"As I was saying," Uncle Humphrey continued to his wife, "the cat was only being a cat, Gwennie. He did not drag the dead mouse to the parson's chair deliberately to embarrass you. It was an offering of the hunt."

Aunt Gwendolyn gave a delicate shudder, her bosom lifting and falling like a wave. "I was mortified beyond words. It happened right when the poor parson was recounting the latest antics of the Stratfield Ghost."

"Not that deuced ghost again, Gwennie. Not in front of Chloe."

Chloe was only half listening anyway, more intent on her own impending doom than a dead man's imaginary exploits. She released a sigh of relief as the carriage rounded the drive and came to a jolting stop. No one would believe that she had hung her chemise from the window to dry—her improper conduct was a source of both prurient interest and kindly concern in this dull backwater parish. Even worse than being shunned, Chloe's country relatives had engaged the entire village to reform her. She was surrounded by moral zealots on every side, well-intentioned people who knew of her past sin.

Caught kissing a young baron in a park, she had been promptly banished from London by her brother, the Marquess of Sedgecroft, to the home of her retired uncle Sir Humphrey Dewhurst. It was the worst punishment imaginable for a social-minded young woman. Chloe might have already considered the rest of the year doomed had she not met the most charming man in Chistlebury at the ball earlier tonight. Her waist still felt warm where he had held her—far too long to be proper, not long enough to be considered an advance by those observing them. It seemed there might be hope for her, after all. Her exile might even provide a little excitement. The village matchmakers had watched in encouragement as she and Lord St. John had flirted across the dance floor.

Practically bouncing out of the carriage, she ignored her aunt's *tsk* of annoyance and made a beeline for the house. She slipped off her high-heeled tapestry dancing pumps at the lichen-coated front steps. It wasn't a proper manor house at all, more of a glorified stone farmhouse with a pond of noisy ducks beneath her window. She missed the smelly bustle and dangers of London, the gossip and daily social rounds. She missed her friends, although most had already forgotten her by now, their lives full of gaiety, parties, and glittering social affairs.

"Chloe!" Her tiny aunt came bearing down upon her like Attila the Hun, her horsehair petticoats bristling against the door. "I noticed that your bedroom window was open before we left tonight," she said, holding her blue-veined hand to her heart as she caught her breath.

Chloe turned, catching the eye of the curly red-haired young woman standing inside the hall. It was her cousin Pamela, who had missed the ball due to a wrenched ankle and who was making strange, undecipherable hand signals behind Aunt Gwendolyn's back.

"It wasn't the bedroom window," Chloe said slowly. She was struggling to interpret Pamela's gesticulations. "It was the dressing closet, and—"

"I opened it to give the closet a good airing," Pamela inserted, motioning for Chloe to be quiet. "The smell of powder and perfume was a bit powerful."

Aunt Gwendolyn was too busy unbundling her petite frame from a fox-trimmed pelisse to take much notice of this secret pantomime. "Well, make sure it is securely closed before we retire. Everyone at the ball tonight was discussing the latest antics of the Stratfield Ghost."

Pamela's eyes grew round, her attempt to help Chloe apparently forgotten. "Ooh, and what has our wicked ghostie done now?"

Aunt Gwendolyn paused for effect, one hand pressed to the onyx buttons at her throat. There was not a woman in the parish, with the possible exception of newcomer Chloe, who had not avidly followed the life and death of the terribly exciting, terribly wicked Viscount Stratfield.

From his war heroics to his brutal murder in bed almost a month ago, there was little the viscount had done that did not titillate the villagers. His killer had not been caught, but bets were still being laid in the local pub that an irate husband had taken revenge.

Naturally, a woman had been at his side at the time of his death. In fact, according to rumor, she had not only been at his side but had lain naked beneath him as he was stabbed. And it was her hysterical recounting of the crime, committed by a masked intruder, that had rocked this sleepy village to its soul.

Aunt Gwendolyn lowered her voice to a rather lurid tone as her husband entered the house. "The handsome devil seduced Miss Beryl Waterbridge as she knelt at her evening prayers last night."

Uncle Humphrey came to a full stop in the crowded hallway, his brown eyes twinkling in amusement at Chloe. "I did nothing of the sort. I was here in this house all last night playing cards with my dear niece. Isn't that right, Chloe? Will you provide my alibi?"

Chloe peeled off her lightweight rose wool mantle; she wondered absently when she would see the handsome Justin Linton, Lord St. John again. As they had parted, he'd vowed he couldn't live without her. Chloe had laughed at his romantic nonsense. "I can vouch for you, Uncle Humphrey," she said stoutly, sharing a grin with him over her shoulder. "You did not seduce a single person that I noticed."

She caught her reflection in the hall-stand looking glass and tried to see herself as Justin would have done tonight. True, he had danced with her twice, but she couldn't help feeling that his attention might have strayed to another young woman whose hair was lighter than Chloe's, whose voice was a little sweeter, whose manner was more demure.

She frowned at herself. Could that be her fatal flaw? Her inability to be . . . demure like other young ladies?

Sadly enough, this seemed to be a family trait, and Chloe wasn't sure she would change it even if she could. She supposed she ought to pretend to be demure to seem more appealing, her sister Emma had always advised this, but deep in her heart she really wished to be loved at her absolute worst.

"And her screams summoned her poor father, who broke a toe trying to rescue her," Aunt Gwendolyn finished, pausing to take a breath from her recitation. "Beryl fainted seven times before she could admit what the ghost had done to her."

Chloe spun from the mirror, her attention captured. "How do you know the woman wasn't dreaming? And did her father actually *see* the ghost?"

Aunt Gwendolyn stared at her with gentle scorn. "Her lips were tingling, Chloe, from the phantasmal kisses. And no, of course Beryl's father didn't *see* the ghost. I imagine he was in too much pain from his toe to care if he had."

"Well, what did the ghost do to her?"

"A decent woman could not repeat his wickedness, Chloe."

Chloe smiled as she handed her scented gloves to the maid. "That's the trouble with this village. Your lives are so lacking in true drama that you make up ghosts seducing women in their sleep. If any of you had any courage, the tiniest bit of daring in you at all, you would have a genuine affair, and—"

"That will be quite enough of *that*, Chloe," her aunt said, her kindly face gone quite pink. "I believe it was your daring nature that got you into trouble in the first

place and is exactly why your understandably belea-
guered brothers have sent you here to—"

"Perish of boredom, all my mental faculties shriveled
up from lack of stimulation," Chloe said with a good-
natured sigh. "Well, it appears to be working. Yesterday
I caught myself talking to the ducks in the pond. My
only hope for salvation is to be found dead in bed myself, ravished, if I have any luck, by the Stratfield Ghost."

Her aunt gave a loud groan of chagrin, which
prompted Uncle Humphrey to absentmindedly pat her
hand while pretending to frown in disapproval at Chloe.
The truth, as her uncle had admitted in private to Chloe,
was that he adored her outspoken views and had not enjoyed anyone's company so much in ages. He claimed
that Chloe had done wonders to draw his daughter
Pamela out of her lonely shell. He appreciated, or so he
said, the unpredictability Chloe had brought to their
home. And Chloe actually laughed at his jokes, Lord
bless her. Her dear uncle was a staunch ally.

"Perhaps you ought to go to bed, Chloe," Aunt Gwendolyn said in a tremulous voice. "Delia can bring up a
pot of chocolate if you wish."

Chloe headed for the stairs, bearing herself like a
heroine in a Greek tragedy. "I don't suppose I could
have a pot of sherry instead?"

Pamela hobbled after her, speaking in an excited whisper. "I'm dying to have another peek inside the two
trunks that came for you today. I've never seen so much
silk and lace in all my life."

"Oh." Chloe paused to glance up the stairwell. "Not
that I'm liable to need them in Chistlebury, but I'm glad

that my undergarments bring you some measure of enjoyment. Between my drawers and your ghost, this should be a year of scandals for your village."

They continued up the creaking oak stairs in companionable silence until Pamela, apparently inspired to wickedness by her cousin's influence, said, "Plenty of women are praying for that ghost, I reckon. Praying that they're the one he visits tonight and has his otherworldly way with."

"His otherworldly way?" Chloe burst into deep laughter at that and veered down the narrow hall to her room. "Heavens, what a thought."

For Chloe's part she did not believe in ghosts. At least she hadn't until last week when, from her bedroom window, she had spotted a lone masculine figure standing on the outskirts of the empty Stratfield mansion in the dead of night.

Was it Stratfield's restless spirit or his human male cousin who had inherited the estate? Strangely the apparition had made her feel more sad than frightened. He had a melancholy air, this spirit, if that's what he was. The viscount had been dead just over a fortnight. Chloe's only experience with the man, unsettling enough, had been during her first days here in Sussex.

She had gotten caught in a downpour on her way back from the apothecary's on an errand for her aunt. The footman who'd accompanied her had run home to fetch her an umbrella.

Stratfield had come thundering across the field on his stallion like Sir Galahad going to battle. Reared in a family of males who excelled in athletics, and a competent horsewoman herself, Chloe had been nonetheless so impressed by the sight that she had stepped up to her ankles in a mud puddle to get a better look at this masculine vision. Unfortunately she did not seem to make a similar impression on him.

Before she could even shake out her cloak, he wheeled his horse to circle her in patent disapproval, his gray eyes as dark and hard as pewter. Chloe found herself at an uncharacteristic loss for words. From all appearances, he was not as easily impressed.

The steady patter of rain formed a veil between them, creating an illusion of a man who was not entirely part of the world.

All the interesting angles and planes of his strong face had arranged into an amused smirk as he surveyed her sodden state. Not perfectly handsome, but compelling. Probably the most unforgettable face Chloe had ever seen, with a clefted chin and those dark slashing eyebrows drawn into an unfriendly scowl.

"Well, get on." He'd extended his leather-gloved hand, not asking, ordering. Not exactly rude but no one's knight in shining armor either. Chloe had the impression that he was paying her only perfunctory attention, that she'd interrupted him in the middle of some important mission, and that he didn't appreciate the interference.

She glanced down at her mucky half boots in distaste, wistfully remembering all the routs and soirées she had left behind in London.

"Hurry up," he added, wiping his hand across his wet cheek.

"But I don't know—"

"Get on, young lady, before we are both soaked to the skin. This is the country, not the court."

Chloe bristled, but the half smile lurking in his eyes took some of the sting out of his command. Having been raised with five roguish brothers had obliterated her most tender sensibilities. Frogs, spit, unsavory jokes. Chloe and her older sister, Emma, had been inoculated against easy insult at an early age.

Still, one should maintain a certain decorum, rain or not, even if one happened to be a young marquess's daughter who was tottering on the thin line of social disgrace. Besides, this Sir Galahad was so full of himself, he could use a little reminder of what constituted good manners.

"At least introduce yourself, sir," she said, the rain cooling the inexplicable heat that rose to her cheeks.

He leaned across the pommel, his lips tightening in a smile. "I am the owner of the property into which you are sinking. Trespassing. In a thunderstorm. In a pretty silk dress. Now that that's out of the way, are you getting on or not?"

"Well, how can I refuse?" she muttered.

That said, she still hesitated, taking a closer look at his face through the curtain of cold raindrops. Preoccupied, self-possessed, with short black hair slicked back on his scalp and his gunmetal-gray eyes regarding her with a detached mockery that appeared to be degenerating into impatience. She glanced toward the stone hedge that enclosed the field. Her footman was nowhere in sight.

"Yes or no?" he asked briskly.

"Yes, but give me a chance—"

To shake the mud off her boots, which evidently

didn't bother him; with one hand he pulled her up behind him, onto his well-trained mount. Chloe's senses registered the scent of Galahad's wet woolen greatcoat, an appealing whiff of woodsy cologne, the intrusive warmth of his elbow joint beneath her breast. She also noticed the way his body stiffened, then leaned back into her with a casual arrogance that made her heart pound. All put together, he was a rather overpowering example of masculinity. She had to restrain the urge to huddle against his hard, muscular body.

She stared at the back of his head in a rather hopeful trepidation. Had she made another of her countless mistakes? Her impulsive tendencies were what had gotten her exiled to this uneventful social oasis in the first place. But Galahad *was* a neighbor. A noble one if she recalled her aunt's passing mention of the man.

Or had it been a warning? Chloe had heard his name even before she had been sent to Sussex. Dominic's younger brother Samuel had died last year alongside Chloe's brother Brandon in the service of the East India Company, which they had joined in search of adventure and the prizes promised them on recruiting posters.

Instead, they had been killed by Gurkha rebels on a scouting mission in Nepal. She remembered her two older brothers speaking of Viscount Stratfield with an admiration rarely displayed toward men of their own class. Apparently the viscount had been instrumental in arranging the memorial service for the two young friends.

In any event Chloe was not at all concerned that her rescuer would do anything so outrageous as to ravish her on his horse, or to abduct her into slavery—until he took off at a gallop in the opposite direction of the familiar bridle path.

"I say . . ." she began to protest before the breath whooshed out of her lungs.

The woods sped past her vision in a gray-brown blur. The horse kicked up tufts of wet turf and sent them flying into the rain. Over a soggy meadow and down a dark humid tunnel of wet honeysuckle that slapped them as they thundered by. She could make neither heads nor tails of their surroundings, but this route did not look anything like the walk home.

She wrapped her arms around Galahad's waist and raised her voice to a shout, her body jostled against his. She felt the muscles in his torso tighten. Did she imagine that he liked her clinging to him for dear life? "Excuse me? I do believe you are headed the wrong way!"

He grunted, or made some such dismissive gutteral sound that indicated she was a feather-brained female for daring to question his sense of direction. Chloe's head began to swim with visions of being abducted by this dark, brooding stranger. Of being dragged down into the bowels of some hidden castle and kept a prisoner of his perverse demands.

Would he keep her naked on his bed, covering her with tender cruelty at night in Russian lynx pelts after he had left her fainting from his ravishment? Would he entice her back to consciousness with pearls and sweetmeats and potent brandy? Or, judging by his hell-bent speed on horseback, would they both be thrown to their deaths before any perversity could be undertaken?

Chloe was contemplating the latter unpleasant possibility when, after flying through a tangled hazel grove, they emerged miraculously onto a clear field.

She stared across the dreary landscape, her heart thumping in her throat. "My house," she said in surprise.

"Imagine that," he drawled, and turned his head slightly to look down at her in a way that let her know he wasn't so preoccupied with his own affairs as to be unaware of how tightly she was clinging to him.

The brown and white half-timbered farmhouse, known by the pretentious name of Dewhurst Manor, withstood the steady rain as it had for two centuries. Chloe imagined she could see her aunt peering through the lace curtains, wondering what had happened to her restless niece. She would probably be soundly scolded for accepting a ride from a neighbor rather than traipsing up to her knees in mud. The poor footman would be dealt a boxed ear.

"You might have told me you were taking a detour," she said under her breath as she unwrapped her arms from the strong male body she had been blatantly using as an umbrella.

He did not turn his head again. She sensed the mockery of his smile as he said, "I see no reason to explain the obvious."

"Of course not," she muttered. An explanation would have involved polite conversation. What a crabby man. She was embarrassed that the possibility of abduction had ever entered her mind. He probably didn't have a castle anyway. At least not in Chistlebury. Perhaps he lived in a cave. He was more dragon than knight. She supposed it was too much to hope he would escort her all the way home, although on second thought, her appearing on the doorstep with Galahad in tow would probably send her aunt into a swoon.

"Well," she said, covering her irritation with a polite smile, "it was very decent of you to take time from your"—From his what? she wondered. From thundering about like an ancient seigneur in search of storm-caught maidens?—"from your duties to rescue me."

He dismounted in silence and helped her down from the horse, lifting her with no apparent effort. The brush against his broad-shouldered body brought another sensation of warmth to Chloe's rain-chilled skin. He had a strong physique, and his touch was surprisingly gentle despite the impatience she sensed in him.

Clearly, although his mind was a hundred miles away, he was still male enough to acknowledge the differences in their sex. He dealt her an infuriatingly dismissive look. "In future, I would advise you not to wander onto my property."

"I hardly did so on purpose," Chloe retorted. "You see, I've just arrived from London—"

"So I've heard."

She stepped away as he turned his lean figure back to the horse. "About me?" she asked in astonishment. Under ordinary circumstances Chloe might have been a little flattered that a man she had never met had taken pains to investigate her.

He turned slowly, looking her up and down as if he had been resisting the urge to do so all along. His face was lean, the masculine features overshadowed by a tension that Chloe could almost feel. In fact, she caught her breath at the suppressed intensity, the male interest that he had not allowed to show before. Had she wondered whether he'd noticed her as a woman? Well, she would wonder no more. Never in her life had a man's gaze left her feeling more seduced and desirable than his brief heated glance. Only when his gray eyes met hers did the faintest flicker of humor appear.

"Yes," he said. "I've heard quite a few things about you, in fact."

"Why should I be of interest to you?" she asked in an undertone.

He hesitated. They were standing in the shadows of the white willow trees that bordered the manor house. Chloe could hear the rain pattering on the silvery leaves, dripping, enclosing them in humid darkness. She sensed he was on the verge of telling her something, a secret, perhaps even the reason why he seemed so preoccupied and impolite. Those soulful gray eyes of his quite softened her heart. Was he sad, stricken perhaps with a terminal illness?

She edged a little closer, hoping to inspire confidence. She had always been drawn to lost animals, to lost people. But there was something else drawing her to him now, a dangerous curiosity, a magnetic heat. If he had been cool toward her before, he seemed to be a veritable hotbed of dark emotion now.

"Why?" she asked again.

She should have been surprised when he drew her into his arms and kissed her. What surprised her more was that she did not melt into the rain, her body suddenly boneless, drugged with the heady sweetness of brandy on his breath. There was power and arrogance and almost desperation in the way his lips took possession of hers. A decade from now she would remember the thrill of that kiss. She struggled for breath. He allowed her but the merest gasp before his tongue drove more deeply into the soft recesses of her mouth.

"Why?" he whispered, holding her as if she were a lifeline, a link to sanity.

And Chloe's own sanity was suddenly in question as his hands drifted down her back, caressing the arch of her spine through her cloak, the contours of her bottom. In her past flirtations she had always felt in control, mistress of her fate. Now her control went up in flames. The dangerous hardness of his body supported and weakened her at once.

She heard him groan into the hollow of her throat. She had not been kissed like this before. She had not been touched like this. Even through her clothing his hands knew where to linger, how to arouse. A raindrop fell on her cheek and slid down against her neck. He licked it, the curl of his tongue sending a deep shiver through her body.

"You shouldn't go out alone," he said, and kissed her again, his mouth wet, his big arms tightening around her.

The sensual rasp of his voice almost brought her to her knees. Her heart was pounding in her throat, her ears. "Why not?" she whispered, taunting him back, not wanting to show how she struggled with herself to stop this from going any further.

He drew away from her with a smile. "This is a small village." His voice was detached again. She might have imagined the heat between them. Before she could even move, he had remounted and wheeled his horse in the opposite direction. "Yet there are dangers to avoid even here for a pretty young woman with a nose for trouble. Stay off my property in future."

A nose for trouble? Dangers to avoid? Meaning what? she wondered. Chloe, the daughter of a deceased marquess, the sister of the current marquess who wielded considerable influence, had been too flabbergasted by his blunt dismissal to ask. She had stood in the rain, drenched and offended, to watch him gallop off as if he were part of the angry storm. She had stood in disbelief, still burning from that kiss, from his enigmatic advice.

How did he know about her? And what was she to make of his melodramatic warning? The only menace Chloe had encountered in this dreary village until today was a parson who loved to spread gossip and a worrisome aunt. Good heavens, was she made of glass?

Without a doubt Dominic Breckland was the rudest and most attractive man she had ever met. Obviously he didn't give tuppence for what she thought. He did not seem to care that she might report his behavior to her brothers, who would probably only defend him anyway, assuming Chloe had been at fault.

Chloe lingered in the rain until he disappeared from sight, no longer feeling the chill. Feeling an extraordinary heat and annoyance, if anything. She had stayed there, and suddenly she realized that she had never dreamed a man like Lord Stratfield even existed, and wished she had never made the discovery.

In fact, she was so put out that she decided the only antidote was to completely forget her arrogant savior, which proved to be exactly the same advice her distraught aunt dispensed a few minutes later.

"I could not believe my eyes, Chloe Boscastle! I could not believe I saw you on a horse with Lord Stratfield. Holding him around the middle!"

Chloe darted to the window to peer outside. "I wandered onto his property by mistake. He brought me home."

"Well, that was a miracle in itself. The man is said to seduce every woman he meets."

"Did he ever seduce you, Aunt Gwendolyn?"

"Do not be impertinent. Stratfield is a neighbor and a nobleman, and as such I respect him. But that doesn't mean I approve of his keeping a mistress on his estate."

"Have you met her?" Chloe asked curiously, turning from the window in disappointment that he had not returned.

"Of course I haven't, Chloe."

Aunt Gwendolyn pulled the curtains back into place, looking indignant at the question. "Parson Grimsby has seen her on several occasions. In the viscount's window, Chloe."

Chloe bit her lip in amusement. "Perhaps the viscount has a sister or an aunt staying with him."

Aunt Gwendolyn's face had colored beneath her rice powder. "I hardly think he would have been behaving with a female relative in the manner the parson described."

"Does he hold bacchanalian orgies in the middle of the night?" Chloe could not resist asking, to tease her.

"I do not have any idea," her aunt sputtered in indignation. "Nor do I wish to know," she added, "and neither should you. The fact that I sense something is amiss at Stratfield Hall should be warning enough, Chloe. Matters are not right with that man. Mark my words."

And perhaps Chloe should have listened instead of laughing. Three weeks later the viscount had been stabbed to death in his bed.

Chapter 2

The news rocked the tiny village of Chistlebury to its roots. Chloe, who seemed to have developed an intolerance to clean country air, had caught a nasty chest cold and could not attend the funeral. The truth was that even before he died, Dominic had become a ghost to her, haunting her thoughts at all hours. She had dreamed of that kiss in the rain. She'd sworn to snub him the next time they met. She'd imagined kissing him again. She had even vowed that one day she and her brothers would hunt down his murderer.

She had cried in bed for two full days after the funeral, privately mourning her rude but attractive rescuer for reasons she could not explain. Her older brothers—Grayson, Heath, and Drake—had made a brief journey to pay their respects. No one appeared to have any idea who had killed Stratfield. His uncle Edgar had rushed all the way from Wales to investigate and handle practical matters.

But the parson had let it slip that Stratfield might have done a little spying during his war days; an old enemy could have resurfaced to murder him. And then his alleged attraction to a few married women had not exactly won him friends. He was a man who had lived as he pleased and apparently lived to please no one but himself. Little wonder he was not widely mourned.

He was dead, and Chloe had no choice but to forget him. She would not have been wise to encourage his attention anyway. He was a man who had lived on the darker side of life. For all she knew, he had done something to merit death. For all she knew, he would have been her downfall. And yet, for many reasons, she hoped his killer would be caught.

Pamela's high-pitched voice drew her back to the less interesting present. "He came here right after you left," she whispered as they entered Chloe's bedchamber.

"Who came here?" Chloe asked blankly, resenting the return to reality.

"Your brother, of course."

For a few irrational seconds Chloe had thought that Pamela meant the Stratfield Ghost. As matters stood, however, she did not have the luxury of worrying about the dead. It was the living who were tormenting her. Specifically, the living in the form of her brother Devon, who had become a wanted outlaw as the result of a prank he'd played last month.

On the way home from a gaming hall in Chelsea, Devon and two of his cocksure friends had held up a carriage that they believed was transporting a young courtesan who had been encouraging their attentions as well as denuding their pockets all evening.

The carriage, however, had belonged to an elderly banker. Shots had been fired, a footman wounded, and Devon had gone into hiding while his brother the marquess pulled strings to smooth down the mess his reckless sibling had made.

Chloe unbuttoned her blue muslin gown and sank down onto the bed with an involuntary shiver, staring at one of the bulging leather trunks that had arrived during the day. The other had been dragged into the dressing closet for lack of space. Her sister Emma had sent a costume to cover every occasion, not guessing how empty Chloe's social life had become.

"I suppose Devon wanted more money," she said, staring around the room. Was it her imagination, all the talk of ghosts, that made her feel edgy and alert? Or was she worried because it seemed that her family was on the verge of falling apart? Except for Grayson, happily married to his clever wife, Jane, all her Boscastle siblings appeared to be unsettled. Perhaps she should concentrate on her newfound admirer Lord St. John. He had the most gorgeous brown eyes and teasing grin, even if he had seemed a trifle shallow. Why could she not be satisfied with a young man like him?

"Your brother came in through the window again when I was sorting out your clothes," Pamela said in an undertone. "The handsome devil has absolutely no sense of propriety, Chloe."

"Propriety?" Chloe gasped, one hand lifting to her mouth. "I absolutely forgot about the chemise Devon left in the window!"

Pamela looked puzzled. "What chemise? I did not notice Devon with a chemise."

"The one that I saw from the carriage. I suppose it doesn't matter now. I suppose my brother thinks he's very funny," she said crossly. "Remind me to remove it before I go to bed. I shall have to push this trunk into the closet anyway."

"Aren't you even going to look through it?" Pamela asked in disappointment.

"Not to—" Chloe rose slowly from the bed, her gaze moving to the closet door. Her gown slid down to her waist, and she shivered. She wondered if she might be coming down with another cold. The strangest prickles had just run down her spine. "What was that noise?"

Pamela glanced over her shoulder. "What noise?"

"It sounded like a man moaning," Chloe said quietly.

"A—oh, that. It's probably the creaky old gate in the drive. Ever since Lord Stratfield was killed, Mama has it locked for the night, though I'm not sure whether it's to keep out his ghost or his murderer. A ghost wouldn't use a gate, would he? Oh, look at this."

Pamela had dropped to her knees, sifting happily through a trunkful of scented fans, shoes, and fringed shawls. Her eyes brightened as she removed a French buckram corset of ivory silk with whalebone supports designed to slim a woman's waist while enhancing the size of her breasts.

Chloe couldn't help laughing at her cousin's expression of shocked delight. Sometimes it did her heart good to see things from Pamela's unsophisticated perspective. "It came all the way from Paris."

"No wonder they had a revolution."

"Why don't you try it on?" Chloe suggested teasingly. "It's not as if I'll have much use for it in the near future."

"Me?" Pamela rose before the oak-framed cheval glass, holding the corset to the modest curves beneath her plain calico bodice. "Can you imagine?"

Chloe slipped out of her gown and stretched across the bed in her own chemise, short corset, and stockings. "Perhaps if I'd been wearing that tonight, Lord St. John would have offered for me on the spot." The thought of which should had made her feel happier than it did.

"Ravish you is more likely," Pamela said somberly. "I suppose you ought to consider yourself honored. Justin seems to think himself a bit above the young ladies of Chistlebury."

"Why don't you wear that corset under your Sunday dress?" Chloe propped herself up on her elbow, deciding she must be desperate indeed if luring her cousin into fashion decadence was her only source of excitement. "Heavens, Pamela, I think you need to position it a little lower. You aren't meant to enhance the size of your chin."

"Lower? But how do you get your, er, bosoms, into position?"

"It looks complicated, but the design really does flattering things to one's figure." Chloe sat up slowly, shivering again for no reason. Just her luck to be coming down with another cold when Justin had mentioned a possible boating party at the end of the week. "The first time I put it on, my maid laced me halfway in and halfway out on the top. I looked like one of those Amazon women who lopped off one of their breasts so they could take better aim with their bows."

Pamela blushed pink to the roots of her auburn hair. "I have no idea what you're talking about, Chloe Boscastle, and I suspect you're making fun of me."

"I'm not, honestly."

Both young women paused, sighing as Aunt Gwendolyn began to shout for Pamela from the bottom of the stairs.

"Well," Pamela said, "that's the end of me for the night." She tossed the corset at Chloe. "And I've never heard of Amazon women, but if they aim their breasts at their beaux, I'm probably better off not knowing."

She swept from the room in such a fit of giggles that the beeswax candles on the chest of drawers blew out. The flames died in a flutter of ghostly vapors.

Chloe slipped off the bed and stared around the smoky shadows of the darkened room. She felt chilly and very aware of being abandoned. She breathed in the scent of melted wax. She was certain she had caught some dreadful ailment.

Then another of those moaning sounds arose in the silence, and this time there was no mistake: the disturbance came from somewhere within her own closet.

Chloe was a city-bred young lady. She did not claim to know the first thing about managing practical matters on a country estate. Nor did she wish to. But one point was clear, even to her in all her blithe ignorance of rustic affairs. The wounded utterance that had just arisen from behind the door of her dressing closet was not anything a rusty gate had made.

Dominic came back to consciousness with a protesting groan of pain. The feminine voice had reached into the depths of his delirium, soft and alluring, reminding him of a time when he had enjoyed basic pleasures. When he had trusted a woman's touch. He wondered where he had heard the voice before, and he wondered briefly where the hell he was before he remembered; Lord help him, he was layered between what he'd dimly identified as female underwear.

He struggled to pull himself upright from the bottom of the trunk. The undignified position reminded him of how he had posed in a coffin and pretended to be dead only a few short weeks ago. The only thing obvious at the moment, however, was that he was feverish and irrational. There was no other plausible explanation for the words that echoed in his brain.

"The first time I put it on, my maid laced me halfway in and halfway out on the top. I looked like one of those Amazon women who lopped off one of their breasts so they could take better aim with their bows."

He frowned, fighting the appeal of that voice, then surged to his feet in a shroud of scented petticoats. For a spell he stood disoriented and shaking, staring blankly at the door. With grim irony he realized that the mortal wounds inflicted by his murderer a month ago might indeed prove his death.

He remembered now. He had been chased earlier in the evening by the man he employed as his gamekeeper. The loyal Irish servant had only been ensuring the privacy of his new employer, not realizing it was his true master he threatened to shoot. Yes, Dominic admitted it had been foolhardy to venture so close to home, for he did not wish to be recognized yet. The world believed him dead. He had no desire to correct that mistake.

He had summoned the strength to climb a tree into this room to hide. Which did not appear to have been a wise move either. It was obvious he was in no condition for any sort of physical confrontation. That day would come soon enough. When he had regained his strength, he would take his revenge on the man who had schemed to destroy him.

For now he needed to heal, to plan, and to deal with the woman whose strange remark had awakened him. Her voice stirred up an enjoyable but elusive chord of memory. The fragrance of expensive soap, a soft female shape, and . . . he was puzzled. How did he know the feel and scent of her?

She had been talking to another person. He had no idea how large an audience he would be forced to entertain. In the event his ghostly presence failed to provide a sufficient distraction, he was reluctantly prepared to rely upon the physical.

Checking the ebony-inlaid pistol in his waistband, he stepped toward the door and braced himself for a dramatic scene.

It never failed to amuse him how hysterically people tended to react when confronted with a dead man.

Chloe heard suffering in that subdued groan, a plea for help she could not ignore. She pictured a man in pain, possibly dying from a mortal injury. A man confused and wounded who had taken refuge in her room. It did not occur to her for an instant that to help him would be to endanger herself. Her heroic spirit rose to the summons.

She pulled on her Chinese dressing robe and flew to the closet without any hesitation. . . . Believing with all her heart that the moan in the dark had come from her own reckless brother, Devon.

Chapter 3

The door opened before Dominic could twist the tarnished knob. It took him several moments to assess the woman's face, heart-shaped, pretty, the refined features reflecting total disbelief. The odd thing was that she had been speaking in a low, worried voice. She had been whispering a man's name as she opened the door. The concern in her midnight-blue eyes had rapidly darkened to horror.

Had she been expecting to find her lover, instead of the Stratfield Ghost, on the other side? The butterflies embroidered on her silk robe blurred before his eyes.

It was impossible to tell which one of them had suffered the strongest shock, the woman or himself.

He knew her, didn't he? He felt a prickle of recognition before self-preservation took over. Now that she realized he was not the man she expected, she was reacting as would any normal female in her place.

She turned in panic to escape.

He would lay odds she'd start to scream before she reached the outer door. It felt like torture to force his abused body into action. It even hurt to breathe. But he could have been dead a hundred times over and still have been able to overpower a woman of her build.

He caught her by the waist and was surprised by the strength of her resistance. She swung her body back at him in reaction. His shoulder burned like hell, aggravated by the movement, but he hadn't held a woman in a month, and his natural instincts ran to inflicting pleasure, not pain. As a general rule, when Dominic wrestled a woman to the floor, she was in for the experience of her life.

Not that such a pleasurable activity was even a remote possibility.

She was half his size, but more than his match in determination. His fingers tangled in her short raven-black hair as he brought his hand up to cover her mouth. It didn't help either of them that she had been caught half undressed, her bottom pressed into his groin. Her soft flesh beckoned him to forget what he must do. He knew what she must be thinking, what he wanted. He felt a fleeting stab of desire as her robe fell open. How easily he could take her. How vulnerable she was, for all her struggling.

He also knew suddenly who she was, the blue-eyed woman in the rain. He remembered the day he'd met her, how angry he had been that she had interfered with his plans. It was the same day he had discovered that someone wanted to kill him. The day he had been shot at while walking in the woods. He had been hunting the would-be assassin when this young woman intruded, tempting him for a few moments to ignore how ugly his life had become.

He'd suspected he had been stalked for weeks. Why?

Perhaps because he'd been about to reveal that the deaths of Samuel Breckland and Brandon Boscastle last year had not been the result of an ambush by Gurkha warriors at all.

Perhaps because he had been gathering evidence that the murder of the two young soldiers had been arranged by their own commanding officer. Dominic had been on the verge of a discovery. He'd sensed it. So had the man who had murdered Samuel and Brandon.

Would a young woman as frivolous and beautiful as Chloe Boscastle have wanted to kiss him in the rain if she knew his life was being threatened? No. Not for a minute. And he would not have wanted her to either. As desirable as he found her, he dared not endanger her. Even his mistress had hinted that she intended to leave him at the end of the month to seek a new protector.

The best he'd been able to do at the time, all he could offer, was to rescue her from a puddle, steal a kiss.

He almost laughed aloud at the irony of it. He had been more than rude and distracted, not giving the exiled daughter of a marquess the attention to which she was accustomed. At any other time he might have flirted at length with her, formally escorted her home. Perhaps turned his charms on her to see if that electrifying kiss he'd stolen developed into something even more interesting.

Well, he was certainly going to make up for that lack of attention now. In fact, he thought as he half carried her struggling form toward the bed, he was going to spend more time with her than any woman he had ever met, whether she liked it or not.

*   *   *

Chloe caught a horrifying glimpse of their shadowy figures in the cheval glass across the room. She was almost grateful for the darkness; it blurred the details of what was happening to her. She'd been so prepared to find her brother hiding in the closet that she hadn't known how to react. Now there was no choice. She was at the mercy of the intruder. She had to rely on instinct to save herself.

A grip like a steel belt squeezed the breath from her body. She stared down at the muscular forearm that held her in a cruel vise. His other hand covered her entire mouth, muffling her angry cries.

She was terrified by his strength, submerged in shock, determined to make subduing her a struggle. But even so, she realized that he was holding back from hurting her. He could have effortlessly snapped her in half. She had wrestled her brothers enough during their childhood to know how easily a man could overpower a woman. She had no idea what he wanted with her, but none of the possibilities that ran through her mind were pleasant.

The pistol in his waistband felt cold and ominous against her lower back. She began to battle in panic again as he moved her toward the bed.

"Stop it," he growled in her ear. "You're hurting me."

She—hurting *him*? she wondered in indignation, then gave his shoulder another good thump with the back of her head. It was a mistake. His hold of her midsection tightened until she had no choice but to go utterly limp, allowing him to lower her onto her own bed. When he leaned over her, his features unmerciful and intense, she lowered her eyes and prepared herself for the worst. Then slowly, as several uneventful moments passed, she found the courage to look up at him.

Their gazes connected in mutual recognition, his gray eyes glittering with irony and something that might even have been pain, her own blue eyes wide with astonishment.

The Stratfield Ghost, she realized with a mixture of relief and anxiety. The terror of the village. The delight of the lonely ladies of Chistlebury. The man whose kiss had haunted, heated her private dreams. He whom she and half the ladies of Chistlebury had secretly mourned. Her Galahad of the soulful gray eyes. But how different he seemed.

He was no more a dead man than she; his body was flushed and hot against hers, his breathing shallow and irregular. The plain fact was that the arrogant man who held Chistlebury in thrall looked ghastly—yes, ghostly, too—almost a stone thinner than the day she had seen him. His skin had taken on an unhealthy ashen tint. A thin stubble of beard gave his angular features a lean, dangerous look.

His expression was hard and unforgiving. Even though she knew his identity, knew he was a nobleman and a neighbor, she wasn't reassured. This incarnation of Dominic Breckland looked like a man driven to the brink of desperation. A man capable of anything.

"Do you remember me?" he demanded in a gruff whisper.

She nodded, realized she was still shaking. His voice wasn't the least bit reassuring either, gravely and raw.

"You—you rescued me from the rain. Yes, I remember."

"I rescued you. From the rain."

He paused a heartbeat. His gray eyes narrowing, he glanced around the room as if to take stock of his surroundings. Chloe was so aware of him, of his heavy male body, that she felt as though her breathing were synchronized with his. And when he spoke to her again, she was so startled that she almost missed the ironic amusement in his voice.

"It seems to be your turn now."

She bit the inner flesh of her lip. "My turn?"

"To rescue me."

"To—" Before she could finish, he lost consciousness, dropping onto her tense body with the impact of an oaken beam, his dark face pressed to hers like a lover in the night. Chloe lay beneath him in a paralysis of horror, wondering in detached anxiety what would happen to her tarnished reputation if she were caught in bed with the Stratfield Ghost.

For the longest time she lay immobilized in that peculiar position, half hoping, half terrified that she was trapped under a dead man. When her nerves finally settled down enough for her to function again in a rational manner, she realized he was still alive. At least she could hear the rasp of his breath in her hair. She made an attempt to slide her hand out from under his hip bone. He gave a low warning growl in his throat.

The weak pulse of his heart beat against her crushed breasts, a counterpoint to the blood rushing through her veins. His fingers were still tangled in her hair. Her body was pressed into the bed. Even if he was half dead, she could feel the latent strength in the muscular torso and thighs that imprisoned her.

"Please get off of me," she whispered, swallowing over the knot that swelled in her throat.

She gave his shoulder a tentative push, only to prod him into rising up with a restrained roar of pain. Observing his reaction, she felt a temporary swell of pity overcome her own fear. He reared back and rolled onto his side, cradling his left arm in a protective gesture.

She stared disbelievingly at her hand, up at his wrinkled linen shirt, back down again at the shiny smear of dark crimson blood on the bed where he had collapsed.

"Oh, dear God," she said, so appalled at the sight that she forgot the danger to herself. "You're hurt. I'll fetch help. . . ." Yes, help. An excuse to escape, to think how to handle this. Helping him perhaps to save herself. With any luck he'd jump out the window before she returned.

"Don't you dare."

He caught the sleeve of her robe and hauled her back roughly between his legs, growling, "Don't you breathe a word to anyone that I am here. Or that you've even seen me."

She felt a little sick, shuddering at the menace in his voice, aware of his breath burning against her neck, the hard, unyielding body that imprisoned her. Was this the same man who had kissed her in the rain? Who had teased and gently tormented her, leaving her aching to meet him again? "But—why must my seeing you be a secret?"

"Because I am dead, my dear, and have no desire to rejoin the living yet."

She drew a breath. He sounded chillingly calm, deliberate, rational even, although his behavior was not. "Well, I have no desire for you to be here, dead or not," she burst out. "What are you doing in my room?"

He hesitated, his deep voice stark in the darkness. "I was chased here. Chased through the woods."

"Chased?" It didn't make sense to her. He was supposed to be dead. He'd hinted that no one knew he had survived the vicious attack. It dawned on her suddenly that there was far more to his murder than anyone in Chistlebury had realized. And now she was caught in his deadly mystery.

Dominic stared back at her, reading the bewilderment on her face. What the hell had he gotten into? Why her, of all people?

He nudged her back against the carved rosewood headboard, his gray eyes pensive. God, what a coil. Now that she knew he was alive, he would be forced to trust her, a complication that could ruin his plans. If she were a man, he would take care of her without a qualm, and in not a very nice way, either.

But Lady Chloe Boscastle, Heath's young wildling sister. A woman a little too bright and beautiful for her own good. The lady appeared to have inherited the family penchant for passion and scandal. Heath would calmly tear him apart with his bare hands if Dominic harmed her, even though in the past he had counted Heath as a friend. In fact, when their two younger brothers Brandon and Samuel had been killed together in Nepal, Dominic had begun corresponding with Heath over their mutual suspicions about the ambush. Yes, Heath was a man to be trusted, not crossed.

But more to the point was whether he could trust Heath's sister. Could the nicely built young lady keep a secret? Could she possibly become his ally? He studied her in silence, suddenly noticing the provocative French corset that sat between them on the bed.

A devious contraption designed to emphasize a lush body that in his hasty appraisal appeared to need little enhancement. An ill-timed distraction if ever Dominic had seen or needed one. Why the devil had such a decent young lady worn it? he wondered in fascination, welcoming the diversion from the dark turn of his previous thoughts.

"This is yours?" he asked quietly.

She hesitated, a dark curl falling forward against her face. He wondered if she was blushing. His own body felt feverish enough without imagining how she would look in this provocative costume.

"I asked you if this was yours."

"What—oh, oh, well, it was sent to me."

"And you've worn it?"

"Umm. I think maybe once. Or maybe not."

He raised his gaze, searching her face for something he had not expected. What had he overheard from the closet? Was Heath's little sister involved in a love affair? Not that he gave a damn one way or the other. But it hadn't been so long ago that he might have thrown himself into a contest for her favor.

His own tempestuous affairs and conquests seemed to belong to another life. Revenge alone had fed him recently. He had thought little about romance and sexual pleasure in the past few weeks.

The reminder of such sweet pursuits came back to him in a rush. Oh, yes, he was indeed alive, perhaps glad for now to be free of the perils and poignancy of a love affair. Under different circumstances, in fact, he might have even enjoyed bringing this young lady to his bed.

But not now. She was as white as chalk, probably terrified of what he intended to do to her, understandably so. There was nothing he could say to reassure her. In the past few weeks Dominic had realized he was capable of acts that previously would have disgusted him. He hoped to God he would not end up hurting her. It was certain that his involvement in her life would not be an enhancement. Not since the gentleman he had once been was gone.

He had no idea himself what he was going to do. He was a man the world believed safely buried in a grave. Perhaps his "murder" had been the death of his conscience, too.

"Where were you tonight?" he asked quietly, curiosity getting the better of him. Warmth and feminine wiles had always intrigued him. "Or is that a secret, too?" he inquired dryly.

Chloe blinked, convinced she was at the whimsical mercy of a certified lunatic. Blast her cousin anyway for dragging out that corset and putting all kinds of sordid notions in this man's head.

He claimed he had been chased here. *Here?* Into her bedroom, of all places. Did he expect her to believe him? He was wounded, but still fast and strong. Stronger than she was. Still, could she make it to the door and down the stairs before him? If she bolted up, threw a pillow in his face, kicked that trunk into his path, well, perhaps. It had worked once when Heath was chasing her after she had stolen one of his coded messages to pay him back for teasing her.

Except that the wretched door to the hall, warped at the hinges, always took at least three good tugs to work free. Dominic would catch her before she could escape, and she would have angered him, not a good risk to take.

His voice jolted her back to reality. "I asked you a question."

"What?" she whispered, stalling for time, hoping that someone in the house would sense her danger, her desperation. _Please let Pamela sneak back up to help me unpack...._

"I asked where you went tonight."

A fresh wave of fear washed over her. Why did he care about her personal life? She suspected he was unbalanced, definitely dangerous. "It was—"

What did he want her to say? The wrong answer could set him off into a rage. Should she admit she attended a local dance? Dull enough in reality, but it might sound a little frivolous and was likely to make him think of romance. Heaven forbid that she put any ideas of that nature into his mind. Let him think her shy and boring, not the wild hellion who worried her family to death.

"I attended a musicale with my aunt and uncle." There. A half truth might satisfy him. He needn't know she'd been flirting her heart out with Lord St. John.

He snorted in derision. She noticed that he had a

beautifully molded mouth, despite his insulting expression as he drawled, "How utterly thrilling. A Chistlebury musicale. And you lived through it." To her mortification, he picked up the corset and dangled it between them. "What, may I inquire, was the point in wearing this?"

She drew back, refusing to follow his thoughts. "You said you were chased here?"

"That's what I said."

He was examining the undergarment in thoughtful amusement, almost as if he were picturing her in it.

She moistened her lower lip. Was he going to insist she put the corset on for him? "Do the people who chased you know you're hiding in my room?"

"No." He glanced up, gazing into her apprehensive blue eyes as he added, softly, "And you aren't going to tell anyone, are you?"

The tension strained her nerves; if he asked her to perform some lurid act, she decided she would rather jump out the window herself. Dealing with five boisterous brothers hadn't exactly left her defenseless. "Why would I tell anyone?" Her voice rose in tart indignation; it wasn't in Chloe's nature to submit to anything without a fuss, another family trait that frequently got her into trouble. "Why should I mind having a man break into my room and bully me about with brute force?"

His thick black eyebrows lifted at her outburst. He cleared his throat. "Would you mind keeping your voice down? I have only done what was necessary. Be forewarned—as I will continue to do so."

"But . . . what do you want from me?"

"I used to own this house, this land," he mused. "Your uncle bought it from me. Are you aware of that?"

"I suppose he told me. I don't remember."

"You do know who I am?" he asked her, more a statement than a question.

Chloe watched him remove his pistol from his waistband and place it beside him on the bed. "The Stratfield Ghost," she said without thinking. She glanced up into his dark sardonic face. "Lord Stratfield, I mean."

"Ah." His gray eyes glittered with irony. "The legend grows. Tell me—gossip reaches me slowly at the grave— am I still up to my nocturnal mischief?"

Chloe actually blushed, remembering the carnal sins her aunt and practically every person in the parish had accused him of committing as a ghost. She had half wished only an hour ago that he would commit those sins upon her romance-starved self. "Shall we just say that you are believed to enjoy an active afterlife?"

He gave her a mordant smile. "If only it were true."

There was silence. Chloe dared another glance at the pistol that sat between them. Sounds drifted from below, the gate creaking open, a horse whickering. Then a man's voice drifted from the driveway, a hard knock at the door . . .

He'd heard it, too. His gaze shot back up to Chloe's, openly hostile, suspicious. "Rather late for a caller, isn't it?"

She could only nod, praying for rescue. Yes, it was late, but if Stratfield had been spotted climbing into her room by an alert servant, then at any moment her uncle would come crashing through the door and she would be—

"Ruined," she thought aloud. "Oh, you *stupid* man. Do you realize what will happen to my name if you're found in here? Do you realize what my brothers will do to both of us? I'm supposed to be behaving myself in Chistlebury."

He grabbed his gun and slid off the bed, flinching in pain. "At the moment your reputation is the least of my concerns."

"Well, thank you so very—"

She gasped as he swayed against her, and lifted her arms automatically to steady him. The instinct came before she could suppress it. She might have done better to let him collapse. The physical contact, the shock of his hard body against hers again filled her with more confusion than she could handle. What in the name of heaven was she to do with him?

"You need a physician, Lord Stratfield."

His muscular weight unbalanced her, forcing them back in a clumsy embrace against the bedpost. He muttered, "Considering the circumstances, I think you should call me Dominic."

"I should call you the Devil, sir."

He glanced at the door, his eyes darkening. Survival had obviously sharpened his animal instincts. "Someone is coming. Hide me."

"I will not."

The pistol pressed into the tender flesh of her shoulder. "I would not enjoy having to shoot the person unfortunate enough to interrupt our 'friendship.'"

"You couldn't," she whispered in dread.

"Believe me," he said, his eyes cold. "I could. If I am

not dead in actual fact, the civilized part of me most certainly is."

She wrenched her arms away from him, her mouth as dry as dust. She could believe him. The lean, unshaven face that stared back at her bore no traces of the elegant nobleman whom she had imagined to be Sir Galahad. An edge of elemental danger had replaced the aloof sophistication that had defined Dominic Breckland, and the transformation made her wonder.

Had he known on the day they met that his life was threatened? Had she walked into more than a mud puddle on that afternoon? Remembering his rudeness, his strange remarks, it began to make sense.

Someone had made a brutal attempt to kill him. She could not blame him for seeking revenge. But not here, not using her as a vessel for his vengeance. And the worst part was that her brothers would never believe she hadn't brought this on herself.

The knock at her bedroom door ended her reverie. She did not know whether to feel relieved or frightened by the hesitant grumble of her uncle's voice. She would not wish the gentle old dear harmed for anything; she did not deem it wise to test Dominic's assertion that he could be driven to desperate acts.

"My uncle," she said in a terse undertone.

He clenched his jaw. "Get rid of him."

"How?"

"I don't care."

"Go back into the closet," she said reluctantly. "He won't come into my room."

He looked around, appraising, clearly not trusting her. "I'll be listening, and watching you."

"I'm aware of that," she bit back.

He tossed her corset onto the bed. "I'll stop at nothing to finish this."

She met his gaze, his cold determination sending a shard of ice down her back. A man with nothing to lose.

Chapter 4

Chloe watched Dominic's shadow shrink back against the wall as she hurried to the door to answer her uncle. Her intruder himself might not be in view, but she felt the dark threat of his presence as surely as if he were breathing down her neck. His menacing promise echoed in her memory. *Would* he harm her or her uncle? Best not to test his capacity for violence.

Her uncle glanced up anxiously as she opened the door a crack. With any luck his intuition would warn him something was very wrong. He would sense her fear and quickly send for help.

"Chloe," he said without preamble, "I would not have disturbed you, but we have a problem on our hands that cannot wait until morning."

She pressed her damp palm against the door, praying he would notice the panic in her eyes. She could only hope that the Stratfield "Ghost" had been sighted near the house. Perhaps her aunt would stage an evacuation for propriety's sake. Heaven knew the woman would fly into the boughs if she guessed the wicked wraith was hiding in her niece's bedroom. She almost smiled at the thought of Gwendolyn taking on the surly ghost.

Her uncle hesitated, his gray-haired head downbent. "May I come in?"

The shadow on the wall wavered, ominous in its silence. Chloe imagined that steel-muscled body imprisoning her again, squeezing the breath from her body like a bellows. Surely he had not always behaved in such a barbaric manner.

"No." She shook her head, her voice catching. How tempting it was to blurt out the truth. How dangerous for them both. "I—I'm not decent, Uncle Humphrey."

"Oh, my goodness," he said in embarrassment. "Oh, dear. Well, it is bedtime, and I would not have intruded, but that was the magistrate banging like a blacksmith at the door. It seems a carriage was held up on Cooper's Bridge only an hour ago. This time the highwayman took only the lady's gloves and garters."

For a moment Chloe forgot her own horrifying situation, following his line of thought. "You don't believe it was Devon—"

"Yes, I do." He began to pace the worn carpet in the hall, glancing down the darkened stairwell as he spoke. "He showed me a sketch, Chloe, the very image of your wretched brother. It seems he's done it again, committed another crime while your bedeviled brother Grayson has barely cleared the smoke away from the first."

Chloe suppressed a sigh; she knew exactly when her eldest brother Grayson had moved from the league of devils into one of its victims. When he'd met his match in her lovely sister-in-law, Jane. Well, perhaps at a later time Chloe would deal better with the anger and disappointment over Devon's behavior, if indeed this recent misdeed could be laid at his door. Perhaps she would understand what demons were driving him to irrational acts. But for now, wasn't it enough to have a rogue taking refuge in her room? Devon would just have to take care of this himself. Chloe had her own personal dilemma to manage.

"Does Aunt Gwendolyn know?" she asked on impulse.

"Good gracious, no," Humphrey replied. "I am afraid to tell her, but—" He stopped pacing, pivoted slowly, and attempted to peer over her shoulder. "I thought perhaps Devon might have come to you? You see, Chloe, I am aware he visits from time to time. No, dear, don't look so distressed. I would never tell your aunt or the authorities. This shall be our secret."

Another secret. Just what Chloe needed to burden her conscience a little more, to complicate her life.

"Our secret?" Stratfield's shadow had moved again on the wall. Not enough to give him away. Only a menacing reminder to Chloe that he was listening to every word, that she could not so much as exhale without his awareness of it. "What secret, Uncle Humphrey?" she asked blankly.

"Our secret about Devon." He gave her an odd look. "I'm not upset at you, Chloe. It's natural to protect your brother. But you must warn him the house could well be under scrutiny. Chistlebury is a far cry from London—"

"You certainly do not need to tell me that."

Her uncle frowned at her. "The authorities here never

have enough to occupy their hours. The silly boy is liable to get shot before anyone realizes he is a young lord in search of idle mischief. Gloves and garters, Chloe. Ah, well. At least no one was hurt this time."

She leaned her forehead on the door. The suspense of knowing Stratfield was waiting for her made it impossible to concentrate on the conversation. Surely he did not mean to spend the night in her room. "Devon is not here."

"I say, is there something wrong with you, Chloe? Your color looks rather off. You aren't taking sick again, are you?"

The closet door gave a distinct creak. Couldn't her uncle hear it? Could he not guess by the panic in her eyes that a man was holding a pistol at her back?

"It must have been that talk in the carriage," she said in an undertone.

"Talk? In the carriage? You mean about the cat dragging a mouse to the parson's chair? I never took you for a squeamish miss."

She resisted the urge to grab him by the lapels of his dressing robe and shake him into understanding.

"Not the cat," she said in a low, precise voice.

"Then—ah, yes." He raised his heavy white eyebrows in disapproval. "That ghost nonsense again. Poor Stratfield. You women are showing no respect for the dead."

Chloe's head began to throb. "Respect?" Her uncle harbored sympathy for a man who was holding her hostage under his very nose?

"Look how pale you've gone, Chloe. Are you afraid of ghosts? If so, I assure you that Stratfield's shade is not about to seduce anyone in this household." He chuckled at the thought. "Why would he sneak about doing in death what he could have done in life? With a snap of his fingers that poor man could have had his pick of our silly Chistlebury ladies. Excluding you and my Pamela, of course."

Spots of light danced before Chloe's eyes. Never mind seduction. Would Stratfield really go so far as to shoot them? If she squeezed through the door and bolted, she might make it down the stairs to hide.

But then Uncle Humphrey would be left standing in the hall, not understanding the danger on the other side of the door. He might try to defend himself against Stratfield.

"It's Devon who should concern us," he added in a somber voice. "Go to bed. We shall have to come up with a plan in the morning to straighten out the young rakehell."

"In the morning," she repeated numbly as he hurried off, his spry figure disappearing down the stairs. Would she even be alive in the morning to hold a conversation? Would she be disgraced by the ghostly Galahad?

She stared after her uncle, torn between a wild terror and self-survival. This was her last chance. No one would venture up to her room again tonight, believing her safe in bed.

Tell him the Stratfield Ghost is holding you hostage. Tell him before it's too late. . . .

"Uncle Humphrey," she called out, "please come—"

Her uncle did not hear her. She realized her cry for help had failed even before she could finish calling to him.

She did not see Dominic spring forward; a flash of motion in her cheval glass was her only warning. The next thing she knew, his heavy weight was pinning her to the door. The impact would have echoed through the house with a telling bang had the wood not been warped.

Caught between the door and Dominic, Chloe found it impossible to move. She could feel the coiled energy in his iron-hard body, and hoped he would not lose control. As for her, she had no choice but to stand perfectly still and pray she would stop shaking. He wasn't exactly hurting her, but the weakness that rushed through her, the heat of his body felt like an attack of sorts. She was embarrassingly aware of how male he was.

If she hadn't experienced the gentle devastation of his kiss that day in the rain, she would have felt differently. Would have been more afraid of him. Perhaps she had imagined his tenderness toward her. Even the memory of it made her dizzy. The sensual power he had wielded had been all too real.

"Is it really necessary to handle me in such a dramatic manner?" she demanded in a burst of anger.

He stared down at her with considerably more self-composure than he had shown before. "As long as you disobey me, I'm afraid it is."

She tensed at the faint pressure in her midsection and looked slowly down in dread. It took her a few moments to realize that the sharp object poking her in the ribs was not a gun, but a pen. Her own *favorite* pen! The nerve of him to take her prisoner with a pen. She snatched it from his hand.

"What were you doing in my desk?" she asked indignantly.

He drew away from the door, pulling her firmly by her forearms into the center of the room. His gaze never leaving her face, he reached behind him to calmly throw the bolt. "I was looking for writing materials."

She stared at him in stark disbelief. Somewhere in her closet he must have found a comb to attend his thick black hair, and a clean bandage to cover—

"Is that my pink Honiton lace petticoat you're using on your wound?" she asked in a scandalized voice.

He gave her a wry smile. "I apologize, but I really had little choice. It was that or another one of your intriguing corsets." His gaze swept up and down her curvaceous form in amusement. "I didn't think I'd fit."

His audacity stole her breath.

She noticed that his gun had disappeared. At least she could not see it on him, and she supposed she could take a measure of comfort in that. But helping himself to her pen and petticoats. What would he demand of her next?

He circled her. The dark was kind to him. Playing dead had not diminished his personal magnetism in the least. Aside from the wadded pink lace beneath his blood-stained shirt, he could almost pass for a gentleman.

"Writing materials," she said. Her brain was beginning to function again, coming to a rather nasty conclusion. "For a ransom note?"

"A what?" he asked, as if he couldn't believe his ears.

She cleared her throat. "A ransom note."

He stopped directly behind her. He was rubbing absentmindedly at the pink lace stuffed under his shirt, and

Chloe remembered how that petticoat had always given her an itchy rash on her behind. She could only hope he suffered as much.

"And pray what would I write a ransom note for?" he inquired, his head bent close to hers.

The dark, her state of undress, imparted an intimacy too distracting to ignore. She could feel her "ghost" smirking over her shoulder. Playing with her, he was, in a very ungentlemanly way.

She straightened her spine and said, "You are aware that my brother is the Marquess of Sedgecroft, a man whose wealth is common knowledge. It is logical to assume he would pay well for his sister's safe deliverance."

He stepped away, kicking the stool out from the dressing table. Contemplating her rigid form, he swung his tall body around and sat to regard her. His heavily lashed gray eyes moved over her like mist.

"*Is* it logical?" he asked in a low voice that seemed to verge on laughter.

She glanced down in disdain at his shadowed form. "Despite your evil intentions, you ought to be warned that there is a good chance my brother would instruct you to keep me."

"To keep you?" he repeated. "Now why on earth would the marquess do such a thing? Why would a brother not want a sister who gets herself in trouble every time he turns around?"

Chloe frowned. If she managed to survive this ordeal with Stratfield, she was going to make Grayson very sorry for sending her to Chistlebury. "It is true that I have not pleased my brother lately," she said reluctantly.

His eyes gleamed in the darkness. "So I understand."

She glared down at him. He sat astride the stool like a prince who enjoyed torturing his subjects. To think she had actually wished that day in the rain that he would ravish her. Chloe cringed at the foolishness of that fantasy. "What do you mean?" she asked in hesitation.

"I know why you were banished to our humble village, darling."

He knew? He couldn't possibly. Grayson and Heath had treated her social disgrace as if it were a War Office secret. Which was quite silly, actually, considering that half of London knew. And this man did not seem the sort who read the scandal sheets, but, still, he *could* have found out.

She dredged up the standard defense. "I was sent to the country to improve my stamina. I—I have a weak chest."

He arched his brow, looking her up and down in a leisurely fashion that brought a hot blush to the surface of her skin. "I do not detect a deficiency in that area of your anatomy, nor in any other part of you for that matter. You look in remarkable good health from where I'm sitting."

"Do I indeed?"

"Indeed," he said heartily, then added as a titillating afterthought, "of course, it is dark, and that robe conceals more than it reveals. I suppose I could light a candle and give you a more thorough inspection. Never let it be said I am one to form a hasty opinion."

"I hardly think we need to go that far," she sputtered.

"No? Pity. Well, you do look fine to me. In the dark, at least. In the rain, too, as I recall."

It was the oddest, most double-edged compliment Chloe had ever received, making her feel she was losing ground before she'd even gained her feet. Never had she encountered a man who poked so brazenly through the social curtain as this one did, except perhaps her own brothers.

"I happen to be prone to coughing spells," she said.

He examined a scratch on his wrist, murmuring, "And to kissing ones, I hear. Behind parked carriages. Tsk, tsk, Lady Chloe."

"How—" Chloe couldn't seem to find the breath to finish.

Dominic gave her a few seconds before he glanced up and studied her face. "Ah, good. Caught you out, did I? Well, your small social sins have nothing on my eventful past. So the young lady likes stolen kisses, does she? I shall have to remember that. For now, however, no female, even one fetching or as forward as you, will distract me from my purpose."

"Really," she said indignantly.

"It is my understanding you were exiled to Chistlebury for indecent conduct in the park." He fixed her with a stern look. "In the middle of the afternoon. What *could* you have been thinking?"

Chloe was beyond outrage. She was actually quite impressed. First, by his devious means of gathering information. Second, that she'd ranked high enough in importance to rate an investigation. Unless, of course, he was criminally insane and would end up murdering her. The thought reawakened all her anxieties.

"How could you possibly—how *could* you have

known about that incident?" she demanded. "I mean, why should my behavior matter in the least to a man I barely know?"

He traced his forefinger along the thin purple scar that crossed his chin. "I have made myself aware of every suspicious activity and person in this village, including you, during the course of my investigation to bring my killer to justice."

"You can't think *I* had anything to do with the attack on you?"

"Of course not," he conceded with a frown. "But you did arrive at roughly the same time."

"It was a coincidence!" she said feelingly.

"Yes. Apparently an unfortunate one for you."

He didn't need to remind her of the potential danger she faced. She had not drawn an easy breath from the moment she'd found him. She glanced at the door of the closet, then guardedly back at him. Her mind began putting pieces together. How could she be standing here so calmly in conversation with a . . . corpse? Only her etiquette-obsessed sister would find a graceful escape in this situation. Chloe's own impetuous tendencies were liable to make the whole thing worse.

"The killer," she said, looking up at his shadowed face, "is that who you meant when you said someone chased you here?"

"Ah, so you are as curious as your brother. I shouldn't be surprised."

She twisted her hands behind her back. Heaven knew she didn't want to set him off again, but . . . "You aren't going to stay here?"

"I'll stay only as long as is absolutely necessary. A day or two at most."

"And you aren't going to . . ."

He hesitated, as if realizing in amused horror exactly what she feared. "Take advantage of you? Tie your frail thrashing limbs to the bedposts and seduce you in secret while the rest of your household snores the night away?" He paused in apparent contemplation of the delicious absurdity of such a situation. "Hmm. It wasn't part of my original plan, but one learns to adapt. Do you think we ought to give it a try?"

Chloe was virtually rendered speechless by the scenario he described. "You wouldn't dare," she sputtered.

"Not unless you have an affinity for dead aristocrats." He shook his head ruefully. "It never fails to amuse me how lascivious I have become in the afterlife."

"You weren't exactly a saint in your living days, were you?"

He lifted his broad shoulders in a shrug. "Neither a saint nor a sinner. I suppose I was—am—only human."

"Why don't you leave?" she asked quietly.

"Because I am not certain that my pursuer has lost my trail." Which was true. Finley, his astute gamekeeper, had chased Dominic practically to the creaking gates of Dewhurst Manor. The irony of it was that his loyal manservant believed he was pursuing his master's murderer, and Dominic was not yet free to enlighten him or enlist his help.

"Your personal dilemma is hardly my problem."

"I'm afraid it is," he said with a dark smile. "Besides,

I will not be much of an inconvenience during my visit. I shall set up temporary headquarters in your closet. You will hardly even know I am here."

"I doubt that with all my heart. Are you serious? Do you expect me to sleep in the room with you? Headquarters—I won't have it. I shall fetch my uncle. Shoot me in the back if you like."

He rose from the stool and stepped in front of her in one fluid movement. His body blocked her from taking another step. "Then I shall have to fetch the authorities."

She stared up at him, more confident now. "To explain that you broke into my room, rifled through my undergarments, and accosted me?"

He stared down at her face, her chiseled cheekbones and strong features. He wondered if it was those dark blue eyes of hers that had gotten her into so much trouble, smoldering with a passionate intensity few men could resist. There was danger in her challenging innocence. Why her? Why couldn't he have broken into the room of one of the dull Chistlebury misses who scurried like frightened little mice whenever he looked at them?

He decided to call her bluff. "I think the authorities would be less interested in the hysterical ravings of a young woman who claims to have been visited by a ghost than by information about our local highwayman."

Chloe's temples began to throb. He couldn't possibly know what her cabbage-head brother had done. His investigation could not have been that detailed. "What highwayman?" she asked in a neutral voice. "I'm sure I have no idea what you are talking about this time."

"Well done." He leaned his hip back against the dresser. "I am almost tempted to believe you. But, yes, I know everything, from the botched holdup in Chelsea to his recent crime in Chistlebury."

"You were eavesdropping on my conversation."

"Of course I was. It happens to be a very helpful habit. I assume you are determined to protect this black-sheep brother of yours?"

"I have no idea what you're talking about."

"Your loyalty is quite touching, really. I hope it is returned. You called a man's name when you opened the closet door. Devon, I think. I don't believe I have had the pleasure of meeting the young devil."

"I want you to go away right now."

He ignored her command and picked up the morocco leather journal he had just spotted on her dresser. "Even from the grave I have a fair amount of money at my disposal. I imagine I could repay his debts several times over and not miss the loss."

She shot forward to rescue the journal from his large hands and stuff it under the bed. Fortunately, it was too dark for him to read her personal scribblings, but the mere suggestion of this rogue being privy to her innermost secrets was an intrusion she would not tolerate.

He watched her in amusement. "One should never record material of an intimate nature on paper."

"One would assume a journal in one's own bed-chamber would be safe from prying eyes."

He crossed his arms over his chest. "If you agree to help me, I might be able to save Devon from his apparent course of self-destruction. Even if the authorities turn a blind eye on his behavior, one of his victims might just decide to shoot him on the spot."

The same fear had entered her uncle's mind. Devon was courting danger, if not death. "Are you striking a bargain with me?" she asked coolly.

And in an even cooler voice, he replied, "A bargain, yes, if you like."

Chapter 5

"Blackmail." Chloe's voice rang out in the shadows. "That's what I would call it."

Before Dominic could respond, the conversation was interrupted by a *ping-ping-ping* that came from behind the closet door. The distinct sound of someone throwing dirt at the window from which Chloe had seen her chemise so provocatively dangled only an hour or so ago.

She stared across the room in an agony of indecision. It was impossible to pretend she did not hear the noise. Dominic clearly heard it, too, his thick black brows lifting in speculation. The disturbance could only be her irresponsible brother trying in his unsubtle way to get her attention.

If she ignored his summons, Devon, the reckless one, would either awaken the entire household or, worse, would decide blithely to climb into her window to find her. Another spray of dirt hit the window.

He would confront Stratfield. Disaster, possibly death, would result.

Dominic whistled through his teeth. "I suggest you

take care of your visitor before the damn fool disturbs everyone in the house."

Chloe pulled the silk robe together, not certain how much he could see of her in the dark. "And what do you suggest I tell him?" she whispered, her eyes narrowing.

He grabbed her arm, ignoring her gasp of outrage, and propelled her toward the closet, muttering, "Tell him the whole British army is watching the house. Tell him to stop robbing coaches! Tell him anything, but make him go away."

"Good advice," she retorted, shaking off his arm. "Perhaps you should take it yourself."

He gave her a little push toward the window, still left open from his entry into her trunk. Chloe leaned over the sill, too benumbed really to feel the cool midnight mist shimmer over her burning face. She started as her chemise snagged in the wood.

She could not believe this was happening to her. To think she had yearned for adventure. To think she had half wished that day in the rain that Stratfield would whisk her away from her uneventful life and . . . have his way with her.

The cloaked figure in the garden shadows below was bending to snatch another clod of dirt to fling at her window. He straightened as he spotted her and broke into a grin.

"Oh, no," she whispered in shock. Another character to add more chaos to her drama. She bit the edge of her lip and stared down at the man with whom she had danced and flirted outrageously only a few short hours ago. She had not believed him when he'd said he would not sleep until he saw her again. What an ignominious start to a love affair.

Dominic, pacing directly behind her, but not in view from outside, stopped and pivoted on his scuffed boot heels. His large frame bumped up against hers. "What is it?" he snapped.

She stiffened her shoulders at the hauteur in his voice. There was something disturbingly pleasant about the support of his body behind hers. "You know everything. Figure it out for yourself."

He lifted the outer edge of the curtain only far enough to peer down into the garden. Then he began to curse under his breath. Chloe raised her eyebrow at him in chastisement. Of course, being a Boscastle, she had heard far worse. In fact, she'd uttered worse herself.

"That isn't your brother," he said between curses.

Chloe smiled, rather enjoying his exasperation. "No, it isn't. It's Lord St. John."

"What the hell is *he* doing here?" he demanded.

"How am I supposed to know?" she asked with an innocent look. "I only met him tonight."

"Did you now?" he inquired in an icy tone.

"Yes, I did."

"You and your corset must have made quite an impression."

"Do you have something against romance, Lord Stratfield?"

"As a matter of fact, I do."

Chloe hesitated. "Well, some of us still believe in the possibility of love."

"And some of us, having been murdered in our beds, are to be forgiven if we are cynical."

"You cannot hold a grudge against the entire world," she said softly.

He gave her a fierce look. "Why not?"

"Well, because—"

"Spare me your youthful idealism and get rid of your unwanted guest."

"Which one?"

"Do not provoke me," he growled.

Chloe glanced down into the garden with an enigmatic smile, which sent Dominic into another round of muttered curses.

"Get rid of him," he said through his teeth.

"And how am I to do that?" she asked sweetly.

"Stop smiling down at him like a siren for one thing." He studied the silhouette of her slender form in the moonlight, at the silk butterflies emblazoned on her curvaceous behind. "I suppose you kissed him, too," he added in a dour voice.

She refused to dignify his insulting remark with an answer, although part of her realized that the situation did appear suspicious. A handsome young buck throwing dirt at her bedroom window this late at night. Dominic would never believe she had not invited him. Her brothers wouldn't have believed her either.

"None of this is my fault," she thought aloud.

Dominic grunted.

"Well, it isn't," she insisted, scowling at him over her shoulder. "I didn't invite him here any more than I did you."

"Perhaps you ought to keep your windows closed," he said in annoyance. "Tell me, are you expecting anyone else to visit you tonight? Should I prepare tea?"

"Only if you have to sail to China to get it."

Dominic took another long look at her silk-draped figure before resuming his agitated pacing. Trust his luck to have a tart-tongued Helen of Troy be the one to discover he wasn't dead. This woman was trouble, which, as he recalled, seemed to be a family trait. Well, more trouble he didn't need. And yet here he was, in the thick of a murder plot, with the village siren and the village idiot on his hands, and his killer on the loose.

"Why couldn't you have fainted at my feet when you opened the closet door?" he asked her. "It would have spared us both a load of grief."

She motioned him to silence with a wave of her hand. "Be quiet a moment."

"What?" he said in astonishment.

"I cannot hear a word Justin is saying with you muttering away. I think he might be asking to marry me."

Dominic stopped in his tracks, astonished at her sense of self-importance. Obviously she did not take his threat to her very seriously, which he suspected might have something to do with that kiss in the rain. He stared at her appealing figure, feeling an unwelcome flush of heat at her flirtatious voice.

Chloe leaned out farther, laughing as she whispered, "A reward? Hmm. What did you have in mind? And, no, of course I haven't forgotten you. What are you doing here?"

"Isn't it obvious?" Dominic muttered in disgust. "A clumsy seduction is under way. Let us all throw dirt at a maiden's window to win her heart. What? No dirt available? Then try duck eggs. Or billiard balls."

Chloe glanced at him from the corner of her eye. "Would you *please* be quiet?"

"Me?" Dominic said, his hand lifting to his chest. "Why don't you ask Romeo to do the same? He's the one making all the racket."

"What are you saying, Chloe?" Justin called up in confusion. "I can't understand you at all. Why don't you come down in the garden so we can talk properly? I made up a poem in your honor."

"A poem," Dominic said, throwing up his hands. His head was spinning. His shoulder was bleeding. And he had to stand by and listen to the local moron spout poetry?

"I like poetry," Chloe said under her breath.

"I don't," Dominic snapped.

"Then leave," she whispered as she braced her elbows on the sill. "Perhaps you had better come back in the morning, Justin."

"The morning?" Justin echoed in disappointment. "Don't tell me I have to wait that long to see you again? I do not believe I can bear this, Chloe."

"Well, that makes two of us," Dominic said darkly.

Chloe tapped her fingernails on the windowsill. "Three." Then, "Oh, Justin, bring your poem after breakfast. I shall be in a better mood."

Dominic scowled in the dark void behind her, his arms folded disapprovingly over his chest. Wasn't this a lovely situation? He could hardly help noticing the wistful catch in Chloe's voice. Nor, for that matter, could even a "dead" man such as himself overlook the suggestive draping of her body as she half dangled out the window to exchange whispers with her admirer.

Which brought him back to wondering about that corset on the bed again. He wasn't the least bit surprised that her brothers had sent her into social exile. Although a castle turret in the Italian Alps would probably not have provided enough isolation to keep this young lady out of mischief. She was too high-spirited and infused with Boscastle passion for her own good.

The mere fact that she had already attracted the interest of Justin, Lord St. John, Chistlebury's most eligible bachelor now that Dominic himself was dead, proved his point. Anyway, wasn't Justin supposed to be engaged to the Seymour heiress, a rather insipid twit who had trouble putting together a coherent thought? What the devil was the boy doing, luring the lovely exile Chloe down into the dark?

"I came all the way here to see you, Chloe." Justin's voice was beguiling in the mist. "Can't you at least sneak outside for a few moments to talk to me?"

"Don't you dare agree to such an indecent demand," Dominic said over her shoulder.

"Why shouldn't I?" She sounded indignant at his interference. "I'm agreeing to yours."

The young lord in the garden below took a few steps back in alarm. "Is there another man in your room with you, Chloe?"

"Tell him there is," Dominic said. "Tell him your lover is an extremely jealous foreigner who fights duels for a living."

"Would you leave me alone?" she whispered angrily.

Justin stared up at her in suspicion. "What did you say? Did I just hear a man's voice?"

Chloe could just see all her hopes for a beautiful romance dissolving before her eyes. In the past she had been drawn to the wrong type of suitor; this seemed to be a trait that her sister-in-law, Jane, had gently pointed out might need to be tempered with a streak of common sense. Chloe secretly suspected that she had fallen into a depressive state since the deaths of her father and younger brother, Brandon. Sometimes she barely felt like living herself. She did not understand why she could not be satisfied as easily as her friends.

She did not mean to hurt her family or to ruin her name. But there were times when she didn't care. Brandon had been killed early last year, and her father had died of a heart seizure barely five months later, when the news of his son's death had reached his country house where he and Chloe had been entertaining. She had been the only other family member present. It had been a brutal shock, learning of Brandon's murder and witnessing her father's death in the same day.

Chloe had not completely recovered. She did not think she would ever recover. She could not say that she and her father had been close. He'd been a distant, hard man who'd withdrawn from his children after his wife's death eight years ago when Chloe was twelve.

Chloe's world had gradually turned gray, and getting into trouble had a strange way of making her feel alive. In a peculiar way she was a ghost, like the man holding her captive.

Both she and Dominic Breckland might be alive in the physical sense, but a vital part of their essence had been damaged, if not destroyed. Chloe could not explain why she felt even the slightest sympathy for a man who could ruin her entire life when any other young lady in her place would react with panic. But then perhaps she was accustomed to being shocked by her brothers. Chloe's family had always flaunted convention.

Which was why tonight she had been so proud of herself for attracting the interest of the lighthearted Justin at the country dance. He wasn't her sort at all. He came from a solid family, didn't drink or gamble, and, as far as she could tell, there did not appear to be a dangerous bone in his body, aside from his lack of judgment in coming here tonight. But passion, controlled, was not always a bad thing, was it?

Her brothers had sworn to see her settled down with an acceptable husband before the end of the year. There might be a chance for a serious match between her and Justin, if he turned out to be all that he appeared.

And if the sarcastic devil practically perched on her shoulder like a gargoyle did not ruin everything.

"It isn't a man, Justin," she explained in a soft voice. "It's only my Uncle Humphrey."

The mention of the stalwart baronet was apparently enough to dim Justin's hopes for a successful midnight seduction. He blew Chloe a string of kisses and promptly vanished into the mist, leaving Dominic to glare after him in satisfaction.

"What a preposterous fool."

Chloe swung around to regard him. "I should have given him the chance to rescue me. I—"

She realized all of a sudden that he was no longer listening to her. He was staring out the window at his estate with an intensity that filled her with apprehension. He looked determined, dangerous again.

"What is it?" she whispered. "Do you see the man who followed you here?"

"Don't worry. I lost him in the woods."

"Don't worry?"

Dominic glanced at her, momentarily distracted by her undeniable appeal to the senses. Little surprise that other men stole kisses from her ripe mouth and prowled beneath her bedroom window. Those deep blue eyes definitely put wayward ideas in a male's mind. In fact, he thought it highly likely she would be swooning in the mist with her admirer at this very moment if not for him.

"My gamekeeper assumed I was a poacher," he said, returning to her question, "and chased me off the estate."

"Why didn't you reveal your identity?"

He smiled. "Because I *am* a poacher, in the process of laying a trap for my murderer. Finley, for all his cleverness, did not recognize me."

"Considering the way you look," Chloe remarked with a grimace, "I'm not surprised."

"Yes, well, we can't all wear decadent corsets and beautify country musicales with our presence, can we?"

Chloe stared past him to the massive outline of his Elizabethan house. He claimed to be well informed. Had he heard the talk that his mistress had been a frequent visitor there in the days following his funeral? It was assumed in polite company that the woman had been advising Dominic's cousin Edgar on her lover's personal affairs. But naturally, in private, people believed the worst.

Especially when the lady had been seen visiting the estate late at night.

"Does Lady Turleigh know you're still alive?" she asked without looking at him.

"No." There was a resigned tone to his voice that discouraged further inquiry.

"It seems cruel," she said, "not telling the woman who loves you that you aren't dead."

The look on his face as he turned to her gave her pause. Yes, she had hoped for a reaction, a clue to his feelings, but not the sudden vulnerability she saw, the raw anguish of a man who had been stripped emotionally to the bone.

"Love," he said in a light tone that belied his expression, "is a ghastly emotion, overrated by poets and idiots who live with their heads in the clouds."

"It's a good thing that everyone doesn't share your cynical views," Chloe said after a moment's hesitation.

"Most people have not had the misfortune to be murdered in their beds."

"That is true," she conceded, "but your friend wasn't at fault for that, was she?"

Again his silence revealed more than words, perhaps even more than Chloe wished to know. Had the fair Lady Turleigh been involved in his murder attempt? No. The thought of a well-bred woman lying in bed while her lover was stabbed to death was so appalling that Chloe preferred to believe his reaction was only a symptom of his cynical nature.

"Your brother fought with my brother Brandon," she said, in a deliberate attempt to change the subject. "Heath said that you had been investigating the attack on their party in Nepal."

Dominic's face darkened at the reference. "Yes," he said tersely.

"Well, what did you learn about them?" she demanded.

"Probably little more than you already know," he answered evasively.

Chloe examined his profile with curiosity. She had always wondered if there could be more to Brandon's death than the reported Gurkha rebel attack on his party. She had suspected that her brothers had been hiding the truth from her. Yet as a young woman in a family of men who restricted her every move, she could hardly sail off to Nepal to investigate.

"You know something," she said softly. Which was half a guess on her part and half intuition; Dominic's shuttered features told her nothing one way or the other.

"What I know," he said, moving from the window to kneel down on the floor, "is that I have told you quite enough for one evening."

"Tell me, and I might gladly help you."

"There's nothing to tell," he said curtly.

There was, and her instincts knew it. For that knowledge alone she would cooperate. Brandon had been more than a brother. He had been her best friend.

But this man was clearly not in a frame of mind to trust anyone, and Chloe might even have felt sorry for him had he not taken over her life in such an abominable manner. For example, the way he was rifling through her trunk again, diving into her most personal underclothes with no propriety whatsoever.

"What do you think you are doing now?"

"Looking for a dressing robe that has a little more

substance. Your state of undress is a distraction I do not feel strong enough at this moment to ignore."

Chloe paused. She might find the underlying sentiment behind that statement very interesting if she actually stopped to ponder it. He found her attractive. Yet obviously he was not going to allow that to interfere with what he needed to do.

"What's wrong with the robe I'm wearing? It's less than a month old."

He glanced up in exasperation. "Be thankful for the mist tonight. If your idiot admirer had gotten a good look at you, he'd be climbing that tree in a trice. I'd have to take care of him, too, and *not* as nicely as I am dealing with you, either."

"Nicely? I should certainly hate to be in your company when you consider yourself in a bad temper." She knelt beside him to rescue a favorite fan from his hands. "Anyway, if you hadn't been leering over my shoulder, I might have had the presence of mind to be properly dressed."

"Would you have gone down to meet him if I weren't here to leer over you? No. There's no need to answer. Your brothers undoubtedly were justified in exiling you."

She gripped the fan in a death vise. "I was sent to the country for the health of my lungs. I am prone to coughing ailments."

"You were caught kissing. A baron, wasn't it?"

Chloe felt suddenly stripped of all her defenses, laid bare before a man it would be impossible to mislead. "I have no idea where you come by this information."

"Suffice it to say that I have."

Chapter 6

Dominic closed the lid of the trunk. He suppressed a feverish shiver; he suspected there was an infection poisoning his body. He needed Chloe's cooperation for a short time, it was true. He required her discretion if his plans were to succeed, and had he been given his pick of partners in revenge, this rule-breaking exile would not have been his first choice.

Was she even capable of discretion?

Could he trust her at all?

It had been a mistake to mention her brother earlier. She had latched onto his suspicions all too quickly for him to be able to deceive her. Yes, Dominic had evidence that Brandon and his own younger brother had been the victims of a heartless plot. No, he did not accept the Honourable East India Company's tidy version of the attack by Gurkha rebels. Could he prove his suspicion? Not quite yet.

Damnation, what *was* he to do with her?

He rose slowly to his feet, aware that she was watching him warily, as one would a wounded animal. He did not blame her. In the past month he had become more beast than man, behaving on sheer instinct. He took hold of her hands and felt her eyes lift to his. Her fingers were so much smaller than his own, yet warm and strong as she resisted his touch.

"Look at me." The protector he had once been would have cherished her innocent fire. The devil he had become wanted to stoke her flames until she burned. "Can I trust you?" he asked, his fingers tightening as if to counteract the tension he felt in her hands.

"I don't know."

It was an honest answer, one that filled him with regret. If he could not depend on her, then all he hoped for would turn to ashes. He would have to find a way to ensure her cooperation until the time came for him to reveal his killer. He might have to take her into hiding until this was finished. Not a pleasant prospect at all, for either of them.

"Can I not win your friendship?" he asked solemnly.

She was cool, this blue-eyed Boscastle in her butterfly robe. "Breaking into my room, tossing me on the bed, and blackmailing me is hardly a prelude to friendship."

"Think of it as one neighbor helping another."

"I want you to tell me what you have learned about Brandon."

He wavered. To reveal what he'd learned might be the undoing of all his plotting. It would also involve her in more danger than she deserved. "Not yet. Don't tempt me to reveal facts that might destroy my chance to avenge him."

She nodded, apparently understanding more than he had wanted her to. "You've said enough for me to know I want to help you."

"The only way to help me is to do as I ask."

"How do I know *I* can trust you?"

"I'm not sure you can," he said. He bent his head toward hers, studying her face in the dark. "No wonder," he murmured.

"No wonder?" she whispered, as if she sensed where his thoughts were leading.

"No wonder that your baron risked so much to kiss you in the park. I have not forgotten the day we met."

He saw the flicker of response in her eyes, and that was all the permission he needed.

His lips skimmed the rim of her ear as his arms closed around her waist. He waited for a reaction. Instead, she went still. The scent of woman stole through his defenses. A month ago his life had taken a hideous turn. Someone close to him had betrayed him. Destroyed his ability to trust. And now he faced an entanglement with the sister of a nobleman he respected, a young lady headed for heartbreak if ever he had met one.

God forbid that he contribute to her self-destruction. But how could it prove otherwise? Chloe stirred in him the ashes of hope if not innocence; her vitality and idealism were traits he once might have shared. He tasted on her lips the poignant qualities of life that he had lost forever. Did she believe in love? In happily ever after? How many stolen kisses and sweet lies whispered in the dark, how many midnight trysts would it take to unmask her illusions?

It was not his place to destroy the dreams society encouraged. Nor did he desire to. Perhaps she would prove more fortunate than he had been. Perhaps her family's famous charm would protect her.

"You're kissing me again," she whispered.

"Yes. I can't help myself." He felt a shiver ripple through her.

"I thought you were going to kill me."

"It doesn't look like it, does it?" he murmured against her mouth.

"I knew you would not . . . could not hurt me."

"I wish I could hold myself in such high esteem."

She pressed her hands against his chest, not struggling, not acquiescing either. His mind registered a shock of pleasure, pain, but even then he desired her above all else. Her warmth, the subtle fragrance of soap on her skin. He ached to draw her essence into his bones. She was a balm, a refuge, more than mere sexual enticement. Soft and comforting in a world of darkness and betrayals. She reminded him of how his life had been, how he wanted it to be again.

He deepened the kiss, robbing her of any chance to resist, of breath. This definitely was not her first romantic interlude, but she was no courtesan either, and he might have been chasing one of the butterflies on her robe for all the hope of a future between them. Yet her body felt so warm and yielding, so lush and inviting, that Dominic craved closer contact. He wanted to peel off her clothes and draw her pink flesh against him. He wanted to beg her to be his, to ease his needs.

It was almost too much for him. His starved senses could not ward off the attack. He hadn't allowed himself to feel anything but unadulterated hatred for almost a month. The silky robe she wore accentuated her breasts and bottom in such a provocative way that her sensual appeal alone could have brought him back from the dead.

From the corner of his eye he noticed a blur of movement outside. It might have been a shadow, a cat on the limb of the tree, anything. But he wasn't about to take any chances. He caught her by her elbows and pulled her straight down on the floor, imprisoning her between his legs.

Chloe jerked her head back in alarm. "What are you doing now?" she demanded.

"The window. I didn't want anyone to see us."

She shifted, drawing her robe together where it had opened to reveal the pearlescent skin of her inner thigh. The muscles in his groin tightened with unbearable tension. She fit so snugly between his legs that he had to draw several breaths to subdue his arousal. He had not touched a woman in weeks, and this one stirred a sexual hunger in him he wasn't sure he could handle.

He didn't know what to make of her, or himself for that matter. He wasn't about to admit that kissing her had left him as hot and explosive as a sex-starved adolescent. But, damnit, she was right. His entire body felt sick and weak. In the past few days he'd been pushing himself to the limit, not sleeping at night so he could watch what happened at his house.

If Chloe Boscastle was as clever as she was attractive, he might have escaped one hazard only to find himself in a worse predicament.

Chloe was afraid to move, not certain herself what had happened or how to react. If he had kissed her to prove how inexperienced she was, he'd get no argument from her on that point. Her lips tingled from the forbidden friction of his, and she wasn't sure why she felt less frightened than before. There was an inexplicable air of intimacy between her and this man. She decided it had more to do with being an unwilling conspirator in his plans for revenge than with romance. How could she hate someone who wanted to avenge Brandon's death?

Captor and captive in a dressing closet strewn with her own undergarments. Only a Boscastle could find herself in this situation. Of course it was appalling that she had allowed him to kiss her again, but deep down inside she still thought of him as the man who had rescued her in the rain.

It would be dangerous to underestimate him, or his effect on her. Sir Galahad, or an embittered ghost? Chloe could not decide if it even mattered. Either identity threatened her.

The unyielding planes of his face did nothing to steady her nerves. The hard determination had settled back over his features even if his eyes smoldered like coals as he settled her back down on the floor in a pile of muslin petticoats.

Petticoats! It took them both several awkward moments to achieve a semblance of sanity. To pretend they might be sitting as normal as you please in a drawing room instead of cramped together on a closet floor. Chloe tugged the dressing robe around her shivery body, clearing her throat to ask again, "What are we supposed to do now?"

He leaned his good shoulder back against the trunk and stared up at the window. "I'm not entirely sure." He gave a start as he felt her kneeling over him, her delicate fingers on his chest. "Hey, what do you think you're doing?"

"How dare you ask me such a question," she said mildly. "Especially after the way you've behaved."

He sat forward with a curse as she finished unbuttoning his shirt to press her fingers lightly against the mangle of inflamed flesh. "That happens to hurt, in case you hadn't guessed. Besides, I don't recall giving you permission to undress me."

"I never gave you permission to break into my room or to kiss me either, but that didn't seem to deter you."

She grimaced, biting the inside of her cheek as she began gingerly to peel off his makeshift bandage and the petticoat fell away from his torso. The vicious stab wounds inflicted on his upper chest and left shoulder should have killed him. His attacker had clearly gone for the heart.

Whom had he hurt to provoke an act of such violent hatred? No small wonder that he'd vowed to find the person who had done this.

"Not a pretty sight, is it?" he asked her.

"The surgeon who attended you did an excellent job of those stitches," she said tactfully, thinking it was a miracle that he had even survived. "I doubt, however, that he would appreciate your ruining his handiwork with all your activity."

"It took hours."

"I still think you need a proper physician. That wound is becoming infected. Look at these red puffy streaks."

"No. No physician."

"What am I supposed to do if you die on me?" she asked in exasperation.

"Throw me out the window for all I care. If I'm dead it won't matter."

"Did it occur to you what would become of me if it is discovered that I am hiding a dead body in my room?"

"Or that you had kissed that dead body? But let us keep that our graveside secret."

"Don't you dare make fun of me, Stratfield. I shall be married off in a trice to some toothless old country squire if I get into any more trouble this summer."

"A fate worse than death. Lady Chloe Boscastle sentenced to the bucolic life. Think of all the crows and cows you can charm."

"I think I am beginning to understand why someone wanted you dead," she said darkly.

"Seriously, my dear, isn't it rather late to be worrying about the small matter of your reputation? I had nothing to do with your exile, after all."

Chloe took a breath to control her temper. "If you're caught in this room, my next exile will be to Tasmania."

"Lady Chloe with all those nasty convicts? Dear me, we can't let that happen to her."

"Is a convict any worse than a corpse?"

"I suppose it depends on the corpse." He paused, struggling, Chloe suspected, to hide how uncomfortable he had become. "Do I take your concern to mean you are really going to reform?"

She met his challenging gaze. "Yes. I am reforming, if you don't ruin everything."

He crossed his right arm behind his neck, cursing aloud at the agony the casual movement caused. "I'm curious. How did I compare to your lover in the park?"

Chloe could not miss the catch of pain in his voice. Like it or not, the man needed medical help, and for the life of her she had no idea how to bring a doctor up here in secret.

"I don't know how you compare," she said. "It's none of your business."

His grin was positively diabolical for a man in so much pain. "It can't have been much of a kiss. I can only assume mine was better."

There wasn't any comparison in Chloe's mind. Baron Brentford's kiss had been uncontrolled and ill timed, nothing that sent sparkling heat through a young woman's body. Nothing that burnished her from inside out like French champagne, even though at the time it had seemed like the most daring risk in the world.

And she'd gotten caught in the act. How would her long-suffering siblings react if they could see her now?

She came to her feet, feeling safer with distance between them. She noticed that he made no attempt to stop her. Was the pain weakening him? Was this entire frivolous conversation designed to distract him from his discomfort? Chloe had to wonder.

"Your kiss," she said softly, staring down at him as one might a wild animal whose nature was unknown, "was much, much worse. Horrid even."

He had the indignity to laugh at her. "Of course it wasn't. Do you remember his name?"

"Whose name?"

"You've already forgotten."

"When are you going to leave?" she asked, twisting her hands behind her back before she strangled him.

"In a day or so."

"A day or so!" she burst out in a half shriek of horror.

He scowled. "Unless you are known to shout in your

sleep, I suggest you keep your voice down. Might I borrow a blanket for the night? For propriety's sake I shall sleep in here."

"For propriety's sake," she muttered. As if there was even a shred of propriety in this man's life. Well, it was a good thing she had been brought up with Boscastle boys, or she might have fallen into a swoon and not recovered.

"Do you intend to sleep on the floor?" she asked.

"Unless you're offering to share your bed."

"I wouldn't share a box with you."

"I didn't ask you to."

Chloe studied his inert form, uncertain what to do. "You ought to put a fresh bandage on your shoulder."

"If you want to be helpful, stop jabbering like a maiden aunt and leave me alone." He felt behind him on the floor with his good arm. Chloe guessed the headstrong monster did not want her to see him in pain. "I don't suppose that wild brother of yours drank any brandy during his visits?"

"I am not running a coaching inn for uncouth men, sir."

"What the devil is this?" His composure was deteriorating; he scowled as he tugged a brass naval telescope out from beneath his backside. "Is this yours?"

"It belongs to my uncle's cousin. I borrowed it." She hoped he could not see the guilty embarrassment in her eyes. The truth was that she and Pamela had smuggled the telescope up here to watch the woods for Devon's arrival.

And to entertain themselves by observing Stratfield's house for his notorious ghost.

"You borrowed a telescope," he said blankly. "Why?"

"For, er, bird-watching."

"Bird-watching?"

"That's what I said."

He gritted his teeth. "Just go to bed. Pull the covers over your head. Please. Leave me alone to be miserable. If I'm dead in the morning, you have my permission to start screaming and pretend to faint. If I'm not dead and you tell anyone—well, I think you know what will happen, don't you?"

Chloe didn't respond to his threat. Somewhere in the last twenty minutes the situation had taken a drastic turn. He was no longer in control. She was. She could stroll out of her room and summon help. She could even tie her captor up in her stockings and humiliate him to her heart's content.

His eyes were sagging shut. He did not look well at all. She backed away from him, her hand lifting to the doorknob. Blustering brute of a man. Poor wretched beast, roaring in misery. Whether he realized it or not, she wasn't his prisoner now. He was hers.

Chapter 7

❦

Chloe stared at the changing shadows on the ceiling until the night lightened into dawn. What *would* happen if she refused to help him? Not only to her, but to him? The possibilities, all distressing, kept her awake. While she resented his bullying and threat of blackmail, she couldn't turn her back on a peer who had suffered as he had. Even if he'd brought it on himself.

Not long ago he had been a respectable member of the human race. He'd befriended her brothers. He had rescued her from a mud puddle, and if he hadn't behaved like a perfect gentlemen that afternoon, he certainly had not acted like a desperate man who would throw a woman across a bed at gunpoint.

She sat up in that same bed. No wonder she couldn't sleep. He hadn't slept either. This she knew from peeking in on him at least a dozen times. Each time she checked, she hoped he'd disappeared, saving her from making any decisions. The sight of that large male body sprawled out on her underclothes gave her a powerful flutter in her stomach.

Part of her wanted to run downstairs like a hysterical

young lady while she could. A stronger part, the part that always got her into trouble, wanted to shelter him.

Until he opened his eyes. His gaze seemed to pierce the dark. Then what Chloe felt was not straightforward or easy to control. What was it about the way he looked at her that set her on fire from the inside out?

She walked quietly to the closet and opened the door, preparing herself for anything.

"Chloe." He beckoned her to him with a wave of his elegant hand.

She hesitated. She felt no safer obeying that summons than any normal female would have when called to the side of a wounded wolf. She didn't want to be his last meal.

"What?" she whispered from the door, staring down at his bare chest. At some point during his restless night he'd removed his shirt and thrown off the blanket that she had draped over him.

The right side of his upper torso was a tribute to the perfect male form, a lean plane delineated with well-toned muscle. But the left side, that mangle of healing flesh and scar tissue. How could one person do that to another? Had he done something horrible himself to deserve it?

He frowned. "What time is it?"

"Almost five." She glanced at the window. "If you're hoping to leave, you had better do so in the next few minutes. Danny exercises the horses early, and—"

She broke off. The faint *clop*ping of hooves from the pasture echoed across the sleeping estate. There was no way now until nightfall that he could escape without being seen.

"What am I supposed to do with you now?" she muttered.

His mouth tightened into a grim smile as he struggled to sit up against the trunk. The telescope lay across his lap. "You can start by bringing me fresh water. Later in the day, if there is an opportunity, you can shave me and bring me all the materials I need. I've made a list."

She started at him, aghast. "Shave you?"

"Yes, shave me. Properly, and by that I don't mean slit my throat at the first opportunity. Please close your dressing robe."

"My—" Stricken, distracted by the heat in his eyes, she was mortified when she looked down and saw how much of her own flesh she had on display. An entire bare breast, the rim of pink nipple exposed. And by the hungry gleam in his eyes when he'd mentioned it, she ought to be grateful he was incapacitated. At least she assumed he had lost his strength. It wasn't a theory she felt brave enough to test.

"It's not that I mind," he added in a low voice. "It's actually a pleasant sight for a man to view first thing in the morning."

"A gentleman wouldn't have noticed."

"Well, isn't it a good thing I left those silly pretensions buried in the grave?"

"It certainly isn't good for me," Chloe said, frowning.

He looked her over before leaning his head back on the trunk. "Perhaps, when the times comes, you would like to stage my resurrection?"

Chloe bit back a retort. Even with her limited knowledge of injuries, she sensed he felt far worse than he would admit. On impulse she knelt and touched his forehead. As she suspected his skin was hot. Too hot.

He groaned and surprised her by turning his face into her palm. "Soft hands," he murmured. "Have you ever hurt anyone in your life?"

Chloe thought of the countless times she had attacked her brothers with her soft hands, whacked them on the behinds with her wooden sword, made rude finger gestures with her delicate white fingers. "No," she lied. "Not on purpose."

He stared at her with his soulful gray eyes, glassy now, yet so intense her belly clenched. "I didn't think so. A woman with hands like yours, Lady Chloe, gives pleasure not pain. I'm glad you've decided to do as I ask."

"I never agreed to anything of the kind." Her expression grim, Chloe eased back onto her feet and glanced around the closet. Dominic's big sprawling body occupied half the space. The other half looked as if a full-scale orgy had taken place during the night. Muffs, shawls, gloves, and shoes were tossed willy-nilly. Her aunt would expire of shock if she saw this.

Chloe wasn't certain she would survive herself. The sooner she got her ghost back on his feet and gone, the better.

"Well, go," he said in a grumpy voice. "Don't stand there staring at me." Then, "Wait. Are you usually up at this hour?"

"Goodness, no. I sleep until noon, take three pots of chocolate in bed, answer love letters for another hour or two. Sometimes I have my hair dressed, or take a soak in a rose-oil bath while my maid massages my toes."

"All that in one day? Poor thing. It must exhaust you."

Chloe narrowed her eyes. "I daresay it is not a good idea to insult the person who has control over one's life."

"Excellent advice," he retorted, flashing her a rude grin. "Keep it in mind when you are tempted to betray me because if you do, I'll come back for you, soaking in rose oil or not. Now busy yourself in some other frivolous pursuit until it is safe for you to go about your affairs."

Chloe ventured a nervous look at her window. "Safe? You don't think the killer will come after me, do you?"

"By safe," he answered, arching his brow at her, "I mean I do not wish you to attract attention by any unusual behavior. And you might avoid taking walks in the woods or talking to any dangerous men you meet."

Why? Chloe wondered in chagrin as she backed into the door. The most dangerous man she had ever met was hiding in her bedroom. Could a young woman have found herself in greater peril?

Chapter 8

Chloe stared at the sumptuous array of breakfast dishes on the sideboard, her stomach churning with anxiety. The smell of kippered herrings made her feel slightly ill. The bite of hot buttered toast she'd taken wedged in her throat like sawdust.

Stratfield might be hungry though; being a surly beast probably worked up a good appetite. She ought to sneak some of those sausages up to him. No. On second thought she ought to let him starve, drive him out like the wolf he was at heart. Heaven forbid she should encourage his insane behavior by feeding him buttered toast. Heaven forbid he regain any weight and grow stronger.

"Dear, dear Chloe, you have hardly eaten a crumb," her aunt chided, expelling a dramatic sigh. "You must have heard the awful news. It has affected my appetite, too."

Uncle Humphrey glanced at Chloe over the top of his newspaper and gave a subtle shake of his head. Presumably he was reassuring her that the awful news did not involve Devon.

"What news?" Chloe asked in a casual voice as she folded her napkin into tiny squares. In Chistlebury a chimney catching fire was liable to be viewed as an earth-shattering event.

Her aunt paused to make sure she had everyone's attention. "The Stratfield Ghost struck again last night."

Chloe put down the mangled napkin, her heart giving a loud thump. "Oh?"

Aunt Gwendolyn nodded. "He seduced another young innocent as she slept."

Chloe caught her uncle rolling his eyes heavenward. "Seduced—"

"Oh, for the love of God, Gwennie," Humphrey said. "Don't fill her head with these lurid tales so early in the morning."

Aunt Gwendolyn looked offended for a full three seconds before continuing her tale. "Rebecca Plumley was seduced last night in bed by the Stratfield Ghost," she announced.

Chloe blinked. "Say it isn't so."

Her aunt nodded. "There was a witness to the deed."

"A married woman in her forties is hardly a young innocent," Uncle Humphrey mumbled into his newspaper. "Besides, Rebecca looks like a scarecrow. I should think even a ghost would show better taste."

Pamela grinned at Chloe over the rim of her teacup. "I wonder what her husband makes of this."

"He is understandably mortified," Aunt Gwendolyn said. "In fact, he was the one to witness the act."

Humphrey lowered his newspaper in exasperation. "Are you telling us that Oswald actually *saw* the ghost having relations with his wife?"

"Well." Gwendolyn paused again. "The ghost was apparently invisible as spirits so often are. But Oswald distinctly heard Rebecca cry out, 'Oh, Stratfield, Stratfield! Do stop that, you daring devil! It tickles so!' And, for your information, the bedcovers flew into the air."

A deep silence swept across the room. Through the crack in the door Chloe saw the maid come to a skidding halt in the hall; her duster was frozen in midair above the bust of Sir Francis Drake, her uncle's personal hero.

Humphrey shook his head in chagrin. "Stop repeating this hysterical nonsense, Gwennie, do you hear me? Stratfield was an honorable man in his prime when he was viciously murdered. I imagine the poor fellow is turning over in his grave at the very mention of—of tickling Rebecca Plumley."

Chloe looked down at the table, suffering a sharp pang of guilty concern. The viscount's wounds had indeed been vicious. He might yet not survive them, and his death would indirectly be on her conscience. He really must have medicine. And sustenance. He had put her in the most precarious position. To think she had longed for some excitement to enliven her exile. Not to turn it upside down. She stared at the steam rising from her tea cup as if the wispy vapors could provide an answer. Could he really hold the key to Brandon's death? She wondered what her brothers would do in her place.

Of course, being young men with a penchant for reckless behavior, they would probably join Stratfield's crusade for revenge. A young woman hardly had that option. What would her older sister, Emma, do? Instruct the viscount in the gentle art of retaliation? Insist he knock before breaking into a lady's bedchamber?

She unfolded her napkin on her lap to catch the sausages and slice of toast she was nonchalantly sliding off her plate. "Does anyone have an idea as to who might have killed him? I should think catching him would be a priority."

Her uncle set aside his paper. "That is the first intelligent thing anyone has said today."

"And inappropriate." Aunt Gwendolyn huffed. "Murder at this hour of the morning."

No one said anything. No one was brave enough to point out that her ladyship had brought up the unnerving subject. Only after Uncle Humphrey raised the paper back to his face did he glance at Chloe to mouth, "It's all most peculiar."

Chloe wanted very much to know what he thought, but even her liberal-minded uncle would be horrified if he discovered what she was doing.

That she had virtually spent the night with a man who was so controversial that someone had intended to stab him to death. A man so strong willed he had risen from his grave to seek revenge.

What was she to make of him? The village of Chistlebury seemed to be divided into those who revered and those who despised him. Neither camp would be surprised to discover that his "ghost" had visited Lady Chloe Boscastle in the middle of the night.

Like attracts like, they would say.

Perhaps they would even be right.

*   *   *

After breakfast, in order to avoid giving her secret away, Chloe excused herself to hide her stolen breakfast in the Chinese vase in the hall and to take a walk in the rambling garden. Without realizing it she found herself standing beneath the scene of her latest crime, her own bedchamber window. The thought of Dominic hiding inside her room sent her into a fresh panic. Prisoner or not, she had to get rid of him.

How precisely was she to bring this about? He needed help. Yet he had forbidden her to fetch a physician, and she could hardly sneak one upstairs without alerting the entire house, if not the village. She considered the wisdom of asking her uncle's advice. But to do so would risk ruining the viscount's plans for revenge, breaking her word to him. Better to get him back on his feet and out of her life.

She turned in hesitation toward the stables. Perhaps she should go to the apothecary's. But a scandalous young lady asking for a salve to treat a stab wound would definitely arouse suspicion. There was little time to waste. She had to exorcise the ghost who had taken over her life.

"Good mornin', Lady Chloe," the undergroom said politely as he noticed her at the door. "Would you like to take an early ride today?"

Chloe stirred from her trance. The brawny young man was diligently currying Pamela's chestnut gelding. She drew a breath and remembered the angry gash the animal had received a week or so ago from kicking at the fence. The horse's hind leg had healed beautifully.

"What was that stuff you put on her leg when she got hurt, Danny?"

"A salve of herbs and oils I buy every year from the gypsies, my lady."

She watched him a few seconds longer. "It certainly appears to have worked."

" 'Tain't nothing better. I used it myself when I got cut up in a boxfight at the fair." He wiped his cheek with his sinewy forearm, motioning with the currycomb to the earthenware jar and green bottle on the rough shelf above. "The ointment and that tonic there'll fix about anything, I reckon."

Chloe stared in fascination at the dark glass bottle. She wondered if she dare. Had Dominic left her with any other choice? Did the arrogant man actually believe that having escaped death once, he could continue to do so?

She waited several minutes until Danny went out into the paddock before helping herself to his gypsy cures. Her mouth was dry as she returned to the house and retrieved the hidden meal from the vase. If anyone asked why she was in possession of breakfast sausages and a disgusting Romany potion, she supposed she could say that she had found a wounded animal and wanted to save it.

It was not, after all, that far from the truth. Dominic Breckland was as wild and dangerous as any untamed animal she would ever encounter.

Chapter 9

Her heart was beating furiously as she entered her bedroom. How still it seemed. The door to the dressing closet was shut, as she had left it. Had he managed to sneak away? How much easier it would be all around if he had. Chloe had not known a moment's peace since she'd found him. A future that involved him did not promise much tranquillity either.

She opened the closet door. His muscular frame was slumped in the corner, one arm draped around her trunk. She was surprised at the reaction of relief that swept over her. His eyes, bright with fever, scrutinized her for several moments.

"Good morning, again," he said calmly, inclining his head. "Are you ready to shave me?"

"Strangle you is more like it," Chloe said in indignation. How could he sit there ordering her about and sounding so collected when she had been worrying herself sick over his welfare? "You are the most troublesome person I have ever met."

A glitter of appreciation lightened his gaze for a moment. "A trait I suspect we share."

"And will undoubtedly pay for," Chloe said, unwrapping her napkin. "Here. Eat these while I look at that shoulder. There's a bottle of brandy in my reticule, too. Add pinching my uncle's possessions to my list of crimes."

"Why do you want to look at my shoulder?"

"I have some horse medicine, you ungrateful, suspicious man," Chloe said in a very quiet voice. "I stole it from the stable, and no one knows a thing. What do you have to say about that?"

He laid his head back rather meekly, his firm mouth curving into a beguiling smile as she unbuttoned his shirt. "I don't know. If I tossed my mane and gave a few good whinnies, would that qualify as an apology?"

He could not stay in her company much longer.

Neither of them had slept much last night. Dominic could see the shadows of fatigue on her pretty, angry face. He knew how often she had checked on him, even though he had pretended to be asleep. What a devilish time to learn that he could still feel such bewildering desire and even tenderness, that he was deeply sorry he had dragged her into his personal hell. Each time she had leaned over him a gnawing hunger had taken hold of him, and it was all he could do not to pull her down onto the floor.

Her body would feel plush against his fevered skin. He could surrender to the erotic images that had haunted his broken dreams.

He could also ruin everything, for both of them, by succumbing to such temptation. It was not only sex he craved. He enjoyed her caring and cleverness but not the weakness she brought out in him.

"Horse liniment," he mused. "I should be thankful that you are resourceful, I suppose."

"You should be thankful you are not truly dead." She paused, her gaze lifting to his. "You must go, Stratfield."

"I know that."

There were muffled footsteps from the hall outside the outer door. Chloe quickly pressed the glass bottle into his hand. "Drink this. My uncle is taking us to a play in the rectory tonight. The servants usually retire to the housekeeper's parlor for cards when they are alone—"

His piercing gaze caught her off guard. She stopped, flustered, as he said, "Should we be fortunate enough to meet again, Lady Chloe, I trust it shall be under circumstances that enable us to finish what we started."

"I—I have no idea what you mean."

Ah, but she did. He could tell by the disconcerted pause she took, the way her fingers stilled on his shoulder. She had enjoyed the sensual aspects of their encounter as much as he. "I mean this," he said.

He took her chin between his fingers and leaned forward to kiss her. He heard the small sigh that escaped her and felt her body arch forward involuntarily. She was primed for the taking, alive and simmering with passion. And her wanted her so badly, it was probably for the best that he could not have her. The more involved he became with Chloe Boscastle, the less control he was liable to have over his own life. She could take over a man's heart without even trying.

He buried his face in her warm neck and brushed his hand down her back. "Stay out of the woods, Chloe. It might seem hard to believe, but there are men who are even worse for you than I am."

*   *   *

The village thespians had staged an amateur production of *Hamlet* in the rectory. The acting was so awful that Chloe had to bite the tips of her glove to keep from giggling. She could not concentrate anyway. The mere thought of Hamlet's ghost only reminded her of her own haunted room.

It was during the gravedigger's scene that she became aware of the buzz of speculation that went through the audience. She turned her head and saw a trim, erect, dark-haired gentleman in a cloak take a seat alone at the front of the theater.

Colonel Sir Edgar Williams, Galahad's uncle and presumed heir. At least he had the decency not to parade his nephew's former mistress in public if she was indeed still in the vicinity. Chloe had not heard anything of her recently and even wondered whether the woman deserved Dominic's bitter unforgiveness. One could make a case that a mistress could not be found guilty of infidelity when she did not know her past lover was still alive.

"Well, my heavens," Aunt Gwendolyn murmured, arching a brow. "Perhaps I can persuade the viscount's uncle to make a contribution to the church rectory. His nephew, despite his other faults, was quite a generous sponsor."

"Do be quiet, dear," Uncle Humphrey whispered. He winked at Chloe. "We wouldn't want to miss a word of this scintillating performance. Anyway, Sir Edgar will not have come into complete possession of his inheritance quite yet. There are legal formalities to handle first."

As he spoke Hamlet accidentally dropped Yorick's skull

on the gravedigger's head. The startled actor swore, rubbing his crown, as the audience broke into unrestrained laughter. Sir Edgar chuckled and started to applaud—until his gaze met Chloe and her aunt's.

He inclined his head and smiled in acknowledgment before turning his attention back to the stage. Chloe felt a rather unpleasant tingle spread through her. That brooding, wandering gaze and strong-featured face—

"That's the ghost's uncle you are staring at, Chloe," Pamela whispered from behind her fan.

Chloe started, realizing that the man did, not unremarkably, resemble Dominic, although a certain vitality seemed to be missing. He was heavier than his nephew for one thing, and years more mature with an old-world gravity about him, a reserve that could be attributed to his military background.

"Why do you think he's broken off with the ghost's mistress?" Pamela asked, her eyes narrowed in speculation. "I mean, assuming that he has."

Chloe's attention was suddenly diverted; Lord St. John had just arrived, his appearance causing a stir among the young female members in the audience. Chloe held back a giggle as he noticed her, grinning at her with complete disregard for the play for several moments before he took his seat. Trust Justin's blustering self-importance to interrupt a performance.

"I don't know," she murmured to Pamela, reluctantly returning her attention to the actors onstage, who seemed far less interesting than the audience. "I suppose he has better things to do than shock Chistlebury by bringing the ghost's mistress to a public performance."

"Or because the pair of them were involved in a murder plot," Pamela said under her breath.

Chloe felt as though a cup of cold water had been thrown in her face. "What did you say?"

"Well," Pamela whispered, wriggling away from her mother's chastising scowl, "it's only a notion. But I do hope they find the viscount's murderer soon. The only place I feel safe these days is in the house behind locked doors. Or in my closet."

Chloe stared straight ahead, afraid her face would give her away. If Pamela and her mother knew exactly who was locked in their house at this moment, they would hardly feel safe. If they guessed for one second that their infamous houseguest from London had been half seduced by the local village ghost—

Heat flooded Chloe as the memory of Dominic's intimate aggression returned in full force. Her hand trembled as she snapped open her fan to cool her stinging cheeks and throat. The desperate hunger in his touch had awakened a dangerous fascination inside her. It was to be hoped that she would never be in a position again to fight such temptation. Or to succumb to it.

He was gone.

She felt his absence as acutely, as powerfully, as she had felt his presence. The moment she walked into her room, she sensed that he had gone. The air still seemed charged with his potent energy, and she was sure she would never forget him, but he had vanished.

She lit three candles and carried one into the dark dressing closet. The window was carelessly left open, and the breeze that fluttered the curtains hinted of rain.

The candle expired almost the same instant as she noticed a piece of small folded foolscap on the floor.

She bent to pick up the paper, then straightened to close the window. There was no sign of him outside. No ghostly figure lurking in the garden to wave good-bye. He had evidently felt strong enough to make a successful escape. But to where?

Perhaps the paper held a clue. She took it back into her bedroom and sat on the edge of the bed, slowly opening it in the candlelight. For a second she did not believe what she read.

"A code," she whispered. A cryptographed message very similar to the ones that she had once found in Heath's personal possessions. Perhaps if two of her brothers had not dabbled in intelligence affairs, the garbled numbers in the cramped columns would not have meant a thing. But as it was, the sight of a coded missive did not shock her.

What shocked her was that Stratfield had obviously dropped it while escaping. And that the handwriting was in her dead brother Brandon's very distinctive script.

"Chloe," a male voice whispered behind her.

She dropped the paper on her pillow, stifling a scream as a dark-garbed figure loomed in the dressing closet door. For an irrationally relieved moment, she thought her ghost had returned, but the shadowy figure soon resolved into the more familiar and far less threatening form of her outlaw brother, Devon. She had practically forgotten all about the rogue.

"Oh, it's you," she said in a soft voice, tucking the

scrap of paper under her pillow. "Why do you have to sneak up on me like that?"

He gave her an engaging grin, his blue eyes glittering. "I can hardly announce myself with a fanfare of trumpets, can I?"

"You shall be announced in prison if you don't stop playing highwayman, Devon Boscastle," she said in a burst of irritation.

He looked genuinely puzzled. "What do you mean? It was once, Chloe. A very bad mistake of judgment."

She jumped up to face him, his equal in temperament if not in size. "Cooper's Bridge. And don't lie to *me*. It isn't funny."

"Cooper's Bridge?" He ran his hand through his short black hair.

"The Kissing Highwayman, Devon. You have to stop."

He blew out a sigh of annoyance. "It wasn't me. . . . I seem to have started a fashion, Chloe. It's a damned embarrassment if you must know. Bored young men are holding up coaches to steal kisses."

"And risking their lives," Chloe said, looking him over.

"Well, I can't stop their stupidity, can I?"

She hesitated. "It really wasn't you?"

"Good God, no. I've been quite a good boy, believe it or not, helping old Cousin Richard pot his orchids. What about you?" He leaned against the dresser, giving her a rueful look. "Desperate for a bit of excitement, are you?"

She glanced away from his shrewd gaze. "You have no idea." And he would not believe her if she told him exactly how much spine-tingling excitement she had encountered since his last visit. *Should* she tell him?

"You've met a man," he said, amused and concerned at once.

She looked up, a little too quickly to hide her guilt. "Don't be silly. In Chistlebury?"

He strolled across the room, eyeing the pillow behind her. "That was a love note you were reading, wasn't it? Lord above, Chloe, don't go falling for some country bumpkin. Our exile shan't last much longer."

"I most certainly hope not," she said. She hesitated a moment. "Devon, no one will talk of it, but you've always been candid with me. Do you think Brandon might have been involved in espionage after he left England?"

"In the Honourable East India Company? I doubt it, although before—" He met her gaze. "It shouldn't be a secret, not from you, not since he's dead. I believe he carried a few messages back and forth for Heath in Portugal. Imagine surviving the war only to be ambushed by fanatics. It doesn't seem right, does it?"

Chloe shook her head, feeling torn between trusting him and the promise she had made to a man she barely knew. Should she break her word to Dominic? After all, she could not be held accountable for a vow she had made while being tossed on the bed and kept a virtual hostage. But . . . a promise was a promise, and if that was the only way to learn what had really happened to Brandon, then so be it.

Besides, Devon might assume the worst. He might believe that Chloe had been compromised beyond repair. The dominant male in him would go after Dominic, and there would be the devil to pay all around. Chloe would be the eye in the center of another storm. No matter what decision she made, she would face controversy and censure.

She looked up. "I suppose you came here for more cash."

He arched his brow. "Actually I came here because I was worried about you. Old Richard is generous enough, but I shan't be responsible for my sanity if I have to pot any more plants."

"Why would you worry about me?"

"Just a sense, Chloe. Oh, all right. I know it sounds daft, but I had the silliest dream that you were in danger." He put his hands on her shoulders. "You aren't, are you? I mean, you're not planning to elope with another cock-brained cavalry officer? Grayson and Heath would have my head if I let anything like that happen."

Chloe felt a cold flush go through her. She'd never lied to Devon before. He had a sixth sense about some things, and deception did not come easily to her now. Now that Brandon was gone, Dev was the best friend she had. Even so, she wasn't quite ready to share her secret with him yet. She had to think it through herself first.

"I did meet a man, if you have to know." She smiled up into his concerned, handsome face. "It's Justin Linton, and yes, he's thrown stones at my window and made up awful poetry in my honor. But he's good fun, Devon. I think the Old Ones might even approve."

The Old Ones included their siblings Grayson, Heath, and Emma, who were not chronologically that much older but who, in the eyes of Chloe, Devon, and Brandon, had always been the family tyrants. Drake had fallen somewhere in between the label of tyrant and troublemaker.

"As long as *you* approve, Chloe," Devon said gently, "then he cannot be all that bad, although I have to say I really took a dislike to that baron you kissed in the park."

Chloe crossed her arms over her chest, the gesture instinctively self-protective. "Yes, well, I'm not liking him all that much myself right now. Look where that indiscretion led me."

The rumble of voices from the stairwell outside her room distracted them. Devon stirred, giving his sister a kiss on the forehead before he stepped back toward the closet.

"All this cloak-and-dagger nonsense, Devon," she whispered at his retreating figure. "I shall be glad when Grayson gives the word, and you are no longer afraid of the authorities."

He grinned before disappearing from sight. "The authorities be damned. It's Aunt Gwendolyn I'm avoiding. The woman will lecture me to death if she gets a hold of me."

Chapter 10

Dominic realized he had dropped the note the instant he reached the fern-shadowed escarpment that marked the boundary of the woods. He could not believe his own carelessness. It was a dangerous sign. He couldn't afford to go soft or grow reckless because a young woman had distracted him. He walked through the dark trees in disgruntled silence.

In fact, even as he approached the park behind his own house, he was thinking about Chloe when he should have been concentrating on not being seen. He had always been an intense, rather private man who did not particularly care for the entertainments common to his class, and he was not particularly proud of his past. Yes, he knew how to attract a woman. Unfortunately, he had not made the best of choices in Lady Turleigh. She had not waited until his body was cold to warm her bed with another man.

He could not forgive her. She was part of the life he wanted to forget.

He didn't care if he was unfair, or if she had been frightened. He did not care if his disgust with her was irrational. He could not blame her for looking after her own interests. But not with his cousin. It turned Dominic's stomach, and he was done with her. The last he'd heard, she had left the village; he did not care whether she returned.

Chloe Boscastle presented an entirely different problem. Infinitely more pleasant and perplexing. She had stirred not only his male hunger, but his more human needs for company and understanding, for intelligent conversation and stimulation. His blue-eyed lady provided for all his private wants in a very provocative package.

He frowned, remembering what little he knew of her family. Rumors had circulated in the ton that one of the Boscastle daughters—he assumed it was Chloe— had been alone with her father when he died. Royden Boscastle had been said to rule his family so tightly that his children were rebelling in public; perhaps something in this explained why the youngest daughter ran a little wild. Her father's succession of mistresses had probably not been of the nurturing nature to replace the mother Chloe had lost.

Of course he could only desire her from afar, thereby frustrating himself to death. With any luck their paths would not cross again. By the time Dominic completed his revenge, which might end up killing him yet, Lady Chloe would be married off and whisked out of temptation's reach. Fortunately for her.

He slipped quietly down the darkened hallway of the unused wing of Stratfield Hall, a living ghost who haunted his own house. Who would think to look for him in the secret passages of the very place where he had been murdered? He rather enjoyed the black irony of it, the village ascribing deliciously wicked deeds to him. In fact, the rumors of his ghostly misbehavior could fit in well with his plans.

If he did not ruin it all with his own stupidity.

He should not have left that blasted note behind. He knew full well when it must have slipped from his pocket. When luscious Chloe had been half undressing him, her capable white hands touching him in a way that had left him breathless with lust. How desperately he had wanted her to keep on exploring his body.

And now those ladylike hands were in possession of a note that might, or might not, depending on its contents, destroy everything he had plotted for. Would she show it to anyone?

Would she keep his secret?

Or would she toss out the paper, thinking it a piece of garbled nonsense? He wondered if the sister of Lieutenant Colonel Lord Heath Boscastle would recognize it for the cryptograph that it was. He wasn't exactly sure himself how important it might prove, or even who had written it for that matter. All he really knew was that it had been found sewn in Samuel's company jacket. His brother would not have gone to such lengths to hide it unless it meant something to him.

He slid his hand along the wall and pressed the lever concealed behind a rough stone alongside the fireplace. The dark passageway loomed before him, empty and uninviting. This was what he had become. A creature of the darkness who must scurry and hide while his enemy feasted at his table, made love to his mistress, planned to spend his fortune.

He stepped into the passageway, allowing his vision

to adjust to the stale airless gloom. He reached into his waistband for his pistol, a precaution lest the dark provide any unpleasant surprises. He had become as skittish as a virgin since his "murder." A gun gave him a measure of security.

His fingers curled not around the pistol's smooth ebony handle but the unbearable softness of a woman's chemise.

The undergarment had fallen out of the window as Dominic made his furtive escape. Not wishing to get his charming if unwilling hostess into trouble, he had stuffed the chemise into his waistband before leaving the grounds. God knew the woman would land in enough trouble on her own.

He examined the delicate fabric. A treasure to drag to his lair? He smiled a little. Not that he required anything to remind him of Chloe. His body provided a painful enough reminder of his desire for her.

It seemed he was not as dead as he had hoped.

He began to descend the impossibly cramped stone stairs that led into a tunnel beneath the house. There he had spent countless hours sitting in the candlelight, studying the cryptic message that was all he had left of his brother.

It _had_ to be vital. Dominic was desperate to solve the code, having come up against a wall in his own inquiries.

It was Samuel's servant who had set off Dominic's suspicions, writing through other British soldiers to reveal that his master had been meeting men in secret in Nepal in the weeks preceding his death.

Hoping to learn more, Dominic had personally corresponded with the British resident of Nepal and later General Ochterlony. He had journeyed to London several times to meet the Board of Control, the company's court of directors, and those in contact with Lord Moira, the British commander in chief in India.

They could not help him beyond reading the official report: Chasing Gurkha warriors into the hills, his brother and Brandon Boscastle had been ambushed and then thrown into an inaccessible ravine, the prey of wild animals and the elements.

By this time a lurid possibility had entered Dominic's mind: his own uncle and Samuel's commanding officer had ordered the ambush in Nepal. Dominic did not know exactly when or how he had begun to suspect the truth. But he did remember that his late mother had never liked Edgar, and had warned her husband more than once that he could not be trusted.

The fact that Colonel Sir Edgar Williams had been in Kathmandu on official business at the time of the ambush did not prove his innocence. There were always renegade warriors for hire in that part of the world if a man offered enough money.

A noise from behind him drew Dominic out of his thoughts. A low whine that was not quite human. He reached for the pistol, then stopped.

The heavy object that butted up against his leg was not a threat. Nor was the cold nose that brushed his hand. He turned swiftly, dropping to his knees in grudging welcome. It was his favorite dog.

"Ares," he said. The big hound sat before him in anticipation of a romp in the woods, his eyes glistening in the dark.

"You should not be here," Dominic said roughly. "I cannot take care of you. There isn't room."

Nor could he take the risk of returning the dog to the house just now, in the middle of the night. Sir Edgar liked to read into the late hours.

"Ares," he said in vexation. "What am I to do with you?"

He straightened and turned back to the stairs. The dog shadowed him as if the matter were settled.

Dominic's mind had returned to a more perplexing problem. He needed that note back in his possession, no matter what risk he must take to retrieve it.

Even more dangerously, perhaps, he would need to visit Chloe Boscastle's room once again.

Less than forty minutes later he was standing in her bedchamber, the letter folded in his pocket. Chloe had slept through the swift theft. He studied her from the closet door, telling himself to escape while he could.

It was too tempting not to touch her. Dominic had promised himself that he would do no more than retrieve the letter and leave her room before she awakened. But once he looked at her, he was transfixed. He pushed away from the door.

Of course she was not arranged across the bed like a typical sleeping maiden. Instead, she sprawled out at an uncomfortable angle, her tousled black curls framing her scowling face. She had kicked one of her pillows to the floor, fighting someone, something in her sleep.

The bedcovers lay twisted around her sleek white legs. He drew a breath, moved by how vulnerable she appeared, not at peace with herself even in sleep. He was not sure how a man would subdue her restless spirit. Or if he should even want to. It might be better to enjoy it.

His gaze followed the line of her bent knee to the hollow between her legs. Her linen nightrail provided little protection from his hungry gaze.

He came closer to the bed. He could see the shadow of dark curls at the juncture of her thighs. His body clenched at the sight. He needed her so badly. He needed to bury his sex in all that warmth and softness.

He sat on the edge of the bed and listened to her steady breathing. What was she dreaming about? After a moment he ran his forefinger gently across her forehead as if to erase her scowl. She stirred, stretching toward him. He stared at her white throat, the bounty of her breasts, her body relaxed and artlessly inviting.

He traced his finger across her collarbone, teasing the dusky peaks of her breasts until they tightened. She was responding to his lightest touch. He felt a dangerous stab of desire deep in his belly. She didn't have to move a muscle to arouse him. He ached for her in every bone.

He leaned forward and rubbed his face against her neck. A mistake. The scent of her obliterated his restraint. She made a little sound in her throat, turning into him. He swallowed, struggling in a battle he had already lost.

He could not fight what he felt for her. She had invaded what was left of his heart, and his body craved her beyond what he could bear. His face darkened with a smile of self-mockery. The Ghost of Stratfield Hall was about to live up to his reputation.

Chapter 11

Chloe dreamed that night that a man was stroking her face with a feather-light touch. His caress made her shiver with longing, and he whispered her name. She moaned, fighting the power of his voice, fighting to stay asleep. His tapered fingers circled the curve of her shoulder, the swell of her breast, teasing her nipple through her nightrail.

Her body responded to her seductor with a surge of uncontrollable lust. Without the inhibitions of her waking self to interrupt, she arched shamelessly against him. She could not see his face in the darkness of the dream. She could only feel the heat and hunger in him.

She wanted to beg him for more. To ask him to touch her in other ways. Her dream self could not stop him anyway. She could only respond to the power he wielded, the needs he had awakened. Her senses answered his unspoken demands without hesitation.

"You have the body of a goddess, Chloe," his faraway voice whispered against her neck. "I could worship you. I could show you pleasure you would never forget."

Her dreamy intellect whispered he was right. When

his hand drifted down her belly and nestled in the warm folds of her sex, she felt herself gripped by a desire so all-consuming she could have wept for it. Her body did weep; in the hollow of her thighs a moist heat seeped, flooding her with longing. A spiraling pleasure spread into the very depths of her. She needed release, a reprieve from the aching inside.

His elegant fingers had found the secret place where no one had ever touched her before. The steady stroking against her mons made her pulsate all the way to the soles of her feet. If not for the frail barrier of her night-dress, she would be completely exposed and open to him. It was the most erotic dream of her life. The blood in her veins thickened as he brought her to a powerful climax. Heat flooded her from head to toe, and her hips lifted; her heart raced as pleasure throbbed in her belly.

She trembled, helpless and yet enjoying every moment of it. *Dominic.* His dark image pervaded her dream. She stirred and tried to speak his name, to ask him why he had returned. She wanted to tell him that she had seen his uncle tonight at the play, and that she did not like the looks of him. She needed to warn Dominic, to hold him. She ached to feel his strength, to demand an explanation of why he had invaded her sleep.

A sensation of chilliness suddenly replaced the intimate warmth she had been savoring. She opened her eyes in reluctance and waited as the pulsations in her belly began to subside. A sensual lassitude throbbed in their aftermath to torment her.

Her dream had seemed so real, and yet she was alone, her body cooling and wide awake—had Devon left the door to the dressing closet open? Hadn't she made sure to shut it securely for the night?

She sat up and fought a shiver as she slipped off the bed.

"Who is it?" she whispered. "You devil, Dominic, is that you?"

No answer. A cursory search proved the dressing closet was empty, the window was closed, and the curtains were drawn. With a troubled frown she returned to her bed, pulling the pillow against her as if she willed the warmth to return to her body.

The note was gone. A single white rose occupied its place under the pillow. Its petals were lightly bruised and fragrant.

She stared down at the bed, her heart in her throat. It could not be. The outrageous fiend couldn't have returned to steal it while she slept. He could not possibly have been here, touching her.

"Oh," she whispered, on fire again, though for a very different reason. "He wouldn't dare."

He had. Frantic, she searched the room, the closet, the floor, still feeling as though she were in a dream.

"And the telescope is gone," she muttered as she wrenched open the window to gaze out into the thin tangle of woods that separated the two houses. "I know you are out there somewhere, probably laughing at me, Stratfield, you—you ungrateful ghost. Is this the thanks I get for helping you?"

Feeling foolish, she backed toward the door to her room. And her dream? How much had been real and how much imagined? How much of her arousal could she attribute to his wickedness as opposed to her own hidden desires?

Well, here was another scandal in the making.

The Stratfield Ghost had struck again, and Lady Chloe Boscastle was his latest victim.

Dominic scratched the dog's ears, his low laugh of satisfaction echoing against the walls of the dark tunnel. "Well, that was a little close, but we've gotten our letter back. I won't be so careless again."

If careless was even the word for it; obsessed seemed a more appropriate description of his behavior. Obsessed with revenge. Obsessed with regaining what was his.

Obsessed, all of a sudden, with a beautiful young woman, who with good reason, should want nothing to do with him. Why else had he knelt at her bedside and tormented himself with those stolen touches? What a stupid risk to take. But look at his hands. He was still shaking from touching her.

She could have awakened. She could have opened her eyes and screamed to bring the house down. Or, as he no doubt secretly wished, she could have submitted to all the things he wanted to do to her. She could, at least in his desperate fantasies, have asked him to give her everything he wanted to.

Clearly she was curious about sexual matters, and he would have loved to tutor her. But just as clearly she was not an empty-headed maiden unable to form an original thought.

She had hidden the note under her pillow. Had she guessed the significance? He doubted it. And yet he also doubted that she had kept the paper close to her as a sentimental memoir of their encounter.

His intellectual nature found her behavior rather intriguing. His body ached for her in a more straightforward fashion.

He lifted the brass telescope he had taken from her room to watch her window. He was rewarded several moments later when she appeared in her white muslin nightrail. Of course she could not see him, hidden like a fox in a ferny hole. She was probably cursing him to the heavens, but not, he hoped, in a too-loud voice.

"Did you like your rose?" he asked the distant image with a chuckle.

As if to answer him she flung a pale unidentifiable object out the window. He could only guess it was the flower he had calmly substituted for the coded letter.

He glanced around. A light had flickered in the window of his estate. In his own bedchamber window. He saw the silhouette of his uncle behind the curtains, a grim reminder that he could not afford to prowl outside Chloe's room like an animal in heat.

He lowered the telescope, his smile fading. "Well, good night again, Chloe," he said in a wistful undertone. "I have some haunting to do . . . and you, my dear, you haunt me, too."

Chloe lit a candle on the nightstand and got down on her hands and knees to reach under the bed. With relief she found her journal where she had hidden it beneath a broken floorboard.

She pulled the slim volume out and carried it back to her bed. On the last page was her most recent entry. An exact copy of the coded letter that Dominic had sneaked back into her room to collect.

Obviously it meant enough to him to take a chance retrieving it. She congratulated herself on having had the foresight to make her own copy. And on forcing her brother Heath to teach her a few tricks on the art of deciphering a code.

It was time to put her knowledge to work on what was perhaps Brandon's last message. She had not helped Dominic without expecting something in return.

Chapter 12

When Chloe came downstairs for breakfast the following morning, it was to find the household in chaos. Uncle Humphrey was hurrying through the hall with his walking stick tucked under his brown greatcoat. His hair was unbrushed, and his cravat was askew as if he had dressed in haste. He gave Chloe a panicked look as he noticed her at the foot of the stairs.

"Fetch your cloak and escape with me while you can, my dear," he said in a stage whisper. "A madness has descended on us, and I wish no part in it."

"What madness?" Chloe asked, but her voice was drowned out by the furor of female voices in the parlor and the yapping of dogs outside waiting for Humphrey's promised walk in the woods.

Pamela appeared in the parlor doorway, her freckled face animated and pink. "Oh, Chloe, at last you are here. The meeting has already begun."

"The meeting," Chloe echoed, her brain still in a fog as Pamela came forward to pull her into the parlor. "What meeting?"

"My mother has called the ladies of Chistlebury together to discuss our common crisis."

Chloe's temples began to tighten with the unpleasant tension of an impending headache. She was cross and tired from laboring unsuccessfully over Brandon's letter until four in the morning. And she was still angry and at odds over whether Dominic had actually touched her during the night or whether she had dreamed those naughty things he had done to her.

She couldn't decide which was worse. She did know she was in no mood to sit and discuss the misconduct of the Stratfield Ghost. The parson's wife rose to shepherd Chloe to the overcrowded sofa, where a matron and her two unmarried daughters sat avidly discussing this frightening threat to the female community. Pamela squeezed beside her.

A deep hush fell over the parlor. All attention moved to Chloe in a combination of sympathetic curiosity and prim disapproval. Almost as if *she,* by dint of her reputation, had brought this scandal upon their excitement-starved village. She cleared her throat and met their stares with a guileless smile.

All at once the women began to speak again.

She rested her head back on the sofa, stifling a yawn. Numbers from Brandon's cryptic message danced behind her burning eyelids. Why had he felt the need to write in code in Nepal? Had Napoleon's agents been sent to that distant outpost to challenge British interests?

She opened her eyes in startlement as the woman seated next to her shook her arm. "He must be laid. Don't you agree, Lady Chloe?"

"What did you say?"

The woman looked at her in concern. "It is our duty to lay him."

"To do what to whom?"

"Lay him. To rest, my dear. The poor spirit is clearly seeking a woman to help him find peace."

To Chloe's way of thinking, the "poor spirit" had been seeking something else from a certain woman last night, and laying him might or might not be the answer.

"How do you propose to do this?" she asked, thinking she probably did not want to be involved.

Before the matron could answer, the room erupted in an uproar. A newcomer had arrived, a striking Gypsy woman in a scarlet skirt and fringed green shawl, gaudy silver bracelets stacked on each wrist. Her sparkling brown eyes, set above a small hooked nose in a thin face, surveyed her audience with amused disdain.

Aunt Gwendolyn pushed a Chippendale chair into the center of the crowded room for her esteemed guest to hold court. "Tell us, Madame Dara," she demanded, clasping her hands to the back of the chair. "Tell us which one of us will be his next victim."

"Madame" Dara, who was probably nineteen if she was a day, circled the chair with indolent grace, recognizing an enrapt audience when she saw it.

"Get me something to drink."

The parson's wife sprang from her chair to pour a cup of tea. She passed the cup and saucer to Pamela, who passed it in turn to the woman beside her, who handed it to Gwendolyn with the reverence one might impart to the Holy Grail.

Madame Dara took the tea and sat. The other women

in the room watched her slurp in fascinated silence as if even this simple act held grave import for their future.

Chloe's eyelids felt heavy with fatigue. She was dying to go back upstairs and work on Brandon's letter, but she had not slept much in the past two days. The strain of what was happening had begun to catch up with her.

"It is . . . *you.*"

She heard the collective gasp that went around the room and looked up in curiosity, alarmed to see the Gypsy pointing straight to the sofa where Chloe sat. Her heart jumped into her throat. The Gypsy could not possibly know. It was a wild guess, an unfair judgment to pass due to the gossip about her scandalous past.

"Now wait a moment," she said, her face growing warm. "Just because I am the stranger among you is no reason to assume—"

She did not have a chance to finish. The chatter in the room rose into a cacophony of voices, shrill, shocked, a dozen women sympathizing with the chosen victim.

"This really is not fair," Chloe said in embarrassment.

Aunt Gwendolyn was veering toward her with such a look of distress that Chloe could not help feeling guilty. Was it possible the Gypsy knew the truth? No. She couldn't know. Labeling Chloe as the ghost's chosen one was—

"A mistake," Aunt Gwendolyn sputtered. "It must be a mistake. Not my innocent little lamb."

Chloe blinked, turning her head to examine the young woman seated beside her. Pamela? The Gypsy had not pointed to Chloe at all, but to her cousin, who was grinning like an elf at being singled out for this unexpected honor.

"I shall fight this with all my strength," Aunt Gwendolyn cried in a militant voice, raising her fist to the heavens. "The Stratfield Ghost will not have my daughter!"

The Stratfield Ghost, Chloe thought cynically, might have a word or two to say on the subject himself. But considering the fact that for the first time in ages Chloe was not the center of scandal, be it real or imagined, she chose to hold her tongue and enjoy a little obscurity.

It would be nice, for a change, to be ignored. It might even give her a measure of liberty. Of course, Dominic would not appreciate having this ludicrous attention drawn to him again. But then if he did not want his spirit laid, he should not sneak into women's bedrooms to take advantage of them as they slept. Someone really ought to put a stop to him. He was certainly more lascivious than he would admit.

Still, he had stolen back his letter, and Chloe thought it unlikely that she would ever have another chance to scold him as she would like. Given the danger that surrounded him, she told herself this was for the best.

She saw him that same night.

She had intended to study Brandon's letter, certain she was on the verge of a discovery that would shed light on the mystery of her brother's death. Perhaps the truth would give her a sense of peace and acceptance.

She had planned on a light supper at home. But her uncle had met Sir Edgar Williams while walking the dogs in the woods just before twilight.

Sir Edgar had invited Uncle Humphrey and his family to dinner that evening. Uncle Humphrey explained to his wife that his first impulse was to refuse, but that he could hardly do so as Sir Edgar was now their closest neighbor.

"Of *course* we cannot refuse," Aunt Gwendolyn said, a crafty gleam in her eye. "It is our duty, after all."

Uncle Humphrey had shared a glance of alarm with Chloe. "Our duty?" he asked cautiously.

Gwendolyn stood facing the parlor window, her voice vibrating with dramatic importance. "If Stratfield has chosen Pamela as his next victim, we must do everything in our power to intervene. Who will court our daughter after a ghost has taken her, Humphrey?"

He glanced again at Chloe. "The same men who did not court her before, I suppose."

But Aunt Gwendolyn would not be dissuaded. The parson and the Gypsy woman had convinced her that drastic steps must be taken to protect Pamela's virtue. As for the prospective victim herself, Pamela could hardly conceal her delight that a notorious spirit had chosen *her*. She even asked if she might borrow one of Chloe's nightrails to wear for the occasion.

The four of them had dressed for dinner. Gwendolyn insisted they must arrive in the carriage, even though Humphrey pointed out that he could practically spit into Stratfield's lake from his doorstep.

"That is crude, Humphrey," Gwendolyn said, her gloved hands folded in her lap.

"It is not crude, Gwennie. It takes us longer to get in and out of the damned carriage than it does to walk to the doorstep."

"Sir Edgar shall not think us yahoos," she replied, undeterred.

During the short drive, Chloe caught herself staring into the moonlit trees. She thought it probable that Stratfield had found a hiding place somewhere in the woods. Was he well? Had the Gypsy medicine done him any good? Where could he spy on his own home and not be observed? She could not imagine how he had arranged his own funeral without help from someone else.

She considered the possibility that he had found an underground smuggler's tunnel or a cave to conceal him. Heath had once told her that some subterranean passageways in Sussex had been reopened to be used in the event of a coastal attack by Napoleon.

The carriage rattled around the stand of silver beech trees in whose glistening shadows Dominic had kissed her. The memory of his gloved hands on her face, his mouth taking hers, unleashed a burst of disturbing heat deep in her belly. He was a dangerous man, all right, in more ways than one, even though she knew what had made him so. Perhaps it was because she could empathize with him that he posed such a danger to her.

She remembered thinking how sad he'd seemed in the woods, and she had begun to understand why. He had reason for his melancholy. No doubt she would have been better off never seeing him again. Yet if somehow his peril involved Brandon, then she was also meant to be involved.

But was desire to be part of the package? Surely she could help while not becoming personally involved with him. Away from Dominic she decided that she could. And yet deep inside she knew it was fortunate she did not have to face temptation again.

*   *   *

She gave a start as Pamela nudged her out of her trance. "Why are you looking so grim, Chloe?" she whispered with a mischievous grin. "I'm to be the sacrificial lamb, as they say, not you."

"You don't look at all grim yourself," Chloe said.

Pamela's grin widened. "Admit it," she whispered. "You're a little curious about what it would be like to be seduced by Stratfield's ghost."

"Of course I'm not," Chloe retorted. Because she already knew. That ignominious privilege had recently been granted to her, and she wasn't liable to forget it in a hurry.

The coach had passed the tall vine-clad gatehouse of the estate. As Chloe smoothed out her gray silk gown, the coachman stopped in the crushed-shell drive before the elegant late-Elizabethan house.

The mellowed stone home with a turreted roof and gables seemed to be as proud and strong as the man who owned it. Chloe could almost see Stratfield standing at the tall bay windows of the long gallery, looking down at his estate with satisfaction. Yes, even a ghost might find peace watching the swans glide on the moonlit lake below the sunken gardens.

An undergroom and two footmen emerged from the top of the stone entrance steps to assist them. Chloe felt a slow prickle of sensation raise goose bumps on her skin. Was someone staring at her?

She glanced up quickly, in the middle of Aunt Gwendolyn reminding her husband not to gulp his food like a wolf. A tall black-haired man was walking toward them, broad-shouldered, with the erect, confident bearing of a professional soldier.

In the dark he looked enough like his nephew Dominic that Chloe caught her breath. Commanding, with those same brooding eyes and arrogantly carved features. His voice was different, though, not quite as deep, with the lyrical lilt of his Welsh origins. He gave his guests a welcoming smile.

"How good of you to come on such short notice," he said, placing his hand on Humphrey's shoulder. "And what lucky men we are to have three beautiful women grace our table."

Sir Edgar smiled most warmly at Aunt Gwendolyn and Pamela, who was explaining that she had wrenched her ankle and was not usually as clumsy as she appeared.

His gaze lingered last and longest on Chloe. She smiled back at him, a polite reflex that had been instilled in her from the cradle. No, the man was *not* as compelling as Dominic, and he was several years older. There was a calculated intelligence in his eyes, as if his every word and deed were carefully weighed. His skin was dark from foreign service, his face more angular than his nephew's. His manners and dress seemed impeccable, from his gracious welcome to his snowy cravat and gleaming boots that clicked smartly on the steps.

"Lady Chloe," he said, his dark eyes kindling, "I have always admired your family. May I offer my condolences on the death of young Lord Brandon. I was in Kathmandu when the savage ambush on his party occurred, but I pray you and your relations take solace in knowing that those responsible paid for their crime."

Chloe stared back at him in numb silence. Her heart seemed to stop, and for an awful moment her throat felt so constricted she found it a struggle to speak. "I don't understand. You—you were in Nepal with Brandon?"

He appeared stricken. "My dear young lady, how bad of me to presume you knew. Your brother and my nephew Samuel served in the company's regiment under my command. I had warned them countless times of the dangers involved in patrolling the lonely native passes, but the brave young devils were intent on proving their prowess. While I was gone on business, they took it upon themselves to play heroics."

"I didn't know," she murmured. "I had no idea." It was not comforting knowledge. In fact, it quite distressed her.

Sir Edgar led them into the screened entrance vestibule. As Chloe regained her composure, she noticed her aunt peering around the Doric columns as if expecting Viscount Stratfield to pop out and yell, "Surprise! It is me, the resident ghost!"

The funny thing was, Chloe could feel Stratfield's presence, too. As least she thought she did. Since he was not actually a spirit, she could not decide what it was she felt. The various emotional states he had incited in her were rather ambiguous and too embarrassing to examine. It was easier to assume she was frightened of him than to admit something more complex made her nerves tremble—something decadent and slightly delicious.

Yes, there *was* an overpowering sense of him in this house. In the dark oak paneling and in the musician's gallery above the dining hall. At any moment Chloe half expected to see his powerful figure appear dramatically on the black oak staircase, ordering everyone to—

"I've been here quite a few times before," Uncle Humphrey whispered over her shoulder. "Stratfield invited me over to go shooting and play cards with his friends. He wasn't as bad as everyone wants to believe, Chloe. He was not the rake he's made out to be, either. All this talk of his ghost—"

"You don't believe any of it?" she whispered.

"Of course not. Why, I remember in the old days people used to whisper this house was haunted by one of the priests who'd gotten himself stuck in a priest hole and could not find his way out. If anyone is seducing women in their sleep, it's probably a randy old cleric's ghost."

Chloe pivoted in the hall where they stood. "A priest hole?"

"Yes. You remember your history, Chloe. The viscount's family came from Roman Catholics. Religious persecution drove many to conceal their beliefs to this day."

Chloe's blood began to tingle. "Was Stratfield a Catholic?"

"I do not think so. I could recall his mentioning his family history only once in passing."

Chloe felt jolted by this discovery and did not know why. What did it matter if Dominic came from a long line of rebels? So did she, for that matter. But she liked knowing a little more about him.

They dined on herbed roast pheasant, potatoes in hot buttered parsley, and apple tarts smothered in clotted cream. A string quartet from the village played medieval melodies in the long gallery above. Sir Edgar could not have been a more attentive host. Yet Chloe's sense of discomfort persisted. Edgar was almost too polite, too at ease in Dominic's role. And Brandon had served under him. She wanted to ask more about her brother, but some instinct stopped her.

Her attention began to wander. Uncle Humphrey and Sir Edgar were speculating on the future of France's aristocracy. She pictured Dominic sitting at the other end of the massive table in evening dress. His masterful personality suited the dark elegance of the house.

She could imagine his holding a silver goblet in masculine fingers, that taunting smile on his face. She could almost feel his brooding gray eyes moving over her in that understated, insolent way he had. She took a deep sip of wine. Had he really dared to seduce her while she slept? As if taking Brandon's letter hadn't been impertinent enough.

The private fantasy, pretending Dominic was sitting here at this table, warmed Chloe's blood. She would dearly love to tell him one last time what a cheeky blackguard he was. Imagine his caressing her dreamy self as she was asleep. What gall, to take advantage of her, to make her respond to him like that. If—

"Are you all right, Lady Chloe?" Sir Edgar's lilting voice intruded on her inappropriate thoughts. "Your face looks flushed. Perhaps it is wrong of us to be discussing the guillotine regime at the table."

Chloe found herself at a loss for words. Unfortunately, Aunt Gwendolyn filled in the awkward void by announcing, "Perhaps she is sharing my unease, Sir Edgar."

"Unease?" Sir Edgar inquired, casting a curious look at Chloe.

"This house is haunted," Aunt Gwendolyn announced, expelling a breath through her nose. "Do you not sense it?"

Sir Edgar looked a little embarrassed. "I cannot say that I have heard any clanking chains in the night or inhuman moaning. Perhaps you ladies need a bit of exercise to chase away these maudlin thoughts. A walk in the long gallery or conservatory while Sir Humphrey and I enjoy a brandy in the library might reassure you."

"That is an excellent idea," Aunt Gwendolyn said, and Chloe should have known from how quickly the woman leaped at the chance that she had an ulterior motive in mind. "Come, girls, let us stroll off the excesses of our excellent dinner."

Sir Edgar rose to escort the three women to the door. But just as they were departing, he said, "One warning, dear ladies. While I do not believe you will encounter my nephew's maligned spirit, there is a remote possibility you will come across that dog of his."

"His dog?" Pamela asked in surprise. "Whatever do you mean?"

He gave a quiet laugh. "That vexing hound he owned. For several weeks it has been tearing up the garden and running loose in the woods. I told the gamekeeper we should have it put down, but he balked until the wretched animal disappeared a day or so ago. I should hate to have it reappear to my guests."

"I am not afraid of his lordship's dog," Aunt Gwendolyn retorted. "The poor creature is probably bereft with grief. The viscount was an avid hunter and horseman," she added with obvious approval. "No matter what has been said about him, he had a way with animals."

"And women," Pamela added in an undertone to Chloe.

Chloe bit her tongue to keep from revealing that she had a little personal experience on the subject herself. Fortunately, this time, Aunt Gwendolyn intervened to offer her own opinion, whispering, "You heard that, girls. The viscount's dog can perceive his master's presence. Animals sense these things, I tell you. That ghost must be laid to rest once and for all, even if I must take him on myself."

That was too much for Chloe and Pamela. They burst into irreverent giggles as Gwendolyn herded them up the wide black oak staircase to the long gallery that overlooked the entrance vestibule. In past days families had taken light exercise and played games in the spacious walkway. Lovers had strolled hand in hand and kissed by moonlight in the alcoves.

Pamela went off into a fresh round of giggling as she examined the ancestral portraits on the wall. Chloe laughed, too, but she was secretly disappointed that she did not find a painting of Dominic to study.

It would have been safer to scold his portrait than to face him in the flesh again.

The sound of Chloe's lighthearted laughter penetrated the walls to the dark gloom where Dominic was hiding. He could feel her vibrant energy lifting his lonely melancholy. The lure of her voice tempted him to leave his prison to see her again. It tortured him to know she was here, in his own house, and he could not take her into his arms.

He wanted more than that, far more, if the truth be told. He wanted passionately to know Chloe Boscastle inside out, to win her admiration and prove himself a hero in her eyes. He wanted to come out of hiding and become a human being again.

He began to pace in the cramped airless space that served as his self-imposed cell. How unfair that he would meet her at the lowest ebb of his life. No doubt he had disgusted her. Even if he managed to have his revenge and emerge alive, he would never be allowed to court her. Her brothers would rightly label him a devil and eat him raw.

Should he survive.

He was willing to see his revenge through to the death. Nothing was going to interfere.

Her laughter echoed tauntingly down the gallery, and he gazed up through the crevice in the wall, aching to see her just one more time. He had tormented himself by re-living their kisses, their heated words, by conjuring up in vivid detail the scent and feel of her supple body. He could not believe she had come here to his house. So near and yet beyond his reach. As if by his desire he had drawn her to him.

And she was laughing. Dining at the table with his enemy. Dancing down the hallway where his murderer had walked. Charming the power-hungry man who could kill a human being as easily as he could a fly.

Dominic had not given her adequate warning.

She had no idea how deadly Sir Edgar could be.

*   *   *

"Mama, where on earth are you going?" Pamela asked in shock, racing to keep up with the petite woman's hurried pace.

"To his lordship's bedroom."

Pamela glanced at Chloe in alarm. "What if Sir Edgar finds us and demands to know what we are doing?"

Aunt Gwendolyn remained oddly unruffled. "We insist that we heard a noise and wandered into the room by mistake."

"Aunt Gwendolyn, really, isn't that the height of rudeness?" Chloe asked, deciding she had underestimated her aunt's determination. That Boscastle blood might be coming through, after all.

"The height of rudeness," Aunt Gwendolyn retorted as she swept down the moonlit gallery, "is a ghost who is bent on ruining my daughter."

Chloe hastened after her. There was no stopping a Boscastle on a mission, not even one whose strain had been diluted. Aunt Gwendolyn had brought along in her reticule a packet of salt, a Bible, a silver bell, and a silk pouch containing the powdered finger bone of a French saint. Or so Madame Dara had claimed when she'd sold Lady Dewhurst the crumbly granules that looked to Chloe suspiciously like oatmeal.

"Well, come along girls," Aunt Gwendolyn whispered upon reaching the closed bedchamber door. "According to the parson's information, this is the room in which Lord Stratfield was murdered."

"Perhaps we should do this in daylight," Pamela said, paling at the mention of the ghastly murder.

"Nonsense," her mother said. "A ghost does his mischief at night, and another opportunity for us to stop him may not come our way. We cannot count on my husband's conversational skills to keep Sir Edgar entertained much longer."

Chloe hung back as Pamela opened the door to the darkened chamber. She had no desire to see the room where Dominic had been so brutally attacked, to imagine him shocked, frightened, in unspeakable agony. Having witnessed the pain he'd suffered from his wounds, she could not remain unmoved by visiting the scene of his intended death.

"Aren't you coming, Chloe?" Pamela whispered over her shoulder.

"I'll stand guard out here," she whispered back. "But hurry, both of you."

After a few moments Chloe found herself drawn to a painting on the wall at the other end of the long gallery. She knew at once that the dashing horseman depicted in a billowing wine cloak was Dominic. The gray eyes that gazed down at her from the portrait held the mocking glint she remembered. The artist had captured the potent energy and depth of Dominic's character.

Almost as if he were poised right in front of her.

"I ought to teach you a lesson," she whispered.

She heard a noise. The faintest scratching, but from where? She followed the sound farther down the gallery to a large unused fireplace flanked by two Italian green marble columns.

"A mouse," she said, peering a little disappointedly into the dusty void. "Probably only a mouse."

She backed away from the fireplace to one of the tall canted windows overlooking the estate. Moonlight glimmered off the black surface of the lake. She did not see her ghost.

"Where are you, Dominic?" she asked in a barely audible voice, pressing her hand to the leaded glass.

"Closer than you think."

She whirled around. A dark-cloaked figure moved toward her in a blur, and her heart leaped into her throat. Before she could speak, a black-gloved hand gently covered her mouth, and she was drawn off her feet into the dark yawning space beside the fireplace.

The column closed in a swirl of dust, and warm, stuffy darkness enveloped her. She felt herself dragged hard against Dominic's chest. His muscular thighs pressed her backward into an airless void. She could not see him at all, but she felt him all over her body. His arms protected her from dangers she could feel but not name. His lips brushed her cheek.

"Oh, my God, Dominic. You are mad—"

"Do not speak," he whispered against her neck.

She opened her mouth to protest the fact that she was wedged between the unfinished wall and his iron-hard body. He pressed his gloved forefinger to her lips, silencing her unspoken complaint. Then his large hand curved tenderly around her jaw. Chloe shuddered, closing her eyes at the appalling thrill of being lovingly abused in his arms.

His hands, encased in cool black leather, moved down her shoulders, to her sides, cupping the cheeks of her bottom. The sensation was at once intimate and impersonal, an invasion that he committed as if he had the right. He had gained strength since the last time she had seen him, in perfect control of his body and fully aware of his power. She was aware of him, too, in the confined space. Aware that he was aroused, his hard male form assuming a dominant position. The darkness heightened her sense of vulnerability, his advantage. She could feel the coiled muscles of his chest, and lower, his thighs pressed to hers.

"I've been thinking about you, Chloe. About how much I liked kissing you."

"I don't know how anyone could think at all in here," she whispered. "It's so dark."

"It's good to see you again." She felt his heartbeat quicken. "It would be good to kiss you, too."

The promise in his voice stole her breath. He slanted his mouth over hers before she could respond. His tongue slid inside her mouth as his other hand drew her closer. His body tightened against hers, a deep moan escaped him, and all she could think was, He's alive. I didn't kill him with the horse medicine, and he's kissing me again.

In the dark, on his own turf, Dominic held all the cards and surely would not hesitate to play them. She was in his power, in *his* closet now, so to speak. He could do as he wished with her. He could keep her in this secret place for days, and no one would guess where she had gone. The possibilities tantalized her. What would he decide to do? His expert kiss had left her aching deep inside and disoriented. Her pulses throbbed through her entire body.

She was not anywhere near as frightened as a proper young lady should be in such an unspeakable situation. She braced herself against the wall, her belly muscles tightening in reaction to the feel of him. "Are we going to stand here mauling each other in the dark?" she whispered. "You could at least bring me a chair." Before she slid to his feet.

"You're not criticizing my hospitality, are you?"

"This is a horrid place to hide. What if I am?"

He twirled one of her glossy back curls around his forefinger. "I should have to punish you if you were."

"Hmm. Punish me?"

"Oh, yes." He tugged lightly on a lock of her hair. "There are a few servicable manacles on the wall in the cellar. A little rusty, perhaps, and certainly not as attractive as the diamonds and gold filigree that usually adorn your delicate wrists."

Manacles. In the cellar. The rogue was threatening to chain her to the wall of all things. That was the thanks she received for aiding him. And what, she wondered, would he do when he got her in chains? Chloe blushed at the erotic images that flitted through her mind, the thought of being restrained and helpless for his enjoyment, in bondage to him.

"Stuff it, Stratfield," she said crossly. "I should hit you if I could see you properly."

"I am right here, Chloe. I could hardly be any closer."

And it was true. The heat of his body stole into hers. The hard pounding of his heart seemed to echo hers.

"Can't you feel me?" he asked, his fingertip tracing the angle of her jaw, the tender rim of her left ear.

"Every inch." Her voice held a breathless quality that he could hardly miss. What had Shakespeare said about the prince of darkness being a gentleman? "The priests didn't put people in manacles, did they?"

"No," he replied cheerfully. "But the smugglers who

followed them two centuries after did. I shall not show you the skeleton I found in chains during my first days of hiding."

"Thank you so awfully much."

He laughed, his warm breath on her shoulder leaving shivers in its wake. "The poor devil wears a placard around its neck which reads 'Release me at your peril.'"

"Meaning what?" Chloe asked, suddenly grateful that she was in the protective reach of Dominic's arms.

"I have no idea."

"Perhaps it means his spirit will be unleashed to wreak revenge on his captors," she said quietly. "Perhaps he's even one of your ancestors."

"I doubt it. Baron Bones seems to have been more an enemy of whoever commanded the dungeon at the time."

"Well, you and the baron might be kindred spirits, if not blood relations."

He smiled at her. "Possibly. Should I release him?"

"Only at your peril, and please, not while I'm present." She paused. "What happens to me now?" she whispered, the words plaintive in the entombing space.

His disembodied voice vibrated with a devilish amusement that made her wish to slap him. "What do you want to happen, Chloe? I'll be as obliging a host as you desire."

Chapter 13

Hiding in the dark for a month played unpredictable tricks on a man's mind. Deprived of human contact, of a woman's touch, of light, who would not be driven a little insane?

Chloe was a man's private fantasy, beautiful and passionate, a prize worth pursuing. And either she was afraid to death of his threats, which he doubted, or she had been unable to stop herself from caring about him. Why else had she not turned him in when she'd had ample opportunity to reveal his secret and run to her family for advice? Was it possible that he had won her wild heart? The possibility of ownership aroused his masculine pride.

"I am happy to see you, Chloe Boscastle," he said between kissing her ripe mouth and taking succulent bites of her neck. She was a banquet for his starved senses. He couldn't even pretend indifference to her presence. His reaction to her was primal and would not be denied.

"There's no air in here, Dominic," she whispered, not exactly fighting him even if she had not granted him permission to ravish her either. "How can you bear this?"

In the dark his senses became too easily inflamed. By the vulnerable softness of her rounded breasts and belly crushed against his, by the subtle scent of her soap on her shoulders. She was all warm flesh and elusive female in his arms. He wanted to devour her from top to bottom, to undress her and worship her creamy body to his heart's content.

"Did you come here tonight to torment me?" he demanded gently.

Of course he knew the answer. Chloe was not capable of such a vindictive act. Any torturing on her part would be pure accident. No matter that she had bedeviled his plans, it was unfair to accuse her of deliberately thwarting him. She might be as undisciplined and impulsively trouble-prone as were her brothers, but he doubted there was a cruel bone in her beautiful body.

"As if I'm as devious as you are, Dominic." She sounded so offended that he almost kissed her again to atone for insulting her, if not to keep her quiet. He couldn't hold her here much longer. Chloe's sparkling personality would definitely be missed at the dinner party. "I had no idea you were hiding in your own house," she added softly.

"And no one else is going to know either," he said. "But if anyone found me, I'm very glad it was you."

"Why?" she asked, teasing him, he suspected.

"You know damn well why," he said roughly.

"Tell me, Dominic." She curled her hand around his neck and went limp against him. "I really want to know."

Boiling heat surged through his blood. What she did to him without even trying. What she could do with a little experience. "Lord, Chloe, you're such a tease."

"Am I?" He heard her breathing quicken, and the sound made him as hot and hungry as a predator about to claim his prize. She desired him, too. He wasn't alone in this maddening desire.

He kissed her again. He knew he was more than a little out of control. He also knew from experience that in the dark she must feel disoriented, afraid to move until she got her bearings. It had taken him days to trust the shadows, to memorize the unfamiliar and become a true ghost. Who could blame him if he took advantage of her? He was so desperate for company, for physical sensation, for a warm, loving woman that he could barely think straight.

It was a tribute to the Boscastle name that he wasn't seducing her senseless where she stood, leading them both down a path of mindless lust. God help him, but how he wanted to bury himself inside her. The accidental brush of her plump breasts against his chest was the most delicious agony he had ever known. The soft weight of her belly against his groin made him ache with desire. She had twisted him into a painful knot of frustration without the least effort. The spell she cast was potent, the ancient alchemy of female magic.

He wanted her naked, at his feet, her blue eyes gazing up at him with adoration and sexual invitation. He guessed he could probably push his advantage. He could keep her here for only a minute more, a spark of light in his dark, ugly world. If he did not stop, he would be groveling and begging for her affection. He pulled her closer, crushing her curves against his hard body.

It was tempting fate for him to bring her to his hiding place. He could endanger her in more ways than one.

And Dominic at his most depraved and maddened worst would destroy himself before dragging Chloe deeper into his private hell. This was not her battle. She was the reward at its end.

"Damnation, Chloe," he said in utter desperation. "Why *did* you have to come here?"

She drew a breath. She seemed more sure of herself again, her instincts for survival reassuringly strong. She was certainly no hothouse flower to wither at the first frost. "How can you possibly hope to remain in this house undetected?" she asked him matter-of-factly.

"Have you *any* idea of the danger you have placed both of us in by coming here?"

"Are you insane, Dominic? Am I being seduced by a lunatic?"

"It is quite possible."

"Hiding in your own home—"

"Don't question me."

"Don't kiss me then."

"Do as I tell you, Chloe."

"Not until I understand."

"You understand far too much. And I shall kiss you if I please."

"You will ask me first—"

As if to prove his point, he cupped her chin in his hands and helped himself to another slow, entrancing kiss. Chloe did a wriggling dance with her hips and shoulders, not certain if she meant to get closer or to escape. Oh, the way this man kissed—an illicit thrill shivered down her spine. Her lips tingled as his tongue slowly traced their outline, licked a path to her earlobe.

Dominic was holding her face as if she were made of the most fragile crystal, his thumbs gently stroking her cheekbones.

But the feelings he stirred up inside her weren't fragile or gentle at all. The flurry of sensation erupted as fierce and unpredictable as a windstorm, raging through her. He seemed to know intuitively how to reduce her to trembling submission. He lowered his left hand and began rubbing his palm with teasing pleasure over her breasts. What a wicked sensation. She felt her knees buckle as sexual anticipation weakened her. Her nipples hardened achingly against her muslin bodice, and her head swam with drugged pleasure. The imprint of his body branded her like a hot iron. She was shivery again, with heat, with cold, with raw desire. Her fingers tightened around his strong neck.

"Don't you dare touch me like that again," she whispered faintly.

He stopped, his gaze narrowing, reminding her of a wolf who was reassessing its prey.

She paused to draw another breath. "At least not until after you tell me more about what you're doing."

In the dark his voice sounded even deeper, hinting at secrets she might not wish to know. "And if I satisfy your curiosity, may I touch you, Chloe?"

"Possibly." She hesitated. Dear God, listen to what she had just said, bargaining her virtue to satisfy her curiosity. "But only a little."

He took her hand, not making any promises on that point, she noticed in alarm. "Be careful going down the steps. You do not mind if I put my arm around your waist to guide you, do you? The timber in this place is rotted in parts. Heaven forbid that you should take a fall and bruise your tender skin."

His low, solicitous voice raised prickles on her nape. Heaven forbid that she should fall, indeed. And asking permission to hold her after what he'd just done. Down, deep, deeper, her dark lord led her into his underground lair, into the subterranean passages beneath the house. How much lower could a lady fall? She could practically feel the flames of Hades under her feet as her wicked prince gave her a tour of his stygian domain.

Would this be the end of her? Would she return unchanged to her dull life as a relatively decent young lady?

Dominic would not let anything hurt her. Chloe believed this or she would not have gone with him.

But would she return as the same unworldly young woman she had been before her descent into Dominic's headquarters?

She was not certain of that answer.

He guided her down into a dusty chalk tunnel where he had left a single candle burning. He saw her nose twitching in distaste at the piles of crumbling mortar and warped brandy kegs that littered the cramped passageway.

A furtive scratching from inside the wall stopped her in her tracks. "Gracious, what was that?"

His smile was apologetic. "Nothing to worry about. Only the rats."

She ducked a rotted beam, murmuring, "Rats," as if she'd just realized he was sharing his quarters with the various vermin a young lady would hope never to encounter in her life. But instead of the expected horror, her voice was filled with pity and a kind of stoic understanding that undid him. "Oh, Stratfield, you tortured devil. How do you manage?"

She was an unpredictable thing was Chloe Boscastle. Not easy to frighten off. The type who'd jump back on her horse after a bad spill. He supposed it had something to do with being reared in a clan of boisterous lordlings. "How do I manage?" he mused. "Well, my valet has a hard job shaving me in the dark, and sometimes I mismatch my cuff buttons, but other than that I am quite comfortable."

"But how lonely for you. What do you think of in all those silent hours?"

He studied her face, noticing how the candlelight gilded her features so that she looked even softer, even more enticing, if possible. "At first there was nothing in my mind but murderous revenge. I dreamed of avenging myself by various means so barbaric I shall not speak them aloud."

She met his scrutiny. "Considering what has been done to you, such thoughts are understandable."

"Perhaps. Recently, however, I find myself struggling to remember that revenge is all I live for. I find my thoughts straying to other matters."

"Oh. How . . . intriguing."

"Is it?" He brought his face close to hers, inhaling her evocative fragrance. He was weak with desire, desperate for her. Surely she guessed that those "other matters" were his rather obsessive thoughts of bringing her down here, undressing her slowly by candlelight, and loving her in every sexual position under the sun.

"Aren't you going to tell me?" she whispered, her breath a caress on his cheek.

His jaw hardened. Her voice challenged him, ignited his smoldering senses. Slowly, his eyes burning, he pulled off his gloves, then curled his hand around her nape and drew her into him.

His mouth touched hers, his tongue slowly penetrated her lips. He shifted his body, brought his other hand around her waist. She moaned so softly he could have cried for wanting her.

"You," he said, the confession wrung from his soul. "I think about you . . . about what I want to do to you. I think about touching you in a hundred different ways, and—"

She kissed him, seducing his mouth into silence. His world shifted. He brought his free hand slowly up her belly to her swelling breasts. Her body softened, yielded to him. Yet at the same time her kiss grew more demanding. Enthralled by her daring, he let her lead the way.

Submission. Seduction. He didn't care which as long as the end result was having her to himself. His breathing quickened as she pressed her breast into his palm. He pleased her. She scorched him to the bone. Her supple body beckoned him, summoned all his dangerous instincts.

He rubbed his thumb back and forth over her nipple, tasted the soft exhalation of breath that escaped her. He moved his hand to the other breast, tracing the weight of her warm flesh, the thin silk of her gown scant defense to what he demanded.

"This," he said, his voice uneven, "is what I think about in the dark. You."

"Not all the time?"

"Enough that I cannot stop myself—"

Before he knew it, he was touching her everywhere, his fingers skimming her stomach, sinking into the silk-clad delta above her thighs. She was warm there, too, making it all too easy to imagine how she would glove his shaft in pure heat.

Sweet torture. They fit so well together. His hard arousal found the soft haven between her legs. Her gown snagged on the rough mortar behind her. She tugged it free, meeting his gaze.

She went still, her lips damp and glistening in the dark. She must have seen the hot need in his eyes. He didn't try to hide it. The urgency of it burned through him, a fever in his blood. He felt the shiver that slipped over her. Was she offended? Afraid? Did she sense that he was close to ripping her gown into shreds?

Her smile broke the unbearable tension. He almost groaned aloud as she moistened her swollen mouth with her tongue. "You can't think about me all the time. What else do you do in here?"

"Sometimes I read," he said. "Or I practice fencing. My uncle was once an instructor of Angelo's technique in Venice. He taught me everything I know about sword fighting."

She rubbed her forearms, peering down the gloomy passageway. "Where does this lead?"

He wavered. He had trusted her this far. If she was going to betray him, it would not matter how much more knowledge she gained. He might be holding Chloe temporarily in his power, but in the end, with a few ill-chosen words, she could bring his destruction.

"It leads to the abandoned mill outside the village via a series of underground tunnels that a smugglers' ring carved into the rise along the estate. The millstream was used to transport contraband items to the sea in the past. For my needs it provides adequate, if cold, bathing at midnight."

"And no one has seen you?"

He gave her a wry look. "Not until the other night when I was forced to take refuge in your room. I knew it was a risk to walk the woods, but I was desperate for freedom."

"How long can you possibly hope to remain in this house?" she wondered aloud.

"Indefinitely, if you keep my secret."

"But Sir Edgar is family, a well-educated military man. Why don't you enlist his help? Or is he one of those rigid types who insists on doing everything by the book? He must have connections, or at least—"

He could see the horror in her eyes as she met his scornful gaze and understood why what she suggested was impossible. She took an involuntary step backward. "Him?" she asked in disbelief. "Your own uncle? You cannot suspect he was involved in the attack on you."

"I do not suspect. I know."

"But why? Are you sure?"

He didn't want to spoil the few moments he had alone with her. "I'm trusting you, Chloe. Now you have to trust me. I heard his voice that night as he stabbed me. His face was masked, but I've known him all my life."

"And with Samuel dead," she said softly, "your inheritance goes to him."

His eyes darkened with sadness. "Yes."

"And Brandon— Oh, my God, Dominic. Did he have anything to do with my brother's death?"

"Come, Chloe. This is not the time to talk. Yes, I believe he had Samuel and Brandon murdered because they had witnessed him selling secrets to the French. Let me show you my private chamber."

"Your uncle," she said in an almost inaudible voice. "I can't believe it."

He brushed a lacy cobweb from her hair, then took her hand, closing his large fingers protectively around hers. She was so quiet that she worried him. He would have spared her the truth had it been possible. He remembered his own shock and bewilderment too well, the feeling of betrayal that had left him reeling.

"Dear Lord," she murmured after a long silence.

"What is it?"

"I was sent to Chistlebury as a lesson for my misconduct. I hardly think this is what my brothers had in mind for self-improvement."

He gave a deep laugh. "So you think this would not qualify as a social call?"

"A young lady must never pay a man a visit, especially at night," Chloe said. "If my sister, Emma, could see—" She broke off with a gasp as a large dark furry object brushed against her legs. "Tell me . . . that is *not* a rat—"

Dominic laughed deeply again. He was impressed that she had not screamed, that she had not asked him more questions about her brother. "That is my dog, whose manners, as his master's, leave much to be desired."

"A dog? Down here with you?"

"Not my choice, Chloe. Ares did not care for the company above, which is understandable, considering the fact that Sir Edgar deems him a dangerous beast and has threatened to shoot him dead."

Chloe stared down in apprehension at the heavily muscled dog. "Is he a dangerous beast?"

He grinned at her. "If he needs to be. For now, I suppose we could call him a chaperone."

"Chaperone? Chef is more like it. He looks as if he's eyeing me for his next meal."

"Well, I cannot say I blame him. You are the most appealing thing either of us have seen in a very long time."

"That is . . . rubbish, Stratfield."

"What are you doing in this house?" he asked, his voice all of a sudden deadly serious. "I thought I had frightened you off forever. I thought you were clever enough to heed my warning."

"You warned me not to walk in the woods."

"And now you know better. Edgar is a coldhearted killer, Chloe."

She shook her head. "I have to confess it's more than I can understand. How did you manage to survive? How could you have arranged your own funeral without anyone helping you?"

"I have one true friend. By the grace of God, he had arrived unannounced the day before I died. I hope I can introduce you to him soon."

A bell began to tinkle above them. Dominic looked up in alarm. "What in God's name does that mean?"

"It's Aunt Gwendolyn," Chloe said after a long pause. "She's trying to exorcise a certain troublesome spirit."

He grinned from ear to ear. "What have I ever done to her?"

"She's convinced you are going to seduce my cousin Pamela in her sleep."

"Cousin who?"

"Stop grinning like that, you demon. After what you did to me in my sleep last night, I should put you back in your grave myself."

He chuckled, leading her back up the steps to the original passage in the wall. "If you were asleep, you could not have known what I did. Assuming that I did anything. Perhaps you were dreaming about me, Chloe."

"Having a nightmare, you mean."

He cleared his throat. How far would she have let him go? He decided it was a good thing that the shadows hid the hungry look on his face. His desire for her was a frightening thing. "Were we intimate?"

"You were, you—incubus."

"And you, poor sleeping maiden, you lay helpless as I took advantage of you?"

"Something like that, Stratfield. Don't you dare ask me to give you any of the details."

He sobered, glancing up at the renewed tinkling of the bell. "Does Edgar have any idea what your aunt is doing?"

"I should hope not."

"Then by all means, stop her. I have never known him to hurt a woman, but let us not take the chance of finding out how far he is willing to go."

*　　*　　*

Chloe decided that *she* was the one who was mad. She could just hear the Spanish Inquisition, also known as the Boscastle family, interrogating her about the whys and hows of this unconventional romance. Heath would probably tie her to a chair in the pantry, as he'd done more than once in their childhood. Grayson would dangle something disgusting over her head like a dead crow to scare her into submission.

Emma, the Dainty Dictator, would do the questioning, pacing around the chair in the hope that Chloe would break down and reveal vital information. Which by miracle of her stubborn nature she never did. "Tell us *exactly* how Viscount Stratfield, a dead man, courted you."

And Chloe would be compelled to answer, "By the usual methods. Blackmail. Threats. Arousing my pity. Kissing me into mindless bliss."

At that point all hell would break loose. Drake, Devon, and Brandon would come charging into the pantry to release the hostage. A terrific fight with the butler's polished knives and forks would ensue until the housekeeper or governess arrived to take control of the uncouth bunch.

Chloe shook her head, smiling at the bittersweet memory. How simple life had been in those days, all her family together. Where—

"Where have you been, Chloe?" Pamela whispered as she noticed Chloe's appearance in the doorway. "You've missed the entire ceremony."

"I, um, was standing guard in the gallery. Did your mother manage to get rid of the ghost?"

Pamela sighed and slipped her candle back into the

wall sconce inside the room. "After all her caterwauling and prayers for his soul to find peace, I think she probably made him glad he's dead."

Aunt Gwendolyn pivoted at the sound of their voices, clutching her Bible and the bell to her chest. "I think I've done it!" she whispered in triumph.

Chloe stared curiously into the empty room, but she managed to avoid looking at the shadowy bed where Dominic had been stabbed. His own uncle. She felt ill at the thought, questions rising like dough in her mind. "How can you tell? It looks exactly the same."

"Well," her aunt said, "you cannot *feel* his presence any longer, can you?"

"I never felt his presence in the first place," Pamela said, not bothering to hide her disappointment. "I was rather hoping we would at least see the ghost before we laid him."

Her mother scowled at her. "Why would you wish to see that irksome spirit?"

"So we could ask who murdered—" Pamela broke off with a horrendous scream as a bulky four-legged shape barreled between her and Chloe to burst into the room.

Aunt Gwendolyn gasped and held her Bible up before her as a shield. Which had little effect on her intruder.

It was a dog. Specifically, Stratfield's beloved hound Ares, who, clearly afraid he would find no welcome from the Bible-wielding woman and her shrieking daughter, had circled back to take refuge at Chloe's side. She stared down in mild panic.

"What are you doing here?" she whispered, covertly giving the sleek tan head a tentative pat. She knew the answer, of course. The dog had wandered out while

Dominic had been distracted sneaking her back into the hall. What should she do?

Aunt Gwendolyn lowered her Bible in relief. The thunder of footsteps on the staircase resounded through the gallery. "Stop that hysterical shrieking, Pamela. It is his lordship's dog."

Chloe released her breath. For all her annoying traits, Aunt Gwendolyn was a true animal lover at heart. She might turn her nose up at a beggar in the streets, but an abandoned kitten would melt her.

Pamela quieted down long enough to collapse on the bed, only to jump up with a squeal as if she had remembered she was lying on the actual scene of Stratfield's death. "Where did it come from?" she asked, eyeing the hound with trepidation.

Sir Edgar's voice cut into the conversation. He had a long dueling pistol in hand, and Sir Humphrey and three male servants were in tow. "What was that unholy noise? What has happened?" He sent a sharp glance around the room before he caught sight of the dog at Chloe's side.

She watched his face harden in anger. "Where did that animal come from? Has it attacked anyone? What are you all doing in this room?"

Chloe noticed that although he appeared to be in control, his hand shook slightly. She remembered Dominic claiming that Edgar wanted to destroy the dog. She felt guilty that Ares had gotten out, that she had inadvertently been the cause of an act that might expose if not endanger Dominic.

"We were walking in the gallery and heard a noise coming from this room," she said calmly. "When we arrived to investigate, we discovered the dog. He has not hurt anyone, Sir Edgar."

Aunt Gwendolyn lifted her brow at this twist on the truth, but gave Chloe a look that might have passed for approval. It was not the most clever excuse in the world, but at least it saved the three women from looking like complete idiots. More important, it did not give away Dominic at all.

Sir Edgar appeared to regain his control and lowered the pistol to his side. "I'd wondered where that wretched beast had hidden itself. One would hope that the servants had checked in here. I should have put it down the day I arrived."

"You most certainly should *not* have done such a thing," Aunt Gwendolyn said in indignation. "The poor creature is mourning his owner. This is a sign of loyalty and intelligence."

Sir Edgar glanced in amusement at Chloe and Pamela, his manners back in place. "As you say, Lady Dewhurst."

"Furthermore," Aunt Gwendolyn said in a pensive voice, "the dog seems to have taken a liking to Chloe. It would appear he is trying to communicate with us."

"Communicate?" Chloe said in disbelief.

Aunt Gwendolyn shook her head impatiently at her lack of understanding. "About his master's death. I believe Stratfield is sending us a message from beyond the grave."

"That he likes Chloe?" Pamela asked slyly.

Sir Edgar glanced out into the candlelit gallery, muttering, "I should have the servants take care of this once and for all."

Aunt Gwendolyn gave a gasp of shock. "You would not put a harmless animal to death? Your nephew adored this hound, Sir Edgar. It would warm my heart to see him running after Lord Stratfield on his frequent rides."

Chloe glanced at the muscular dog from the corner of her eye. She was not an avid animal lover herself, but she would not wish to see one hurt. And there was little in the mastiff's menacing bulk to warm her own heart. But what the beast's owner did to her heart was another matter entirely.

Moreover, for all her aunt babbled on about loyalty and intelligence, Chloe could not be sure that the dog would not eventually lead Sir Edgar to Dominic's hiding place. And if Sir Edgar were capable of butchering his own nephew, there was no telling what he would do when confronted by the resurrected Dominic in the flesh.

"I have always wished for a dog like this of my very own," she blurted out, sounding so much like a feather-brained female that she cringed inwardly.

Aunt Gwendolyn stared at her in a combination of disbelief and delight. "Have you, dear?"

Pamela narrowed her eyes.

"Oh, yes," Chloe gushed, going so far as to clasp her hands to her heart. "Papa had promised me one right before he died."

Which was probably the biggest lie she had ever told in her life. Chloe had been demanding a diamond tiara, not a dog. As if disgusted with this turn of events, Ares sank down on his haunches beside her.

"I should be happy to find a suitable lapdog for you, Lady Chloe," Sir Edgar said, his mouth curling into a faint smile. He took a step toward Ares, then stopped as the dog bared his teeth. "You see, this animal is unpredictable."

"He is not unpredictable at all," Aunt Gwendolyn insisted. "The animal is already serving his duty as a protector." As if to prove her point, she swept past Sir Edgar and knelt to scratch the dog's ears.

Ares consented to this nonsense with a look of utter resignation. Chloe wondered suddenly what she had gotten herself into. What was she to do with a killer dog?

Or a killer.

She glanced up at Sir Edgar's face, attempting to understand what hid behind his mask of unctuous agreeability. Could her well-mannered, accomplished host be capable of murder? Was it possible Dominic had made a mistake? It had been dark in this room the night of the attack.

"What do you make of this, Sir Humphrey?" Edgar asked the other man hovering in the doorway behind Chloe. "It's up to you whether you wish this animal in your house."

"I have never been able to refuse my wife when it comes to rescuing a stray, Sir Edgar," Humphrey answered with a good-humored shrug. "I should not be wise to start now."

Sir Edgar shook his head in defeat. "Then by all means, take the beast. But do not say I did not warn you if it turns on you."

Sir Edgar stood alone with Chloe on the stone entrance steps while the rest of her family climbed into the carriage for the brief drive home.

"Thank you for the pleasure of your company, Lady Chloe. I wish I could have offered you a more entertaining evening."

She forced herself to meet his regard. He seemed gallant, refined, and yet the seed of distrust, of horror, had been planted in her mind. "I was well entertained, Sir Edgar," she replied cordially.

Heavens, that was true enough. Thinking of the way Dominic had kissed her in the dark, had caressed her body, brought a searing blush to her skin. No one had *ever* entertained her like that. And now she knew the basis, if not the details, of his story. Her curiosity had been satisfied while other parts of her nature were aroused.

Sir Edgar smiled. "I wonder if Chistlebury will hold either of us here much longer. I begin to miss the art of battle, and you clearly belong in London, Lady Chloe, where you can be admired."

For a moment Chloe wondered if he was warning her away. "You flatter me, Sir Edgar." And frightened her even more.

To think that such a distinguished man could be a killer. Or that he'd played a hand in Brandon's death. Was it possible? Had Dominic made a terrible mistake? Yet someone had made a monstrous attempt to murder him, and Sir Edgar stood to gain a great deal from his inheritance. Chloe decided to put her trust in Dominic. She was not about to take any chances.

"You sweet little thing," Aunt Gwendolyn cooed to the massive dog who sat in watchful silence at the mossy steps of Dewhurst Hall. "Look how obedient you are."

"Look at the size of him," Uncle Humphrey said in a disgruntled voice. "I don't suppose I'll be having steak chops this week."

"You ate enough at Sir Edgar's table tonight to last you until Christmas."

Sir Humphrey ignored the insult, watching as Chloe and Pamela entered the house arm in arm, Ares following in their shadow. He cared deeply for those two young women and was surprised how determined he was to guard them. "I did not take to our new neighbor, Gwennie."

The usual argument that he expected from his spirited wife did not come. "Nor did I, to be frank," she said in an undertone. "A man who dislikes dogs cannot be trusted."

Dominic watched the carriage disappear down the drive, craving one last glimpse of Chloe's face. Her taunting smile was an image to keep with him in the darkness. When the shadows began to suffocate him again, he would think of her and how she had brightened his hellish realm. He would remember how it had felt to laugh and be himself, to lower his guard and trust another as he had once done so easily.

In a way he was glad that Ares had gone with her. The damned dog had become a liability. But no more so than Dominic's involvement with the desirable lady who had learned his deepest secrets.

His mood sinking, he returned to his hiding place. In the drive below he could see Edgar staring after the carriage. The perfect host. The perfect soldier. The man who had betrayed his own country and family for gold, who had killed without conscience. It made Dominic's flesh crawl to think of his uncle staring at Chloe.

He stood for a moment inside the passageway. He needed to work on the coded letter—it required a focus he did not seem to be able to muster. It fit somehow into the puzzle of Edgar's treachery, but who had written it? Who was it meant to reach?

He trudged down the steps to the cellar. God, no wonder he could not think clearly in this dank hole. The oppressive gloom muddled his mind. He needed to breathe. He needed the brisk night air.

Almost a half hour later he crawled from the chalk tunnel that had been carved into the down and emerged from a wooden trapdoor on the floor of the abandoned mill. The journey seemed endless tonight, and he was almost drunk with relief as he broke outside into the night.

A twig snapped in the dirt. He reached inside his waistband for his pistol. For the second time that evening he had company.

Aunt Gwendolyn's bloodcurdling scream echoed through the house. Chloe had barely sought her bed when the shrieking awakened her. By the time she found her dressing robe and made her way to the door, tripping over Ares, the screams had subsided.

In fact, Aunt Gwendolyn appeared quite calm when Chloe and Uncle Humphrey traced her to the parlor.

"My God, woman," he said, fumbling to put on his spectacles. "What is the meaning of this? Why are you standing there in your cloak screaming the house down?"

"I saw him, Humphrey," she said excitedly, dragging him to the window. "I saw him riding through the woods on his horse. I saw the *ghost*."

Humphrey and Chloe exchanged glances. "It wasn't the ghost, Aunt Gwendolyn," Chloe said in hesitation. "If you saw anyone at all, it was probably Devon."

"Devon?" her aunt asked in a puzzled voice.

"Yes, Devon," Humphrey said irritably. "The rascal was most likely coming to us for help, and you frightened him away with your screaming."

"It was *not* Devon," she replied. "I know my naughty devil. This apparition was bigger than Devon, as big as that bad boy might be. Furthermore, he was riding Stratfield's horse."

Uncle Humphrey shook his head in concern. "Perhaps I should take you away for a month. We could visit our friends in Dorset and have a quiet holiday."

"No," she said with such vehemence that Chloe turned around from the window where she had been sneaking a look outside. "Are you completely insensitive, Humphrey? We cannot go away now. Our Chloe has fallen in love."

Chloe's heart missed a beat. In love? Her first irrational thought was that her aunt had found out about Dominic. Yet that was not possible. Gwendolyn would hardly give her blessing to such a romance. Besides, Chloe didn't love him, did she? Love surely did not describe the acute distress that made her feel like laughing with abandon one moment and weeping in frustration the next. In love. With Dominic. Her brothers would go wild. They would start another war.

She could imagine having to explain her actions. *Yes, I would like the family to meet the man I love. He has been dead for several weeks, but don't let that put you off. It didn't discourage me. Where did we meet? Er, in my trunk of undergarments. Where does he live? Well, in his ancestral home—inside the walls, that is. . . .*

"Yes," Aunt Gwendolyn continued, "I believe Chloe has lost her heart to our own Justin, and a delightful match they make, even if Pamela does not like him. I think this is a union the entire family can approve. Let us not crush it in its infancy."

Chloe did not know whether to feel relieved or to burst out laughing. "Heavens, above. I am not in love with Justin. I've only known him—" Well, less time than she had known Dominic, but she could not compare the two men, or what each of them made her feel. Dominic was so much more complex, so dark and alluring. Justin was the man her father would have wanted her to choose. Not that long ago she had been considering him a good catch herself.

She took a breath. "I think it's time I tell you the truth, Aunt Gwendolyn. Devon has been coming here secretly to me for help. Yes, I know it was wrong of me to take advantage of your hospitality, but he is, after all, my brother, and—"

"He's my nephew, too," her aunt broke in rather impatiently. "And I do believe I love the scamp as much as you do, Chloe. I am perfectly aware that Devon has been coming to your room on the sly. Consider it an act of kindness on my part that I have not intervened."

Chloe felt heat warming her cheeks. "I cannot believe you knew. It seems I'm a disappointment again."

"I do understand discretion, Chloe, and the meaning of family loyalty. I have a bit of Boscastle in me if you recall."

"Yes," Chloe said meekly, noticing her uncle's amused look.

"I am not stupid, Chloe," Aunt Gwendolyn continued. "Nor are my senses impaired. You and Devon made quite a racket the other night in your room. It sounded as if you were practicing a country dance."

A country dance. Chloe's face was positively on fire now. Her aunt could only be referring to the night she had discovered Dominic in her dressing closet. The night he had tossed her on the bed and scared her silly. An interlude that had changed Chloe's life forever.

"I'm sorry if I disturbed you," Chloe said after an awkward pause.

Aunt Gwendolyn's sweet face darkened in a mixture of distress and annoyance. "You and Devon did not disturb me. What disturbs me is this ghost."

"Do you really think it is Stratfield's ghost you saw, my dear?" her husband asked in a tentative voice. "And why would he be riding in front of our house if it were?"

"I should think the answer is obvious, Humphrey," she retorted. "The man is begging to be put out of his misery."

"Aren't we all?" he murmured.

"And I," she claimed, "obviously did not do a proper job of laying him tonight." She turned to Chloe and Humphrey in chagrin. "I fear I may have stirred him up instead of settling him. He's coming to me for help, Humphrey, and I cannot fail him."

*   *   *

Dominic watched as the tall blond-haired figure swaggered into the dilapidated mill house. "I almost blew your pretty head off, Adrian," he said in annoyance. "What the hell are you doing here at this time of night?"

The unannounced arrival was Adrian Ruxley, Viscount Wolverton, professional mercenary, prodigal son, and heir to a dukedom. With a wry smile, he pulled off his leather riding gloves and squatted down in front of the trapdoor from which Dominic had only recently emerged. His short blond hair accented the hard angles of his sun-bronzed face. His hazel eyes reflected a good-natured concern. "Dominic, my old friend, now you have me truly worried. We arranged to meet at nine tonight in the woods. I do not believe I misunderstood the time. You were unable to make our meeting?"

Dominic glanced up grimly. "My uncle was giving a dinner party."

"So I noticed. The estate was ablaze with expensive candles. I almost invited myself over just to see Edgar's reaction." Adrian whistled softly over his shoulder, and the steed he'd ridden moved into the protective shelter of the mill house. "It must have been quite an interesting affair for you to miss our appointment," he said in a cautious voice.

There was silence. Their friendship had been forged years ago in the same Prussian military academy where they had met Heath Boscastle. The two of them had only recently been reunited since what seemed to be another lifetime. Rejected by his proud, embittered father, who believed Adrian to be the product of his young wife's illicit love affair, Adrian had spent the last eight years of his life in self-exile. Only three months ago he had returned to England at his father's request. No fool, Adrian was intrigued by the promise of a fortune.

Rake, rebel, mercenary, cynic, he was one of the most talked-about men in London—and the only person Dominic trusted with his life.

He put down the pistol he had removed from his waistband. "The truth is that I *forgot* I was supposed to meet you."

"Well, it isn't the end of the world," Adrian said mildly. "If you were spying on Edgar, I would not have wanted you to lose some vital information. It's not like the old days when we snubbed each other for anything in skirts."

"Isn't it?"

Adrian's expressive hazel eyes narrowed in speculation. "You *aren't* serious? You were with a woman? How could you risk everything? I mean, I know how one would be tempted, a month without sex in a stuffy hidey hole, but for God's sake—I *hope* the lady does not know anything."

"She knows everything."

"You bloody desperate fool," Adrian said in amazement. "Well, I pray to God we can buy her off or send her away at least until this is over. Who in heaven's name is she anyway? One of your housemaids?"

"Lady Chloe Boscastle." Dominic closed his eyes and drew a breath. There were traces of her unforgettable scent on his shirt. God, his entire body pulsed from holding her. All his longing bottled up, ready to explode. He felt like some sort of wild animal, so hungry for his mate that he could howl beneath her window.

"Boscastle? Not Heath Boscastle's line?"

"I'm afraid so."

Adrian laughed in stunned admiration, his white teeth gleaming. "You are the only man I know who, being presumed dead, could somehow manage to seduce one of the most desirable ladies in London. From the grave of all places. God help you, Dom."

"It wasn't part of my original plan. I . . . fell into this, so to speak."

Adrian sobered as if he could read volumes in what his friend left unsaid. "Hard to resist, is she?"

Dominic rubbed his stubbled jaw. "Impossible. Not that I can carry on a satisfying courtship as a corpse, as you so tactfully pointed out."

"I imagine there are ways."

"She's worth the effort."

"Let me do more to handle Edgar."

"You've done enough," Dominic said slowly, staring out at the moon-dappled stream. "I could not have survived without your help."

"I'd cheerfully tear out his heart with my bare hands to avenge you if you would permit me."

Dominic looked at Adrian with gratitude. Even in their younger years Adrian had always been an outcast to Dominic's traditional English lord. His friend had spent lonely years in India and foreign outposts as a mercenary when his father had sworn to disown him. No doubt Adrian would murder Edgar if he were allowed.

"The day may come."

"Then let it be sooner rather than later," Adrian replied. "It is repugnant to me to see you living like this while Edgar enjoys the fruits of his evil."

Dominic's expression did not change. Somber, intense, determined. Adrian would do exactly the same thing in his place, and they both knew it. The bitter vagaries of life had rendered them each capable of unimaginable deeds. "I assume you haven't learned anything else about Edgar?"

"Not much that you didn't already know. He was by-passed at Corunna for a promotion by Wellington. He spoke rather rashly to the wrong men about it. It seems as if his defection to the Honourable East India Company was a reaction to being snubbed by his superiors. Then again, a man can pocket a tidy fortune by taking foreign prizes if he's willing to leave the regular army." Adrian hesitated. "He could not have acted alone. Not with the kind of critical information he sold."

"I know, but who helped him? Who?"

"I have no idea, but there are men who will want to find out. I'll do all I can before I meet my father, although I have limited contacts in London. Not everyone welcomes a mercenary home with open arms. In the meantime, enjoy this young lady with caution. I hope to God you can trust her."

Dominic laughed quietly. "I have no choice."

Adrian's smile was rueful. "I don't suppose we can send her away for a few months."

"I wouldn't want to if I could."

Chloe had no idea whether her aunt's ceremony in Dominic's bedchamber had "stirred him up" or scared him away. Or even if he had been the spectral rider whom Gwendolyn had seen in the woods that night. She doubted it.

Why would he risk being seen riding when he wished the world to believe him dead? Unless this was part of his elaborate scheme to expose Sir Edgar's treachery. Somehow Chloe thought that an aloof professional soldier like Sir Edgar would not be the type to fall for ghostly theatrics.

Still, if not Dominic, then who was the mysterious rider in the woods? Not Devon. Not Justin, whom Aunt Gwendolyn would have recognized. A friend visiting Edgar? A stranger passing through the village? Chloe burned with frustration that she could not contact Dominic directly to caution him.

He might as well have been truly dead. With every hour of silence that passed she began to fear that she would never see him again. He seemed to think that his quest for vengeance would protect him.

Over the next few days she thought about nothing but Dominic, what he planned to do. At church while the parson's thundering sermon startled the congregation of Chistlebury. Lying across her bed while by candlelight she worked on Brandon's code, sensing she was near a breakthrough. In the overgrown rose garden where she walked for hours on end in a futile attempt to lure her ghost into at least giving her a sign he was safe.

He was silent, uncommunicative, and when she wasn't angry at him for not contacting her, she worried that he had gotten into trouble and could not reach her. How would she know if he was lying helpless in his tunnel? It was wrong of him not to ease her anxiety.

More than once she was tempted to send for her brother Heath, a master of discretion, to help. Her promise to Dominic stopped her.

She understood that to a man like him, whose trust in virtually everyone had been destroyed, another betrayal might be the end of any tenderness that had survived in his heart. She would not dare violate his rigid Draconian Code. The passion of his honor was all he had left. It was a double-edged virtue she intuitively respected even if it exasperated her.

Still, she waited for him. She found herself awakening in the middle of the night, restless, smoldering with the urges he had aroused and left unfulfilled. Unable to go back to sleep, she would pace at her window to scour the misty woods for a sign of him.

Once or twice, just before dawn, she even waved her chemise at the woods to see if he would respond.

Four days later her subtle efforts to attract attention worked, although on the wrong man. Lord St. John called on her late one afternoon while she was exercising Ares in the apple orchard.

"Put that dog away, Chloe," he said as he came up behind her. He was dressed in a white linen shirt and nankeen breeches, a wrinkled cape hanging over his broad shoulders. His boots were muddy and scuffed. "I can't even pretend to be romantic when I'm afraid the beast is going to take a bite out of my bum."

Chloe laughed, tugging the dog's leash closer to her side. She had forgotten how boyishly simple Justin could be, how informal he was compared to the bucks in London who tried to impress her with their lineage and elegant clothes and only ended up looking like prissy fools.

"He hasn't bitten my bum once, for your information," she added.

"Then he's not dangerous, only stupid," he said, a sparkle in his eyes. "If I were your dog, I'd—"

He stepped toward her. Their gazes locked, and Chloe realized with a pang of alarm that he was working up the courage to kiss her. She wasn't shocked by the prospect, no one could see them in the high-walled garden, but Ares suddenly sprang into a half crouch and growled.

Justin emitted a yelp of mock alarm and jumped back behind a gnarled apple tree. "Hey! That wasn't my bum he's snarling at. That was another part of my anatomy I cherish even more dearly."

Chloe bit her bottom lip in amusement. "Do you think I might start a new fashion for chaperones?"

"Do you think you could tie him up so I can talk to you without fear of castration?" Justin asked half jokingly.

"Don't let my aunt hear you using such frank language."

He grinned. "Your aunt was the one who sent me out to find you."

Chloe glanced in surprise at the house. "She did?"

"My parents have invited you and your family to come to supper at our house tonight. Tell me you'll accept." He took her hand and brought her fingertips to his lips. "Please, Chloe, please. I shall throw myself in the stream if you don't."

Chloe felt a sudden impatience to be by herself again. What was wrong with her? Not long ago she had found Justin good fun. Why did she keep comparing him to a shadow lover who represented everything she should resist? Why did he suddenly seem like an overgrown schoolboy and not a man? Specifically a dark, intense, and disconcerting one. "I really will have to ask my aunt—"

"Chloe!" her aunt called out from the parlor window. "Ask Justin if we are expected at six or seven this evening."

He chuckled. "Well, there's your answer." He kissed her knuckles before he released her hand. "Leave the beast behind tonight if you don't mind. I aim to take a nibble of you myself."

Chloe watched him swagger out of the garden, his wrinkled cape twisting around his waist. When he reached the gate, he stopped to blow her another kiss. She raised her hand to wave back only to be distracted by the sound of Ares whining low in his throat.

She laughed as he tugged eagerly against the leash. "Stop it, Ares. You aren't going to eat Justin or anyone else for that matter. You'll have to behave—"

She broke off, slowly lifting her head. The dog was not facing in Justin's direction at all but toward the woods. As if he recognized someone she could not see.

"Stratfield?" she whispered, her pulse accelerating. "Dominic, is that you?"

She ran to the far end of the orchard, Ares bounding at her side, but there was nothing to arouse suspicion in the woods that she could see. The peaceful shadows looked undisturbed. She couldn't hear even a leaf rustle, only the hopeful pounding of her own heart. Whoever had been there was gone.

Ares sat obediently at her side.

Pamela began shouting at her from the house. "Have

you seen my new gloves, Chloe? I hope that dog of yours didn't eat them."

She released her breath. "Damn you, Dominic," she said into the silence that mocked her disappointment. "Damn you, you devil."

Chapter 14

Supper with Justin's parents proved to be an awkward affair. Chloe kept sensing that they disapproved of their son's interest in her, and their few veiled remarks made it clear that in their view a lady from London might not find country life to her liking at all.

Justin tried to apologize by making fun of them, and stole a kiss from Chloe in the hall when it was time for her to go home. "Are you angry at me, Chloe?"

She wasn't angry at him. She didn't feel much for Justin one way or the other; her mind just kept straying to other matters. How could she explain she had fallen in love with a man he thought was buried in a grave? She could hardly believe it herself.

"You seem so preoccupied lately," he said as he drew away from her.

Her aunt overheard this last comment, approaching them after her husband had wrapped her in her heavy woolen cloak. "The girls are afraid of the ghost."

Uncle Humphrey ushered his harem outside. "Rubbish. Chloe has her feet firmly planted on the ground. I wish I could say the same of my wife."

*   *   *

Chloe did not feel as if her feet were planted on the ground at all. All throughout the ride home she kept searching the moonlit wayside and leafy hedgerows for the least sign that Dominic was still alive and haunting the area. When a lone cloaked horseman appeared at the fork in the road to block their way, she went still, willing the carriage to stop.

The elderly coachman halted the vehicle in obvious annoyance. For an instant Chloe convinced herself that the mysterious rider in the road was Dominic. She glimpsed in the stark, shadowy angles of his face the image she had been willing to appear. She leaned toward the door in anticipation. Her heart raced with hope even though she knew it was unlikely he'd reveal himself in such a dramatic fashion.

The resemblance to Dominic was, unfortunately, only an illusion of night and bloodlines. Her hopes sank as the rider's features came into sharper focus. The chiseled planes of Dominic's face blurred and became those of the last man on earth she would want to meet at night.

This could not be a good omen.

Sir Edgar patrolling alone in the dark. What was he up to? What had he been looking for?

Her uncle voiced his own disapproval from the carriage window. "My God, Sir Edgar, I could have shot you for a highwayman."

Sir Edgar nodded in apology, sitting straight-backed on his horse. "You need remember that the villain who murdered my nephew has not been caught."

On closer inspection Chloe wondered how she could have mistaken him for Dominic. She couldn't detect the tiniest hint of passion in Edgar's eyes, not a speck of warmth.

"Do you hope to find him single-handedly?" Aunt Gwendolyn asked, her voice a trifle aloof. She had not forgiven him his dislike of dogs.

"The local authorities have proven rather unhelpful, Lady Dewhurst," he replied in a polite tone. "Their investigations have led them to the conclusion that my nephew was killed by a stranger to the area, quite possibly a deranged soldier. As there have been rumors of suspicious activity in the woods at night, my gamekeeper and I have decided to do our own investigating."

"How brave of you," Chloe murmured, her fingers curling tightly inside her gloves. Brave was hardly the word. What was he looking for this late at night? Did he suspect Dominic was not dead? Or had her ghost begun to lay his trap?

Edgar glanced down at her, a smile hovering on his thin lips. "I should wish my land a safe place for young ladies to stroll and take the air."

"And to exercise their dogs," Aunt Gwendolyn added, politely challenging him.

He laughed as if to concede defeat. "Of course."

A minute later the carriage was rumbling down the road, passing under the gentle rise of Stratfield Hall. Chloe stared out the window as if she could see through the dark gray stones into the very heart of the house. She sighed wistfully as her aunt and uncle began to bicker and the great house disappeared from view.

Dominic, if I ever see you again, I may kill you myself . . . Where are you?

* * *

Lord Devon Boscastle was waiting in the parlor for everyone to come home from the supper party. Tall and arresting, he was dressed in a black greatcoat, pantaloons, and polished Hessian boots, his thick black hair wind-blown, his blue eyes brimming with good spirits.

At first, in the firelight, he so resembled her older brother Heath that Chloe's heart took a plunge. He's found out about Dominic and me, she thought in panic. Or something awful has happened at home. Why else would he appear to the family without warning?

Then he turned, and she recognized Devon by his dia-bolical grin. She backed into the sofa to sink down in relief. Her nerves seemed so on edge these days that she expected the worst every time she turned around. Aunt Gwendolyn and Pamela quickly covered their own pleased surprise with warm hugs and welcoming chatter. Women had fallen in love with Chloe's brothers from their first days on earth in the Boscastle nursery when their blue eyes had stolen the nursemaids' hearts. Who else but Devon could be forgiven for holding up a car-riage as a prank?

"Have no fear, everyone," he said, looking pointedly at Chloe over his aunt's shoulder. "I've only come to say a proper good-bye before I return to the bosom of the family. I have paid my penance potting orchids and am ready to be unleashed again upon the world."

Chloe studied him fondly. He looked more at ease with himself than he'd seemed in months. "Is everything cleared up in Chelsea?" She was of course referring to his debacle debut as a highwayman.

He gave her a pained smile. "Yes. I owe Gray a debt that he shall probably never let me forget. I'll do my best to convince him it's time for you to come home, too. The pair of us have rusticated long enough."

Time to come home. Chloe's heart turned cold at the thought. Only a short while ago she'd been desperate to escape Chistlebury. Now she was determined to stay, no matter what she had to do. Nothing could make her abandon Dominic in the middle of his crisis. Who would have imagined how her life would change in the course of a few weeks? How the focus of her world would shift. Harder still to imagine was what the future would bring, and whether Dominic's dark quest for revenge would succeed.

At that same moment, in the same house, Dominic was waiting impatiently inside her room for Chloe to retire for the evening. He'd fought with himself for hours before breaking down and climbing through the window into the closet.

He knew it was a risk. He knew Adrian would throw up his hands in despair at his irrational behavior. But Dominic had stayed away from her as long as he could stand it. He had to see her again if only for a few minutes. She gave him strength and an emotional foundation besides hatred to anchor him. He was obsessed with her, insane for her company, for the sight of her. He wanted to hear her laugh, to hold her again.

She had been taunting him for days with her subtle little methods to draw him to her. Yes, he appreciated her attempts at discretion. No, he could not resist her, waving her chemise from her window like some impertinent Circe luring a sailor to his doom.

Not that he needed any reminders of her existence or

her appeal. When he was not wholly absorbed in watching Edgar, he was thinking about Chloe, about how much he wanted to see her again. He could not believe how desperately he craved her when they had been together only a few stolen hours.

He leaned against the windowsill and stared outside. Where the devil *was* she? Her room was a tribute to female vanity—stockings, fans, shoes strewn about as if she had tried on every article of clothing she owned to make the perfect impression.

But on whom?

His black eyebrows rose in displeasure. Was her scandalous corset missing? No. There was the provocative garment on the wardrobe floor, and a bloody good thing for her, too. If Chloe was going to model that for any man, it would be him and him alone.

"Where is she?" he muttered.

He'd heard the carriage rattle home almost two hours ago. Hiding behind the door, he had waited and waited for Chloe to come up to her room, but something, or someone, was keeping her downstairs.

He hated not knowing where she was. He had seen Edgar ride from Stratfield Hall earlier in the evening and wondered if it were possible that his uncle and Chloe were together in the parlor. He hadn't noticed anyone else riding from his estate, but a visitor could have arrived before he climbed the tree to her room. He should have thought to check the stable. The problem was that she was the only thing he could think about.

Ares lifted his head toward the window, releasing a soft growl of warning.

Dominic drew back the curtain with a scowl as he recognized the fair-haired masculine figure standing under the tree. "Not again," he said in disgust.

"Chloe!" Justin called up in a ridiculously seductive voice. "Don't hide from me, you little flirt. I see your pretty shape behind those curtains."

"If you see a pretty shape," Dominic muttered to himself, "then you need a good pair of spectacles, you moron."

"Are you playing coy, Chloe? You weren't coy at dinner when I fed you that cake."

Dominic grunted. So *that* was where she had spent the evening, being spoon-fed by this colossal fool. He folded his arms across his chest and glared daggers at the window as the revealing one-sided conversation went on.

"I won't go away until you talk to me, Chloe," Justin whispered loudly. "I want to know you're not upset with me for stealing that kiss in the hallway." He paused. "Although it did seem to me you enjoyed it. All the ladies in Chistlebury enjoy my kisses."

Kiss in the hallway? Dominic's jaw hardened as he envisioned the passionate Lady Chloe locked in the embrace of Chistlebury's fair-haired Lothario. No doubt he was the only person in the village who did not think Chloe and Justin were a delightful match. Being dead, however, he would likely not be allowed a say in the matter.

On impulse he raised his voice to a warbling soprano and sang through the curtains, "Go home to your mother, Justin. I've had all I can take of you for one night."

Justin blinked owlishly up at the window. "What in heaven's name happened to your voice, Chloe? You sound so queer. Are you taking sick again? Do you think it might be catching?"

"Yes. Yes. I'm sick, dear," Dominic trilled, fluttering his fingers out the window. "I'm sure it must be horribly contagious."

"You didn't seem sick when I kissed you, and anyway I'm as healthy as a horse. Let me look at you just once before I leave."

"Ooh, gracious, no, Justin, you naughty thing! I've just gotten into my nightrail. I'm really not decent at all."

Justin clutched his hand to his heart in melodramatic angst. "I refuse to budge until I'm allowed one last look." He broke into a boyish grin. "Pamela said you have some interesting garments in your trunk."

Dominic gritted his teeth. "If you bring everyone outside with your antics, it will be your last look, I swear to God."

Justin stamped his foot in a feigned display of temper. "I shan't go. I shall throw a great big nasty tantrum until you give in. Anyway, your aunt likes me."

"Well, I don't," Dominic said under his breath. It was insulting, honestly. Did Chloe really find this annoying infant attractive? She had kissed the fool?

"What, Chloe? Oh, come on. One peek is all I ask for pleasant dreams. It won't hurt anything."

"Oh, hell," Dominic said, snatching a frilly night cap from one of Chloe's trunks. Jamming it down low on his forehead, he reached for a pink silk shawl and threw it on over his wide shoulders.

"I'm waiting, Chloe," Justin whispered in a petulant voice.

Dominic smiled with evil intent, poked his head through the curtains like a turtle, and disappeared just as quickly back into the room. "There. Are you happy now?"

"That was cheating, Chloe," Justin complained. "I couldn't see anything but a big pink blur."

"Sweet dreams, Justin," he muttered, yanking the curtains together.

Dominic pulled off the cap and shawl, turning his head. Footsteps sounded lightly in the hall outside Chloe's bedchamber. The doorknob turned, and he heard her grumbling in annoyance about uncouth country houses as she pushed repeatedly against the warped doorframe.

He stood in the dressing closet, suddenly unsure of himself, of how she would react, of what excuse he could give to explain his presence. The truth of his need, his hunger, might frighten her. He knew it frightened him. He could not promise her anything. Not the future her family desired for her. Not a sweet courtship. Not a future at all for that matter.

He could offer her nothing but trouble.

As Chloe opened the door, a chill slid down her back. Someone was in her room. Not Devon, whom she had left downstairs with her uncle. Not just the dog, who seemed to have taken a fancy to her bed. The fine hairs of her nape stirred in awareness. She felt her heart beat harder with a delicious anticipation. She was almost afraid to hope. She couldn't bear it if she was disappointed again.

"Good evening, Chloe," said the deep, familiar voice from the depths of her dressing closet.

She hesitated before closing the door carefully behind her. She had promised herself she would tell him to go to the devil if she saw him again, but at the mere sound of his voice, her composure begin to crumble. All the hours of anxiety, of waiting, of not knowing how he was. And he sounded in perfect health, the beast.

So many conflicting emotions cascaded through her, it was hard to control herself. She wanted to rail at him. Run into his arms. Demand what he thought he was doing in her room again and where he had been while she'd been half out of her mind with worry.

She did none of these. It took enough out of her to manage an answer in a normal manner at all. He was safe. He was here. "How nice of you to call, Lord Stratfield."

He gave her a slow smile. "How nice of you to allow me."

"I haven't allowed—" But she had. What was the point in pretending? She'd been dying for word of the devil for days. She kicked off her shoes and pushed them under the bed. Had she remembered to hide her journal? Yes. He knew enough about her as it was. A lady had to keep some secrets to herself. Especially from him.

He opened the closet door, his pose arrogant, intimidating. His gaze traveled slowly over her as if he were studying every detail of her appearance down to the seams of her yellow muslin dinner dress. Did he approve? Apparently, to judge by the gleam in his gunmetal-gray eyes. Heat swirled in her belly. Her breathing quickened.

"What were you doing downstairs for so long?" he demanded softly.

She frowned at him. Trust him to disappear for days

while expecting her to sit here moping by the window. "My brother Devon came to say good-bye. Apparently all is forgiven and forgotten, and he has been called back to London. You cannot hold the threat of exposing him over my head."

He studied her face. There were no more threats of that nature between them, and they both knew it. "Was Edgar there, too?"

She stared back at him, barely paying attention to what he had just asked. He was so devastatingly male, he took all her breath away. She was suddenly afraid of what might happen if she stopped being angry at him, of how easily he could make her forget everything else. "Why would Edgar be there?"

"He left the house earlier in the evening. Alone. I was concerned he may have come to call on you."

Chloe's heart gave a nervous flutter. Had he been worried? Jealous? He who claimed to have no decent feelings? He was like her brothers who hated to show any weakness. But . . . was it possible that she had become a weakness for him?

"We met him on the road a little while ago. He claimed he was looking for your murderer."

"Isn't he the essence of chivalry?" Dominic asked darkly. "I don't want the swine anywhere near you or your family."

"I don't particularly care to be in his presence myself," Chloe said in a subdued tone. Her anger was draining away. She could feel herself drawn by dangerous degrees to Dominic. She wanted to touch him, to lay her head on his chest and breathe his scent, to make him stay.

A plaintive voice floating up to the window from outside saved her from making a rash move. Chloe's mouth opened in shock. "Heavens, that sounds like Justin."

Dominic sighed in irritation. "It is Justin."

She swept around him into the dressing closet. "What does he think he's doing?"

Dominic pivoted slowly, an evil grin on his face. "The twit wanted to see me in a nightrail."

"What?" It took several seconds to put two and two together. "You *are* trouble, Dominic Breckland, trouble from beginning to end. I cannot believe you would do such a thing. What a blackguard you are. I mean it."

His devilish chuckle burned her ears as she hurried to the window and crossly pulled open the curtains. "Be quiet down there," she whispered, peering through the branches.

Justin gazed up at her in unconcealed disappointment. "I thought you'd changed into your nightrail, Chloe. That looks like the dress you were wearing at supper. Were you only teasing me all this time?"

"Teasing you?" Chloe turned her head to glare at Dominic across the closet. He pantomimed a puzzled shrug. "Apparently I was, Justin. Everyone in London knows what a wicked tease I am."

Justin threw up his hands in surrender. "You can tease me all you like, Chloe. I'm a good sport about that sort of thing."

She shook her head. What was she supposed to do with two unruly men? "Not at this time of night, Justin," she said firmly. "I'm closing the window now. Go home, please."

"Good for you," Dominic said behind her, pretending to applaud. "That's the spirit. Put him in his place."

"It's you I'm putting in your place," she retorted, turning to confront him.

"Dear me," he said with a mocking grin before he pulled her into his arms. "But I do believe it's going to be the other way around."

Her startled gaze lifted to his. He was holding her so tightly she could not lift her arms, and she didn't really try. "What do you mean?"

"Let's go back into the bedroom, Chloe. I'll show you what I mean."

He carried her to the bed and, between long, hungry kisses, removed every article of her clothing. Her yellow gown, her petticoats, her garters, her lace-trimmed chemise.

When he had rolled off her last stocking, he caressed and studied her nude body as if she were a work of art to admire.

Chloe smoldered under his dark scrutiny. Her breasts felt heavy and swollen, the tips aching for his touch. He'd never looked more intense, more dangerous, not even on the night she had found him in this room.

"I should leave," he said quietly as he ran one hand up her thigh to the soft curve of her hip.

"No, Dominic."

His eyes searched her face. The tension deep within her mounted. She bit the inside of her lip. His hot gaze traveled over her body again. How exposed she felt, how vulnerable. Yet deep inside her she found her very helplessness exciting.

"If I stay," he said, "we both know what will happen.

You will never belong to anyone but me until the day I die."

"Take me," she whispered.

He leaned over her and claimed her mouth in a kiss that sealed the pact she had made. It was a kiss of possession, deep and intoxicating. The wicked pleasure of it left her without a single defense.

She could not think. He dominated her mind, her senses anyway. The taut-muscled strength of his body. His virile magnetism. In the deepest part of her, she already belonged to him, ached to be his lover.

She sat up slowly to kiss him back, whispering against his bruising mouth, "Touch me all over. Take me now. I need you as badly as you need me."

"Do you?" His voice was rough, but his hands felt gentle as he held her face. "Do you need me, Chloe?"

He drew her into his lap so that she straddled him like a wanton. "You know I do," she whispered, her breasts crushed to his chest.

He shifted position, lifting her with his powerful thighs. He wrapped one arm around her waist to anchor her. She might have fallen back onto the bed otherwise. His free hand caressed the curve of her backbone, the globes of her bottom. She arched her neck and shivered in unbearable anticipation.

Ever so subtly he moved his hand across the sensuous angle of her hips, to the sleek front of her thigh. She tensed, throbbing deep inside. She was embarrassed he would discover how damp she was in the aching hollow of her womanhood.

When his fingers found her, it was as if a flame caressed her. Her flesh burned; she melted into him. In that moment he could have done anything to her he desired.

He was aroused. She could feel his thick member as he repositioned his thighs to open her wider. He groaned into her hair, stroking the damp curls above her cleft, slipping his fingers slowly inside her.

"Sweet Chloe," he whispered. "You are so soft in there. Put your hands on my shoulders."

She obeyed and felt his iron-corded muscles tighten under her fingers. The pleasure of his probing touch took her breath away. She sank into his caress, boneless, silently pleading for more. Yes, more. She wanted to follow this. Completion.

"Is this what you need?" he asked softly, lust glittering in the smoky depths of his eyes as he lowered his head.

More than anything, yes, she needed him. There was a rightness to their mating. An inevitability that she had felt from the start. He would possess her. And then she would possess him.

"Are you going to undress?" she whispered.

He smiled and brought his mouth to her breast. "In a moment. I'm a little preoccupied right now."

He drew her nipple between his teeth, and she gasped as sweet pleasure seared her. Her head fell back as he began to suck her breast into his hot, wet mouth. Within moments she sagged against the support of his arm. The suction of his lips tied her nerves into straining knots. It was too much. Not enough.

"Chloe."

She stared up into his dark, hungry face. "Don't you

dare leave me like this, Dominic," she whispered in a husky voice.

"No," he said, shaking his head. "I can't."

He leaned back and pulled his white linen shirt over his muscular shoulders, then unbuttoned his snug black pantaloons. As he bent to remove his black leather boots, she studied his shadowed form in wonder.

It was the first time she had seen him completely naked. His body was even more breathtaking than she'd imagined—lean, sculptured sinew and graceful bone. She remembered the chiseled musculature of his chest and shoulders from the night she'd found him, the athletic strength. The healing scar did not disfigure him as much as it marked him a survivor.

He glanced around, his eyes narrowing. She did not avert her gaze, but looked her fill, showing him her desire, her approval. Hard angles and firm muscles defined his lower torso and legs. She worked to control the rhythm of her breathing. It was all she could manage not to moan in pleasure as he moved toward her.

She reached out to him. She needed to feel him again. He caught her fingers as she touched the hard plane of his abdomen. She could tell that he was struggling with himself. That he desired her and did not wish to do the wrong thing.

She leaned back against the pillows, disentangling her fingers from his, her body arranged in a pose of age-old feminine invitation.

"Dominic," she said in a whisper, "this is what I want."

He could not satisfy his senses fast enough with the offering before him. The sound of her beguiling voice.

The velvet softness of her skin. The secret hollows of her body. He wanted to experience it all at once, to submerge himself in pure Chloe and yet to take her slowly, savoring every moment they had together.

There was not enough time to sate his craving for her. There would never be enough time.

He knew they dared not disturb the sleeping household. Their sense of caution seemed only to enhance the sexual mood, to heighten the sharp pleasure of every touch. She was a woman worth whatever risk he must take to have her. Strong, beautiful, and caring.

He stretched out alongside her on the bed. The anticipation in her lovely blue eyes intensified his desire for her.

"You drive me mad, Chloe," he said with a rueful shake of his head.

Her smile tantalized him. "You were mad when I met you."

He gathered her soft, warm body in his arms. "Well, I'm a raving lunatic now."

She caressed the powerful line of his shoulder with her fingertips. "What does that make me?"

He forced her back down onto the pillows. "Mine." She was liquid fire beneath his hard, aroused body. Soft and fierce. He wanted to explore, to exploit her sexual weaknesses to bring her pleasures she had never known.

"I cannot take another moment of this," she murmured. "You're a cruel man, Dominic."

He blew the lightest breath across her taut belly. He meant to show her just how cruel and kind a lover he could be. Of course it was a game that could all too easily backfire. "Be patient," he whispered against her soft flesh, when he wasn't sure that he could hold out much longer himself. His sex strained against the inside of her sleek thigh, heavy and engorged with blood.

Loving Chloe reminded him just how desperately human he really was. His desire for her brought out not so much his strengths as his vulnerabilities. How could he explain, without sounding like an utter fool, that being with her gave him the courage to return to his dark prison? Without his fantasies of her to fill in his bleakest hours, he would lose his mind. Could she possibly understand that she alone had proven the antidote for the hatred and despair that threatened to destroy him?

He was ravenous for her.

She had the body of a siren, plush pink-tipped breasts and rounded hips that invited thoughts of sex. The fragrance of her inflamed his senses. Soap, fresh air, and musky sweet arousal. He wanted to bury his face between her thighs and breathe her perfume into his lungs.

"Dominic?" she whispered, her sexy blue eyes mirroring his hunger and confusion.

He stared at her. She was so ready, so lush for the taking. He wanted to make love to her with a desire that made his body burn like a torch, but he hated the thought of not being able to stay with her afterward, of being denied the privilege of holding her through the night. He wanted all of her. He wanted an intimacy that went beyond a sexual act.

"Why do you look at me like that, Dominic?" she asked in an undertone.

He drew a breath, parting the soaked curls between her thighs with his thumb. She went perfectly still as he pressed up against the tender bud of her sex. She was already sensitive to his touch. Pleased at her response, he slipped his fingers into the swollen folds of her labia. Her eyes drifted shut in drugged enjoyment.

He bent his head to kiss her, tasted the pleased gasp she gave as his fingers quickened their movements. She was the sweetest thing he had ever touched. Tight. Creamy wet. He shuddered at the thought of being gloved inside her tight woman's body, of sinking into her heated depths. By the time he brought her to a climax, he was so desperate for relief that he was practically rubbing himself against the bed. She was made for passion.

"What are you waiting for?" she whispered as the last contraction ebbed from her body.

He leaned down to kiss her pouting mouth again. "Do you really want to give yourself to a man like me?" he asked softly.

"Only to a man like you," she said without hesitation.

He closed his eyes. "You honor me, Chloe."

"I don't want to honor you, you scoundrel. I want you to . . . to finish what you started. Dominic, for God's sake, have a little mercy. I have *never* felt like this before."

"My God, I hope not." The thought was intolerable to him. If he had met her before his life had fallen apart, he had no doubt he would be approaching her brothers for her hand. "Chloe," he said, the intensity of his expression easing, "you're the best thing that has ever happened to me. I'm afraid the same does not hold true in reverse."

"You're wrong," she whispered. "And you aren't going to change my mind."

"God help me," he said in a low voice. "I don't intend to."

She watched his face as he rose up onto his knees and pushed her pale legs apart, exposing the wet crevice of her womanhood. He drew a sharp breath. He was so hard he feared he might explode before he even entered her.

He made a hoarse sound of pleasure deep in his throat as he positioned his shaft against the entrance of her drenched sheath. She felt like bliss, but she was tight inside, and he was afraid he would tear her, so fierce was his need.

"I'll try not to hurt you," he said, and lowered his head to kiss her.

He felt her tense at the powerful thrust that drove him into the depths of her body. He could feel him stretching her, forcing himself past her maidenhead, but it was too late to stop. His mind emptied. His kiss muffled the soft gasp she gave. When she began to relax a little, he whispered against her mouth, "Wrap your arms around me. It doesn't always hurt. It won't last."

"It doesn't hurt you, does it?"

"God, no. It's heaven."

He withdrew from her only to sink back inside with a slow forceful thrust. He felt her quiver, but she didn't tighten against the invasion, and then he was oblivious to everything except his own need, his urgent quest for relief. She moved slightly, meeting his movements.

"Chloe," he said, his arms straining to hold his weight, "you feel so good."

"So . . . do you"

That was all it took to push him over the edge. Those three erotic words. His body stiffened; he slammed into her one final time, a climax wrung from the depths of his shuddering body. He felt as if he would flood her, as if he would come forever. When it was over, he sank down beside her and wrapped her in his arms, gripping her so tightly he suspected he was hurting her. She said nothing. If she felt like him, it probably took all her energy to breathe.

He didn't know what to say. He might have ravished her body, but in the end she had conquered his heart.

Chloe finally broke the silence, lifting her head from his shoulder. Her hair was damp around her face. Her blue eyes pierced him, and he wanted her all over again. He was already hard.

"When will I see you again?"

"I don't know. Not soon enough for me."

She attempted to sit up, tousled, sexy, her temper flaring. "How am I supposed to know if you are in trouble or even alive?"

"It might be better if you don't."

"*Dominic.*" She pushed his arm away. He saw the pulse beating at the base of her throat. She was breathtaking, his, her body flushed with his taking. "I think you're right. You are dead, you fiend. You don't have one decent feeling left inside you, and what we just did doesn't count."

"I tried to warn you." His heart was thundering in his chest, in his ears, in his temples. "I should never have come here tonight, Chloe. I had no desire to cause you so much distress."

"It's a little late for that, isn't it?" she whispered in a wry voice. "You should have fallen into someone else's window." She pulled the coverlet up to her chin as if suddenly conscious of her nudity, of how far they had gone. It hadn't been enough for him. He wanted to take her in every way a man could take a woman.

"I wish this could be different," he said. "We'll just have to do our best."

"What a mess," she whispered.

"Chloe." She was angry and upset, and he couldn't blame her. His life was in shambles. He was a threat to everything she was.

"Don't worry about me, Dominic," she said tartly. "My trunk and undergarments are always at your disposal. You can wear my petticoats whenever you please."

Her wounded indignation struck him as both unfair and well deserved at once. There wasn't time to soothe her feelings as much as he might like to, or to convince her of what she meant to him. He took one last look at her before he slid off the bed. He couldn't be sure, but he thought there might be tears in her eyes. God help him if she started to cry. He'd weaken, and be back in bed with her until the morning.

"Don't get out of bed, Chloe."

"Not even to push you out the window?"

He bent to kiss her. At least her humor had returned, although it might have been flattering to remember her heartbroken and naked on the bed where they'd made love. "Try to go to sleep," he said gently.

"Go to—"

He escaped into the closet, pausing to pat Ares on the head before he braced himself for his exit. The dog barely moved except to follow his movements with liquid brown eyes that seemed to accuse him. "Jesus," he said, "even my own damned dog has turned against me."

He climbed onto the windowsill, felt the night breeze on his warm face and throat. If Chloe had any sense, she would bar this window behind him so that he would not be able to return until he could offer her a proper future. Or chop down the tree that gave him access to her room. He couldn't stay away from her.

He hooked his leg across the sill and around the nearest branch. As perverse as it seemed, his sexual encounter with her had energized him, restored his vitality. He was boiling with frustration for more of her, but his spirits felt better than they had since his stabbing. The inner strength he needed to confront his opponent was back in spades. He could channel all his physical needs now into revenge. How he handled his heart was an entirely different matter.

Chapter 15

Chloe should have known that when she fell in love, she would fall hard and with all the impulsive passion of her Boscastle heart. Naturally she would choose the worst man in the world for her. Naturally the course of their love would not run smoothly. She sat for a full thirty seconds, lamenting her fate, stunned by his departure, by what had happened between them.

Then she sprang off the bed and pulled on her yellow dinner dress to go after him. She wasn't the type to lament for long. She felt abandoned, afraid for him and herself. She couldn't believe they had come together in a blaze of sexual intimacy, and then he had climbed out the window, leaving her to smolder in her bed like a live coal. She could not let him go without—something more. More of him. More of his tormenting, the trouble he brought. A reassurance that he would return, or that nothing would happen to him while they were apart.

On a more practical note, she noticed that he had forgotten to take the telescope he had stolen from her on his first visit to her room. She picked it up from the floor on her way to the door.

Her heart racing, she slipped into the hall and stole downstairs through the darkened house, then outside into the night. The damp grass pricked her bare feet as she threaded her way around the muddy duck pond to the garden. Dominic had just landed on the ground when she reached him, rising from a crouch.

"God in heaven!" he exclaimed when he saw her. "Are you trying to ruin us both?"

She held out her hand to him. "You forgot the telescope."

Frowning at her with concern, he took the instrument and tucked it into his waistband. "Thank you."

"You cannot continue like this, Dominic. Living in a—a wall is not normal."

"I realize that." He ran his hand through his black hair in exasperation. "Do *you* realize what you are doing to me? Every time I see you I'm tempted to throw down my cards for the chance to regain my life."

"But you can't," she said quietly.

"Not if I mean to bring Edgar and those he worked with to justice. I can't trust the authorities to do it for me. I have no idea how many friends he might have, or whom he might hurt next. He doesn't exactly play by the rules."

She would not argue the point again. He was as stubborn-headed, hell-bent, and honor-bound as any of her brothers. "At least you can make some sort of arrangement to let me know you are well."

He gripped her by the shoulders. The moonlight did not soften the uncompromising angles of his face. His ordeal had left its mark in an attractive austerity. "I'm in no position to be promising you letters, Chloe. I told you once there is only one man I trust. His name is Adrian Ruxley, Viscount Wolverton. He's the man who helped me stage my own funeral. Should something happen to me, you may go to him, but *not* until I've done what I need to do."

"If he's a trusted friend, perhaps I can persuade him to talk some sense into you."

"Don't get more deeply involved in my problems than you already are. Go back to being the high-spirited lady you were when I first met you. When this is all over, I shall give you anything you want."

"I haven't been high-spirited for a long time, Dominic."

He released her with a sudden curse, his gaze focusing on the back of the house. "Someone's coming out here," he said. "Don't give me away."

"What—"

"Don't say anything."

Chloe whirled around, instantly recognizing her aunt's petite figure charging down the garden path. "What do I do?" she whispered to Dominic's retreating figure.

"Use your wits, Chloe," he said unhelpfully, before ducking behind the tree.

"Do you not see him?" her aunt shouted. "Right there, you dunderhead! Behind that tree."

"Who are you calling a dunderhead?" Chloe demanded.

"You!"

"I don't see anybody." Which was partially true. Dominic had disappeared behind the tall row of trees that flanked the entry gate, his lean figure blending into the long shadows.

To her astonishment, Aunt Gwendolyn reached around and grabbed Chloe's arm to yank her in the direction of Dominic's shadow. "There! *There*. Now do you see?"

What a dilemma. Chloe had no idea what to do. If she admitted she could see Dominic, then his secret would unravel. If she pretended he wasn't there, her aunt would have good cause to call her a dunderhead.

"I'll get the parson," Aunt Gwendolyn said in excitement, her silver-streaked curls disheveled. "Come with me. No. On second thought, stay here. Guard him."

"Guard whom?"

"The ghost!"

"What ghost?"

"The ghost right in front of your face."

"How can I guard him if I can't see him?" Chloe asked.

At that moment Dominic stepped forward, dramatically, his cloaked figure overshadowed by the gatehouse. "Madam," he addressed Aunt Gwendolyn, "she cannot hear or see me. Do not waste precious breath."

Aunt Gwendolyn glanced at Chloe from the corner of her eye, murmuring, "Incredible."

Dominic inclined his head in a grave nod. "Quite."

"Why, you poor tragic man—er, ghost," the older woman said anxiously. "Are you having difficulty on your passage to the other side?"

"The other side of what?"

"Oh, dear," Aunt Gwendolyn said nervously. "It never occurred to me that he might be trying to go up when he's meant to go down." She cleared her throat. "Lord Stratfield, I must warn you that I am a married woman."

Dominic looked blank. For an awful moment Chloe thought he would burst into laughter. "Married?"

"Married as in faithful to my husband. I cannot consort with you, my lord."

"Consort with me?"

"I know of your reputation for seducing women in the parish," Aunt Gwendolyn said in a tremulous voice. "Tempt me not."

"To do what?" he asked, in genuine confusion.

"It was not my daughter at all, was it?" Aunt Gwendolyn said with a gasp of understanding. "It was *me* you sought."

Dominic was edging back into the shadows. Chloe could only be grateful that because of their evening out, the gate had not yet been locked. He would be able to escape before her aunt grabbed him, too, and found out he was no apparition.

"I must leave you now, madam," he said with a melodramatic wave of his cloak.

"Leave me?" Aunt Gwendolyn cried. "But I do not know why you came or what help you desire from me."

"Well, I . . ." Chloe enjoyed the look of uncertainty on his handsome face. "I have to go. I have tarried too long as it is."

Aunt Gwendolyn put her hand to her mouth. "Then does this mean—my lord, please tell me, does our meeting mean you have been successfully laid?"

"Ah, madam," he said as he squeezed out of the gate. He shot a wry glance in Chloe's direction. "Alas, that is too personal a question to answer."

He vanished into the trees.

Aunt Gwendolyn stood shaking her head in disbelief. "He's gone. Our ghost is gone."

And Chloe could not have been more relieved. Of course since she had not "seen" him, she had to pretend continued bewilderment. "Are you sure, Aunt Gwendolyn?" she whispered, staring up at the sky as if somehow Dominic's spirit had taken flight.

Her aunt followed the direction of her gaze and frowned. "I don't think he has floated up to heaven, my dear," she said in irritation.

Chloe glanced down questioningly at the ground. "Then—"

The woman sighed. "Apparently he has not disappeared down there either, although one might understandably conclude that Hades would be his most likely abode."

Chloe paused. "Where do you suppose he went?"

"It would seem, Chloe, that the afterlife is more complicated than the human mind can comprehend. Where did he go?" Aunt Gwendolyn waved her hands back and forth in the air. "He went neither here nor there. Into the unknown ethers."

"What unknown ethers?" Chloe could not resist asking.

"If I could answer that, then they would not be unknown, would they?"

"I suppose not."

"Bah. I shouldn't expect one of your tender experience to understand the mysteries of life." She gazed hard at Chloe. "Under the circumstances, perhaps it is best if we do not reveal this encounter to anyone else. We must *not* tell anyone that we saw him."

"But I didn't see anything," Chloe said.

"Exactly. And if he is to come to me again, then he must feel he can trust me."

Chloe glanced into the woods where Dominic was presumably hiding. "Do you *want* to see him again? It seems rather a frightening thing to befriend a ghost."

"My dear, if that is the sacrifice I must make to protect you, Pamela, and the other ladies of the parish, so be it."

"It shall be our secret," Chloe said stoutly.

"Very well." Aunt Gwendolyn cast a sharp glance around the quiet garden. "I must admit I am puzzled by one thing, Chloe."

Chloe's heart began to race again. Had she really thought to escape so easily? "What would that be?"

"What were *you* doing in the garden at this hour, Chloe? What brought you down here, if not his lordship's ghost?"

Chapter 16

Two days later Lord Devon Boscastle strolled up the steps of his brother Grayson's Park Lane mansion. It was the first time Devon had been officially welcomed home since his public disgrace. The distinguished Boscastle head footman, Weed, ushered him into the drawing room with a warm smile.

A battalion of servants was preparing to close up the house for the marquess's stay at his country estate. The housekeeper, Mrs. Soames, brought Devon a thick wedge of raspberry pie and dabbed her eyes at the sight of him. A pair of parlormaids made a point of plumping the cushions before he lowered his backside onto the sofa.

The black sheep was formally embraced back into the bosom of the family. As ridiculous as it seemed, Devon felt a sense of overwhelming gratitude and relief to be welcomed home. This brood might behave badly at times, but there was always a sense of acceptance and warmth among them, and the worst sins were eventually forgiven.

His sister Emma swept into the room a few minutes

later, her curly apricot-gold hair drawn back from her finely boned face. If there was any lecturing to come, it would be from her, he thought with an inward groan. Emma, the Dainty Dictator, she of the sprite's form and warlord's lack of mercy. The young widow who had buried her husband and opened her own Scottish academy to train untamed maidens on the path of the social straight and narrow. She was currently staying with their brother Heath until she decided where she would set up permanent residence.

"Devon," she said, clasping her hands behind her back to examine him.

"Emma." He stood to embrace her. "How charming you look."

"Do I?" She leaned back a little to study his face, not at all moved by his flattery. "Fair warning, Devon. Gray has called a family cabal to discuss our crisis. Battle plans are being drawn. An attack is imminent."

His blue eyes clouded. "I thought I was forgiven—"

"Not you, silly." She shook her head in chagrin. "It's Chloe. What a man does to his reputation is one thing, but a young lady is another matter altogether. Grayson is of the opinion, and I cannot disagree with him, that Chloe will continue her unhappy behavior until she has settled down in marriage."

Devon examined the watercolor of a Scottish landscape above the fireplace. "Have you never given in to a foolish impulse even once in your life, Emma?" he asked curiously.

"Of course I have."

"What?" he teased. "You wore pearls to church?"

"Why?" she asked, folding her slender arms, "does everyone assume I am a paragon?"

He tugged the pale curl that fell against her cheek. "Perhaps because you are?"

She grinned. "I should teach you all a thing or two. I think I could probably set London on its ears if I gave in to my true self."

"Do it, Emma," he said as a knock sounded at the door. "It's almost time for a new family scandal."

Lord Heath Boscastle gazed out the window as the rest of his family assembled in the private drawing room. He knew the reason he had been summoned, knew that he held the deciding vote on Chloe's future. For once he wished that things could be as simple as they appeared on the surface.

He wished he could believe that Chloe had met a decent young man and that love appeared, as Devon believed, to be in the cards for his beautiful little sister.

Could it be that easy? he wondered, his dark blue eyes cynical. Send the wayward young woman to the country for several weeks or so and, voilà, she meets the aristocrat of their dreams, and all her demons are subdued.

Possible, but not likely. Not for a Boscastle, at least.

His older brother Grayson, the Marquess of Sedgecroft, took a seat on the blue tufted sofa, his leonine presence indicating the cabal was about to proceed. He had always reminded Heath of a medieval prince, blond, confident, eager for action. Drake and Devon, darkhaired and restless with abundant energy, preferred to stand at either side of the sofa, as if they might bolt at the first opportunity.

Emma, the widowed Viscountess Lyons, sat alone by the fire in a high-backed tapestry chair, a notebook and pen in her lap. Heath worried about her future as much as he did Chloe's. A fair young widow was easy prey for the wrong man.

Emma glanced around the room. "Isn't your wife joining us, Grayson?" she asked in concern.

Grayson grinned a little sheepishly. "She hasn't decided whether she could in good conscience join a family conspiracy behind Chloe's back."

Drake gave a deep appreciative laugh. "Jane being a victim of a similar conspiracy herself?"

Grayson pretended to take offense. He and Jane had married not long ago, after a courtship that had been more a battle of wits than tender wooing. The lovely honey-haired marchioness was probably the only woman alive who could keep her husband in line. And have him love her for it. "Are you saying that marriage to me is something of a punishment?"

"Being your brother is," Devon said feelingly. "At least at times."

Emma cleared her throat. "May we proceed with the matter at hand? You, Devon," she said, inclining her pen in his direction, "please tell us your opinion of Chloe's young man."

Devon hesitated, as if he felt that to share this information might be a betrayal of his younger sister. "I don't exactly know what Chloe thinks of him—she wasn't quite herself when I last saw her. Perhaps that is a symptom of true love."

"What is *your* opinion of him?" Heath asked.

Devon shrugged. "I don't know him well at all. Justin and I met at a shoot a few summers ago. He seemed all right, didn't he, Drake?"

Drake shook his head. "A bit spoiled, arrogant as I remember."

"Are you discussing my husband?" a feminine voice teased from the door. "Or would this personage be any of his brothers?"

Heath glanced up with a grin at his sister-in-law. "Do come in, Jane. You'll bring a fresh perspective to our debate."

The Marchioness of Sedgecroft entered the room, her gaze going straight to her husband, who, along with the other men present, had risen at the sound of her voice. "I daresay my opinion will not be welcome. I have never made a secret of the fact I disapproved of banishing Chloe in the first place."

"Very well," Heath said, guiding her by the elbow to a chair. "You shall be the single voice of dissent."

Drake smiled. "The voice of reason."

Jane came to a halt and laughed. "Then let me say from the start I shall *not* sanction any more of my husband's sneaky and heavy-handed tactics in regard to holy matrimony."

"Heavy handed?" Heath said, barely suppressing a chuckle.

"Sneaky?" Grayson looked genuinely affronted. "I prefer to think I proved the desperate lengths to which a man in love can be driven." Everyone present knew he was referring to the fact that he had tricked Jane into marrying him.

"Which brings us back to the subject," Emma said. "Does this young man *love* Chloe? Is he a match worth pursuing?"

"More to the point," Jane said, arranging her rose-pink skirt around her ankles, "is whether this is a match worthy of a clandestine marriage contract made at midnight in a parked carriage?"

There was only a moment of silence as the family remembered how Grayson had turned the tables on his devious Jane during the turbulent days of their courtship.

"Darling," Grayson said, his gaze openly adoring, "are you complaining?"

She gave him an intimate smile.

Emma shook her head in chagrin. "If I have any say in this, there will not be another cause for notoriety. Shall we introduce ourselves to this brave young man? Drake? Grayson?"

Grayson's broad forehead creased in a frown. "There can't be many chances for misconduct in Chistlebury."

"How does the old saying go?" Jane asked her husband. " 'An idle mind is the devil's workshop?' "

Grayson laughed. "Why do you look at me when you quote that?"

She smiled again. "Experience, my love."

Drake glanced over at Devon. "Is it safe to wait to make a decision?"

"This young man hasn't formally made a proposal," Emma pointed out. "I hope they haven't decided to elope."

"I don't remember Chloe flirting with anyone at Dominic's funeral," Grayson said thoughtfully.

"Only because she wasn't there to flirt," Heath said. "She was unwell on that day as I remember. From what I understand, they have not found Dom's murderer yet. Sir Edgar wrote me that he suspects a dishonored soldier or sailor. Strange. The whole thing is entirely strange and disturbing. I suppose I should offer to help Edgar."

"Flirting at the poor man's funeral," Emma said, incensed at the very notion. "I should hope not. What has happened to this family in my absence?"

Grayson settled back against the sofa. "Aunt Gwendolyn says that this St. John is the most eligible bachelor in the parish."

"He's probably the only bachelor," Devon said. "The village must boast a population of twenty-five."

"Perhaps I shall ride down to introduce myself," Grayson said.

"Scare him off like a field mouse is more like," Jane murmured. "I do recall how you frightened off her poor cavalry officer with your shouting in the pavilion at that breakfast party."

Heath looked over at Drake. "Whatever happened to that baron who kissed Chloe behind the carriage?"

"I believe he's been silent about the whole affair," Drake replied. "Considering the circumstances, he probably considers himself fortunate that Grayson did not kill him."

"I say we should wait another fortnight to decide Chloe's fate." Heath stroked his upper lip. "Something may change by then."

Grayson shrugged. "That's reasonable."

Emma nodded. "Waiting is often the wisest course—

anything to avoid another wedding scandal. It would be the absolute end of us."

Grayson stared across the room at his elegant green-eyed wife. "I don't know about that, Emma. A wedding scandal was the start of a very happy life for me."

Chapter 17

Two uneventful days had passed since Aunt Gwendolyn's ghostly sighting in her garden. True to her word, Chloe's aunt had managed to keep her secret. She had not managed to curb her curiosity, however. From her window Chloe had spotted the woman skulking about the rosebushes several times late at night. What her aunt planned to do with Dominic if she caught him was anyone's guess. The irony was that she and Chloe both wanted to get their hands on the same elusive devil and subdue his restless spirit.

"If you find our ghost," Chloe whispered from the windowsill as she gazed out in the dark, "give him my best wishes, won't you?"

It had not escaped her notice that Dominic had deserted her again without making any promises for their future whatsoever. Even if he managed to see through his dangerous scheme, she could not be sure where they would stand. She wondered what their wild night of passion had meant to him. His body may have healed, but his mind was still at the mercy of his demons.

Would she find that their association had been built on nothing more than a man's desperation and a strange series of events? Certainly there would be no easy way to explain to her family how she and Dominic had become involved with each other. Chloe could not let him take all the blame.

There was no guarantee that he would not end up truly dead from his game of vengeance, and that these other fears of hers would never even have a chance to come to pass. She told herself she should be glad he'd refused to draw her any deeper into his perilous scheme. She should appreciate his stubborn resolve to protect her. None of which changed how she felt about the infuriating man.

There were times such as tonight when she stood at her window and swore she could feel him watching her; her skin would tingle with anticipation.

At other times the sensation of being observed became unpleasant and intrusive, and she wondered whether Edgar was gazing out into the evening woods as she was, both of them searching for the man who haunted them.

"I know you are there, Dominic," she said with a heavy sigh as she closed the curtains for the night. "I hope your enemy is not as aware."

Could Chloe be deliberately taunting him? Dominic wondered from the leafy embankment of the wood that concealed his presence. Did she guess that he was ready to break into her room and damn the consequences? Was she trying to lure him again, or was that idiot Justin courting her in the dark?

If he had the opportunity, he was going to teach Justin a thing or two for trying to tempt Chloe. Not that Dominic had any objection to tempting her himself, but he would fight to deny any other man the privilege. Especially after she had given herself to him the other night. She belonged only to him, and when his affairs were in order, he would make sure the entire world knew it. He would never be forced to leave her again.

He smiled at the image of her in the telescope. He could see her silhouette behind the lace curtains; her unstudied movements made him feel breathless, weak and powerful at the same time. He remembered the milky texture of her skin, the throaty gasp she had given when he had thrust into her strong body, the fragrance of her, the bruised look in her eyes when he'd forced himself to leave her room.

He lowered the telescope with regret. He could torture himself all he desired at another time. This evening a far more unpleasant task awaited him. Edgar had been exploring the areas around the estate late at night recently, and Dominic wondered why.

Was his uncle meeting someone? Or had he begun to suspect that he was under surveillance? Had he realized that the house he claimed as his inheritance did indeed have a very active ghost? Edgar might even be planning a quiet escape. He had friends and valuable property in India. An Englishman could live as a king in a foreign land.

Dominic debated whether to follow him on his nocturnal explorations or to take the chance of examining Edgar's personal papers while he was gone. The possibility of a trap always existed, that his uncle had begun to sense he might not have been as successful in his plans as he assumed.

Edgar might even have begun to believe in ghosts.

The day of the picnic dawned fair but not overly warm. Chloe dressed in a cloud-blue woolen walking dress with a fringed paisley shawl and soft leather half boots. Beneath her beribboned straw bonnet, her eyes were reflective. Both her anxieties and foolish hopes had been awakened when she'd realized that the picnic would be held not far from the abandoned mill house where Dominic went when he was desperate to escape his confinement. Of course, he would not make a public appearance at a picnic. She had little chance of seeing him today.

Even so, she hoped for a sign of him as she and her family rode through the oaks and beeches that formed a leafy canopy of branches overhead. The hedges burst with clusters of wild white roses. At last the parish church and thatched cottages fell behind, and the pleasant sounds of birdsong competed with the clatter of carriage wheels and conversation. For the first time Chloe realized that she was missing London less and less, that her own unruly nature had begun to take root in this unlikely setting.

"Chloe," her aunt called back meaningfully as they rode over a sturdy footbridge toward the millhouse, "keep an eye out, won't you?"

She turned her head. "An—"

Her aunt gave her a dark smile. An eye out for a cer-

tain irksome ghost was obviously what she meant. As
if Chloe were not already obsessed with searching for
the smallest sign that Dominic was still alive. Hadn't
he mentioned that there were tunnels, honeycombs of
underground passages in this area, hidden vaults where
smugglers had stashed their loot?

A jolt of excitement chased up her spine. Was it possible that he was lurking in the depths of the very earth
beneath her? What a thought, to imagine herself riding
right over his hiding place. It was intriguing to picture
him in some underground labyrinth plotting to bring
his enemy to justice. Chloe and the entire Boscastle family's enemy, if it was true that Sir Edgar had been involved in Brandon's death. The idea conjured up images
of Dominic in dark and strangely seductive terms. Of
Hades and Persephone, and their underworld love affair.
How frightening to think that the French could attack
the sleepy villages of Britain from subterranean burrows.
She was suddenly glad of the sacrifices her brothers had
made to protect the country from invasion.

Yet on such a mild day, with the peaceful setting disturbed only by frivolous chatter and the distant tatting
of a spotted woodpecker, Chloe could almost convince
herself that none of it was real. Her personal dilemma
might have been something she'd dreamed. Could any
man be so wholly evil as Sir Edgar? Could a man betray
his country, commit murder, and calmly go on with his
life? She knew the answer in her heart.

Evil occurred every day, but she was young, and her
instincts ran to thoughts of life not to death or sadness.
She had lost both her parents and her brother. She did

not want to dwell on such unsettling things during a picnic.

The picnic goers, who included most of Chistlebury's gentry, competed in a boisterous one-legged race and an ugly-face contest. Despite her worries, Chloe managed to enjoy herself, and to her surprise she even began to relax as she, Justin, and a circle of young people drank spiced ale in silver cups and toasted one another with outrageous compliments.

And then she noticed Uncle Humphrey look up with a sharp frown as a distinguished-looking horseman crossed the footbridge to the grassy clearing behind the millpond. Sir Edgar had arrived with a manservant who retreated into the background with the horses.

The tall and darkly elegant Edgar looked enough like Dominic from a distance that Chloe's heart twisted in wistful longing. Older, more restrained, such an unpleasant reminder of pain and loss that she felt as though a cold shadow were moving over her.

"Have I missed the fun?" he called out. Without waiting for a reply, he strode to the trestle table where she sat with Pamela, another young woman, Justin, his brother Charles, and Justin's elderly aunt.

"We're just going off on a treasure hunt for Miss Redmond's glove," Justin said with a friendly smile. "Would you like to join us?"

Sir Edgar laughed, his black brows lifting. "Compared to the rascals I have chased down in my career, it is indeed tempting to enjoy such a frivolous pursuit. What does this missing glove look like?"

"It's butter-yellow leather with tiny pearl buttons," Pamela answered.

Sir Edgar glanced down at Chloe, his smoky eyes uncertain. "Is there a prize for finding this lost treasure?"

Charles held up his hand. "A bottle of my aunt's famous blackberry wine."

"And Miss Redmond's eternal appreciation," Justin added with a grin, motioning to the laughing young lady at the table behind them.

There was an hour time-limit set on the hunt, and the afternoon had turned cool as the sun lowered behind the trees. Chloe and Justin had partnered off, but separated when he had an impulse to go off to the pond's edge and search among the reeds and cattails for the treasure.

"I'm not ruining my shoes and stockings for Georgina's glove," Chloe called after him with a slight shiver. Her shawl was too thin for the damp chill.

"We could drink the blackberry wine together, Chloe," he said, a dimple showing in his cheek.

"Not if you drown, Justin."

"I'm not going to drown."

Chloe frowned. She had no intention of venturing into either the cold murky water or the overgrown woods to hunt for a silly glove. Somewhere in the stand of long sessile oaks she heard Pamela giggle, and the carefree joy of the sound brought a smile to her face. At least one of them was still enjoying the afternoon, and Chloe might have, too, if there hadn't been such a cloud of dark worry hanging over her head. She missed Dominic, could not be completely at ease without knowing where he was or what he was doing.

She watched Justin wading between the straggly reeds

for a few minutes before she turned, her patience at its limit.

The mill tower stood behind her, abandoned and compelling.

"The perfect place to hide a treasure," she thought aloud.

Chapter 18

"Are you here?" she whispered almost inaudibly into the dusty gloom of the mill tower house. If anyone asked what she was doing, she would of course claim to be hunting the glove. But it would be a lie. She hoped desperately to find evidence that Dominic had been here in recent days.

There was no answer, no sign of him. Broken boards, some cord, a post, and several rusted axles forced her to tread a careful path into the tower house. Already the hem of her light wool dress wore a ruffle of gossamer strands of dust and cobwebs.

Dominic had left no evidence of his visits to this desolate place.

"Where are you?" she whispered.

A rectangle of light fell to her left as the tower door creaked open. She turned, heart in her throat, at the gruff questioning voice behind her.

"Did we find what we are looking for?" Sir Edgar asked in a stage whisper.

She pivoted, trying not to show he had startled her,

how reluctant she was to be alone with him. "The glove—"

"Is this it?"

He entered the tower, bending at the waist to pick up the pair of gloves Chloe must have dropped. "These are blue, and a pair. I thought—"

"Oh, they're mine," she said in embarrassment. "Miss Redmond's glove is yellow."

"Shall we put them back on you?" he asked, the perfect gentleman. Stately, trim, his bearing erect, his demeanor gallant. Holding aloft her delicate gloves.

"No." She had answered too fast, but she did not want him to touch her. She could not bear to be touched by the hands that might have caused her brother's death and scarred Dominic in body and soul. Just being alone with Edgar in this isolated place made her eager to escape his company.

He glanced around. "Someone said that this tower is haunted. There have been lights seen here at night."

Chloe's heart skipped a beat. "I hadn't heard."

He gazed at her directly. "Do you believe in ghosts?"

Where was he leading? "Perhaps," she replied. "Certainly there are people who haunt us all our lives."

He smiled, considering her more closely. "A provocative answer."

"It was a provocative question." She edged away with a giggle, playing the lighthearted female to the hilt. "I thought the glove might be hidden in—" She held her breath. The floor had moved. She was sure of it. The floorboard beneath the broken window had . . . lifted. Dear God. Was Dominic about to pop up like a jack-in-the-box? Had she led Sir Edgar to his hiding place? Well, at least she knew now he was still alive and up to his usual dangerous mischief.

Edgar's alert gaze followed hers. "What is it?"

"A . . . a . . . a rat, I think."

"A rat?" He looked amused. "Are you—"

She screamed at the top of her lungs and lunged into his arms, hitting him in the chin with her reticule. Her shriek nearly brought down the dusty rafters of the tower. Sir Edgar blinked in surprise, then started to laugh.

"There! There!" Chloe shrieked, pointing in horror to the opposite side of the tower.

Edgar swung around.

"He's gone," Chloe breathed, crossing her hands over her heart. "Oh, thank goodness. How brave you were, Sir Edgar. I swear the thing was enormous—with burning red eyes and long yellow fangs."

He took her elbow, clearly comfortable coming to the rescue of a helpless female. A commotion of footsteps resounded outside the unhinged tower door, and Justin appeared with his brother and Pamela beside him. "Even a seasoned officer such as me is afraid of rats, my dear," Edgar admitted with a deep chuckle. "Disgusting creatures, living in dirt and darkness."

Justin waved the hidden glove over his head. His boots and the hem of his cashmere pantaloons dripped water onto the floor. "I found it! I knew I'd seen Tom in those reeds. Come on and claim the prize with me, Chloe."

She did not resist as he drew her away from Sir Edgar's side. It took all her willpower not to glance back at the floorboard that had moved. She was positive it had not been her imagination.

Did Sir Edgar know anything? He had given her no indication that he suspected that Dominic was even alive; if he did, he was practiced enough in deception to hide his thoughts. Chloe couldn't help wondering how he'd react if he learned that she had become involved with the nephew he'd intended to murder.

Her fingertips felt icy as she slipped her gloves back on. "Do join us outside, Sir Edgar. This place is oppressive."

Had she sounded convincing? She thought she saw him glance once again in the corner before he turned toward her.

Pamela pushed the tower door open and light poured into the penumbral gloom, illuminating the angular planes of Sir Edgar's face. He smiled at Chloe, but not before she caught the hard glint in his eye.

Even her return into the sunlight did not make her feel any warmer. Her coldness came from within. It was only a matter of time until Edgar discovered the truth and reacted. Dominic would have to bring his deadly game to an end before much longer.

Dominic unclenched his fist one finger at a time. He felt the chill sweat of relief break out across the tense muscles of his back. From his cramped position beneath the trapdoor at the back of the tower, he had overheard every word of the conversation between his uncle and Chloe. He had listened with a blood rage filling his mind.

If Edgar had touched her, had threatened her in any way, it would have been all over. He would have died at Dominic's hand before he realized what had happened.

Only now that Chloe had safely gone did Dominic loosen his death grip on his dagger. The stinging surge of blood returning to his fingers helped to restore his sanity.

"I cannot go on like this," he muttered as he blindly felt his way back along the chalky tunnel. He would have to wait until evening before he could return to his house. Hours of claustrophobic impatience, of not knowing what Edgar was doing, where he was.

Yet Dominic had never been closer to bringing his vengeance to fruition than he was now. Two nights ago he had discovered documents hidden in Edgar's campaign chest that provided more evidence of his crimes, how he had paid to have Gurkha rebels ambush Brandon and Samuel, how he had sold military secrets to the French. In his arrogant belief that he was too clever to be caught, Sir Edgar had put more than a few condemning details of his treachery to paper, clues to the identities of the agents who had worked with him during the war, of the information he had revealed in Portugal while he served in the regular army.

With Adrian's help, Dominic had gained enough knowledge to fill in the gaps and instigate a formal Crown investigation. It was time to play his hand.

Chapter 19

She should have known that her aunt could not remain closemouthed about her ghostly encounter in the rose garden for long. The day after the picnic, Chloe arrived home from an afternoon walk with her uncle to find the parlor once again in utter chaos. The clink of teacups could barely be heard between the excited flow of female chatter. Every matron in Chistlebury appeared to be in attendance for this emergency meeting.

"Ladies, please, let us have order," implored the sensible Widow Roberts. "Madness will not catch a ghost. Nor will it assist our fund-raising attempts to repair the church steeple."

"Shall we lay a trap?" one lady asked quite seriously.

"A trap?" Aunt Gwendolyn pursed her lips as Chloe swept into the room with a frown of disapproval.

She was sorely tempted to shake the gentle-hearted woman for this impulsive betrayal of Dominic to her friends. She could only hope that when word of this reached Edgar, he would pass this development off as so much feminine hysteria. Would he really believe that his middle-aged neighbor had spoken with Dominic's spirit in the garden?

The robust red-haired Lady Ellington shook her head. "One of us would have to volunteer to be, well, the bait."

"I'll do it," Pamela offered through a mouthful of gingerbread, her freckled face ingenuous.

"You shall do nothing of the sort," her mother said in horror, flinging a napkin between them.

"Why not?" Pamela asked. "I'm the one Madame Dara said he wanted. It would seem I should be the logical choice of bait."

"You are far too young to face such danger," Lady Ellington insisted. "It will take a woman of some experience to lay this spirit to rest."

Lady Wheaton, a baroness with five daughters of her own, added her agreement. "This a dangerous endeavor. An older woman would be better able to handle him in the event he turned on her."

"Did Stratfield . . . attempt to force himself upon you?" Lady Ellington asked Gwendolyn.

"I took my precautions, my dears," Gwendolyn replied rather smugly.

The eight ladies in attendance leaned forward from their chairs as one.

"Precautions?" whispered the baroness.

Gwendolyn nodded. "I sprinkled a protective powder of salt in a circle around my feet before I began the ritual."

The group glanced expectantly at Chloe, who raised her brow and murmured, "Well, don't look at me. I did not see the ghost."

Which she would not qualify as a lie. The Dominic Chloe knew was a breathing, infuriating, flesh-and-blood human being. A man capable of inciting very carnal, earthly emotions indeed. There was certainly nothing ethereal about the way he had taken over her life.

"How do we set this trap?" Lady Wheaton asked.

"Are we all to be involved?"

"Should the parson be present?"

"Will it be necessary to lure him? This Stratfield Ghost, I mean, not the parson."

Another squall of conversation broke out. The ramifications of such a courageous sacrifice were discussed in the frankest detail. The assembly concluded, not unhappily, that the ghost would most likely continue his nocturnal seductions until he was stopped.

The exact plan for setting the trap was temporarily put aside as the discussion veered to settling on the identity of the ghost's next victim, now that Pamela was under her mother's protection.

"I don't know why he should come to you in the first place, Gwendolyn," said Lady Harwood a trifle sourly.

Pamela leaped to her mother's defense. "We're living in his former house, for one thing. We were his closest neighbors."

"And we have taken his beloved dog to our bosom," Aunt Gwendolyn added.

The ladies glanced at the rather overweight dog sprawled out across the hearth as if it had only now occurred to them to associate the beast with his wicked master. Ares, a few moments ago regarded as a benign mutt, suddenly assumed the menacing appearance of a hound from hell.

"Do you think that animal communicates with the viscount's spirit?" Lady Ellington whispered behind her hand.

Aunt Gwendolyn nodded. "Naturally."

Lady Fernbrook narrowed her eyes. "Why don't we ask him to show us his master's next victim?"

"An excellent idea," Aunt Gwendolyn agreed. She closed her eyes. She pressed her fingertips together in a prayerful attitude.

The cozy parlor grew so quiet one could hear only the popping of the coals in the grate. A bottle fly buzzed against the window. Then even the insect fell silent as if caught in the spell of suspense.

"Ares," Aunt Gwendolyn said in a low, breathy voice that made Pamela elbow Chloe in amusement. "Communicate with your master. Ask him the name of whom he will seek solace from next."

Her nostrils flared with emotion.

The hound lifted one eyelid and gazed indolently around the room. His tail thumped the carpet.

"Show us," Aunt Gwendolyn commanded, her voice rising. "Show us the person your master seeks if she is in this room!"

Of course there was no contest.

Chloe's lip curled in disgust as the lazy cur, who must have gained half a stone since coming to Dewhurst Manor, deigned to rise from the hearth to scratch its rear end.

Chloe had walked that dog for hours. She had brushed

and petted the useless hound, allowed him to sleep in her room. But Aunt Gwendolyn had been sneaking Ares sausage bits under the table for days.

The dog padded straight across the carpet and poked his muzzle between her knees.

Aunt Gwendolyn cleared her throat and nudged the animal discreetly to her side.

"Perhaps we should move on to the matter of the annual *bal masqué*?" Lady Ellington suggested with a faint sneer.

Sir Humphrey voiced his doubts about the existence of the Stratfield Ghost that evening in the parlor. Chloe and Pamela were playing an unexciting game of piquet in the corner. Aunt Gwendolyn was trying unsuccessfully to communicate again with Ares, who was staring wistfully at the door with his head buried between his paws. It was past the time for his nightly walk.

"I feel he is trying to say something," Gwendolyn said, on her hands and knees before the hound.

"Probably 'Help! I am being accosted by a lunatic,'" her husband muttered from his armchair. "Damnation, Gwennie, do get up from that humiliating position. Are you even sure it was a ghost you saw in the garden the other night? How do you know it was not the dog hiding in the trees?"

Aunt Gwendolyn gave him a frosty glare. "I daresay I know the difference between a dead man and a dog." She glanced past him to the window. "And once again, I sense that something is not right with poor Stratfield."

Humphrey snorted. "Well, he's dead, for starters. How much more 'not right' can the poor sod be?"

"Language, Humphrey!"

He put down his book. "I'm taking the dogs out for a walk."

Ares and the two sheepdogs dozing by the fire sprang immediately into action and raced to the door. Chloe looked up from the card table, her face brightening.

"This late at night, Humphrey?" Aunt Gwendolyn asked in concern. "Do you think it is safe?"

"My family has lived in Chistlebury for half a century, and the viscount's murder is the first of its kind. I doubt that his death was anything but an aberration."

"May I come, Uncle Humphrey?" Chloe called after him.

"Certainly not!" her aunt replied before Humphrey had the chance. "I have just received a letter this morning from Heath and Emma in London. As I have already written back to reassure them that you are enjoying a peaceful retreat from your former, let us say, attraction to misfortune, I feel compelled to assure them that it is true."

"So I cannot go?" Chloe asked in disappointment.

"There is absolutely nothing in those woods or its environs that should attract a young lady at night."

"Except for the viscount's ghost," Pamela said softly behind her hand of cards.

Sir Humphrey let the dogs sniff ahead as he took a detour off the familiar footpath through the woods. There was little moonlight to guide him to the ferny escarpment that marked the edge of Stratfield's estate. But he had often walked this pleasantly overgrown track, using his stick to shove the occasional blackberry brambles out of his way. He knew the hidden tracks by heart.

He had met Stratfield on this path more than once in the past, along with that dashing young hothead brother of his Samuel, who could talk of nothing but his upcoming adventure in Nepal. In Humphrey's opinion, the brave fool had met his death defending a handful of greedy merchants who would annihilate the entire world in the British Empire's interests. More than once Humphrey had tried to persuade Samuel to seek out a different career. But posters promising adventure and fortune lured innumerable young men into joining the Honourable East India Company.

Samuel and his two older brothers, the late Michael and Dominic, were cut from a different bolt of cloth altogether. Dominic and Michael had been more reserved and logical, thinking out every aspect of their lives. Humphrey had always liked Dominic. He could not quite believe he was dead.

In fact, he did not believe it at all.

He stopped, his nape prickling, and stared behind him. Ares was exploring the earth around a foxhole.

"Something caught your fancy, Ares?" He turned a pile of humus over with his stick, his face reflective. "Those toadstools have been trampled since two nights ago when we were last here. Odd, isn't it? I'd say someone besides us is sneaking about."

He heard branches rustling in the undergrowth behind him, a man's crisp voice calling out, "Stop right there. I've a gun— Oh, it's you, Sir Humphrey. I wish to

Hades you'd stop giving me these scares. I've orders from Sir Edgar to shoot any trespassers on sight."

Sir Humphrey raised his walking stick and turned to greet the Irish gamekeeper who worked at Stratfield Hall. "Ah, Finley. Just the man I was hoping to meet. I'd like to have a word or two with you."

Chapter 20

Another week passed. Chloe felt herself slipping back into the restive state that had dampened her spirits after her father and Brandon had died. The world gradually began to look gray again. She felt uneasy, on edge, as if she had been turned inside out.

She had not heard a word from Dominic.

Did he realize how she worried about him? Did he know that she was on the verge of staging a private hunt for him? He probably wasn't thinking about her at all. True to Chloe's habit of making horrible choices, she had lost her heart to a phantom, a man who had no room in his life, or what was left of it, for love.

But life for the rest of the world continued on. In the midst of Chloe's private conflict, she was dimly aware that the ladies of Chistlebury had thrown themselves heart and soul into planning their annual *bal masqué*. The local assembly room was swept of its cobwebs and dust balls, the century-old chandelier was polished and restored with fresh candles, chairs were brought out of storage.

If anyone asked, the village patronesses claimed they

were hoping to raise funds from the ball to patch the schoolmaster's roof, to provide a few more coal braziers for the chilly parish church, and to repair the steeple.

In reality, the masquerade dance provided the perfect background for all the matchmaking mamas whose debutante daughters had returned from their last London Season without the coveted marriage proposals they'd been sent to procure.

As Chistlebury boasted only a few eligible young men, the annual ball had become a frantic competition of sorts. This year's event promised to be even more intense than usual. For one thing, the desirable Viscount Stratfield would not be present. For another, the lovely Chloe Boscastle seemed to be in the lead for Lord St. John's affection.

Then last, but not least, an exciting newcomer had just landed in Chistlebury on his way to London. A duke's heir, it was said, who was in the market for a quiet country home. The fact that this magnetic adventurer, Lord Wolverton, had a tainted reputation did not discourage the league of wedlock-obsessed mothers from placing him at the top of their lists to impress.

Who among them would not secretly wish her daughter to become a duchess? The little matter of Lord Wolverton's murky past as a mercenary could be tidily swept under the Aubusson carpet of his Mayfair mansion. His exploits in foreign lands could be considered heroic, if one chose to look at it that way, and not believe the rumors of his dealings with opium-eaters and pirates.

For her part Chloe paid no attention at all to their chatter. It had become an effort to engage in civilized conversation at all, and she alone knew the reason for

Adrian's appearance in the village. Her aunt was so concerned about Chloe's lapse into despondency that she wrote to Grayson in London, asking his advice. Yes, the entire family knew Chloe had been a little moody for some time, but she had seemed to be so uplifted lately, and she and Justin were clearly not as friendly as they had been.

Chloe woke up on the day of the ball and decided she would throttle the first person who asked her if she felt better. She went straight to her dressing closet and opened her trunk, as she had done every morning. Of course there was no sign from her elusive Dominic. No way of knowing when or if she would ever see him again.

The only thing that had kept her grumpy spirits going was the fact that she had almost broken Brandon's code. She had found the numbers that represented *a* and *e*, and from there her work should become easier. Heath had studied the art of cryptology at college. He'd taught Chloe that the codes used during the war were not as complicated as one would imagine.

There was usually no time to decipher a message in the middle of the battlefield, or when a young corporal captured a dispatch. Most of the ciphers were mathematically based, using a chain of numbers. Even so, it took Chloe forever to figure out that the number 2 represented *h* in one column. In the next column, three letters down, the number 2 had become *j*.

It took a certain perception, a methodical and intuitive skill, to see patterns that others missed. She did not look forward to explaining to Heath how the code had come into her possession.

Dominic's secret had complicated her life in ways neither of them could have foreseen. The day passed slowly. As evening fell, she bathed and put on her costume for the masquerade ball, a pink gauze dress with silver tissue wings to represent the fairy queen, Tatiana. Even the circlet of pink silk rosebuds on her head looked wrong to her. She didn't feel in the least bit airy or playful. She wanted to bite off someone's head.

She had no reason to look forward to the ball.

"Wear your scandalous corset tonight," Pamela urged her as the maid dressed her hair. "It might put you in a better mood."

And so Chloe did, either as an act of protest against Dominic leaving her to worry or as a talisman to lure him back to her, she could not decide.

"All right," she whispered as she and Pamela crowded into the carriage together for the ride to the assembly room. "I took your advice. I'm wearing a certain shameful garment under my costume, but don't you dare tell anyone, or else."

Pamela, dressed up as a medieval princess, grinned in illicit approval. "Perhaps the soon-to-be duke will take a fancy to you."

Chloe's heart missed a few beats. "What are you talking about?"

"The rogue every woman in Chistlebury has been talking about while you were locked away in your tower, Rapunzel. Honestly, Chloe, he's probably the last man your family would want you to marry. He has a perfectly sinful reputation, but I hear he's as handsome as they come."

All of Chloe's senses went on the alert.

"He's coming to the ball?"

"That's what I was told," Pamela whispered.

Gooseflesh prickled Chloe's arms. Adrian, attending the ball? Was it a good sign or a bad one that he was appearing at a country dance? She wondered if he would give her a message from Dominic, whether it was news she wanted to hear, or whether Adrian attending was merely to alleviate his boredom. Chistlebury's social life did tend to put one to sleep.

Pamela nudged her. "What do you want to wager that he'll dance with you?"

Chloe made a face. She supposed it was another sign of her decadent nature, but the French corset had lifted her mood a little, that and the hope of hearing from Dominic. "Perhaps he'll take a fancy to *you,* and I shall become the governess to your children to escape my own family."

"Are you serious, Chloe?" Pamela's eyes widened. "I'd give anything to have Drake and Devon as my brothers. They're so manly and protective."

"Only when they're not ruining your life," Chloe grumbled, and then, for the first time in a week, she started to laugh. "It's always been a mystery to me why other females find the rogues so attractive."

"Are you missing your baron in London?" Pamela asked in sympathy. "Is that why you seem so sad lately?"

Chloe was tempted to laugh again and ask, "What baron?" But she simply shrugged and let her cousin draw her own conclusions. Suddenly she was eager to reach the assembly room and put her corset to good use. They had been waiting out in the carriage for what seemed like forever because Aunt Gwendolyn could not find her wig—she was dressed as the Greek goddess Hera—and Uncle Humphrey, costumed as Zeus, had discovered that Ares had hidden the mangled hairpiece under the sofa.

"Why would the dog steal my wig?" Aunt Gwendolyn asked in distress as the carriage set out for the ball. "Is he upset at me? Was not Ares the son of Hera in legend? Haven't I fed the ungrateful pup my choicest bits of sausage?"

Her husband grunted. "I imagine he thought your wig was a badger. He is a hunting dog, after all. Now would you kindly get off my lightning bolt? It took Mansfield all day to whittle those zigzags."

The small brick assembly room at the village outskirts blazed with candlelight when they arrived behind the procession of other vehicles. Tea, lemonade, coffee, and light dishes were offered in the refreshment room, which was really a drafty hall where the elite of Chistlebury and a nearby hamlet shivered in their finest evening apparel and heirloom jewels.

The ball itself opened on a disastrous note. No sooner had the steward signaled the band on the dais to begin than a cloud of choking black smoke filled the ballroom. Chloe's throat tightened and she fought to breathe, as much from anticipation as from inhaling the noxious fumes.

She couldn't help wondering if Dominic and his friend had planned some dramatic spectacle. Would he emerge from the billowing puffs of smoke like Mephistopheles? She was afraid for him, and yet at the same time she hoped his risky charade would soon end. She would never complain about her life being too dull again.

But Dominic did not appear in a dramatic puff of smoke. Nor did Sir Edgar or Adrian. It seemed that a pair of youthful pranksters, disgruntled boys who had been punished by the parson, had taken revenge by stuffing several old sheets down the chimney to the fireplace, then setting them aflame.

By the time the air had cleared, the arrival of Lord Wolverton was announced, and Chloe had her first curious look at the mysterious man who had befriended Dominic. He cut an undeniably attractive figure as he strode into the ballroom in the blond wig, knee breeches, white lace-trimmed shirt, hat, and black velvet mask of a seventeenth-century highwayman. She wasn't the least bit surprised to see him immediately surrounded by the village patronesses. His instant popularity did make her wonder, though, how she would be able to get him alone for a few minutes.

Adrian solved the problem for her, appearing very discreetly beside her on the dance floor.

How he managed to escape those fierce-hearted dragonesses without offending anyone and make it to Chloe's side to walk her through the steps of the quadrille was a feat she could only admire. He did not speak for several moments. Nor did she. Instinctively she felt safe with him, at ease. He seemed to be the sort of man who lived by his own rules, and those rules included unswerving loyalty to his friends. She knew that he had sought her out for a reason.

Her mouth went dry as his perceptive hazel eyes examined her through the slits of his half mask. He was tall and well built; he moved with power and purpose, a man to stir a lady's blood, but it was news of Dominic she wanted and sensed that Adrian had brought her.

"Chloe, I have heard a lot about you from our mutual friend." His voice was low-pitched and attractive. "Forgive me if I step on your toes. I do not dance well at all."

"A duke's heir? Not dance—" She could not stand it another second. She could not flirt or be herself when her heart was filled with this horrible apprehension. She dropped her voice. "Please tell me this is not your way of preparing me for bad news. Is he here? Has he sent you to fetch me? Is he all right?"

His deep laughter made her dizzy with relief. "Yes. Yes. And yes. Is that all you wanted to know?"

Her gaze scanned the dance floor, assessing every costumed guest, every masked face for her elusive Dominic. "Where is he?"

His mouth curled with a gentle smile of reproach. "Do not be so obvious, Chloe. He isn't ready to share his secret with anyone else but us just yet. The time is almost here for him to come out of hiding. I think Dominic is more than ready for this to be over."

She drew a breath, her attention returning to his masked face. "When?"

"Sometime in the next few days. You will not want to be involved in the actual confrontation."

"Not involved." She held out her skirts and muttered under her breath as she executed a perfunctory curtsy. "You do not know much about my association with him, do you?"

His dark hazel eyes glinted in good humor. "I know that he is in love with you."

Chloe fought to hide the pleasure that flooded her. "He told you that?"

"Sweetheart, he did not need to tell me. Why do you suppose I am here?"

"But—all right, if you are his closest friend, then you know better than anyone how dangerous it is for him to confront Edgar alone. You don't support this mad scheme of his, do you?"

He glanced over her shoulder as if assessing whether it was safe to continue their conversation. Chloe realized vaguely that they had broken the formation of the dance and were drifting in subtle degrees toward the door, presumably unnoticed in the crush of the crowded dance floor. "Of course I support him."

She looked around in confusion. Justin frowned at her, then turned to bestow a smile upon his dancing partner. Her aunt and the other patronesses were watching Pamela dance with Justin's younger brother, Charles, a serious law student. The only person who seemed to be paying any attention to Chloe was her uncle.

"I'll take care of him," Adrian said quietly, following the direction of her gaze.

She looked up at him in alarm. "That's my uncle. Don't you dare do anything to hurt him."

Adrian's chuckle brought a blush to her cheeks. "I meant that I shall distract him."

"Why?" Chloe whispered, her voice low with the anticipation that had wound her nerves into knots. Where was Dominic hiding? What was he planning to do? When would she see him?

The dance ended, and before another could begin, there was a commotion at the back of the ball. A woman shrieked, other guests started to laugh as a huge sheep trundled down the center of the crowd, having escaped his costumed shepherdess.

Chloe, whose nerves were on edge enough as it was, shook her head in amusement and glanced back up at Adrian. "That's all we need, a barnyard—"

Her voice died to a soft gasp of startlement. She knew instantly that it was Dominic, not Adrian, who swept her into his strong arms for the next dance. He wore the exact costume of a dashing masked highwayman as Adrian had, but she knew the difference to the core of her being. No one had ever held her with such arrogant possession. No other man's touch told her she belonged to him, sent a thrill of sensual excitement through her.

And his eyes, she could never mistake the mocking masculine gaze that melted her and made her heart pound in fierce longing. She faltered a step. He caught her, steadied her, his mouth grazing her ear. The intensity of being so near him stole her strength. Her belly quivered in response. She was magnetized to him, to the steely length of his body, and nothing could weaken the power he wielded.

"Chloe," he murmured, "how good it is to see you again."

"Why here?" she whispered, her eyes sparkling with excitement.

"Edgar made plans to attend. I can't be sure whether it is for pleasure or whether he's meeting someone."

She laughed softly, so happy to see him that even their enemy could not spoil her mood. "It might be sheer boredom—although Chistlebury's annual *bal masqué* is hardly where one would go for pleasure."

His eyes darkened. "Unless he wanted to see you."

"I doubt it, Dominic."

"Why?" he teased. "I can't stay away from you."

"You didn't even know I'd be here."

"Didn't I? The Belle of Chistlebury mope in her room and miss the ball?

She caught her breath, waiting for the dance to bring them back together before she whispered, "There have been some very interesting things going on in my room recently, for your information."

"Haven't there, though?" he said in an undertone. "Now listen closely. There is a side door to your right. You are going to slip outside first, and then I will follow."

"What if we're seen leaving together?"

"It will appear that you have gone to the cloakroom to primp and fetch your fan. Adrian will cover my absence."

"Adrian?"

"To your left."

From the corner of her eye she saw Adrian's shadowy figure standing guard in the dimly lit hall outside the door. Disguised alike, the two men appeared similar enough in height and build to pass as the same person. Unless Sir Edgar suspected that an intricate trap was being laid. Chloe glanced around the crowded dance floor in search of Dominic's uncle.

She looked back at Dominic. He was staring intently over her head, presumably watching the dancers for the perfect moment to execute their escape. He seemed so in control of the situation—she could only wish that he had gone to all this trouble, involved Adrian in this elaborate charade, just to see her. She wanted to be alone with him, held in his arms again, all their problems behind them. She did not want to think that he might confront Edgar at the evening's end.

She felt a stab of apprehension as she met her uncle's questioning gaze from across the room. Surely he did not recognize Dominic in the masked disguise. It wasn't possible, not at this distance. Her uncle was only staring at them because Aunt Gwendolyn had made him promise to keep an eye on her. There. He had finally looked away. It was merely Chloe's guilty imagination that made her think he suspected anything. She was on fire with impatience to be alone with Dominic.

Her heart thumped hard against her breast as the steps of the dance drew her closer to his iron-hard frame. His eyes burned right through her. "What are you going to do if Edgar's friend doesn't appear?" she whispered.

"Spend a few minutes with you. I hated leaving you after what happened, and I'm not sure that Edgar isn't watching you."

"Watching me? Why?"

"You're Brandon's sister, for one thing, and you have an interest in how he was murdered. And you're damned desirable for another."

A surge of irrational happiness swept over her. She wanted to pull him against her and kiss his beautiful mouth, untie his mask and caress his face and his thick hair, revel in the burning heat and power of his body. He seemed stronger than ever. He was well, whole again. Hers.

"Did you think I could stay away from you?" he demanded in a soft seductive voice that raised shivers on her skin.

"You've done a fair enough job of it." She stared into his eyes. "Are you really ready to face Edgar now?"

"No more talking, Chloe."

She knew the answer in her heart anyway. She sensed that something grave was about to happen, that he was ready to take the risk. A chill of fear slid down her backbone, threatening the joy she felt at seeing him again. This was the moment he had struggled to bring about. The moment she had prayed would never come to pass, when he would face Edgar and demand retribution.

His hard gaze caught hers. He was determined, dominant, confident he would succeed on his own terms. "*Now*. Don't hesitate. Don't look back. Turn to your left as soon as you pass the cloakroom."

She barely heard the music ending above the pounding of her pulse in her ears. There was a collective rush to the door for the refreshment room, and this helped to cover their exit. She moved as one with the swell of guests who surged out for a drink of lemonade, a chance to flirt over wafers. Pamela waved gaily over the heads of the guests who separated them.

"I'm going to fetch my fan," she said at her cousin's questioning look.

Dominic had disappeared. How or to where she could not guess. She obeyed his order to appear as normal as possible. Without him in sight it was easier to control her actions, but her mind was preoccupied. Considering his utter lack of moral conscience, Edgar was not an enemy to underestimate, but then neither was Dominic.

She squeezed between the line of people outside the

refreshment room and forced herself to walk as calmly as possible toward the cloakroom. A darkened passageway loomed to her left, quiet, deserted, and suddenly Dominic was grasping her hand, leading her away from the murmur of voices behind them. Almost at the same moment she saw Adrian emerge from the cloakroom and blend back into the crowd.

The reappearance of the duke's heir did not go unnoted. Lord Wolverton was, after all, the plum prize of the ball, encircled by females young and old, who pleaded for him to describe his adventures.

Dominic grinned. "A pity we cannot watch him fend off all the she-wolves."

Chloe gave him a playful poke. "Spoken as one who has been in his position?"

He flashed a grin in answer, and before she knew it, she was being drawn into a small dark room that had clearly been used for storage by the look of the furniture covered in musty sheets.

"What about my aunt and uncle?" she asked, staring back at the door.

"They shall be well distracted by Adrian, I assure you."

"Is he as good at distraction as you are?"

He laughed. "Perhaps you're the best judge of that."

"Have you been in here before, Dominic?" she demanded.

"Er, yes. As a matter of fact, I have."

"With another woman?"

He chuckled, pulling off his mask and hat. "*Hiding* from a woman as I recall. These annual balls can be murder on a bachelor, I tell you."

"Murder." Her eyes darkened in distress. "Do you have to use that word?"

"A poor choice, I agree," he said, turning back toward her.

She stared up at him, not even attempting to hide how she felt. It was all she could do not to give in to the temptation to wrap her arms around his neck and kiss him until neither of them could breathe. She was only responding to the possessive heat in his eyes, the memory of the night they had made love. She needed to be passionate with him again tonight, to show him how she felt. Of all the men she had known, he was the only one who understood and accepted her for who she really was, who fanned the fire in her heart instead of trying to dampen it.

"Waiting for you has put me in the worst mood, Dominic."

"Perhaps one day soon I can make it all worthwhile."

She saw the sparkle of mocking approval in his gaze. "Don't make fun of me," she retorted. "The horrible fact is that . . . I need you." She covered her face in her hands. "Oh, how awful to admit it."

For a moment he did not move. She thought, half hoped, that perhaps she had spoken those three humiliating words in such a low voice that he might not have heard them.

But he had. She lowered her hands. She could tell by the muscle that tightened in his masculine jaw, the flare of answering fire in his eyes as he gazed down at her. He bowed before her, his tricorn hat in his hands.

"When this is over," he said quietly, "you shall not be able to get rid of me."

He had already taken the precaution of locking the door, and now he wedged an old oak settle up against it to ensure their privacy.

She stood in silence as his dark muscular figure moved with purpose around the confined space. His lithe elegance stole her breath away. She was embarrassed by how the sight of him weakened her, made her ache to know him in the most primal, intimate way she could imagine. Her breasts felt swollen, waiting for his touch. Her body craved him, needed him so badly that she began to shake.

When he held out his arms to her, she was afraid her knees would fold beneath her. How could she bear letting him leave her again? Masculinity dominated every feature of his face, his hard angular jaw, the stark symmetry of his cheekbones, his firm mouth. The hot yearning in his eyes set all her senses on fire.

"I don't have much time," he said. "If Edgar doesn't show up soon, I shall have to return to the house. It's past midnight."

Her emotions, so long held in check, threatened to spill over. "Are you going to leave a glass slipper on the stairs for me to remember you by?"

"Chloe, please." He stroked the short curls that framed her face.

"I shan't cry over your grave again if you get yourself murdered, Dominic. I mourned you when I thought you had been killed the first time," she said. "I cried myself to sleep over you, and I don't know why."

"I'm sorry I made you cry," he said, drawing her against him. "I'll make it up to you."

Their eyes met and held.

"I want you, Dominic."

"But I didn't bring you here to—"

"Please," she whispered. "Hold me."

She was his. She accepted that from the moment he took her back into his embrace. Her entire body warmed, melted against the hard planes of his torso. "What are you going to do when you meet Edgar?" she whispered as he deftly unhooked her gown. The gossamer wings of her costume fell to the floor. Her pink gauze gown soon followed, puddling around her ankles. In trembling acceptance, she allowed the heated claim of his capable hands on her body, putting his brand on her, preparing her for his possession. But no matter how she desired him, she would not enjoy this with her whole heart while she feared for his life.

She pulled his cloak off his shoulders. "What am I going to do?" he mused, watching the garment fall to the floor to join her costume. "I'm—" He held her away from him, his eyebrows lifting, his gaze dark with desire. "Dear heavens! That scandalous corset, Chloe. I hope you had a premonition that you would see me tonight and weren't wearing that for anyone else."

It was her turn to torture him now. "Hmm. I might have."

He smiled slowly. "I always wondered what it would look like on you."

"Well, now you know."

"Which is why I am going to take it off," he said roughly as he reached for the silk lacings that bound her in the tightly boned buckram.

Chloe swallowed a moan. No man had ever made her appreciate her own body. Her breasts felt indecently full against the confines of her corset. She lowered her gaze as he loosened the last of her laces, then slowly removed her chemise.

She heard his sharp intake of breath and lifted her gaze. His eyes shone like graphite. The look he gave her sent a bolt of heat to the secret reaches of her body. A look that marked her as his.

He caught her by the shoulders and drew her against him. His hands moved with tender desperation over her pale arms and back, sculpting the cleft of her buttocks, the curves and hollows of her shape like an artist bringing life to his most prized creation.

"This is not how it should be for us, Chloe," he said with a rueful smile. "A woman like you deserves a gallant courtship, but I can't help myself. You see, I need you, too."

"I don't know about a gallant courtship. Some ladies find the Stratfield Ghost very exciting."

"Your aunt, for one?" he teased.

"Wait until she finds out you're alive."

"Perhaps I'll keep pretending to be dead."

She caught her breath as he went down on his knees to take off her garters and stockings. With a sigh of longing she let him lower her slowly to the bed they had made on the floor with their clothing. Despite their attempts to lighten the moment, neither of them could know how his game of revenge would end. He pressed a warm kiss on her belly, and her head fell back as pleasure shot through her.

"I don't want to lose you, Dominic."

The black velvet cloak beneath her felt cool on her bare skin. He stood over her and swiftly removed the rest of his own clothes. Chloe drank in the hard beauty of his body, the athletic grace of muscle and bone that made him every inch a dominant male and aggressor. He was built with power and masculinity from his broad shoulders to his tapered hips and heavily muscled thighs.

"When you look at me like that, Chloe," he said with a wicked smile, "I do not know if I will find the strength to leave you."

"Then stay," she said, raising up on her elbows. "My brothers will help you."

"Of all the men in the world who would understand what I have to do, it would be your brothers. Now touch me, Chloe, with those daring hands of yours, as I have dreamed you would do."

She rose onto her knees, murmuring, "Dominic."

He gave a shudder as she began to explore the planes of his nude body, tracing the healing scars on his chest, memorizing the ridges of solid muscle and sinew of his biceps and back. He felt warm and hard like polished wood, his heart beating against her fingertips. The thought of belonging to him thrilled her. She wanted him all to herself, wanted to feel every inch of him inside her again.

She thought of the first time she had seen him on his horse. She sighed at the memory of finding him in her room, of how easily she had fallen in love with him, of how she could not bear to see him hurt again.

She wrapped her arms around his waist, whispering, "I'm not letting you go until you seduce me, Stratfield."

He smiled down at her.

"I mean it, highwayman. Stand and deliver."

*   *   *

Dominic marveled at the female perfection of her form, that a woman so delicately made could harbor such a warrior's spirit. She had no idea how she had saved him. If not for Chloe, he would have lost all hope, all faith that life held any goodness for him.

She had believed in him when he had treated her with undeserved cruelty, when he had behaved no better than an animal. He had not earned her loyalty, but she had seen through his mask of pain and rage to the man underneath. When he had gone on the attack, she had stood up to him and shown him reason.

He loved the contradiction of courage and softness that made her so intriguing. He loved the way she touched him. When she pressed her palms against his belly, her fingertips brushing the arrow of hair that lay above his groin, his mind ceased to function. His lower body clenched in anticipation. It took all his restraint not to urge her hands lower to his thickening rod. His hips flexed in shameless enjoyment. The fragrance that drifted from her skin made him burn. How could the woman who rendered him this helpless have given him so much strength?

"Chloe," he said, his spine arching, his shoulders tensing at the sexual hunger smoldering in his blood. "We don't have enough time, and I need you so badly."

She pressed ardent kisses on his strong throat, his chest, and when her soft lips brushed the base of his penis, every muscle in his body constricted as if in pain. Fluid heat flooded him, engorged his veins. He could barely breathe, stricken with a need he had never known. Her tongue curled against the crown of his erection like a wet flame. He was stunned, his body shaking. Passion came naturally to her. She was a born seductress, this woman he loved.

"Chloe," he murmured, his voice hoarse and uneven as he lifted her up to kiss her erotic mouth. His other arm locked around her waist, supporting her. "Chloe," he whispered in her soft black hair. "My God, what you do to me."

She arched upward, her belly pressing to his. His hand tightened around her waist, locking her to him. He kissed her and cupped her plump breasts in his palms. Her nipples hardened between the agile pinching of his fingers. She gave a deep moan, folding under him, vulnerable and inviting.

He was on top of her. All over her. Holding her down with one hand against her midriff, parting her thighs wide with the other. His heart pounded as he stroked the wet curls of her sex. She melted against his fingers like honey, completely open to him, moist flesh that beckoned a man's touch.

"Dominic," she whispered, her hips moving against his fingers. "I think my heart is going to stop."

He felt an incredible surge of power, of pleasure. He might have wished for finer surroundings for her benefit, but for himself he did not care. All of his attention was focused on Chloe, her ivory body nestled invitingly on the darkness of his cloak, her thighs spread wide to him, her blue eyes drugged with helpless passion. "What would you like me to do?" he whispered, teasing her. "If it's too much, I could stop—"

"If you dare . . ."

He had no intention of stopping. He couldn't. He was going to take this as far as he could. He brought her again and again to the brink, loving the breathless whimpers that broke in her throat. His fingers sank into the engorged folds of her sheath. He played with her until she was weeping for him to be inside her. She was his woman to worship, to please.

She gave a cry as he slipped his hands under her bottom to enter her. She was so tight, he could have come on the first thrust. Instead, he braced his palms on the cloak and concentrated on controlling his movements, rubbing his shaft between the folds of her slick entrance before giving her what she wanted. The slow friction teased her until she was practically begging him to enter her, shuddering with lust. "Do it," she said.

His mind reveled in the sensation of wet heat. She was completely open to him, her graceful body pinned to the floor, shaking with uncontrolled sensuality. He was going to learn how to pleasure her inside and out; he would make loving her an art. With tantalizing restraint he slowly embedded himself inside her.

"I could die like this," he said, his head thrown back, the muscles in his shoulders contracting in pleasure.

He was lost in her. He loved how her body welcomed him. He loved the feel of stretching her to the hilt, filling her. This act he would not rush, no matter what awaited him afterward. His only thought was to sensitize her, to give her pleasure; he stroked her channel with slow, steady pressure, claiming her one inch at a time. She tensed, and he felt her inner muscles stretched by his thick member. He growled softly and rotated his hips, teasing her just a little more, sinking ever so slowly, so deeply inside her.

He watched her eyes close in enjoyment, her neck

arch, her belly tremble at his relentless attack on her senses. Each thrust tested his willpower, inflamed him. He felt the exact moment when she began to shatter, her womb convulsing, gripping him until he, too, was overwhelmed by sensation, overpowered with need. The world exploded, his hips bucked as he emptied his seed into her body.

He had never known such earth-shattering eroticism in his life. He could not believe that their mating had been such a wild delight. He rolled onto his side, their bodies still joined, fragrant with the perfume of sex. He cradled the back of her head in his hands and lowered his head to kiss her. She was warm, shivering a little, but deliciously responsive. He forced himself to ignore the stirring of desire in his groin. He would grow hard inside her too easily. He wanted more of her.

"Chloe, my love," he whispered, stroking her face. "I don't want to leave you."

She went still, her blue eyes shimmering with tears. "Then stay."

He brushed her black curls back from her forehead. "You have no idea how much I wish I could, how you tempt me. Be strong. When Edgar is exposed, my life will return to normal, and nothing will keep me away from you."

"Except four arrogant brothers and a sister who faints in shock when someone drops a knife from the dinner table."

He grinned. "I'll help you put on your costume. It sounds as if confronting Edgar might be good practice before facing your family."

They finished dressing in absorbed silence, Dominic

distracted, aware they had been gone longer than was wise, that he always lost track of time when they were together. She's changed since I first met her, he thought. But then so had he. God knew this exile her brothers had imposed on her was not what any of them had in mind.

And now his attention must return to a darker matter. Edgar had been corresponding with a man in London or its environs. This, Dominic had deduced from the speed by which Edgar exchanged letters with this unknown person.

The person's identity? Dominic did not know. Edgar appeared to burn the messages as soon as he read them. But Dominic had found a partially charred letter in the fireplace that Edgar had drafted instructing his factor to withdraw a large sum of money from his bank.

Was Edgar planning to escape or to pay off an accomplice from his past? Was he plotting another murder?

Perhaps Dominic would never know. But he would stop his uncle from destroying anyone else.

"Chloe," he said, in hesitation, his large hands closing around her softly rounded shoulders, "I want you to go back to London, or wherever your brothers are as soon as possible."

"Do you think they'll give me any choice in the matter?"

His gaze darkened with concern for her. "Convince Heath you must."

"And pray share with me the magic words that will open the iron doors of his heart to allow me home?"

Dominic's mouth tightened into a thin line. "Tell him he *must* bring you home. You can convince him."

"I doubt it."

"Try, damn it. When word of Edgar's treachery is exposed, there will be a scandal. Remove yourself from it now."

"I don't care about scandal, Dominic. I care about you and what happens when you face the man who killed Brandon. Did you ever finish decoding his letter?

He looked at her sharply. "*His* letter?"

"Yes, the letter, or partial letter, you left in my room and stole back. It was written in my brother's hand. I cannot tell if it was meant for you or Samuel."

He shook his head in disbelief. "How do you know?"

"I recognized Brandon's handwriting, and, well, I made a copy of it to decipher. He seems to be referring to something Edgar planned to do. I shall give you the translation when I finish."

"You are an amazing woman, Chloe."

"I shall be amazingly miserable if anything happens to you. Why won't you let me help you confront Edgar?"

"No."

"Am I supposed to sit by and do nothing?"

"If anything happens to Adrian and me, it will be up to you to get your brothers involved."

Her heart missed a beat. "What are you going to do to Edgar?"

"Convince him to do what is right."

"And if he refuses?"

"I'll do whatever I must."

She pulled away, her blue eyes a little angry, bright with anguish. On another woman the winged fairy costume would have looked airy, ethereal. But Chloe more resembled a Roman goddess about to start a war. Strong rather than insubstantial. Frail on the surface only. The sort of woman some stuffy old earl would love to indulge, to spoil, to show off on his arm. The thought turned his stomach. He didn't want to lose her to another man. He wanted to triumph and claim her for himself.

He gripped her hand, drawing her back from the door, his body close to hers. "I will come back for you," he said, his gray eyes glittering. "One way or another. Don't go kissing anyone behind carriages or in hallways again. Be mine always. I *will* come back."

She bit her lower lip. Her face was pale. He had the oddest feeling she wanted to hit him. "Just make certain when you do come back," she whispered, hiking up one of her rather mangled wings, "that you are not a ghost."

Chapter 21

When Chloe emerged from the room, she found that the receiving hall was still crowded with guests who did not care to dance, chatting over a glass of lemonade. The band was just beginning another set, but the last thing she felt like was whirling around after what she and Dominic had just done. She felt light-headed enough as it was. She wanted to be alone, to ponder what was happening between them, to steady herself. To be ready in case he needed her help to finish this thing with his uncle.

Perhaps she should have been more concerned over the loss of her virtue and her fallen status. She wasn't. What was gone was gone. She simply wanted to sit quietly for a while and relive every decadent detail before she began worrying about what would happen to him. Would tonight be the night he would finally confront Sir Edgar? What was he going to do if Edgar did indeed have an ally waiting in the wings? What if he and Adrian failed? Her throat closed at the thought.

"Well," one young woman murmured, bumping into Chloe's back, "my mama says that if the Stratfield Ghost has his way, there won't be a virtuous lady left in the village."

Chloe released a wistful sigh and adjusted her wings back over her shoulders. If she had her way, Dominic's haunting days would soon be over forever, and his vices would be reserved for one woman alone.

"I do not believe there is a ghost at all," a disgruntled gentleman said in a loud voice. "I think the whole thing is nothing but female hysterics. What is your opinion, Lady Chloe?"

Chloe glanced around at his unfamiliar florid face. She didn't even know his name; he was one of Justin's cohorts, which reminded her that she hadn't danced with Justin all night. He had completely ignored her. Not that she minded. In fact, she hadn't even thought of it until—

"Ah, so there you are, Chloe." She looked up to see her uncle elbowing his way from the refreshment room. "I wondered where you had gone."

"I was here," she said vaguely, glancing past him.

"Here?"

"Well." Oh, she hated being deceitful. "I thought to fetch my fan. Silly me. I had it on my wrist all along."

His gentle eyes looked thoughtful. "Silly you."

"Yes." Her pulse began to pound. "Silly me."

"Has your Lady Dewhurst had any more luck laying our naughty ghost?" a guest asked with a grin from behind the older man.

Sir Humphrey turned away from Chloe to answer, and she felt a profound if temporary sense of relief. He might have suspected something was off in her reply, but he wasn't going to press her. Chloe was thankful for that. She despised lying to one who had been as kind to her as her uncle.

He placed his hand on her arm. "Let me get you a glass of lemonade, Chloe. You look a little flushed."

Lord. If only he knew why. He wasn't *that* kind as to accept what she and Dominic had been doing. She would rather die than to distress him, to disappoint her one champion in the house.

"Lemonade would be perfect, Uncle—"

She stopped cold. She had just noticed Sir Edgar Williams emerging from the cloakroom, elegant in black evening dress and a flawlessly white linen neckcloth. Obviously no one had informed him this was to be a masquerade ball, or he considered himself too dignified to appear in costume. But then, Chloe thought, his entire personality was a facade. A heartless killer disguised as a knight of the realm, a gentleman with gutter instincts.

She watched Sir Edgar glance around the hallway, studying each masked guest in turn. Her heart pounded erratically against her ribs. Had he discovered that Dominic was alive? That he was here tonight? Or was his mysterious friend in attendance? It did not seem likely that Edgar would do his secret dealings in a place like this. If he made a move toward the room where she had left Dominic, should she try to waylay him?

She felt her uncle's hand tighten around her arm. Puzzled, she glanced up at his face.

"Let us get that lemonade, Chloe," he said quietly.

She nodded, looking around to see Sir Edgar disappear into the ballroom. A lean cloaked figure in the corner caught her attention, and she felt a wave of heat engulf her as she realized Adrian had resumed the charade. He looked directly at her, gave a barely perceptible nod, then smiled down warmly at the cluster of chattering women surrounding him.

Was that nod Adrian's subtle way of telling her that Dominic had safely hidden himself? Yes. Adrian must have seen Sir Edgar, too. He would not be standing there flirting so outrageously with all those females if he feared for his friend's welfare.

She could only pray that the rest of Dominic's plans went as well.

· She turned back to her uncle. "Lemonade, yes, that's just what we need."

He stared at her for a few seconds before guiding her to the refreshment room. "It's good to see you happy again, Chloe. We've all been worried about you this past week or so. This dance appears to have done you a world of good."

She did not dance again with Adrian. He was surrounded by admirers for the rest of the evening, which she took as a reassuring sign. Surely he would not appear so relaxed if Edgar's cohort had arrived. In fact, the last she'd seen of Sir Edgar, he had been in conversation with the pastor.

Neither she nor Adrian made any more attempts at conversation with each other. It would be unwise to draw attention to their association. She did not know him at all, she had not even seen Adrian's face unmasked, but he was the kind of man who effortlessly made a woman feel protected, defended, safe from danger.

Perhaps this was because he had spent his life fighting

for others, using his body and his wits as a shield. In fact, he was the last man in the world one would peg as a potential duke. He looked and behaved more like the mercenary rogue he was reputed to be. His history of unconventional conduct and adventure in foreign lands was infamous, the stuff of popular fiction that Chloe and her friends devoured in the newspapers. Some of those wild tales must have been true.

Yet she could not help liking him. He was a person one trusted instantly, and if Dominic had only a single ally, she was glad that it was Adrian Ruxley.

She turned from watching him to discover Justin standing right behind her. For the first time since she'd known him, he did not smile as their eyes met, did not appear carefree and young. She felt a prickle of apprehension crawl down her spine. He looked so uncharacteristically serious.

"So it's true," he said, shaking his head in disapproval.

Chloe blinked. She seemed to be hiding so many secrets these days that she had lost count. "What is true, Justin?" she asked guardedly.

"You're in love with him."

"Er, him?"

"Yes." He sniffed, nodding in Adrian's direction like a spoiled child. "Do not try to deny it."

Chloe glanced around in embarrassment. Justin's voice was getting louder; fortunately, they were standing alone. "I have only met him for the first time tonight."

"Which makes it all the worse," he burst out, his sultan's turban sliding down over his forehead. "I defended you, Chloe, when everyone warned me you were fast."

A few guests had begun to look at them. Chloe contemplated pushing him behind the potted palm. Didn't she have enough to worry about tonight without Justin throwing a public temper tantrum?

"I have no idea what you are talking about, Justin."

He pushed his jeweled turban out of his eye. "I saw you, Chloe Boscastle. I saw you sneaking off with that duke to be."

"For your information Lord Wolverton merely escorted me to the hall while I went to fetch my fan."

"Ha! You were both gone long enough to take a tour of the Continent."

"Stop behaving like an infant," Chloe said under her breath. "I did *not* go on a tour with Lord Wolverton." Which was absolutely the truth. She had been touring with Dominic, and if Justin did not control—

The menacing shadow of a man fell between them, saving Chloe from giving Justin that well-deserved push. The interruption might have been welcome except for the fact it was Sir Edgar's presence that stopped Chloe from committing an overt act of violence. She would gladly face one hundred of Justin's tantrums rather than this foul man.

"A lover's spat?" Sir Edgar asked with a wry smile. "Shall I play the neutral party?"

Chloe gave Justin a quelling look. Perhaps she could turn his outburst to an advantage. As long as Edgar was here, he could not harm Dominic. "It was a misunderstanding."

"I'll say," Justin muttered, but he was apparently enough of a gentleman to leave the matter at that. "You will excuse me then, both of you?" he asked, backing up several steps. "I think my mother is calling to me."

Sir Edgar glanced down at Chloe with a resigned sigh. "Well, it is not London, is it, my dear? These country bumpkins do not understand the sophisticated art of social etiquette. I suppose you are accustomed to breaking hearts."

Chloe watched Justin march right up to another young lady and ask her to dance. The nitwit apparently was not going to nurse a broken heart for long. Well, she'd always known that she was a little too wild for him.

"Do *you* plan on leaving for London in the near future, Sir Edgar?" she asked pointedly, her gaze avoiding his. She could not bring herself to look him in the eye. She was not a good enough actress to hide her contempt.

He shook his head. "Alas, it is taking longer to attend to my nephew's estate than anyone could have predicted. I have found—"

There was a sudden lull in the buzz of laughter and conversation around them. The house steward was about to award the prize for the best costumes. Guests swelled forward, forcing Chloe and Sir Edgar into separate channels.

He gave her an apologetic shrug as they parted. She felt awash with relief and hoped he had not sensed anything suspicious in her behavior toward him. The idea of engaging in lighthearted banter with the man who had stabbed Dominic half to death was more than she could stomach. She could murder him herself with her bare hands.

The guests were clapping wildly for each costume presented. Chloe spotted her uncle edging toward her, using his lightning bolt to clear a path. Adrian stood at the far end of the ballroom, his pose relaxed, one broad shoulder pressed to the wall. Chloe noticed him glance her way, then toward Sir Edgar, as if he were focused on keeping them both in his scrutiny.

Yes, it was a good feeling to have a friend like Adrian in one's sight, even if it was true that he had spent an entire summer on a Chinese pirate ship. Still, as long as he was here protecting her, he could not aid Dominic. Her brows furrowed in worry.

Was Adrian going to help Dominic execute the final step of his scheme? If not in physical deed, Adrian must have been involved in plotting Edgar's downfall.

How would they do it? she wondered, a knot rising in her throat. Dominic had been careful not to give her the details of his final plans. She gripped her fan tightly in her fingers. As long as he came back to her alive, she was almost glad she did not know.

Dominic walked as quietly as a ghost into the darkened bedchamber of his own home. He did not have a moment to lose. A quarter hour at most, to be on the safe side. He had taken a detour home from the dance. The servants had retired to their hall. He knew their habits down to the exact minute his footmen extinguished the candles in the long gallery before turning in for the night.

Adrian would do what was required to keep his eye on Edgar, but Dominic's uncle was no fool. For a week he had been questioning the servants about Dominic's friendship with Adrian, when they had last met, what they had discussed. It was clear that Edgar viewed Adrian's stop in Chistlebury with suspicion. Yet for tonight Adrian's primary function was to ensure that no harm came to Chloe. Fortunately, while Dominic's beloved might be a little rash in matters of romance, she did show good sense when it came to her survival.

Edgar's mysterious acquaintance had not shown up at the ball, after all. Perhaps Dominic's hunch had been wrong. Perhaps the dance was not private enough for their meeting. Or perhaps Edgar knew he was under suspicion and wanted to appear as normal as possible by attending a social affair. It seemed likely he had warned his contact to stay away.

Dominic would leave that matter to the agents of the Crown who dealt in subterfuge.

He laid his brother's bloodied and torn military jacket across Edgar's pristine white pillow. From the small urn in his hand he sprinkled a trail of white sand out into the gallery, all the way up to the portrait of himself on the wall. It was sand that had come from Nepal, sent by Samuel's faithful servant for the memorial service that had been held. He wondered if Edgar would know what it represented. A gauntlet thrown down in challenge.

He propped the empty urn on the floor in front of the secret passageway leading to the stygian vault that had hidden him for over a month.

If fate was kinder than it had been in the past, this would be his last night of being entombed in darkness. If fate proved unkind, it would simply be his last night.

He slipped between the crevice in the wall and waited for his senses to become accustomed to the grainy dark. In this he had the advantage over Edgar. Dominic could orient himself to the gloom within seconds now. He knew the exact depth of each stair, the twists and turns of the old smugglers' tunnels. Where the mortar and dirt would collapse if disturbed. Where to duck his head.

Indeed, Dominic had become quite intimate with all the appointments of his secret hell. He had looked evil in the eye and survived, as one who'd walked through flames might emerge scarred but stronger.

Until he had met Chloe, he had not even taken time to analyze what he had become, and she had been the bridge between the man he had been in the past and the one he hoped to be in their future.

A man who could approach her brothers and convince them why he was worthy of her hand. He grimaced inwardly at the thought of presenting his case and explaining their courtship. No matter how he phrased it, he would come out looking like a veritable devil. Heath would poke holes through his defense, if not literally through Dominic himself.

No, the Stratfield Ghost was hardly the type of man one would choose to give one's sister to in marriage. Of course, it would be claimed, quite accurately, that he had ruined Chloe. Well, she had ruined him, too. She had ruined him for any other woman, and when he was free, he would move mountains if necessary to claim her. The blood in his veins still burned from their coupling. She had held nothing back tonight. How he wished there had been more time for them.

He peeled off his black velvet cloak and tossed it over the skeleton propped up against the tunnel wall. The leering skull and bleached remains had been his silent if not agreeable companion for most of Dominic's concealment.

"Here, my friend, you looked a little cold."

Dressed only in the ruffled white lawn shirt, knee breeches, and jack boots of a dashing highwayman, Dominic did not feel the cool of his hiding place tonight. Making love to Chloe had invigorated him and poured energy into his very marrow. The bright warmth of her being had stayed with him.

He picked up his sword and bowed deeply before the cloaked skeleton. "Dear Baron Bones, this will either be the last time we practice together, or I shall soon be joining you in your unclad state. Help me if you can. If I survive, I give my word to lay your remains to rest in a place of honor."

Chapter 22

Was it her imagination, or was Uncle Humphrey subjecting her to more than the usual questioning looks tonight? Chloe had the unfortunate feeling that he wished to speak to her. She also had the feeling that it was not a discussion she would enjoy.

Hence, she made a quick escape up to her room as soon as they reached the comfortable old house. As she hurried up the creaking stairs, she sensed her uncle watching her from the hall below.

What was wrong? Had he seen her sneak off with her masked highwayman at the ball? If so, he could only assume she'd had an assignation with Adrian, which she could quite honestly state was untrue. After all, she had only met the man tonight at the ball, and he had returned to the ballroom to cover her interlude with Dominic.

Unless Uncle Humphrey suspected something else. He was an intelligent man, an intuitive one. She hesitated at the top of the stairs, tempted to peek down at him. She could hear her aunt and Pamela laughing in the parlor, in high spirits because Aunt Gwendolyn had taken first prize for her costume and Pamela had found an ardent admirer in Justin's brother, Charles.

But what could her uncle have discovered? The encoded message from Brandon? No. That would not put him in such a brooding mood, Chloe decided as she put her shoulder to her warped door and pushed.

The door was already open, and she flew across the chamber, stumbling over the inert warm body lying on the floor. She went down on one knee, her wings flapping around her face.

"Dominic?" she whispered hopefully, knowing of course it could not be him.

Ares leaped up to give her a slobbery kiss on the mouth.

"Ugh. You've been eating sausage again." She swiped her gloved hands across her wet, pork-scented lips. "I don't suppose we have company?"

The hound padded after her as she stood and went straight into the dressing closet, searching in vain for a sign that Dominic might have come or left a message.

"He hasn't been here," she murmured. "I shall have to console myself with his pudgy dog."

She pulled her trunk to the window and sank down with a pensive frown. How could he win this battle by himself? she wondered. No, not by himself. With Adrian. She could only pray that the pair of them were as clever as they believed themselves to be.

My uncle was once an instructor of Angelo's technique in Venice. He taught me everything I know about sword fighting.

Dominic's words came back to her as she rested her chin reflectively on the windowsill. She did not underestimate Dominic's strength and determination, but Sir Edgar had a killer's instincts and no conscience whatsoever. If Dominic cornered him, his uncle would fight to the death. Both men would. She draped her arms across the window, poised on her trunk to watch the woods, his sleeping estate, for a sign of him.

What did she expect?

A fireworks display? An honorable duel at dawn in front of the duck pond? Dominic had become skilled at moving in shadows. It seemed likely he would take his revenge on a private field. Chloe decided that at the first sign of trouble, she would make up some excuse to go straight to Stratfield Hall. She refused to submit to the waiting, the not knowing.

Ares settled down beside her for their vigil. All through the night she would doze for a few minutes, wake up with her heart pounding, and watch.

Dawn came, and nothing had changed. There were no signs of any disturbance from Dominic's estate. The sun rose on the mellow stones of Stratfield Hall, sheltering whatever secrets it held.

She stretched her cramped limbs and rose stiffly from her uneventful sentinel. It was Sunday morning. She told herself the quiet meant that all was well.

There was something reassuring to Chloe about the familiar chaos that greeted her as she walked into the family parlor later that same morning. Ares had apparently stolen one of Aunt Gwendolyn's shoes and hidden it. Aunt Gwendolyn, in a feathered bonnet, gray silk dress, beaded pelisse, and the other shoe, was sending all the servants and her husband on an emergency hunt.

"You have more shoes than any woman I have ever met," Uncle Humphrey muttered. "Three cobblers have retired in Chistlebury from your business alone. Why is *this* shoe so essential?"

She straightened one of her feathers. "Perhaps this missing shoe is a message from his master. The dog may have been instructed to hide it from me for a reason."

"A message from his master?" Sir Humphrey glanced at Chloe in exasperation. "Do you suppose Stratfield has taken to wearing women's shoes in the afterlife?"

"He might be giving me a sign," Aunt Gwendolyn said.

"A sign?" Her husband shook his head in bafflement. "With your shoe?"

"Yes. A shoe could be an occult representation of the next step Stratfield wishes me to take to help him."

Sir Humphrey threw up his hands. "I wish to God he'd help me. An occult representation. A shoe."

Pamela stuck her head into the room. "We're going to be late to church. Do hurry, all of you."

Chloe had to smile at that. Pamela was always a slugabed who found any excuse to avoid going to church on Sundays. This change of attitude could only mean that love was in the air, that her cousin hoped to meet Charles there to continue the romance that had been sparked at the previous evening's ball. She felt a faint pang of envy. Chloe was never going to have a normal courtship with a sweetheart gazing at her like a mooncalf from a church pew.

No, she thought wistfully. Her own courtship consisted of a man dressed as a highwayman whisking her off for an illicit interlude, which, now that she contemplated it in the aftermath, really had begun to take on a rosy glow of romanticism. She could hardly believe they had danced together, made love with such desperation. And yet she could still feel the hard weight of Dominic's body on hers, his hands in her hair, on her face.

"We are looking for your mother's lost shoe," Sir Humphrey informed his daughter. "The misguided woman refuses to leave the house without it."

"I saw her shoe in the middle of the stairs just a few moments ago," Pamela said.

"Was it going up or going down?" her mother asked.

Pamela shrugged her slender shoulders. "What does it possibly matter? Do hurry, Mama."

Chloe wandered over to the window and gazed outside. Where was Dominic now? She ought to be furious at him for putting her in this situation. Even if she did decide to ask her brothers to help, there was no guarantee any message she sent would reach them in time to save him. He might have confronted Edgar before they left London.

"Are you coming, Chloe?"

She glanced around at the sound of her uncle's voice. They remained alone in the room, and she could hear the carriage drawing to the front of the house.

"Yes. I'll be right there."

"Anything interesting outside that window?" he asked quietly.

She managed a wan smile. "There doesn't seem to be. Did Aunt Gwendolyn ever find her shoe?"

He frowned at her in concern. "Your head is up in the clouds this morning. Pamela just told us it was on the stairs. Didn't you hear?"

She moved past him with her gaze averted, aware that he knew her better than anyone in the house. After last night, with Dominic occupying her mind, she must seem more than a little distracted. "Come on. Let's suffer the parson's sermon for the sake of our souls."

He touched her lightly on the shoulder as she passed. "Chloe, my dear, if you ever need someone to help you, I shall be here."

Uncle Humphrey involved in a scheme of duplicity and murder? Chloe could not resist turning to smile at him, regretting that her secret had built a wall between them. "Thank you. You have been kinder to me than I deserve."

The congregants of Saint Luke's Church sat in a dazed trance, apparently not recovered from the previous evening's exciting masquerade ball. Of course sleeping during a sermon was not an unusual occurrence. On any given Sunday the parson's vigorous pounding on the mahogany pulpit was routinely interspersed with an errant snore from the oaken pews.

Chloe found it impossible to focus on Parson Grimsby at all with his thin pointed nose and buckled shoes even though she guessed that his sermon on virtue was directed at her.

Well, it was too late, she thought rather unremorsefully.

She fiddled with an onyx button on her glove, the moments dragging by. Somewhere in the back of the church a small boy broke wind and was soundly slapped by his mother. Lord, what if *she* conceived a child as a result of her love affair with Dominic? If such a thing did happen, her brothers would personally escort him to the altar, and Chloe would let them, too, although she had no reason to think he would not come willingly.

"Is there something wrong?" Pamela whispered as they knelt together to pray.

Chloe glanced up. She'd just realized that neither Adrian nor Sir Edgar had attended the overlong service, but then that shouldn't surprise her. "Why do you ask?" she whispered back to her cousin.

"You keep sighing and fidgeting."

Chloe lowered her gaze. There *was* something wrong with her. Here she sat in a quiet ivy-smothered parish church, her head piously bowed, on her knees, praying for the soul of a man who had debauched her in the dark, on a floor, less than twenty-four hours ago.

She ought to be praying for forgiveness. Or praying that her family would never find out what she had done.

But no. She was praying that Dominic would not go out and get himself killed in earnest, thereby remaining alive to debauch her all over again. And offer her a decent future.

He'd said he would come back to her, hadn't he?

She shifted on her knees. She felt a little cold, from anxiety and lack of sleep. How much longer could Parson Grimsby go on praying? He must have covered every sin twice over by now.

"Chloe." Pamela nudged her as the lengthy prayer finally ended and they settled back into their seats. "Do you want to know something?" she whispered.

Yes. She wanted to know that Dominic would be waiting for her when they returned home, and that Sir Edgar would pay for all the evil he had inflicted.

"What?" she whispered back.

"I borrowed your corset."

Chloe sat up a little straighter, examining her cousin from the corner of her eye. "Oh? Is there another dance upcoming?"

"No." Pamela blushed attractively under her creamy freckled skin. "I'm wearing it right now."

"You wicked thing," Chloe teased.

"It was your idea."

"Mine?"

"Don't you remember? You suggested I wear it to church. Do I have it on properly?"

"It's rather hard to tell under your spencer, Pamela."

"Oh. Right." Pamela wriggled around for a few moments before whispering again, "Do you want to know something else?"

"Why not? It has to be more interesting than this sermon."

"Justin is going to marry the Seymour heiress. His brother told me last night. I am sorry, Chloe."

"Such is life, Pamela."

"Aren't you at all upset?"

"Not over Justin. I cannot imagine marrying a man who stamps his foot to get his way. It's rather like being betrothed to your first pony."

"I've thought of something else," Pamela whispered.

Aunt Gwendolyn made a face. "Do be quiet, girls."

"What?" Chloe whispered to her cousin.

Parson Grimsby gave the pulpit one last resounding bang. The congregation gave a collective sigh of relief.

"All the women in the parish were hoping Lord Wolverton would come to church today so they could see what he looked like in the daylight." Pamela paused. "I expect he's off to grander things."

Chloe forced a smile. Grander things. "I expect so."

The sky was overcast when the service ended. The cawing of crows in the distant fields greeted the congregants who filed outside. Chloe's spirits had plummeted at Pamela's rather irrelevant observation, and the words echoed a disturbing refrain in her mind.

I expect he's off to grander things.

What grander things could Adrian be doing on a quiet day like this? Not helping Dominic to challenge Edgar. Their encounter would occur in the dark, not on a peaceful Sabbath morning when practically the entire village was strolling benignly down the church footpath, past the lopsided crosses in the churchyard, to the line of parked carriages and carts.

Aunt Gwendolyn was still talking to anyone who would listen about the significance of her misplaced shoe.

Chloe's heart fluttered. How silly she was. Why was she allowing Pamela's thoughtless remark to upset her? Dominic would *not* stage his confrontation on a Sunday afternoon, when everyone could see or hear— Everyone was gathered here. No one could witness anything that went on at Stratfield Hall.

She stared at the clusters of people assembled on the church porch, around the footpath. Servants and gentry, young and old.

Sir Edgar was not here.

"It's happening right now," she said, gazing toward the main road. "While I stand here like a ninnyhammer listening to my aunt talk about her haunted shoe. They're together at this very moment."

Her uncle was suddenly at her elbow, his face grave. "What is it?"

"I—" She shook her head, her instincts struggling against the promise she had made. "I cannot tell you."

"Tell me," he said. His voice was very low. "I know he is alive if that is what you are trying to hide from me."

"What?" she whispered, her face turning gray.

"I know Stratfield survived the attempt on his life, and I believe I know who wanted him dead. What I do not know is how *you* became involved with him, Chloe. Your aunt watched all your comings and goings from the house like a hawk. How could you possibly have established a friendship with the man from your room?"

Chloe stared miserably at the row of uneven crosses in the churchyard. "It doesn't seem possible, does it?"

"How?"

"Well, he fell into the situation, so to speak."

"Fell?"

"Umm."

"Into . . . the—"

"The trunk of my underthings from London, all right? Now you know the sordid details. He did not plan it. I didn't plan it. In fact, I was sitting in my room, minding my own business, on the road to reform—"

"Your room," Sir Humphrey said, hitting the heel of his hand on his forehead. "I should have guessed. It wasn't Devon, was it? It was Stratfield. You . . . oh, how could you, Chloe?"

"Are we going to stand here berating my behavior

all day?" she demanded. "Dominic is with Edgar right now."

He took her arm. "No. I shall berate you on the way home."

He marched her past Pamela and her friends, all of whom gave Chloe a sympathetic smile. Chloe could only assume that they assumed she had gotten into trouble again, and—

"Why don't we take the carriage, Uncle Humphrey?"

"Because your aunt will not walk a mile in her haunted shoe, that's why, and because I know a shortcut that is much faster."

"Shouldn't we at least tell her that we are leaving?" Chloe asked with an anxious glance over her shoulder.

"And spoil her dramatic moment?" Sir Humphrey shook his head. "We'll leave word with the driver to bring her and Pamela home. Wait here."

"But—"

Chloe stood alone on the footpath as he hurried off toward the line of waiting carriages. In the distance she could see the tips of the trees that encircled Stratfield Hall. Of course Dominic would have planned the details of his revenge down to the hour.

He couldn't confront Edgar at night, when the servants might hear a disturbance, or the sound of a pistol shot would carry in the silence. He had chosen instead a Sunday morning while everyone was at church.

"All right," Sir Humphrey said, huffing a little for breath as he rejoined her. "We want to be gone before anyone asks to come with us."

Chloe fell into step with his brisk strides. "What are we going to do?"

His mouth firmed. "*You* are doing nothing, young lady. It seems to me you have done quite enough already. I shudder to think how I shall explain this to your aunt, let alone the rest of your family."

A chill seeped into Chloe's bones. "Do you really *have* to tell them?"

"I'm afraid you have crossed the line this time, Chloe. A kiss behind a parked carriage is one thing."

"You might as well put a noose around my neck," she said glumly. "Or toss me on a ship to be transported to the colonies."

"I doubt the colonies would know what to do with you."

"Uncle Humphrey," she said in despair, "I thought *you* understood. I did only what I had to do."

He decimated a crop of toadstools with his walking stick. "You might have sought my help, Chloe."

"He wouldn't let me."

"But he let you help him?"

"He didn't want to do that either. But when I found out about Brandon—"

"Brandon?"

"Dominic believes that Edgar had Brandon and Samuel killed in Nepal because they found out he had betrayed the British army to the French. Edgar planned the ambush."

"Dear God."

"He doesn't have a conscience, Uncle Humphrey."

"Dominic," he said, shaking his head in dismay. "On a first-name basis with a ghost now, are we?"

"How did you find out he was still alive, Uncle Humphrey?"

"His gamekeeper Finley and I put our heads together. I had suspected for some time that Stratfield's death was not as simple as it appeared. Finley and I both felt that more than a mere poacher was haunting the woods."

"*Haunting* is the word."

"After Finley and I talked, he did a little investigating inside the house late at night. He knew his master was alive but would not betray him for the world."

"As his uncle did," she murmured.

"Yes." He threw her an irate look. "Which does not excuse the fact or explain why *you* became involved with him."

"It doesn't, does it?"

Chloe felt a little breathless by this time, from practically running through the tall grass, from defending her position, from trying to convince herself that Dominic was not fighting for his life while she and her uncle argued with each other.

"I thought you and I understood each other, Chloe. I thought you were on the path to reform."

"I thought so, too, Uncle Humphrey."

He grunted. "And hiding a man in your room was supposed to help you in exactly *what* way?"

Chapter 23

All through the night Dominic had played a game of cat and mouse with Edgar. Leaving one tantalizing clue after another, he had laid a trail from his bedchamber to the secret passage in the long gallery, through the narrow tunnels beneath his house to the underground dungeon where he had plotted his revenge.

Now, on this quiet Sunday morning, he would end the game. The estate was empty; only the black swans gliding on the lake remained in place to witness what would happen. The neighbors had trundled off to church; the long-winded parson had just begun his sermon.

Chloe was probably fidgeting in her pew, perhaps even flirting with that fool Justin to alleviate her boredom. Dominic had watched through the telescope to see her climb into the carriage with her relatives. The carriage had not returned. At least he could act knowing that she was safe with her family.

Adrian stood guard inside the gatehouse.

Edgar was so close now that Dominic could hear him breathe, could feel the vibrations of his cautious footsteps on the secret staircase that led to Dominic's lair.

"Where are you, damn it?" his uncle muttered into the airless void. "Come out and show me your face. Let this be done in the open."

"Why?" Dominic called up quietly. "Why, when you have worked in darkness for years to destroy so many lives?"

He heard Edgar hesitate, sensed him studying the shadowed chasm below him to discern Dominic's exact location. "What nonsense is this, Dominic? Why are you hiding from me?"

"I'm not hiding, Edgar. I am merely waiting for my guest to arrive."

"Why?"

"To give you a chance to explain yourself, to deny what we both know is true."

Edgar hesitated. "I deny nothing."

"Turn yourself in, or I shall take you in myself."

Edgar forced a laugh, descending another step. "A gun is so much more efficient than a dagger." He lifted his right hand steadily; the ebony barrel of a dueling pistol gleamed in the dark. "I should have used this the first time on you."

Dominic slowly uncurled his body from his crouching position in the corner. "But how efficient is a gun with a safety that has been jammed, Edgar?" he asked slowly.

Edgar's voice shook in fury. "I had my pistols locked away—"

"In *my* desk. Did you forget that you are only a guest here? A most unwelcome one, at that."

Panicking, Edgar raised the pistol to Dominic's face and pulled the trigger, only to fling it to the steps when it failed to fire.

"You're insane, Dominic. Who but a madman would hide in the walls of his own house? I should have you put away. After all, you staged your own murder in order to seduce the poor sleeping women of this village. You are a certified lunatic."

"Without doubt. Perhaps it is a family trait that we both share."

"Go to hell."

Dominic laughed at the unintended irony of his uncle's words. "Where do you think we are?"

"I should have cut your heart out that night."

"And kept it in a casket under your pillows?" Dominic's voice was almost detached. "Who was coming here to meet you last night, Edgar? Who helped you betray your country?"

Edgar did not answer.

"I know why you had my brother and Brandon killed."

Edgar paused. "They knew, too, but it didn't help them."

"How many people were involved?"

Edgar laughed bitterly. "Why? Do you think you and your Boscastle friends can conquer the world? Your brother believed that Brandon Boscastle would protect him, and they both died."

Dominic would not allow the taunt to weaken him, knowing that Edgar would pay for that, too. Involving the Boscastle family only made him more determined to bring his uncle to justice.

"I hoped you would turn yourself in, Edgar."

"I'd rather see us both dead."

"All right. Here." Dominic threw a sword into the air.

"Catch. This will be our final lesson. Do you remember our practices? You made me fight you blindfolded. It was an excellent discipline for fencing in the dark."

Edgar cursed in anger, his hand lifting reflexively to grasp the hilt. "Do you really think to beat me?" He descended the remaining stairs with cautious grace. "I taught you everything you know about fencing. I studied your weaknesses, Dominic. I learned your vulnerabilities."

Dominic drew his sword. "One fights with the mind as well as the body, is that not what you used to tell me?"

"I'm flattered that you remember." Moving with an agility that belied his age, he opened with a straight thrust and disengaged inward. "The pity of it is that I have studied other techniques since your schoolroom days."

"Show me."

Edgar circled the shadowed form in front of him. Once in Paris he had been a *maître d'armes,* which was when Dominic suspected he had made his French connections. "Samuel thought he could bring me down, too. Do you know exactly how he died?"

Dominic did not waver. There was no emotional manipulation or mental torment that could break his concentration now. He had come back from the grave for this moment. He had sat in this unbreathable hole for weeks, picturing the exact scene as it unfolded before him. He had planned how he would execute each move. He had prepared himself for every eventuality.

Not even hearing the vile description of how Samuel had been ambushed and brutally killed could distract him. Edgar's taunts fell on his mind like raindrops on a stone, not penetrating his hardened emotions at all.

"Do you know what his body looked like when he was found, Dominic?" Edgar asked, attacking with feint and disengaging.

Dominic balanced his weight and lunged. "Perhaps you should be more concerned with how you will look when we are done."

Edgar had stripped down to his boots, shirt, and pantaloons. He had not slept all night. For hours he had been following clues that confirmed what the backward village of Chistlebury had claimed all along.

Stratfield was haunting his own home. His spirit would not rest until he had confronted his killer.

Of course what this village of peasants did not know was that Dominic had never been laid to rest. Edgar had been unable to attend the funeral because he was allegedly in Wales at the time of the murder. To be present at the burial would have aroused suspicion, and Edgar had foolishly assumed that Dominic could not possibly have survived the slashing he had dealt him.

But the stubborn bastard had refused to die, unlike his two brothers who had very obligingly gone to the grave. Michael, of an accident in which Edgar had played no part. Samuel, by the assassins he'd hired in Nepal.

It was in the midst of war-ravaged Portugal at Corunna that Samuel, nothing more than an inexperienced messenger boy at the time, had discovered that Edgar was trading military secrets to the French.

Samuel and his brash young friend Lord Brandon Boscastle had followed Edgar one morning to a small village church and caught him in conversation with a Portuguese priest who in secret was working for the French.

The two men had confronted Edgar in private that same day, requesting a clarification of why Edgar had met secretly with a priest, and conversed in French.

Edgar confessed that his family had descended from a long line of Roman Catholics. He did not practice his faith in the open; in fact, he had converted to the Church of England to become a soldier, but in a moment of weakness he had thought a few prayers would not hurt. Samuel should understand; he was, after all, his own nephew, and the family descended from a line of Roman Catholics.

It was a plausible explanation.

Samuel and Brandon had even appeared to accept the story at face value and never questioned him again. A few years later, when Edgar angrily resigned his commission in the army to accept a better-paying post with the Honourable East India Company, the adventurous pair asked to again join his regiment.

Edgar had not dreamed that the seemingly boyish young soldiers had been commissioned by British Intelligence to spy on him, to gather information proving he had sold information to the French after he had been bypassed for the promotion he believed that he deserved.

A young inexperienced aristocrat who'd won Wellington's favor had gotten the job that Edgar coveted. The years he'd worked so diligently for the army counted for nothing.

Now, ironically, with Dominic's death, Edgar had stood

poised to receive everything he had earned. A title, land, riches. Damn it to hell, he had *killed* his own kin for his reward.

It did not bother him at all that he would kill Dominic for a second time.

Chapter 24

Chloe and her uncle reached the weathered stone gatehouse of Stratfield's estate within twenty minutes. Catching her breath, she stared at the elegant Elizabethan house. It seemed too benign a setting for the violent confrontation she feared had happened within. There was no movement behind the windows, no cheerful smoke rising from the chimneys . . . no sign of life or death anywhere. Her heart felt as heavy as lead.

"What are we going to do?" she asked her uncle as she tested the heavy wrought-iron gate and found it chained shut.

"You shall do nothing," Sir Humphrey said, "unless it is to wait here in this gatehouse while I investigate."

"But the gate is locked."

Sir Humphrey began to bang his walking stick against the iron bars. "Finley! Open up right now! Finley, this is urgent—you must let me in."

The door to the gatehouse swung open, but it was the strong figure of Adrian Ruxley, not Dominic's short, wiry, Irish gatekeeper who appeared before them. "Quiet down, Sir Humphrey," he said as he approached the gate. "You're making enough racket to raise the dead."

Chloe met his confident gaze, her spirits lifting in hope. He looked so unconcerned. Did it mean Dominic was all right? Was his ordeal with Edgar finally over?

"Lord Wolverton," Sir Humphrey said in an urgent tone, "I do not think you would be standing there making jokes if you understood the gravity of the situation."

"I understand," Adrian said, his voice respectful.

Sir Humphrey subjected the man standing before him to a somber scrutiny. "Then why are you not with Stratfield at this very moment?"

Adrian removed a heavy brass key from his vest pocket. "I promised him I would not interfere."

"So did I," Chloe said in a barely audible voice. She gazed past him to the house. "But he seems to think he's bloody immortal," she murmured. "Just because he's come back once from the dead does not mean he can do it again. There is such a thing as tempting fate."

"It's different this time." Adrian regarded her closely. They both knew different aspects of Dominic, his strengths, and his vulnerabilities. "Dominic is not at the disadvantage. He's planned this engagement as carefully as Edgar planned his brutal murders."

Chloe tried to take comfort in what he said. There was something reassuring about Adrian's confidence in Dominic's ability. Perhaps it was a male attribute she did not understand. She wanted to share his faith and courage, but she was certain she would not take an easy breath until the moment she saw Dominic again with her own eyes.

The feeling returned to her that Adrian was a powerful ally, a man apart from others. He was athletically built, a mercenary who had fought fierce battles in foreign lands. His strong-featured face and dark blond hair would turn heads at any ball in London. He would draw admirers to his charismatic personality despite, perhaps even because of, the controversy that surrounded him.

Yet there was a gentleness to him that had nothing to do with his past. Chloe could see it in his appealing hazel eyes. A quality that balanced out the rumors of his dark history.

"I don't care what we promised him," she said as the gate swung open to admit her. "You have to at least make sure he doesn't need help. Edgar is a desperate man. He'll realize he has nothing to lose now that his treachery has been discovered. He'll fight to the death—"

"I made Stratfield no such promise," Sir Humphrey said in a decisive voice. "Move aside, Lord Wolverton. I am obligated to come to my neighbor's aid in times of crisis."

Adrian wavered, glancing back reflectively at the house before he stepped aside to let Sir Humphrey go through the gatehouse door. There was enough uncertainty in his gaze that Chloe's desire to intervene was reawakened. It wasn't over. Adrian would not look like that if it was.

"Be careful, Uncle Humphrey." Chloe's heart ached with love for him. Then, to Adrian, "I can't bear the thought of anything happening to either of them."

Adrian studied her for a few moments, then shook his head in defeat. "I will go to protect your uncle, but if Dominic thinks I broke my promise, I shall never hear the end of it."

"Thank you," Chloe said, staring past him at the house. Somehow she had to go inside, to be close by if Dominic needed help.

Adrian touched her wrist. "Finley is missing. He was supposed to guard the gatehouse, but he's been gone a little too long. I thought you and your uncle were him coming now."

She looked up into his face. "Perhaps I can find him."

"Dominic will not wish you to place yourself in danger."

"Nor would I," her uncle said feelingly. "I'd prefer that you wait inside the gatehouse."

"I shall be fine. Do what you must do."

Wait. No, she could not wait. Certainly not outside. She could at least locate Finley and send him to help. Not that she had a particular desire to come face-to-face with Edgar, to expose her part in this, but she'd be damned if he'd ever hurt anyone she loved again.

And she loved Dominic.

She began to run toward the house in her Sunday dress, up the stone entrance steps, into the dark oak-paneled hall. How still the place seemed. As empty and quiet as a burial vault.

"Finley?" she whispered, pivoting as she heard the front door creaking open.

There was no one behind her.

She edged toward the vast unlit fireplace and covertly bent to pick up a blackened poker from the hearth. "Who is it? Who's there?"

No answer.

She backed into the hall, stifling a gasp as she stepped

over a man's brown woolen cap on the carpet. She stared down, sickened, at the small pool of blood beside it.

It was a gamekeeper's cap. She could not look at it without seeing Finley's leathery features, his shock of red hair, his hesitant smile. What had happened to him? Had he been trying to help Dominic?

"Where are—" She felt a hard muscular force against her legs and whirled, the poker uplifted, to look down at the heavy tan hound sniffing the carpet.

"Ares, not you . . . yes, *you.* It was you at the door. Come along. Earn those sausages you've been eating. Help me find Dominic and Finley."

The dog led her down the hallway, around the corner, to the library. She could not see any more blood, but it occurred to her that there might be more than the one hiding place Dominic had shown her in the house.

The logical choice would be the library, where a man might spend hours alone and unobserved. The door was already opened. The room smelled pleasantly of brandy fumes and musty, old leather-bound books. It was a dark retreat, the heavy drapes closed against the daylight.

Papers lay scattered across the floor. A chair was overturned as if there had been a scuffle.

"Dominic?" she said in an undertone. "Finley, are you in here?"

She stared around the room. Ares pushed past her, his nose to the floor, picking up a scent.

"Find them," she said, gripping the poker in her gloved hands.

Not the fireplace, she thought. The dog moved right

past it without stopping. She watched him walk straight to a corner bookshelf, then disappear.

The panel gaped open. She followed the dog into the dark crevice, all her senses on the alert.

"Dominic?" she whispered, staring down into a musty black void.

A rough calloused hand closed around her ankle. She cried out, pitching forward with the poker, before she hit her shoulder on a beam and regained her balance.

Ares whined plaintively from the shadows. Below her, at the bottom of three wooden steps, a man moaned. She went down on her knees and pulled from his mouth the cravat that had been used to gag him.

"Finley," she said in horror as he lifted his battered face toward her. "What happened? Where is Lord Stratfield?"

"My knife is over there in the corner. Cut my hands and feet free so I can be of use. Sir Edgar found me snooping about and took me by surprise. It won't happen again."

She scrambled down the steps and felt around in the dirt for his knife. "Where is Lord Stratfield?"

"In the smugglers' vault. I sat here helpless and could hear him moving about. Hurry, Lady Chloe. Cut harder. Ye'll not hurt me."

Chapter 25

The two men, uncle and nephew, circled each other in the darkness, relying on their intuition, on training, on survival instinct. Over a decade had passed since they'd parried together in the salon, since they had chased ruffians through the streets of Soho for sport. The rules of correct swordplay neglected, they fenced relying on sheer reflex and physical strength. Once Dominic had struggled to impress his uncle with his fledging skill, hoping to earn a word of praise, a toast at the end of a lesson.

Now he fought with but a single goal, a fire that burned in his heart. To challenge the man he'd admired and who had betrayed their blood bond in the most coldhearted way imaginable.

He sensed, rather than saw, the moment when his uncle began to grow careless, to weary. Edgar had lunged in a move known as the final thrust; Dominic had deftly twisted his trunk to the right to protect himself, anticipating the strike.

"Not bad, Dominic," Edgar murmured, "but I have to ask, is this the best you can do?"

Edgar's blade came out of nowhere, slicing a thin layer of skin at the base of Dominic's throat. The heavy spill of lace of his highwayman's costume probably deflected a deeper cut.

At any rate, it caught Edgar off guard long enough for Dominic to balance for his own final thrust, ignoring the blood that trickled in a stinging rivulet down his throat.

Mercilessly he advanced, his body bent in a lunge. He could feel Edgar's desperation now, his realization that he was overpowered.

"You were always my favorite, Dominic," he said, his breathing uneven.

"Your favoritism sent me to hell."

"It isn't too late—"

Dominic did not hesitate. Positioning his left foot forward, he attacked. He felt his blade bury itself in skin, muscle, the tendon of Edgar's shoulder, heard the surprised curse that came from his uncle's throat. It was not a killing blow, but a disabling one. He stepped back, sweat burning his eyes, his arm lowering.

"For Samuel. For Brandon. The authorities can decide what to do with you now. You must answer for your other crimes. Be glad I did not murder you. I considered it."

He stood in absolute stillness to reflect on what had happened. He had wanted to kill Edgar. Something had stopped him at the last moment, a scrap of humanity left in his soul.

He heard a faint, unfamiliar disturbance from the heavy floorboards above. Edgar dropped his sword and staggered back into the bony arms of the skeleton chained to the wall. The impact of his fall wrenched one of the manacles from its rotted beam.

Dominic lit a candle and gazed dispassionately at the macabre scene. Edgar sagging to his knees, drawing the leering skeleton to the dirt with him. The sight sickened Dominic. All that had brought him to this moment sickened him. He had done what he had to do, and now he felt drained. He was desperate to escape.

He turned to the flight of steps, then paused at the peculiar noise that arose from behind. He glanced back, his gaze disbelieving.

As the skeleton swung free, there resounded the hollow clank of a chain being released inside the wall, followed by a rusty hinge snapping loose from the ceiling.

"A trap," he said, and watched in detached horror as a wooden platform poured a crushing load of stones upon Edgar's body. Dislodged chalk and mortar flew everywhere, filling the hole with billows of dust. It stung his eyes, clogged his nose as he hastened to flee for fear the whole damned vault would collapse.

The dust settled like a shroud on the scene below. The beams holding up the remaining walls seemed stable.

Edgar lay buried on the floor, crushed to death, his sword glinting in the dust. On the last step, Dominic slowed to bid his silent companion Baron Bones a final tribute.

"Well, we are both released at last, good friend, but it doesn't seem right to leave you in such an undignified pose. Not after we have shared so many confidences. At the very least you deserve a decent burial for listening so patiently to my tale of woe. It was what I promised you."

"That's where I come in." A shaft of light filtered down from the crevice cut into the wall; Finley stood peering down at his chalk-coated master with a relieved grin. "Looks as if you've a carcass that needs to be carried off, my lord."

Dominic glanced up in gratitude at the bruised face of his middle-aged Irish gamekeeper. "Finley, what perfect timing. Do be careful of the skeleton, won't you? The poor fellow has suffered long enough. As for my uncle, well, he is done inflicting pain."

Chapter 26

Chloe and Finley had just left the library when a deep rumbling came from within the walls of the house. It was an unnatural noise, the warning groan of hell being unleashed. Chloe's heart seemed to cease beating as she sprinted up the seemingly endless staircase to the long gallery, Finley overtaking her, Ares staying at her side.

They were not alone.

Behind her the servants of Stratfield Hall had just returned from church, their carts clattering through the open gate. In a matter of minutes they would resume their positions in the house. The housekeeper would put on her apron and ask Sir Edgar if he cared to take his luncheon in the dining hall or in his office.

Unless Sir Edgar's days of dining as a usurper at Dominic's table were done. Chloe did not pause to take a breath at the top of the staircase. Sunlight poured in through the glazed windows of the gallery. But the silence felt ominous, worse even than the rumbling that had preceded it. The entrance to Dominic's secret hiding place was wide open, dark and uninviting.

She rushed toward it.

She was not alone.

Behind her Dominic's well-trained servants, sensing something was amiss in the house, came surging up the staircase in a wave of indignant apprehension. Had the murderer struck again? Why else had the gatehouse door been left open, with Finley nowhere to be found?

Would they discover Sir Edgar stabbed to death in the same bed as their former master? The butler and footmen took command of the irregular army. The housemaids brought up the rear, wielding dusters and mops. And then an authoritative voice broke through the anxious whispering.

The small figure of Lady Dewhurst in a feathered bonnet and beaded pelisse shouldered a path straight to Chloe. Her daughter, Pamela, followed, panting for breath, accompanied by her bewildered-looking sweetheart, Charles.

"Aunt Gwendolyn!" Chloe said, steeling herself at the grim expression on the woman's face. This was not at all the way she wanted her aunt to find out the truth. "What are you doing here?"

Gwendolyn peered over Chloe's shoulder. "I should ask you and my husband the same thing. Where is the rascal?"

"Which rascal would that be?"

"Do not play innocent with me, young lady. I am not stupid. I asked Pamela what everyone was hiding from me, and that is why I am here."

Chloe glanced helplessly at Pamela, who had launched into another one of her indecipherable pantomimes behind her mother's back.

"You're here because . . . because . . . because I lent Pamela my scandalous corset?"

Aunt Gwendolyn swung around to study her daughter's figure. "What corset?"

Pamela shook her head. "I've no idea what anyone is talking about."

Chloe edged closer to the entrance of the hiding hole. Adrian, Finley, and her uncle would not have remained inside the vault all this time if Dominic were hurt.

Unless they were covering his body, tending his injuries. Unless they'd had to subdue Edgar, and . . . Chloe's head swam with unspeakable images. Dominic *would* prevail. He had the advantage this time over his uncle. He'd had weeks to prepare, to plan. He had promised to come back to her, and he was a man of his word if nothing else. He was determined, her devil, the other half of her wicked soul.

She went still at the heavy tread of a footstep from inside the hidden passage. She knew in her heart it was him. She spun around, her entire focus on the figure that emerged into the light.

For a frightening second she did not recognize him.

Her mouth opened on a soundless laugh. His tall, lean figure was coated in a heavy layer of white grainy dust. A ghostly shroud from top to bottom. His thick black hair, his eyebrows, his cheeks, the shoulders and sleeves of his lace-trimmed highwayman's shirt, the black knee breeches and jack boots.

But it was him, safe, whole, walking toward her while she stood transfixed by the sight, by what it meant.

"Dear God, have mercy!" a kitchen maid shrieked

from the bottom of the stairs. " 'Tis himself—the Strat-field Ghost!"

Aunt Gwendolyn put her arms around Pamela, the feathers on her bonnet quivering. Chloe covertly dropped the poker on the floor.

Silence engulfed the gallery. No one moved. No one dared to speak again. A smile broke across Chloe's face. Covered in that chalky film, he did indeed look like a ghost risen from the grave.

Then Dominic's mocking gaze found Chloe's face, the pure fire of passion and resolution smoldering in his gray eyes. She was not conscious of moving, of walking toward him. He had come back. He had kept his word, and suddenly all was well in the world again. Her mind began to function once more. Joy bubbled up inside her, fierce and cleansing. There were suddenly new problems to face, consequences to consider.

If she went to him, then everyone would know, would realize that they had been having a romantic relationship. Everyone would guess that she loved him, that the fast young lady from London had become embroiled in another scandal. That this time she had gotten involved in the worst, the most wicked trouble of her life.

And everyone would be right.

Dominic did not give Chloe the option of pretending they had not been lovers, of waiting until they were alone to hold her. He walked straight to where she stood and pulled her into his arms. He needed to feel her warmth, her approval, to reassure her that everything he had promised her would come to pass. She was staring up at his face in amazement, in relief, her beautiful blue eyes bright with tears.

"It's over," he said, and lowered his head to kiss her. "Marry me, Chloe Boscastle. Be my wife."

Lady Dewhurst and her daughter gasped in unison at this shocking development. The entire staff of Stratfield Hall, who apparently were still unsure whether Dominic was man or ghost, watched in speechless fascination.

Dominic did not pay any of them the least bit of notice. He was too intent on kissing the woman who had given him strength, the woman who had been the only reason he had survived for so long and kept his sanity.

"Chloe," he said, his large hands sculpting the delicate bones of her face. His touch was tender yet fiercely protective. He had been filled with admiration and concern when Finley explained how Chloe had found him in the library and released him, quick thinking and caring.

Dominic loved the wild stubborn side of Chloe, and he loved the part of her that was vulnerable and a little overwhelmed by life, that had gotten her into trouble. He was only sorry that he had not met her years ago, when he would have made a better impression on her family. Yes, winning over the tightly knit Boscastle clan was definitely his next monumental task. Perhaps it would be his hardest feat ever.

"Dominic," she whispered against his mouth, "don't you dare ever put me through anything like this again."

He laughed, his voice low and husky. "I don't think there's any chance of that."

Her blue eyes sparkled with embarrassed amusement. "You do realize we have an audience?"

He glanced up briefly, only then realizing what he

must look like to the stunned crowd of onlookers in the gallery. "Carson, don't stand there gaping like a carp. Fetch me some bathwater and a fresh change of clothes."

The astonished footman blinked. "But . . . but . . . you . . ."

"They think you're still a ghost," Chloe whispered, trying to stifle a giggle.

Dominic smiled down at her, pulling her harder against his lean body. "I don't suppose I could fool them long enough to get us both out of here without having to explain myself?"

Chloe glanced at her aunt from the corner of her eye. "It doesn't appear to be a good possibility." She hesitated. "Where is my uncle? And Adrian?"

Dominic tenderly framed her face in his hands. His gaze absorbed every detail of her features. He had lived for this moment, to return openly to this headstrong woman he loved. The passionate relief in her eyes was all the reward he needed, the proof that everything had been worthwhile.

Now it was his turn to protect her, to court her in a more befitting manner and prove to her he could be very human indeed.

"Chloe," he said gently, placing his hands on her shoulders. "I should like to go on kissing you forever and send these people away, but it looks as if by coming back to life I shall have to take up all those gentlemanly pretensions again."

She sighed as they moved apart. "If you must."

He straightened his shoulders. Now that his ordeal was over, it would be a physical ache even to let her out of his sight. He had watched his enemy die, and perhaps he should have felt more remorse. Certainly he hoped he would never have to look such evil in the face again, but confronting Edgar had been the only way he could live with himself and honor his brother's memory. He could go on now. He wanted to put what had happened out of his mind, to concentrate on the good in his life, on Chloe.

He looked away from her pale face with regret. Her aunt was regarding him with a rather menacing expression. Adrian and Sir Humphrey had just emerged from the hiding hole, brushing dust off their clothing and discussing, of all things, the political situation in China. Finley followed, carrying the cloaked skeleton in his arms, a sight that evoked another collective gasp of horror from the people gathered in the gallery.

Dominic suppressed the urge to throw back his head and laugh. How would he explain what had happened to the village? He had not thought this far ahead. He could just imagine the rumors that would start to fly about the Stratfield Ghost, his bony companion, and the notorious young lady from London who had loved him.

"Stop it," Chloe whispered, biting her lip.

"Stop what?" he asked.

"Stop that . . . that grinning."

"I wasn't grinning."

"Yes, you were."

"I was trying not to laugh."

Aunt Gwendolyn, apparently recovered from her bewilderment, had taken it upon herself to confront Dominic. "Well, my lord, you show yourself at last, appearing a good deal more down to earth than when I last saw you."

He looked genuinely contrite. "I assure you, Lady Dewhurst, that there is an explanation."

"There will have to be."

Chloe put her hand on her aunt's arm. "Aunt Gwendolyn, please understand, we never meant to deceive you."

"Deceive me? What are you talking about?"

Chloe lowered her voice. The butler had pulled himself together enough to order the staff to resume their duties, but a few servants still lingered on the staircase, casting mortified looks at the skeleton in Finley's arms.

"What I mean," Chloe said in an undertone, "was how we allowed you to believe that Dom—er, Lord Stratfield—was a ghost that night in the garden."

"A ghost?" Aunt Gwendolyn said, scoffing. "I never believed it for a minute."

"What gave me away?" Dominic demanded, his voice warm as he addressed the older woman.

Aunt Gwendolyn narrowed her eyes. "Yes, I believed it at first, but then the next day I noticed there were big footprints around my mint garden. No one in my house is allowed to pick my herbs under penalty of death. Suddenly I remembered how you had always enjoyed chewing mint leaves, my lord."

Dominic grinned again.

"I decided not to give you away," Aunt Gwendolyn added, "although if I had known you were involved with my niece, I would not have been so understanding."

Dominic graced her with his most charming smile. "Then I am forgiven for my little masquerade?"

Aunt Gwendolyn did not return his smile. "I have not

forgiven you anything yet, my lord. In fact, it remains to be seen exactly what and how much I am expected to forgive, and even if I decide to forgive you, it does not absolve you of your responsibility to Chloe's family, and the matter of whether they choose to forgive you." She paused to take a breath. "Assuming of course there is anything to forgive, which by the look of the kiss you just gave my niece, I assume there is."

"Oh, goodness," Chloe said, realizing that the road ahead would be challenging.

Dominic's grin faded. "I am not exactly sure what you just said, madam, but I *assume* it does not bode well for me."

Lady Dewhurst directed a stern look at her niece. "This is not something we should discuss in public. You will come home with us right now, Chloe, so that your uncle and I can decide what to do with you."

Dominic straightened, his eyes darkening. "What do you mean?"

"I mean," Gwendolyn said, "that her future is for her family to decide."

"Then I request the right to be included in the decision," Dominic said.

"Might I voice an opinion?" Chloe asked in irritation.

"Not in public," her aunt retorted. "I do not think the world is ready for your opinions yet."

Dominic almost smiled at that, but refrained, not wishing Chloe's aunt to think him disrespectful. "Forgive me, madam," he said, "but my ability to follow the rules of polite society has grown rusty during my . . . retreat. Of course there is a proper protocol to follow in these matters."

Of which he knew absolutely nothing. He had never been wildly in love before. He had never been so absolutely besotted with a young woman to the point that he would cheerfully endure a public tongue-lashing, that he would go down on his knees to plead for her. And he had never become romantically involved with a Boscastle princess. Heaven knew what that entailed.

Yes, he had known there would be repercussions, consequences to becoming her lover. He was prepared to face them. He had just rather conveniently pushed the thought to the back of his mind. It was now time to polish off all his noble pretensions and resume his former life. He could no longer climb into Chloe's bedroom or whisk her away from balls to love her senseless.

It was going to be harder than he'd realized.

For one thing, he was not willing to relinquish her for even one day.

For another, he did not want to give her family a chance to investigate his behavior, to decide he was not a desirable match for her. Chloe could well be carrying his child. He wanted to pamper and protect her, to start life over with her as his wife.

Simply put, his resolve had found a new challenge, and he could only hope he was as successful at playing a suitor as he had been a ghost.

Chloe felt so relieved to have found Dominic safe that she did not even demur as her aunt hustled her and Pamela out of the gallery. Her last wistful glance at her lover was of his helping Finley lay Baron Bones on the Turkey carpet. Who but a man who'd been believed dead would form a friendship with the remains of another who had died in such a horrible manner?

It was a rather poignant and ridiculous sight, Dominic respectfully placing the skeleton in a peaceful pose, then looking up to wink at her. She and Pamela had started to giggle, a little irreverently, which seemed to give Aunt Gwendolyn the impression they'd become hysterical at the sight of the cloaked skeleton.

"What a dreadful thing to see on a Sunday morning!" the woman exclaimed. "In my day, a young lady would never have been exposed to such horror."

Chloe and Pamela grinned at each other as they were shepherded down the stairs. Chloe could have pointed out that her aunt had dared to confront a very troublesome ghost and had thought nothing of it. That Boscastle streak of stubborn bravery apparently ran through everyone in the family, male and female, young and old.

"Thank you, Aunt Gwendolyn," she said on impulse as they reached the carriage waiting outside. All of a sudden Chloe realized how lovely, how enchanting Dominic's estate appeared when viewed in the sunlight. The gardens offered a variety of hidden arbors and splashing fountains, shady walkways and even a maze in which children could play endless games.

"Thank me for what?" Aunt Gwendolyn asked suspiciously as she straightened her bonnet.

"For your wonderful hospitality, for allowing me to stay at your house, for giving me the chance to reform myself."

Aunt Gwendolyn harrumphed. "Stop it, Chloe. I am not the fool you and your uncle assume me to be. You are no more reformed than that poor devil Stratfield."

"Are you angry at me, Aunt Gwendolyn?" Chloe asked innocently.

Aunt Gwendolyn scowled. "I shall leave anger to your brothers, who will probably never speak to me again after they learn about what has happened in my house."

Pamela glanced at Chloe in protective sympathy. "Do we really have to tell them anything?"

"I do not see how we can avoid the inevitable," her mother replied.

Chloe did not see how either, although she racked her brain during the short ride home. Naturally the whole world would soon know that Dominic was not dead. His story would become a sensation in London, and the part she had played would be the making of another scandal.

Yes, she realized that she would have to face the inevitable sooner or later, but she did not expect to find the inevitable waiting for her in the parlor, in the intimidating form of her older brother Heath.

She should have guessed one of her male siblings had arrived by the presence of every maid in the house pretending to tidy the parlor while he sat perusing an outdated newspaper. From an objective point of view, Chloe could see the attraction. He was an arresting figure, well muscled, elegant, and unfailingly polite. His chiseled features and heavily lashed blue eyes melted female hearts on a regular basis.

But to Chloe he was simply Heath, the most enigmatic member of the family, and, presumably, her judge and jury. And there he sat, as silently awe-inspiring, as immovable and inscrutable as the Sphinx at Giza.

"Chloe." He laid down his paper and rose from his chair to regard her, hands clasped behind his back.

Chloe's heart began to thunder. Did he know? How *much* did he know? Was he angry? How angry? Those deep blue eyes of his never revealed anything unless he allowed it. His superior officer had once said one could apply hot coals to the soles of Heath's feet and his expression would not change, which reminded Chloe he had been tortured while he was briefly imprisoned by the French.

"This is a surprise, Heath."

"Yes. Surprises seem to be in the air lately, don't they?" He turned, cast a fleeting smile at the bevy of maids and said, "I do appreciate your diligence, but would you please return at another time? I should like some privacy with Lady Chloe."

Chloe felt a chill as the room emptied, the maids crestfallen but obedient. "Surprises?" she said, determined not to let him undo her.

"I know, Chloe."

"You know . . ."

He motioned her to the sofa, his voice even, his manner so composed she wanted to hit him with a bookend. "Tell me how it happened."

"How did what happen?"

He smiled faintly. "Did I mention that I just spent a very enjoyable—and enlightening, if short—meeting with an old friend of mine? Lord Wolverton. I believe you have met."

"I believe he is fond of Dominic."

His smile widened. "Yes. Aren't we all? Our dear resurrected Dominic. So, tell me, how did it happen?" He settled back in his chair. "Sit down, Chloe. You look quite uncomfortable standing there. Sit down and explain the situation to me."

She steeled herself. "I came to the country. I fell in love with a viscount, and I expect we shall be married if Grayson does not banish me again or frighten him away. What else is there to know?"

"Oh, there's his sneaking in and out of my sister's room for a start. Your disappearing from a ball with a mysterious masked guest. Consorting with"—Heath threw up his hands in exasperation—"with a ghost."

"Well," Chloe said. This was the most volatile display Heath had shown anyone in ages. Perhaps in his entire life. Probably that, more than anything, was what had her worried. "It all sounds so much worse than it actually—"

"How did you manage it, Chloe?" Heath asked, lifting a dark brow. "I am truly amazed at your ability to seek out the most compromising situations imaginable. Do you stay awake at night plotting trouble?"

"How insulting."

"I am serious, Chloe."

"When are you not?"

"How on earth did you manage to ruin yourself so completely in such a short time?"

She flung herself down in a chair, resigned to her fate. "Fine. I shall tell all. My original sin was to leave my window open for Devon to climb in."

"And?"

"And? Dominic climbed in instead."

"And?"

"I felt sorry for him?"

"You felt sorry for him," Heath repeated slowly. "Is that all there is to it?"

"Hmm. There might have been a little more."

"A little more?" Heath contemplated a spot on the ceiling. "Heaven help me. Now I know what Grayson was complaining about before he got married. This family is careening down the road to ruin. You, Devon, and who can guess what Drake is up to? How much more, Chloe? To what extent have you become involved with Stratfield?"

"I'm not entirely sure what you mean."

"I'm entirely sure you do."

"I really don't."

"Perhaps the journey back to London will refresh your memory."

"London? But why? Aunt Gwendolyn could use my company here what with her fund-raising and— I have no new clothes." She had almost run out of excuses. "The Season will almost be over before I have a decent wardrobe made."

"Life as you have known it may well be over, my dear," Heath said unsympathetically.

"What are you suggesting in that ghastly tone of voice?"

"Your stay in Chistlebury was meant to be a retreat from temptation."

Chloe watched as Ares nosed open the door and stared up at her, wagging his tail for a walk. "And so it was. Buried in Chistlebury. That's what my friends thought."

"For God's sake, Chloe."

"I don't think I like the way you said that, Heath."

He leaned forward to watch the hound waddle into

the room and collapse at Chloe's feet. "I was the neutral vote when your exile was decided. I believed you were serious about reform."

"I was. Honestly, Heath, none of this was my fault."

"Was it Stratfield's fault? Should I call him out? Friend or not, if he has wronged you, he shall pay."

Chloe went down on her knees to draw Ares to her.

She wondered if Dominic would mind eloping to avoid facing her family. He might not appreciate the excitement so soon after his own drama, but then he had no idea how excruciating it was to be the subject of a Boscastle Inquisition.

"I should like at least another week here, Heath, to say my farewells to the friends I have made."

"No," he said, his voice unequivocable.

She stared at him. "Why not?"

"Because in a week you'll have gotten yourself into another scandal."

"I don't see how."

"I don't either; it doesn't seem possible, but the fact is that you will." He paused, frowning down at the floor. "That dog is enormous, Chloe. Someone needs to put him on a slimming regime and give him regular exercise."

"I have to pack my things," she murmured.

"Your belongings are in the process of being packed as we speak. The carriage will come for us tomorrow."

She stood up, her hands on her hips. "I cannot leave Dominic without telling him where I'm going."

Heath remained unmoved. "Dominic is a capable man and may visit you, in a proper manner, whenever he desires. If he wants to find you, he will do so. I shall inform him of our decision."

"Did Adrian explain to you that Dominic risked his life to destroy the man who killed Brandon and Samuel? Doesn't his bravery count for anything at all?"

"I would have helped him. Every one of us would have helped him. He did not have to play the hero alone."

"Are you saying that the only way he may see me is by asking your permission?"

"Precisely," Heath said. "If he will not submit to the rules of Society, he will at least submit to our family wishes."

Chloe groaned inwardly at the thought of Dominic submitting to anything. "For your information he's already asked me to marry him, and I've accepted without any reservations."

Heath leaned back in his chair, his long frame relaxed. "How nice for you, Chloe. Now let us give Dominic the chance to impress the rest of your family and see whether *we* shall accept him." He smiled. "Without any reservations."

Chloe spent her last night in Chistlebury in her empty dressing closet, gazing out the window at Dominic's estate. The house was brightly lit in celebration. Guests had been coming and going all day, some in expensive carriages, others on horseback. She wondered whether his past lover Lady Turleigh had been one of the recent arrivals, and how Dominic would react if she appeared at his door, contrite and begging his understanding.

Chloe hoped the woman would take one look at Baron Bones and run screaming into the woods.

A clod of dirt hit the window.

Startled, she leaned over the sill and looked outside, whispering hopefully, "Dominic?"

The man standing below dropped the handful of dirt he had been about to pitch. "No. It's Justin."

"Justin?" She peered down at the fair-haired figure lurking under the tree. "What on earth are you doing here? How did you get past Heath's guard?"

"One of the servants felt sorry for me and sneaked me around the garden." He stepped into the moonlight. "Pamela told me you were leaving in the morning, Chloe. I wanted to say that I'm sorry for everything."

She sighed. He was rather sweet in his own annoying way. "I'm sorry, too, Justin."

He looked unsure of what to say next. "What are you going to do in London?"

"Be miserable and repent for all my sins."

"I'd ask you to marry me, but my parents have another match in mind."

"Oh." Chloe hoped she sounded disappointed. She saw no reason to tell him she wouldn't accept his reluctant proposal if he offered it to her on a silver platter. "I suppose we'll both recover over time." He appeared so relieved to be excused that easily that she ached to laugh out loud.

"I suppose we will. In a few years, perhaps."

A few minutes seemed more likely.

He glanced over his shoulder in the direction of Dominic's estate, lowering his voice. "You'd wonder if it was the Lord who'd come back to life for all the people visiting Stratfield." He hesitated. "I think he ought to marry you."

"I think so, too, if my awful family doesn't interfere."

Another voice joined the conversation, deep, cultured, amused. "Your awful family is going to interfere again, I'm afraid. Lord St. John, I am Chloe's brother. Would you mind removing yourself from the premises immediately?"

Justin flushed a deep red. "Of course, my lord. I only wanted to say good-bye. I did not mean any disrespect to your family. I—"

"Good night, Lord St. John," Heath said, his pleasant voice underlaid with steel. "A shame we had not met under more . . . appropriate circumstances."

Chloe drummed her fingertips on the sill as Justin made a hasty escape, stammering apologies with each step. So began her restricted life again.

"Juliet," Heath called up with a grin, "I suggest you get some sleep before our journey tomorrow."

Chloe woke up in the middle of the night and gazed around the room. All her belongings had been packed into her trunks, with the exception of her journal, which she would not allow anyone to touch, and her corset.

She had bequeathed the scandalous garment to her cousin Pamela.

She lit a candle and opened the journal to the page marked with a red ribbon on which she had copied Brandon's partial letter. In the past few days she had been unable to concentrate on it, despite the fact that she had come close to breaking the code he had used.

Suddenly, in the stillness, without even trying, inspiration came. The words were clear, horribly so. She took out her pen and slowly began the translation.

> *. . . and so in closing I have enough faith that you will do what must be done. Pray God we will not be dead before this finds you. In this land of brutal beauty death comes as swiftly as a shadow. In any event, I trust that your cunning will save you, for he means to kill you and I do not know when or by what means. Use the information revealed above.*
>
> Brandon

Chloe closed the book, her throat aching. She could hear Brandon's voice. She could feel his spirit as intensely as she had in life.

"A warning, Brandon," she whispered. "I'm afraid it came too late."

The following morning she awakened early and dressed, leaving the room with the copied letter in her hand. She found Heath in the parlor, reading a book on Egyptian artifacts.

"This is a copy of a partial letter found in Brandon's belongings. Dominic has the original, encoded, in his possession."

Heath frowned as he scanned the paper. "You did this?"

"Yes."

"Does Dominic know what it says?"

Chloe shook her head. "I think we should show it to him before we leave."

"I shall send this to him right away." He looked up at her. "By messenger, Chloe."

"Tyrant." She watched as he folded the paper and put it into his pocket. "What do you think?"

"I would like to see the rest of it before I make a judgment."

Chapter 27

Dominic had risen early the next day to write some desperately overdue letters to his solicitors and personal contacts in London. Edgar had already run through a great deal of Dominic's money, ordering furnishings for what he assumed would be his new home and for his existing sugar plantation in Antigua, as well as his holdings in India. Dominic's secretary would have on his hands a hell of a mess to untangle.

Business affairs were actually the last thing he cared about. After breakfast and a shave, he intended to go straight to Dewhurst Manor to visit Chloe, and not by climbing in her window either. He would present himself formally on her doorstep. He had hoped to see her last night, but a parade of well-wishers had descended on him, and he had been obliged to welcome them.

He hoped Chloe was not planning a grand wedding. He was done with waiting for what he wanted, and what he wanted was her as his wife. Convincing her family of his credibility was another matter.

He put down his pen as his footman appeared at the office door. "I sent the message to Dewhurst Manor as you requested, my lord, but Sir Humphrey said he regrets the young lady is gone."

Dominic came out of his chair, his heavy eyebrows knitting into a frown. "Gone? As in gone to the village? Gone for a walk?"

"She's apparently been taken to London, my lord."

"London? Did she leave word for me?"

"Not that I know. But her brother did, and I have been instructed to give this to you." He handed Dominic a sealed letter. "Shall I wait to send a reply?"

"To London? No. Go, please."

He opened the note, his instincts preparing him for bad news.

Dominic,

The last time I saw you, or thought I saw you, was at your funeral. While I congratulate you on your resurrection, I condemn your seduction of my sister. Let us meet again, on my turf and on my terms.

By the way, I am enclosing the partial letter from Brandon which my sister has decoded. What an industrious pair you and she have been in uneventful Chistlebury.

I trust there are no more surprises in store for any of us.

H

With a rueful smile Dominic unfolded the enclosed letter, the translation of Brandon Boscastle's code, and read it. It was an unmistakable warning, and he could not help wondering whether it had been meant for Samuel, himself, or someone else.

Presumably, with Edgar dead, it no longer mattered. In any event, Dominic had a more pressing problem on his mind—an unplanned trip to London to face his final judgment.

He was surprised to find himself slipping back so easily into the role of gentleman. There was comfort in the rituals and traditions of his old life, and knowing the order of things. In fact, he rather looked forward to the whole rigmarole of ton society and its frivolities. Temporarily, that is. He would always remain a rebel at heart, a private man who preferred the companionship of a few true friends to an overcrowded party. He decided he should be grateful that the most fashionable set had not yet learned he was alive.

Still, for the present, here in London, it was time to put his aristocratic pretensions to the test, as rusty as they might be. He'd never had to prove himself to an entire family before, and what an intimidating family to have to impress. He had no idea how he would explain his brief sojourn in hell without sounding insane, and how Chloe had helped him escape. Her brothers deserved the truth, would demand it of him, and he did not intend to lie.

He only hoped he could persuade the Boscastle clan to focus on the future he had planned, and not on one violent chapter of his past.

He was led through the spacious corridors of the Marquess of Sedgecroft's Park Lane mansion and into a private study where, his back to the door, Grayson Boscastle sat behind an enormous rosewood desk. Grayson had always seemed to be a gregarious, charismatic man, whose rakish tendencies had apparently been subdued by marriage to Lady Jane Welsham.

Grayson raised his head the moment Dominic appeared at the door. There was nothing gregarious about his openly hostile expression, and the manner in which he uncoiled his large frame like a lion about to attack.

"Stratfield," he said, his blue eyes as friendly as a frozen lake.

"How are you, Sedgecroft?"

"Considerably better than you, it seems."

Ah, Dominic thought in grim amusement, as he glanced around the room at Heath and his fair-haired sister Emma strategically positioned in matching chairs that flanked Grayson's desk. This must be what Chloe meant about the Spanish Inquisition. He wondered when they would bring out the thumbscrews. Look at the three of them. A man would confess to seducing the pope under their basilisk scrutiny.

"Where are Drake and Devon?" he wondered aloud. "Stretching the rack to accommodate me or trying on executioners' robes?"

"They are standing guard outside the door," Grayson replied in a crisp voice, his long fingers tapping the desktop.

"In case anyone tries to enter the torture chamber or I escape?"

"Both. Either."

He found himself more at ease than he expected. Perhaps, after his recent ordeal, there was little left to rattle him. Perhaps he desired Chloe enough to walk through fire to win her. Or rather the firing squad, he thought wryly. The resentment toward him that smoldered in this room could burn down the whole of London.

"Lady Lyons, I believe," he murmured, bowing to Emma. "It is my pleasure to meet you at last." He turned to regard the elegantly poised black-haired man on his left. "And how are you, Heath?"

Grayson continued to glare at him, his firm mouth pursed as if he were refraining from making a rude remark. Emma, a very delicate woman with strawberry-blond hair, cleared her throat, fussed with her shawl, then skewered him with the most unsettling look he had ever received in his life. It was a combination of a schoolmistress's fondness and severe disappointment, as if a favored student had done something unspeakably wicked, and she did not quite know how to react.

And Heath, his friend, or was it *former* friend now, regarded him levelly, those Boscastle blue eyes cutting straight to his very soul.

Not much friendly warmth there today. Not murderous anger either, but rather an impartial assessment that left Dominic unsure of where he stood.

"Heath," he said again, breaking the silence that was undoubtedly part of the torture process to wear down his defenses, "it has been a long time."

Heath lifted his brow. "Rather too long it seems. You have been a busy boy since we conducted business at the warehouses on the wharves. Getting yourself killed, haunting your own house, not to mention your dramatic resurrection—"

"And ruining our sister," Grayson interjected, clearly impatient with Heath's wry commentary.

Emma's polite voice offered another perspective. "And,

lest we forget, bringing to justice the man who murdered Brandon and Samuel. They gave their lives trying to catch a traitor. Dominic risked his to finish the job."

"Thank you, Emma," Heath murmured. "It certainly portrays Dominic in a different aspect than that of a mere rake and villain, doesn't it? Dominic, I have explained the details of Brandon's murder as I understand them to the family. It was a little more challenging to explain the part that you and Chloe played in this affair."

There was a deep hush. The long case clock in the corner on lion-clawed feet chimed the hour. Grayson looked away as if he were struggling to hold his feelings in check. Only Heath maintained his steady gaze on Dominic's face as if weighing the situation.

"You might have involved us," Grayson muttered. "We would have helped."

"Without involving Chloe," Emma said in distress. "Goodness, what if something dreadful had happened to her? What if this mad Welshman had gotten his hands on her when she was alone?"

Dominic's eyes flashed with emotion. They had no idea how deeply their accusations wounded him. Of how he and Adrian had kept Chloe under their constant scrutiny, practically to the point of obsession. And if even once he had suspected that Edgar intended to harm her, Dominic would have revealed himself and ended his game. Fortunately, her own instincts had kept her from taking any rash chances. He owed her so much, loved her so deeply.

"Never would I have put Chloe in any danger. I did not set out to involve her in my plans. But once I met her . . ." He shrugged helplessly, and thought he saw a glimmer of amused sympathy in Heath's eyes. How could he possibly explain that he had been unable to resist Chloe from the start? In those early days of his recuperation, he had been half animal at heart, acting on only the most primal instincts of survival and revenge. Perhaps if he hadn't met Chloe, he would never have recovered from his pain and rage. It was unthinkable that she would be punished for her part in his redemption.

"I don't know how it happened, but I am prepared to accept full responsibility. Chloe did nothing wrong."

Grayson snorted. "And snowflakes do not melt in the sun. Listen, Stratfield, Chloe was sent to Chistlebury to behave herself. Compared to the scandal in which the pair of you are embroiled, her original crime of being kissed behind a parked carriage looks laughably innocent."

"Then perhaps it was an overreaction to send her into exile in the first place," Heath said in a thoughtful voice.

At that moment the door opened. Grayson's wife, Jane, the Marchioness of Sedgecroft, took a few steps into the room. Her honey-colored hair was drawn back from her face in a frame of soft waves. "Is this a closed conspiracy, or can anyone join in?"

"Do come in, Jane," Heath said, rising with Grayson to greet her.

She gave Dominic a warm smile, almost as if she sympathized with his position. "Be forewarned, all of you. I am taking Chloe's side."

"Without knowing all the facts?" her husband challenged her.

"That's right," Jane said, unruffled by his stern demeanor. "I am supporting her on general principle alone."

She directed a mock frown at the handsome marquess. "As well as on my past experience with the devious ways of its senior member. That would be you, Grayson."

"My darling devil's advocate," Grayson said, his own look for her warm and admiring.

"Someone has to bring a sense of fair play to this family," Jane said.

"I always play fairly," Heath said with a laugh.

Emma glanced over at him. "In both love and war?"

"I don't believe Heath has ever been in love," Grayson said offhandedly. "Have you, Heath?"

Heath directed an enigmatic smile around the room. "My private affairs, or lack of them, are not the purpose of this meeting. Do have a chair, Dominic. There's no point in pretending we are going to do you physical harm."

"Why not?" Grayson asked darkly.

Jane walked over to her husband's desk. "Because he loves Chloe, and she loves him, and I suspect their association has progressed beyond your control." Her voice was gentle and more than a little understanding. "Am I correct, Dominic?"

He smiled at her. "Lady Sedgecroft, you have looked into my heart."

Grayson made a face. "Well, it's damned lucky for you I didn't remove it. Sit down at the desk, Stratfield, and have a drink. My secretary will be here with the contract in an hour. Heath wishes to discuss some details regarding Sir Edgar when the two of you are alone."

Dominic felt as if the weight of the world had been lifted off his shoulders. Of course he did not want to sit. He wanted to see Chloe. He wanted to take her to his town house, so much smaller and less impressive than this mansion, but far more intimate for the purpose he had in mind. The anxiety he had felt for her throughout their ordeal had lessened, but had not gone away completely. He would always want to keep Chloe in his sight. Some of the fears he had developed would probably stay with him for the rest of his life.

There was no denying that his experience had changed him as a man. He could only hope it was for the better. Certainly having Chloe as his wife was a vast improvement over his past life. Where was she now? Had they punished her? Made her feel ashamed of what she had done? He could not bear the thought of being apart from her. She had to be hidden away in this house somewhere. He glanced up at the high plastered ceiling, knowing that if Chloe had her way, she would be listening to this conversation with her ear to the floor.

He smiled at the thought.

"Where is she?" he asked Grayson.

"Resting in her room," the marquess answered.

"When may I see her?"

Grayson shrugged. "As soon as the contract is signed— I don't suppose I could stop either of you anyway."

Chapter 28

Chloe had dozed off fully dressed across the four-poster bed. She had been too restless to sleep the night before, too hopeful that Dominic would stage a last-minute rescue from the fate of returning to face her family.

When she had finally gotten out of bed at dawn, she had curled up in her chaise and listened to the sounds of London stirring. Carts and hackneys rattling over cobbles, cows being led to market, the chatter of street vendors setting up their wares, merchants calling to one another. The wonderful chaos of the city, her city, and yet . . . well, who would have thought she could miss her dreary village this much?

She had dressed and fallen into an exhausted sleep after the maid brought up her tea and a mountain of letters from old friends and admirers. An hour or so later she opened her eyes to find Heath, Drake, Devon, and Grayson seated around the four-poster, waiting patiently for her to awaken.

She slid up against the pillows and stared up at each of their handsome faces in turn. So similar and yet distinctly different. She sighed. "There are four corners to my bed. There are four devils at my head."

Heath laughed. "Devils who care about you, I might add."

"And this devil does not like being excluded from your confidence," Devon added gently.

She turned her face into the pillow. "Devils or angels, does it matter? There should have been five of you."

Brandon, she meant. The adventure-seeking sibling they had lost and only now could properly be mourned. There was healing in the truth, no matter how painful it had been to face. The family could take pride in Brandon's bravery. The missing pieces of his young life could be put into place and contemplated. His death had been unfair, but at least they understood why it had happened, who to blame. Together last night they had discussed Brandon's coded letter, his dedication, and had vowed he would not be forgotten.

"I want to go back," she said, glancing at each of her brothers again.

Drake shook his head. "Chistlebury will never be the same. The papers are already talking about it."

"I'll never be the same either," Chloe said. "Has Dominic arrived yet?"

"I think," Grayson said carefully, "that it might be a good idea if you did not see him for a month or"—he stopped cold at the look of panic in Chloe's eyes—"or not. I had no idea you felt this strongly about him."

"Isn't passion a family trait?" she asked, challenging him.

Grayson shook his head. "I cannot deny that, but

Chloe, do you not think that you should at least follow our advice for once in regard to your admirers?"

"You have made a few poor choices in the past," Drake added, his blue eyes more mirthful than admonishing.

"Her very first-time love was our old butler," Devon said in amusement. "The poor fellow could hardly polish the silver without Chloe hanging on his legs."

"Emma wants you to meet one of your most ardent admirers in the garden," Grayson said in a gentle voice. "He's—"

Chloe sat up straighter. "No. Absolutely not. No admirers."

"He's an old family friend," Grayson finished. "Yes, we know you prefer your darling Stratfield Ghost, but this man—"

"He's old," Chloe said. "You want me to marry a relic. He's really old."

Drake grinned. "Ancient."

"Practically one of them Egyptian mummies," Devon said with a sly grin. "He's brought all his vital organs along in jars."

Chloe scowled at their four grinning faces. "What color are his eyes?"

Heath shrugged his broad shoulders. "It was hard to tell behind those thick spectacles."

"At least he has all his teeth," Grayson said.

Drake nodded. "Indeed. He was complaining about how much it cost to have them made."

"Is Chloe ready to come downstairs yet?" Jane called from the doorway, apparently unaware of the conversation inside the room.

Chloe slid her feet to the floor. "Would you help me pack, Jane? I'm running away. I shall send you my address when I know it. If Dominic can be bothered to find me, I shall wait a reasonable time for him to fetch me."

Jane swept into the room, appearing not at all intimidated by the four handsome men grinning at her, one of whom was her husband. "What is she talking about? Have I missed something?"

"The elderly suitor in the garden," Drake replied, struggling to appear serious.

"What elderly suitor?" Jane asked, looking baffled.

"The one I helped to the garden bench." Grayson winked at her. "The one whose hand shook when he signed the marriage contract."

Jane stared at him. "The one—oh, Grayson, do grow up." She took Chloe's hand. "Do you remember what happened in Brighton?"

"When my hideously evil brother Grayson tricked you into thinking he wanted to make you his mistress? Yes, I remember. I daresay it was an experience I shall never forget."

"And I had only one true friend at the time, a woman with the courage to risk her family's anger by telling me the truth."

Chloe sighed.

"Yes," Jane continued, "it was *you,* and now I shall repay the favor—there is no elderly suitor waiting for you in the garden. It is your Dominic."

"Dominic, in the garden?" Chloe ran to the window and pushed aside the heavy damask curtains. "I don't see him anywhere. Is he in one piece?" She turned to her brothers in panic. "What did you do to him?"

Heath rose from his chair. "Let us just say he won't be giving the family any trouble again."

"You've given us all we can handle," Grayson said bluntly.

Chloe broke into a jubilant grin. Her Dominic was here, downstairs. She felt weepy and joyful. "Oh, look at the pot calling the kettle black." She glanced at herself in the mirror, then bent to slip on her shoes. She was too happy to care about what they thought, too intent on finding Dominic to stay angry at their silly prank. They would not have been her brothers if they hadn't teased her. Poor Dominic. Now he'd had a taste of the torture she had endured—and inflicted—for years.

She stopped at the door, giving Jane an impulsive hug. "Wait a minute. Did one of you mention a marriage contract?"

"I don't know," Heath said. "Did we?"

"Just go," Jane urged her.

Devon called after Chloe as she left the room. "At least we did not frighten him off. That's a good sign, I'd say."

Chloe burst into peals of laughter, lifting the overskirt of her peach silk gown to race down the stairs.

Emma met her halfway up. "Good heavens, Chloe. Decorum, please. That handsome man in the garden does not wish to be mown down by the woman he intends to marry."

Chloe laughed again, her heart lighter than it had been in ages. "Decorum? I shall give the lot of you decorum."

Chapter 29

The sight of Dominic standing alone in the garden stole her breath away. England being England, it had started to sprinkle, and raindrops spangled his crisp black hair and the shoulders of his charcoal single-breasted tail coat. He turned when he heard her footsteps on the gravel. He looked relieved, his gaze holding hers.

For a moment neither of them moved. Chloe was struck by how compelling he was in his tight gray pantaloons and black Hessian boots. Every inch the gentleman? Well, not quite. There was a very ungentlemanly side to this man, several inches of barbarian if the truth be told, and Chloe was not entirely sure he had laid all his demons to rest.

But he reminded her of the man she had fallen in love with on that first rainy day. He was real, and she was more convinced than ever that no one like him existed in the entire world.

She tried to slow her pace as she approached him. She really did try to show some decorum. But the problem was—her fatal flaw had always been—her inability to be demure, and in the end she ran into his outstretched arms and laughed with sheer abandon as he swept her effortlessly into the air.

He kissed her face, her neck, his fingers brushing through her short dark curls. "Chloe, for a few minutes, I was afraid you wouldn't come. I thought you'd changed your mind."

She stared up at his masculine face. He had put back on the weight he'd lost, but he still looked a little dangerous and intense . . . until he smiled, his gray eyes both mocking and tender. "I was waiting for you to drop into my closet."

"Don't tell me you're disappointed."

She arched her neck for him to kiss her again. The burning warmth of his breath against her skin made her melt inside. "Perhaps a little."

He drew back slightly to smile at her. "Ah. The lady is not averse to having an intruder in her bed?"

Chloe sighed and brushed a raindrop from the lapel of his coat. "I thought it was all rather terrifying and exciting."

"Exciting? Finding a half-dead man in your French drawers?"

"Not just any man, Dominic. I'm rather particular as to whom I invite into my closet."

"I should hope so."

It took her a moment to realize that he was fighting to control himself. He had lifted his face to the sky as if he welcomed the cool sting of rain. She felt her eyes fill with tears. This was only the second time she had seen him outside in the daylight. It would require patience for him to forget his endless days in darkness.

"Chloe." He glanced down at her face, in control again, more at peace with himself than she could ever remember. "Do you think you can bear to raise our children in a house that is haunted by a ghost?"

"As long as it's not your ghost who's doing the haunting," she teased him. "Has the scandal died down yet in Chistlebury?"

"Hardly," Dominic replied, "although Sir Edgar's death has been announced by the authorities to have been an accident. It seems he was crushed to death by a load of mortar while exploring the hidden recesses of Stratfield Hall."

"And Chistlebury's notorious ghost?"

"Ah, yes. My resurrection is still the talk of the village. However, after the promise of a generous donation to the church, even the parson has chosen to overlook certain inconsistencies in the explanation of my apparent demise."

"Is it safe to say that scandal is behind us?"

He gave a devilish laugh. "Scandal will follow us forever, I'm afraid. In later years the legend of the Stratfield Ghost will grow."

"Are you telling me that his wicked behavior will become worse?"

"Not exactly. But people will swear that Stratfield's spirit was seen carrying his own skeleton through the gallery."

Chloe smiled. "I saw him myself at the annual *bal masqué* dressed as a highwayman. He's quite a virile ghost."

Dominic drew her against him. "The dates and details will become blurred. Our story might be exaggerated.

But one fact will remain undisputed: Viscount Stratfield, whether mortal man or ghost, fell in love with a very wonderful young woman from London."

He returned to his town house a few hours later, his heart considerably lighter than when he'd left. A hundred duties awaited him. The evening passed before he knew it.

He swiveled around in his chair as the bedchamber door of his town house creaked open behind him. Hard to believe it was almost midnight. There was a gun on his desk amid the clutter of papers—official inquiries about Samuel, a letter from the company's board of directors, fresh notes of condolences as the news of his death plot spread around town. By now the report of Edgar's treachery had undoubtedly reached those secret contacts who had betrayed England alongside him if they had not long since scattered to hide.

The sounds within his London town house were harder to identify than those of his country estate, but there was something in the cautious tread behind him that alerted all his senses . . .

In anticipation of pleasure.

The spicy scent of Chloe's soap drifted enticingly across the room, awakening the sensual aggressor inside him. He would know her fragrance anywhere, would respond to it. He heard her silk-lined cloak slither to the floor. A chill of raw desire chased down his spine. What a delicious surprise this was.

He leaned back, enjoying the moment. "I hope to God you did not come out at night alone, Chloe."

"Jane brought me in the carriage."

He rose and looked out the window. Jane gave him a jaunty wave from the carriage, and, before he could react, the crested vehicle took off into the London streets.

He pivoted, his laugh incredulous. "How do you intend to go back home tonight without my escorting you?"

"I don't."

"And—you're planning to spend the night here?"

She was advancing on him, her blue eyes brimming with wicked fun. "What's the matter, Stratfield? Are you the only one allowed to be an uninvited guest?"

Dominic's heart began to pound. By the look on her face, he decided that even if he had to explain the situation to her brothers, an evening alone with Chloe in this seductive mood would be well worth it. He couldn't resist her, would never be able to refuse her anything for the rest of their lives. "Won't your family be frantic if they find you gone?"

"Umm." She began to unbutton his crisp white linen shirt, her fingers deft and quick. Sexual heat rose to the surface of his skin. "Jane promised to take care of them for me."

His senses swam with the subtle scent of her. How he loved her touch. "Quite a brave woman, this Jane."

Chloe smiled up at him, her voice catching with emotion. "You have to be brave to marry a Boscastle."

"I think I knew that."

"It's too late if you didn't. I love you, Dominic."

He put his hands around her waist, gathering her soft body to his. It *was* too late. Dominic had lost his heart to Chloe the day he had rescued her from a mud puddle. He had known then and there that he wanted her, that he would pursue her if he ever managed to sort out his life. But he hadn't guessed that his fantasies would be fulfilled in such an incredible way, that he would fall so deeply in love with her.

"I see the darker side of Dominic again," she whispered, wrapping her arms around his neck. "Don't go into hiding on me again."

He ran his hands down her strong back, lingering over the rounded rise of her bottom, drawing her into the heat of his body. He moaned softly at the perfect fit of her curves molding to his hard torso. "Not bloody likely. Chloe—" He shuddered as she pulled back to finish unbuttoning his shirt.

"Stop worrying, Dominic. Jane is very clever."

"So is Heath."

"And what will he make us do? Get married in the morning? Oh, good. Then perhaps I won't have to listen to Emma lecture me on wedding decorum and guest lists and— What are *you* doing?"

"I've taken your advice and stopped worrying." He unhooked her gown and pushed it to her waist, cupping her ivory-white breasts through her chemise. By the time he had backed her against his bed and kissed her, Chloe did not seem to remember what they had been discussing.

Nor did Dominic for that matter. Chloe had truly become a temptress, with her ripe body and bold curiosity. His chest muscles tightened in pleasure as she traced her fingertips tenderly over his hideous scar. Her touch had always aroused him, but her aggressive pursuit of him set him on fire. He would never be able to deny her. His attraction to her had been both his weakness and his strength from the start.

She kissed his chest, licked and bit gently, and he began to shake. She looked incredibly desirable with her soft pink mouth wet and swollen and her gown shoved down to her waist. Her lips felt moist and warm on his skin, and his heartbeat quickened. He lowered her to the bed and captured her mouth in a deep, hungry kiss, leaning over her languid body.

"Chloe, my love," he said as he casually untied her chemise and garters. "I'm so glad you decided to drop by."

He had her naked in seconds.

The sensuality of her smile unleashed something edgy and powerful inside him. She shifted her shoulders deeper into the pillow in a pose that was as challenging as it was submissive. "Take off your clothes, Stratfield."

"Did you have something particular in mind?"

"I have everything in mind."

"I see."

He pulled off his shirt and pantaloons, allowing her gaze to travel over his nude body. He felt himself grow hard under her scrutiny, the unfettered desire in her eyes. When she arched off the bed and began to kiss his belly, he was so consumed with lust that he couldn't move, could only submit and enjoy himself.

Her mouth drifted lower. At first he could only groan in pleasure. When her soft lips closed over his thickening shaft, he shuddered and gripped her shoulders, his hips bucking against her. Her tongue circled the knob of his sex. His spine curled in reaction. The sensation rocked him to the core.

If he had hoped to reduce her to tears of delight, it seemed to be turning out to be the other way around. He caught her chin in his hands. "Who taught you that anyway?" he demanded.

"Audrey Watson," she whispered, her blue eyes provocative.

"Audrey—*the* Audrey Watson?"

"So you've heard of courtesans in Chistlebury, have you?"

Dominic grinned. "I've heard of *that* courtesan. Why on earth did she tutor you? I've heard she selects only one or two students a year."

"She didn't." Chloe looked sheepish. "I eavesdropped in Brighton when she was giving my sister-in-law lessons on seduction."

"Your sister-in-law?" he asked incredulously. "Jane, the elegant marchioness who stood up to her husband and who brought you here?"

"Yes. One and the same. Jane, my dear ally."

Dominic shook his head in wonder. He could feel the fierce beat of his heart throughout his whole body. Chloe was his world, the flame that had given him hope in darkness. She was also a strong, earthy woman with a passionate nature, and the thought of spending forever with her left him breathless.

He nudged her onto her back. He was shaking again, his need for her intensifying, growing more urgent with every moment. His hands moved over her body, her heavy breasts and swollen nipples, then lower to force her legs apart. He stroked her intimately, taking shameless advantage of having her in his bed for the first time ever. He felt virile, capable of having sex until sunrise, his body hot and hard.

Just touching Chloe's warm smooth skin and ripe curves infused him with lust. Her sexual instincts heightened his own hunger until the blood in his veins pounded with it. He wanted her vulnerable, open and helpless like this. He wanted to do everything imaginable to her. The pleasure of her mouth on his shaft had sharpened his desire to a degree he had never before known.

He spread open the inner folds of her sex and eased his finger inside her sensitive passage. Her tender muscles tightened at the friction. He felt the tremor that shook her, teasing her until she was writhing against his hand. She was surrendering to him completely, being her most sensual self.

"Chloe," he said in a hoarse voice, "I love you so." He bent his head to suckle gently on her breasts. She responded with a low-throated moan that tightened every muscle in his body in anticipation.

The cream of her arousal had soaked his fingers. He had to be inside her or he'd go up in flames. He needed her, and she was begging him to take her. Still, he wouldn't hurry. He wanted to drive her as wild as she could be. He wanted her to ache for sex with him until she would do anything he asked.

A woman like Chloe could never be taken for granted. She had to be pleased, pampered, seduced in body and soul.

"Dominic, I think— I'm going—"

It excited him to see her lose control, the way she moved her body, her voice becoming deep and breathless. He clenched his jaw when she climaxed against his hand, shivering with desire, with a need that matched his own. He studied her face, his fingers quickening, not releasing her even then. Twice more he brought her to a climax.

At last he moved over her. His own need had grown too great to control. He heard her whispering his name, her body straining. He caught her hands over her head and stared down into her eyes. She bit the edge of her lower lip.

"What are you doing to me, Dominic?"

"Whatever I feel like. Any objections?"

She closed her eyes, gave a breathy sigh. "None at all."

He eased the thick head of his shaft into her cleft. She was so dewy and warm he almost exploded on the spot. He arched his back and drove inside her passage with a powerful thrust.

"Dominic."

She caught her breath. He thrust again, deeper, deeper, until there was no breath left in her body. She surged upward, meeting him, only to subside with a gasp of pleasure. He drove his tongue into her mouth to deepen their kiss, pumping himself into her wet sheath with abandon. She locked her legs around his hips, absorbing the impact of his body. He could not stop himself. He was impaling her to the bed, lost in her, his hips flexing in a relentless rhythm.

He had never needed her more than he did now. Her body not only welcomed him, but encouraged him, gloving him so perfectly that he had to slow his movements or he would tear her into pieces. This was elemental, a storm out of control and yet in harmony with all of nature, a beautiful fury. He fought to keep himself in check.

"What a woman you are, Chloe," he whispered hoarsely, lifting her legs up over his shoulders to give him better access.

"Your woman," she whispered back.

Her voice, husky with pleasure, urged him to bury himself even deeper. When she began to move against him, he wanted to growl with pleasure. He threw back his head and braced his body for a climax that seemed to be wrung from his very soul. He could feel her splintering beneath him, feel the damp suction of her squeezing him dry.

He heard her sweet cry of pleasure as he poured his seed into her. She looked so beautiful, gave herself to him so unhesitantly that he would have moved heaven and earth to keep her. He loved her so much it frightened him, and yet the thought of not having her in his life was unbearable.

She smiled up at him, tendrils of damp black hair caressing her cheeks. Her vibrant blue eyes reassured him that she shared his intense feelings. They had been meant for each other. Finding her had been the one good thing that had come out of the tragedy of Brandon and Samuel's brutal deaths.

"That was quite a lesson in seduction you learned, Chloe Boscastle," he said softly. "Remind me to thank Audrey later."

Chloe could not even find the strength to tease him back. The dark passion in his eyes, the love, immobilized her. She felt his burning gaze to the core of her being. He made no secret of his desire, his emotions, and even now she could feel herself responding to him all over again. That was how it was between them, would always be. One look from Dominic, and she came apart.

He was different than when she had first met him. He had changed. They both had. He had risked his life for what he believed in; she had risked her reputation because she believed in him. Tonight she could even feel the difference in the way he had made love to her. He was stronger, more sure of himself. He would never completely return to acting the perfect gentleman who lived within the rules of Society. There would always be a little wildness, a rebel, in both of them. But only with Dominic could Chloe at last begin to find peace from her own restless nature and the spells of sadness that had overshadowed her in recent years. They deserved the happiness that awaited them.

"So thoughtful, Chloe," he said quietly, rolling onto his side to look at her. "I didn't hurt you, did I? For a while there I lost complete control."

She sighed in contentment, snuggling against him as if she could stay in his arms forever. "I'm fine, Dominic. Are we going to sleep here tonight?"

He subjected her to a rueful smile. His body was hardening again as he held her. He could not get enough of her, and knowing that she would soon be at his side night and day only intensified his need for her. He sucked in his breath as her hands began to explore his body.

"You aren't sleeping here at all, Chloe. At least not tonight."

Her hands stilled their arousing quest. "Why not?"

"Because, my darling temptress, I made a promise to your family only this morning that I would protect you, and so far I fear I have fallen short of that goal."

She gripped his hips in her hands, her blue eyes narrowing. "Are you really going to make me leave?"

The possessiveness of her touch sent a thrill of heat through him. "I'm afraid I am."

"Right now?"

She sprawled back against the pillows, deliberately inviting, testing her power over him. His throat tightened as he stared at her invitingly posed body, studying her through heavily lidded eyes. Her desire for him inflamed him. What man would not respond to her lush sensuality?

He moved over her, kissing her breasts, then her quivering belly, the tangled curls of her sex. He felt her resist this new invasion, raising her hips off the bed, but he was faster, pinning her down easily with one hand. He nudged her completely open with his other hand, blowing lightly against her swollen cleft. Chloe trembled uncontrollably, twining her fingers in his hair. Her excitement intoxicated him. When his tongue penetrated her sensitive folds of flesh, she gave the sweetest groan he had ever heard.

The taste of her, her honeyed moisture, made him hungry for more. He buried his face between her legs, pushing her knees farther apart, licking her.

"*Dominic,*" Chloe said in a strangled voice, twisting futilely against the hand that held her down.

He nibbled tenderly at the nub of her clitoris, his tongue stabbing deeper and deeper inside her passage. Chloe had subsided back onto the bed with her face in the pillow. Her entire body trembled with pleasure until the moment when he pushed her over the edge, and she convulsed in helpless abandon against his face.

"God help me, Chloe," he muttered, dropping his head down on the bed. If he did not take her home soon, her family would be at the door, demanding her safe return.

She sat up, looking dazed, tousled, her black curls damp around her face. "What did you just do to me?"

He grinned up at her. "Didn't you like it?"

"What do you think, you devil?"

He reared up, his erection painful. "It's a damn good thing I have work to do tonight. I won't be able to sleep after this."

"Are you really going to take me home?" she demanded.

"I shall deliver you safely to the doorstep." He slid off the bed to struggle back into his pantaloons. "Put your dress back on, Chloe."

"What if I refuse?"

"Then I shall have to throw you over my shoulders as you are and let your brothers figure out how to dress you."

She threw a pillow at him. "That's a nice way to restore our respectability, parading me bare-bottomed through the streets of London."

Yet less than an hour later Dominic made good his promise to take her home, and Chloe stood, fully dressed, in front of him on the doorstep of Grayson's elegant mansion. Apparently accustomed to situations that would shock the average servant, the Boscastle butler did not blink an eye.

Nor did Heath, who sauntered out of the library to greet his sister, a book in hand. "Ah, Chloe. Our black lamb home at last." He glanced up past her to the dark figure who stood behind her like a sentinel. "Thank you, Dominic."

Dominic nodded, reading approval for bringing her back in Heath's eyes. "I'm sorry if you were worried."

"Actually, I wasn't. I knew she was with you and that you would bring her home in due time. Do stay a while. I have a few things I'd like to talk to you about alone."

Chloe looked indignant. "How did you know where I was? Did Jane spill the soup?"

"Of course Jane did nothing of the kind," said the marchioness herself from the middle of the staircase. "I would not betray you even under penalty of torture. The coachman, however, is another matter." She swept down the remaining stairs in a silver dressing robe and pearl-seeded slippers. "So, Chloe, how was your visit with dear Aunt Rosemary?"

Chloe hid a smile as she slipped around Heath. "The poor thing was exhausted by my company. She begged me to leave so that she could rest."

Dominic's eyes widened. The shameless little baggage, mocking his virility to the world. As if Heath and Jane had no idea who "Aunt Rosemary" was and exactly what Chloe had done to overexert the old dear. He would show her overexertion the next time she came to his bed.

Jane's eyes danced with delight. "Do come up and share your visit with me. Did you fire off any Congreve rockets?"

Chloe smothered a giggle. "At least one," she said mischievously as she followed her sister-in-law up the stairs.

Dominic glanced disbelievingly at Heath. "Does that phrase mean what I'm afraid it means?"

Heath attempted not to laugh. "You might have to ask Grayson about that."

"Yes." Dominic shook his head in disbelief. "What was it you wished to discuss with me?"

Heath's amusement faded. "Come into the library, Dominic. We can talk in private there."

Dominic cast an appraising glance around the room. Carved rosewood bookcases with brass-trellis doors stretched toward the vaulted ceiling. Rampant lions and plump amorini adorned the gilded stucco. A circular gilt mirror of Greek design hung over the chimneypiece. Below, a modest fire smoldered in the ornate marble fireplace.

He looked at the man sitting opposite him in an armchair. This was a room that suited the vigorous Marquess of Sedgecroft far more than his reserved, quiet-spoken brother. "I assume you have quite a few questions for me regarding Brandon. I shall offer as much information as I can, but I'm afraid I know little more than I have already revealed."

Heath did not appear surprised. "There are many questions to be answered, yes. But not for you, perhaps. Your part is done, Dominic, and quite effectively, I have to admit."

Dominic stared into the fire. "Sometimes it seemed I was possessed to the point of madness. I could think of nothing but revenge." And Chloe, he mused, although this he could not add.

"All with good reason," Heath said. "But often it

takes a man possessed with a worthy objective to see justice served."

"Which is where you will take over," Dominic guessed, referring to Heath's involvement in British Intelligence. Was Heath still in commission? He did not ask, suspecting he would receive only an evasive answer. And was his own part truly done? He rather hoped so. He preferred to live the rest of his life in peace.

Heath shrugged. "I don't know whether I shall be involved in a formal investigation. Personally, I have questions that I will seek to answer. Officially, I am not sure whether I will be needed. As close as I was to Brandon, I did not know his involvement in espionage was as dangerous as it was. I suppose he wanted to prove himself without help from his family."

Dominic reached into his vest pocket. "I appreciate you sending me Chloe's translation of Brandon's coded letter."

"I should very much like to see the original," Heath said, leaning forward with his hand outstretched. "Is that it?"

"Yes. I confess I am a better swordsman than cryptographer."

"And a damn good thing for all of us," Heath said with feeling as he tucked the letter into his pocket.

Dominic paused. "Where do you suppose the other half of the message is? It ended on a rather ominous note. The more I think about it, the warning could have been meant for any of us."

"Indeed," Heath said darkly.

"Edgar could not have worked alone."

"No. That is the troubling part of what is left on our

hands. Perhaps the men who helped him are still in military service. One of my superiors believes there might be a soldier, subaltern, who could testify that he saw Edgar exchange information with a French spy in—"

Heath stopped in midsentence as the door opened behind Dominic. It was Grayson, dressed only in his shirt, pantaloons, and boots, a bottle of brandy in hand. He looked pleasantly surprised to see the two other men sitting alone.

"Stealing a few moments of peace, are we? Not a bad idea, considering how the females of the family tend to dominate our lives." He looked directly at Dominic. "A fate I suspect you are only *beginning* to learn."

"Pour Dominic a brandy, Gray," Heath said with a smile. "He needs a few moments in male company to prepare him for the weeks ahead."

"The weeks ahead?" Dominic took the brandy glass that the marquess had removed from the lacquered Chinese cabinet. "Is there some sort of secret initiation into the family that Chloe failed to warn me about?"

The two other men chuckled. "The wedding preparations," Grayson said as he took his chair.

Apparently Heath did not drink. He removed a cigar from his pocket instead. "Emma is in her element planning every last detail. I trust you do not mind."

"It's Chloe who should be consulted," Dominic said without thinking. "As for me, I should happily marry her in a meadow." He looked a little embarrassed when he realized what he had revealed, that he wanted Chloe as his wife whatever he must do to claim her.

Grayson did not seem at all offended. Perhaps he was so besotted with his intriguing Jane that he understood.

Heath's reaction was harder to interpret. He did not appear to show his feelings easily.

"Alas," Heath said, "once the idea of a wedding was put in Emma's mind it ceased to be a matter of what you or Chloe desired."

Dominic laughed. "Should I be frightened?"

"You should run for your life," Grayson confided.

"Speaking of running away," Heath remarked as he lit his cigar, "where the blazes has Adrian gone? I'd only learned he was in England days ago, and now he's disappeared."

The remark made Dominic realize what a small circle of men made up his elite class. They attended the same schools, the same social functions, christenings, weddings, funerals. "He's gone off to make peace with his father, which ought to be an interesting reunion, considering the fact that the old duke has been calling Adrian a bastard for years. He promised to be back for the wedding."

"We should all run off," Grayson joked. "Go on a lengthy shoot in Scotland until an hour before the ceremony."

"I wonder which one of you is going to make me an uncle first," Heath mused.

Grayson's broad grin gave him away.

"You devil," Heath said with a laugh, lowering his cigar.

"I haven't said a word." Grayson shook his head somberly. "I am the keeper of family secrets, and Jane's physician said it is too early to be sure."

When Dominic rose to leave, he was surprised to see by the clock that two hours had passed. It felt strangely pleasant to be included in this close-knit clan with all its joys and troubles. It reminded him of the two brothers he had lost. The funny part was that he found he wanted to impress these men, to prove himself. He was *not* going to be an irresponsible rake for the rest of his life, not with Chloe at his side. And now, for a short time, until she came to him for good, she was home. Safe and protected until he took over.

"Good night to both of you."

"Have we scared you off?" Heath asked.

"Not that easily. But—" Dominic hesitated at the door. "Well, I know I shouldn't ask, Grayson. I have an awful suspicion what the answer will be—but does the phrase 'setting off Congreve rockets' mean anything to you?"

Epilogue

❦

Chloe was drowning in a sea of female attire, knee-deep in the waves of promenade dresses, shawls, corsets, and petticoats that covered her bedchamber floor. Somewhere in this embarrassing mess of fashion excess she had lost her journal. Heaven forbid her scandalous confessions should fall into the wrong hands just when she was about to become a respectable matron.

It was the day before her wedding, and the dressmaker had just left the house after making a last-minute alteration to Chloe's wedding gown, all because Emma, the Dainty Dictator, had decreed that the Belgian lace border of the low bodice was lopsided.

"By a hair," Chloe murmured. "Who would have noticed?"

And in the midst of the furor to make the adjustment, she had lost her journal with all its unspeakable secrets.

Jane popped her head into the room. "Your Dominic is downstairs, Chloe. Are you going to the park for an hour?"

"Why go to the park?" Chloe muttered. "My room is

a veritable jungle. We could wander about here for days and not be found. We—"

She turned from the wardrobe, realizing that Jane had wandered off, presumably to join Emma downstairs to attend to another crucial detail of the next day's event.

She reached into the depths of her wardrobe. "Where are you?" she muttered. "Buried where no one except me will find you, I hope."

"Now *that* is a sight for sore eyes," Dominic said, leaning his elbow against the doorjamb.

Chloe shot to her feet. "Emma's going to kill you if she catches you up here."

"Emma sent me up."

"Emma? You *must* be mistaken."

"No." Dominic's eyes gleamed in amusement. "I marched in the back entrance with Grayson's tailor and assistants. I don't think she recognized me."

Chloe eyed his compelling muscular form, impeccably clothed in a double-breasted tail coat of superfine and tight pantaloons. His short black hair was brushed back from his angular face. Would his devilish gray eyes always do such disconcerting things to her vital signs?

"How could she not recognize you?"

He shrugged. "I had a pile of boxes in my arms. I hid behind them. What were you looking for on the floor anyway? Another half-dead man in a trunk?"

"I'm looking for my journal, if you must know."

"Why?"

"Why?"

He came into the room, closing the door behind him. "I could help you with the contents if you care to rewrite the original."

Chloe paled. "I hope to heaven that does not mean what I am afraid it means. Do you have my journal, Dominic?"

"Of course not, darling." A slow grin spread across his face. "But I do remember by heart a few of the more striking entries, if that helps."

"You sneak. You couldn't possibly have read it."

His deep chuckle gave her chills. "Let me think. Ah, yes. 'My fatal flaw is my inability to be demure. No decent man should want me, I am sure . . .'"

She gasped. "You did read it!"

"It was rather sweet."

Sweet. Chloe could only thank her lucky stars that he hadn't read her later entries concerning her attraction to him.

"Did you really want me to ravish you that day in the rain?" he asked, drawing her into his arms.

She resisted. He pulled her closer. The warm strength of his arms surrounded her. His hand slid up her nape to cradle her head. A shiver of anticipation shot through her, and her breathing quickened. In another moment she would not be able to remember that she was disgusted with him for invading her privacy.

He nibbled at her ear. "It's a good thing I'm not really a decent man."

"Why did you come up here anyway, Dominic?" she asked.

"I wanted to give you something."

"What?" she said, curious despite herself.

He lowered his head, his eyes glowing with love, and kissed her with such fierce possession that she forgot all about her missing journal. Was she angry at him? It didn't matter. What mattered was that this was the man she would pledge her heart to in the morning.

She laid her head on his shoulder and listened to the murmur of voices in the hallway. She had never felt safer, more at peace in her life.

"The wedding should be a quiet affair," Emma said, sounding more hopeful than convinced.

"In this family?" Jane laughed. "I trust you're not laying odds on it."

"I would be mortified," Emma said. "All my old friends have come back into town for the occasion. Chloe looks like an angel in her gown. Dominic is a handsome devil, and they are in love. The breakfast dishes promise to be divine, and the cake is perfection." She paused to squeeze in a breath, sounding as if her maid had laced her a little too tightly into her corset. "Could anything possibly go wrong?"

Dominic looked down into Chloe's eyes and smiled.

"Not for us," he promised her. "Your wedding dress could be made of sackcloth. The breakfast dishes could be dust, and the cake can collapse before it's even cut. It won't change what really counts. Everything is going to be right from now on."

He was so different from when they had first met, his vital energy harnessed, his heart cleansed of revenge. He was still her dark, soulful Dominic, the man she would be with forever, but no longer haunted. She smiled back at him, taking his hand in hers. "Everything has been right for me since I met you."

Read on for
a sneak peek at

The Wedding Night of an English Rogue

the final novel in Jillian Hunter's
Boscastle Trilogy!

Julia stood concealed behind one of the columns in the ballroom, watching the two men on the balcony above her. It was impossible to decipher their conversation. She could hardly see their faces from this distance, but she would have recognized Heath Boscastle anywhere. The handsome devil still drew attention. Several debutantes, in fact, had made a show of walking back and forth directly beneath him.

Her fiancé was drawing attention, too. Julia frowned as two giggling young women stopped directly in front of her.

"Do you think they noticed us?" one of them whispered.

Her friend glanced up at the balcony. "Boscastle is looking *right* at me."

"What about Sir Russell?"

"I heard he'd gotten engaged, but he's looking, too."

"Let's look back. They're like gods."

Julia cleared her throat. The two younger women appeared startled, taking a step into each other. "Ladies," she said rather coolly, "haven't you been told that it is not only impolite but unforgivably forward to stare—even at the gods."

As they scurried away, duly shamed, Julia, hypocrite that she was, resumed staring at the two compelling figures on the balcony. They couldn't be discussing her all this time. They seemed perfectly calm, which meant that Heath could not have told Russell their secret.

Heath looked down to the exact spot where she stood. She slipped back behind the column. If Russell found out what had happened between her and Heath years ago, he would be understandably appalled. The mere fact that Julia had kept it a secret would seem to compound her guilt.

She had good cause to feel guilty. For heaven's sake, she had shot a man and practically invited him to ruin her all in one unforgettable day.

Her blood still went cold when she remembered Heath lying between the rocks, silent and unmoving. How relieved she'd felt when she had flung herself down on the ground and discovered him still alive. Very much alive, in fact. His blue eyes had seared her like a naked flame, disbelieving, furious . . . and disconcertingly male.

She'd had the distinct feeling he was undressing her with those eyes despite the fact that she could have blown him to kingdom come.

"You *shot* me."

"Well, no wonder." She was terrified. He had a magnificent body, and she'd probably scarred one of those muscular shoulders. Her father would hide her gun again. "What were you doing jumping out at me from behind that carn?"

"I thought you were someone I knew."

"Well, I thought you were the rabid fox that had attacked the livestock last night."

"Do I look like a rabid fox?" he demanded.

No, she thought, biting the tip of her tongue. He looked like a lean, angry wolf who would leap up at any moment and eat her. Even wounded he gave the impression of dangerous strength. And sensual appeal. She had been warned about him, of course. Every debutante wished to snare a Boscastle. Well, she had just shot one. Did that count?

Then, to make matters worse, she had proceeded to pull off his shirt. Her relief that the wound was only superficial gave way to a sting of pleased shock to discover that he was every bit as gorgeous as she'd suspected.

"It doesn't look as bad as I feared."

"That's easy for you to say."

She was beginning to feel better. She hadn't really hurt him. "I am sorry."

And that had been the start of it. A humiliating incident that had led to the most magical interlude she had ever experienced.

The eroticism of his kisses, the sinful thrill of being captured against that hard male body, still haunted her like a sensual dream. She'd never imagined, before or since, that she could respond to a man that way.

She certainly couldn't imagine what she would say when she came face-to-face with him tonight.

But she was about to find out.

Sometimes, examining how her life had turned out, she wished he had told. She might never have gone to India. Her father would probably have forced her to marry Heath and advised them to make the best of it.

She would never have shot that soldier in the buttocks. Of all her sins, that was the one that had shocked Society the most.

She realized in alarm that he and Russell had left the balcony. That Heath was suddenly standing at the opposite end of the hall. Just that one glance at his profile, the hawklike nose and strong, clefted chin, made her heart beat a little faster. She leaned against the wall, watching him in resentful fascination. Why couldn't he have grown fat, or lost his teeth? Perhaps he had. She could not properly see his mouth from where she stood. She remembered it, though. His firm, sensual lips with the small white scar, his beguiling smirk, the dizzying kisses they had shared.

She had never met a man who possessed the lethal elegance of Heath Boscastle, or who even came close. A man who had once seduced her down to her stockings at a hunting party when they both had been too young to know better. Or had it been the other way around? Had she clumsily attempted to seduce him? Wild Miss Hepworth her friends had called her in those days. They probably called her far worse now. The Wicked Lady Whitby.

She'd had plenty of time to reflect on what had happened between her and Heath. Years, in fact, for reflection and regrets. Naughty woman that she was, there were moments when her truest regret was that the two of them had not followed their heated encounter to the end. She hadn't always felt like that. It had taken a lonely marriage to make her face what she had wanted, what she could have had. That there wasn't only one path to contentment.

But on the day that she and Heath had parted, she had felt only an overriding panic and a guilty relief that they had stopped themselves before anyone discovered them.

And that he had kept his promise that he'd never tell.

Heath was coming closer.

He walked toward the column with the same languid grace that had once set her nerves on fire, that took her breath away even now. He was tall, broader in the shoulder than she recalled, a little leaner perhaps, but still dangerously attractive in a long-tailed black evening coat and pantaloons. Older, more experienced, more on edge, as elusive to the female heart as ever. Her throat closed as she stared at him. She'd believed she would never see him again. The ache of unresolved feelings inside her made her wish that she had not. It hurt to realize what might have been. And yet she could not deny the anticipation that rose inside her. Clever, handsome, an irresistible rogue. How silly to assume he would remain preserved as he was in her memory.

Six years, she thought, astonished that so much time had passed. She had been married and widowed in India. She had seen a side of life that the haut ton could only read about in the newspaper and gasp at in horror.

What had Heath heard about her?

She knew he could see her, that he was perfectly aware of who she was. His stride was unhurried, yet powerful.

Did he remember what they had done together that day in the library?

She steeled herself to look up into his heartbreakingly beautiful face, the chiseled features, the hard, sculpted chin. His dark blue eyes danced with restrained amusement, answering both her unspoken questions. He stopped as she stepped into his path.

He knew everything about her.

And he remembered perfectly well what they had done.

Furthermore, he hadn't lost even a single white tooth.

Even worse, she couldn't stop staring up at him, drinking in all the details of his appearance. One would think she had never seen a handsome man in her entire life. Of course, there was a little more to it than that. They shared a secret.

"Julia," he said in the deep, cultured voice that brought another rush of forgotten memories to the surface, teased her starved senses. "Still hiding, are you? I trust you aren't armed tonight. Should I search you?"

She studied him in feigned puzzlement. "I'm sorry—do I know you? Have we been formally introduced?"

He took her by the hand, drawing her forward without a qualm. "Very funny, considering the fact that you almost shot me dead the first time I saw you."

"You shouldn't have been hiding behind that rock. I thought you were a fox." Now that she found her voice, she seemed to have turned into a chatterbox. The warmth in his eyes made it too easy to talk to him. "Oh, Heath, have you forgiven me? Did I leave you with a scar?"

"Yes. And yes. Actually I have gotten several scars since we met, but yours is the only one associated with a pleasant memory."

There was a pause. She was aware of how hard her heart was beating, of other guests glancing at them, that time had only intensified his personal magnetism. She'd been surprised when Russell told her that Heath had never married, but then he was young enough and could afford to wait, could take his pick from the entire female population of England. A man who looked like Heath Boscastle would hardly have to search for a companion.

She was staring at him again. And he was smiling, although not out of any sense of superiority or conceit that she could tell. A perfect gentleman, he didn't launch into gloating reminiscences of their sinful interlude.

It was more emotionally charged than she'd imagined it would be, meeting him like this, and she had imagined it countless times. He was the same charming rogue she remembered. The war had changed so many of her male acquaintances, and Heath had been captured, had survived a great deal.

He cleared his throat.

She gave herself a stern mental shake and glanced away.

"Would you care for something to drink?" he asked, drawing her to the end of the corridor.

"A drink?" She wished she would not keep remembering how he'd looked half naked, how the hand that was guiding her in such a gentlemanly way had plundered the private recesses of her body. He was so poised. It must amuse him to remember what they had done.

"Yes," he said in a light voice. "A beverage. You know, that liquid stuff one swallows from time to time."

"A drink," she repeated.

"Do you need me to draw you a picture, Julia?" He waved his free hand in front of her face. "Julia?"

His voice was warm, teasing, as seductive as she remembered, had tried to forget. He'd always had a wicked, wry sense of humor, and it took all of her wits to pretend she was not affected, that every word he said, every gesture, did not take her back to the past. The lure proved too strong. She adverted her gaze, afraid she would give herself away, afraid that he was too intelligent to deceive. How humiliating that she could still recount every word.

I had one glass of claret, Heath.

Yes, well, it's all gone to your head.

No, it hasn't.

It most certainly has, or you wouldn't be kissing me like this.

Do you mind?

Of course I don't mind, but I daresay you will tomorrow.

I won't. I never do anything I regret. Well, until now . . .

He'd threaded his long fingers through her hair and pulled her back into the sofa, his sensuality overpowering, the heat of his chiseled lips on her throat drugging her senses. The other houseguests had gone off on a hunt, and she and Heath had been locked together in the library for three hours, unable to open the door, or at least pretending that the lock was jammed. Three fateful hours. Her life had never been the same, the stolen pleasure of their interlude overshadowing her to this moment. The ache inside her became more persistent, bittersweet and unfulfilled. There was something about him that inspired confidence and penetrated her defenses. Yet he had kept his promise to her.

She forced her mind back to the present. He was no longer holding her hand, but she had felt the warmth of his strong fingers all the way down to her knees. A blush of pleasant awareness washed over her.

She met his curious, perceptive gaze and sighed inwardly. It was far too easy to lose herself in those eyes as she had once learned. Guests were milling around them, staring at them in recognition now. Clearly those in the know had heard that Julia was engaged to Sir Russell, and Heath was a Boscastle male—eligible if elusive, a conquest to be pursued by the marriage-minded at any price.

She started to laugh. "Yes. I'd like a drink—anything as long as it's not claret."

A flame kindled in the depths of his dark blue eyes. His mocking smile was irresistible. "Ah, yes. I've heard it goes to one's head."